DONUM - THE GIFT

— . —

OMNIA VINCIT AMOR, BOOK I

MAXIME JAZ

MAXIME JAZ

Cover design by: Kon Blacke

To my readers

ACKNOWLEDGMENTS

Huge thanks go to all my Writing Community friends on Twitter, too numerous to name, but I'll name a few, still: Bjorn, Krystle, Susan, Gabriel, Boots, John, Rebecca, Kira, Aud, Chase, Dan, Em, Alistair, Luke , Connor, Jayme, Travis, Mario... Basically, the whole community in Kira's accountability thread too.

The #WRITEboyslove community has been a huge support too, and a welcoming, safe community. I have to highlight the founders of this amazing community, Kon and Amy, and thank them for their everlasting support and enthusiasm.

I especially have to highlight Kon Blacke here, as he has become a trusted friend, even though we live on opposite sides of the globe, and have never met. He has also become an invaluable beta reader of my works, and has been all but supportive and enthusiastic of my writing, and a fan of some of my characters. Kon also designed Donum's cover, and not only that, he also designed the covers for Book 2 and 3 of the trilogy, as well as promotion materials. I cannot be thankful enough to him, as without Kon, I would still be struggling to get these books out to readers. His grasp of the story, the characters and their relationships all made for wonderful covers which he should be deservedly proud of. I am also eternally grateful for his beta reading comments and sharp insights into how my writing could be improved.

I have to thank separately my other trusted friend and beta reader, Dr. Susan Hancock, who wrote beautiful literary analysis of my works each time she had finished reading them (and twice, nonetheless!). Susan is a gem and I trust her with all my stories, knowing that her feedback will be invaluable. Thank you from the bottom of my heart!

Finally, these books would not be with you now without the support of my husband and my kids, and them letting me have some time to write, with minimized interruptions. Love you!

To my readers, I am forever grateful to you for wanting my books, and awaiting the next ones.

FOREWORD - CONTENT NOTES

This book contains graphic depiction of violence, abuse, death and grief, as well as explicit sex scenes.

For a more detailed list, please scan this QR code.

CONTENTS

PREFACE

This book's story is set in Ancient Rome, loosely based on the times during Trajan's reign. However, the emperor and all the characters are fictitious, and do not reflect real historical events of those times.

"Donum" is not a historical fiction, but rather a queer romance set in a historical setting, depicting fictitious events.

The language of the book does not reflect the language used during ancient times. When Latin words are used, those can be found in the glossary at the end of the book, otherwise, the book was written in modern English, following US spelling, but UK turn of phrases might still appear. It is the author's choice to spell "grey" with an "e" instead of an "a". Celtic language, although various languages and dialects existed, is represented in this book by Scottish Gaelic and Irish.

Some other adjustments have been made to fit our modern times. Even if adulthood technically started way earlier in Ancient Rome (between twelve and fifteen years of age), all characters have been aged up in the story to fit the standards of our times in a European setting. This also means that the coming of age ceremony for boys takes place at eighteen, and not fourteen to fifteen, which would be the historically accurate version.

Roman names have been sometimes adapted to fit the story, and some of them are purely fictional.

"Donum" is the first book of the Omnia Vincit Amor trilogy, but can be read as a standalone.

I

Marius walked into the ample room, his mood dark. He was tired and the last thing he wanted was to attend this reception, but he had to, Lucius being his host on his voyage to Rome. He was coming back from campaign and his army camped outside whilst he enjoyed Lucius' hospitality.

Now, after having bathed and changed clothes, he was ready to attend the festivities, though he was not looking forward to them at all. He lay down on one of the beds where a young slave had led him, and he let him fill his cup. He swirled the rich wine, looking around, vaguely bored already, this life seeming surreal after the realities of war and endless marches. There were various countryside nobles lying around, their ages differing, and soon, he presumed, dancers, slaves, and drunk guests. He knew where this would lead, and his mouth turned sour.

He raised his head when Lucius entered, a small smile on his long face with a nose like an eagle's beak. The man was in his fifties and well-known for his ambitions. Marius knew exactly why he had invited him to stop at his estate, as he was close to the emperor, and Lucius undoubtedly was looking to gain some favors. He didn't really care, and his eyes drifted to the slave walking behind Lucius, a young man by the looks of him, though it was difficult to judge, his eyes downcast, his head so low Marius wondered how he could see where he was going at all. A thick metal collar circled his neck, and a chain dangled from it, leading to Lucius' hand. The slave was only wearing a thin white tunic, mid-thigh, baring one of his shoulders. Marius checked him out, his lean body, his light brown hair, cropped short. He could not see his face. *Probably a fuck toy*. His mouth twisted into a sour smile. Lucius lay down on the bed next to him, tugged on the chain, and the slave wordlessly sank to his knees in such a fluid motion that Marius didn't even catch it. He remained with his head down, his hands on his thighs, kneeling next to Lucius.

Lucius greeted him, an amused light in his eyes. "Greetings, Marius Ulpius Lupus. I hope you are satisfied until now with my hospitality?"

He raised his cup, and Marius did the same. "Yes, thank you, Lucius."

The older man smiled. "You will see, this is going to be something tonight... I have some surprises when everybody's in the mood..."

Marius just nodded but didn't comment. He was already fed up. His eyes drifted back to the slave who was sitting on his heels, motionless, barely breathing, and Lucius noticed it, his eyes twinkling. Food was brought then, and Marius sighed, relieved, that it was excellent.

The night grew on him, the wine slowly warming his dark mood. He noticed, though, that Lucius was not feeding the slave at all whilst they chatted, mainly about politics in Rome and the Empire. His eyes drifted to the slave's ribs, too visible under that thin layer of muscles, the skin taut on that meagre flesh, and his brows furrowed slightly, catching a scar on his bony shoulder, faint and white. *Surely more on his back...* Marius had always had slaves back at home and on his campaigns too, but he hated the whole concept and definitely couldn't bear people mistreating them... apparently, Lucius was one of those.

He pried his eyes away from the kneeling young man and focused on the dancers in the middle of the room. Oriental slave girls with luscious curves, barely dressed. The guests were becoming rowdy a bit, some groping at the slave boys serving food, some pulling them in their laps, and he had to shift his gaze away. Not that he was a prude, but he had never liked public sexual acts at parties, and he was dreading them now, slowly chewing on his lower lip.

Lucius turned to him, his cup in hand. "Do you like my slave?"

Marius looked at him, completely caught off guard, but maintained a straight face, blessing his training quietly. He pretended to take a sip of his wine before replying, trying to sound casual. "He is quite pretty."

Lucius' lips curled into a smile. "Yes, he is... quite delicious too..." His eyes wandered to the kneeling man who had stayed still, seemingly not even hearing them. Marius forced his face to stay neutral, but his blood was boiling at Lucius' words, even if Marius had guessed the slave's true purpose from the start. Lucius continued, his voice languid. "I was planning to have him fucked senseless on stage tonight by some of my willing guests but... if you're into boys, I would like to gift him to you for the night."

His dark eyes bore into Marius' and Marius swallowed. *What the....* His eyes drifted to the kneeling man, catching a slight movement of his shoulders, his breathing faster a bit, but his eyes were still on his knees. He had had his fair share of boys when he had been younger, but now... it had been a while and he was not sure. Then again, he didn't want to anger Lucius either... *and it might save this slave from whatever Lucius had planned for him tonight...* He swallowed, looking at Lucius. "Would you really? I'd be delighted..."

Lucius smiled, and they raised their cups to drink.

Lucius pushed the chain into his hand, talking to the slave. "Tonight, you are going to stay with my noble guest, and you are going to fulfill whatever he wants or desires. Understood?" The slave nodded and Lucius' eyes blazed, his voice cold. "Answer me."

"Yes, dominus."

His voice was soft, but deep, and instant pity seared into Marius' heart. He hid it though and his face stayed a mask.

Lucius smiled. "Good boy..." He looked at Marius, his eyes amused. "You can do whatever you want with him. He is very well trained. And if he doesn't obey, just let me know." His eyes went back to the slave, a cruel light in them. "But he will. He knows what awaits if he doesn't..."

Marius looked at the slave's shoulders, and he saw him shudder slightly. He put a small smile on his face, just to fool Lucius. "Very well... we shall see." He rose then, a sudden urge in him to leave the hall, this whole feast already turning wrong, the moans and cries of slaves being pummeled senseless filling the room. He turned to Lucius, smiling. "I am going to retire and try out your treat."

Lucius smiled back, raising his cup. "Enjoy."

Marius looked at the slave, gently tugging on the chain. "Get up and follow me." He watched him rise, his knees red from kneeling for so long, barely shaking as blood flew back into his legs. His face was still down, not looking up at all. They walked away, Lucius' eyes on them.

Marius walked down the airy corridor to his room and opened the door, leading the slave in. He turned and closed the door, whilst the slave sunk to the floor, his hands on his thighs, eyes downcast. Marius let the chain rattle to the floor, taking in the room, when there was a knock on the door.

He opened it and a young slave bowed, a plater full of food in his hands. "Dominus Lucius said to bring you this, you might need it tonight." He let the slave in, and he put the platter on the table, quickly leaving, backing out of the room, bowing. Marius closed and bolted the door, walking to the bed, his toga already too heavy.

He turned to the slave. "Come here and help me undress."

As soon as he'd said it, the young man rose and walked up to him, dragging the chain on the floor. Marius sighed and reached to unclip it from his collar, noticing how the metal had chaffed his skin, swallowing his anger rising in his throat. He let him take his toga down, the man skillfully unfolding it and folding it to put it on a shelf. Then he walked back to Marius and stood, his eyes downcast. Marius pondered what to do... he obviously didn't want to bed the slave... but then again, if he didn't, would he tell on him?

He sighed, turning to the young man. "Look at me." Marius saw him freeze, his shoulders tensing, and he didn't obey, making the soldier in Marius sigh in frustration. He repeated it, sharper, digging his fingers into the man's chin, forcing his face up. "Look at me!"

Slowly, he raised his head, grey eyes looking ahead, wide with terror, not daring to look into Marius' eyes, looking into the void behind him. Marius studied his pale face, his smooth skin, his well contoured lips, and jaw. His hand went to his mouth and pushed it open. *Nice teeth*. His eyes roamed his body, almost as tall as him, meagre muscles, a shadow of what they had maybe been once. *Way too lean... starved, maybe*. Marius sighed, letting the slave cast his eyes down, his shoulders slouching with relief.

Marius breathed out, trying not to sound too annoyed. "Your dominus told you to obey, so when I ask you to look at me, I mean it. Do not disappoint me again." The slave nodded. "And... I would like you to talk when I talk to you. I might have questions, and you need to answer them."

This time, he spoke softly. "Yes, dominus."

Marius sighed, eyeing the dishes on the table. "When did you eat last?"

There was a pause as he waited for the answer, seeing the young slave's shoulders rise faster, panicking, but he answered, his voice barely audible. "Three days ago, dominus"

Marius froze... *three days*... his anger boiled slowly, but he didn't say anything, just sat down and gestured the slave over to his feet. "Kneel." As soon as he'd said it, the young man was on the floor next to him, waiting. Marius pulled the roasted chicken apart, pulling strands of meat off, and gently touched the slave's shoulder. "Open your mouth." He did, and Marius pushed a piece of meat in, watching him chew slowly, his shoulders trembling.

Marius kept at it, feeding him whilst he ate, making sure they ate slowly, not too much. He then poured a full cup of water and handed it to him. "Drink. Slowly." He did, his hands shaking, and handed him the cup back. Marius saw that he was fighting his tears but didn't comment.

Now what... He looked at the slave, slowly pondering, finally giving in. "I know your dominus told you that you're mine for the night, but honestly, I'm too tired to do anything. Can you do a massage?"

The slave nodded, his voice a bit more assured. "Yes, dominus."

Marius smiled. "Perfect. Let's go to bed then and you can massage me... nothing else for now."

The slave nodded and Marius walked to the bed, taking his tunic off, laying down on his stomach, sighing. The slave climbed up next to him and straddled his thighs, making him shift in discomfort, but he didn't ask him to climb down.

Marius heard the popping of the oil bottle and felt the slave's warm hands on his shoulders, kneading, putting his weight into it and it felt divine, his hands gliding on his back, shoulders, massaging out the stress and pain, the strain from his trip, days, and days of riding. Marius had to admit, he was a talented masseur, and he sighed, content, half asleep already. The slave's hands roamed all over his body, ending with his feet and Marius turned, his eyes closed, feeling his hands on his chest, slowly going to his abs.

He opened his eyes and watched the slave work his muscles, the dim glow of the candles lighting his face, his hair lightly on his forehead. He continued downwards and stopped over his cock, lifting his eyes into his, the first eye contact since they'd met, and Marius shook his head. "No, not now..."

The slave continued then, kneading his thighs and calves, his feet, and he was in heaven. He realized then he would not stop until asked to, so he spoke, his voice thick. "Just cover me and let's sleep..." He did and Marius felt the bed move as the slave climbed down. Marius opened his eyes, wondering where he went as he could not see him.

He leant over the bed and his eyes grew wide when he saw the slave curled up on the marble floor next to the bed, his eyes closed. "What are you doing?"

In a flash, he was on his knees, his voice filled with fear. "Sleeping, dominus."

"On the floor?!"

Marius hadn't realized the anger in his voice, too stunned by what he had seen, and the slave stammered, unsure. "You said we should sleep... that's where I sleep usually, dominus..."

Marius swallowed and realized he was freaking him out. He patted the bed, his voice strained. "Well, not tonight. Climb up, you'll sleep with me."

He obeyed, hesitating, not understanding at all what was happening. He lay down with a shaky breath and Marius pulled the covers on them, staying away from his body but feeling his heat under the sheets. *Damn this whole thing!* He fumed silently, watching the slave's shoulders rise and fall. He didn't move, possibly waiting. "I won't touch you. I'm too tired. Just sleep."

"Yes, dominus."

Marius drifted off to sleep, not caring anymore, his whole body relaxed and pain free.

Marius woke with the sun at dawn, as if in his camp, and watched the slave quietly sense it and slip off the bed to kneel on the floor. He sighed and looked down at him. "You don't have to kneel as soon as I'm up. Come here."

He obeyed again, wordlessly, and knelt on the bed, waiting.

Marius looked at him, curious. "What's your name?"

"Kyle, dominus."

"You're a Celt?"

"Yes, dominus."

"Captured in war?"

"In a raid, dominus."

"When?"

"Three years ago, dominus."

"How old were you?"

"Eighteen, dominus."

Marius saw his struggle, his eyes welled with tears, pushing the answers out, wanting away from his memories, and he decided to stop, not wanting to torture him further. He sort of knew anyway what had happened to him, probably raped to exhaustion until he had given in, and then sold... He was also mildly irritated at himself for caring at all. He would leave anyway today and not see him again, sick to his stomach to leave him here with Lucius. Then again, the slave had been here for years, anyway...

Marius rose, not wanting to talk further. "Come and help me with my clothes and armor."

The slave hurried to his side, slightly confused but quickly composing himself, and Marius watched his hands as he helped him dress and buckle his armor, his eyes shining with tears. Marius stopped him, his hand on his arm, and the slave lowered his head, waiting.

Marius sighed. "I did not touch you last night because I'm guessing you are used enough as it is... but your dominus should not know this, he would be upset. So, just tell him we had a great time."

The slave nodded; his voice choked. "Yes, dominus."

Marius pinched his lips. *Damn it.* He walked over and picked up the chain, reluctantly putting it back on the collar, gently sliding his fingers under it, grazing the slave's chaffed skin. "Do you have this on all the time?"

The slave nodded, unable to talk, and Marius led him out of the room, grim, looking for Lucius.

He found him on his terrace, overlooking his estate, a slave boy fanning him.

Lucius looked at them, his eyes gleaming. "So, noble Marius, liked my treat?"

Marius pushed a wicked grin on his face, his hand roughly kneading the slave's back, up and down. "Yes, you can say that. He is something..."

Lucius watched them carefully, the slave's eyes welled with tears, and his eyes gleamed. *He'd roughed him up good.* He smiled, a cruel smile tugging at his lips, a sudden idea in his head, wanting to gain Marius' favors, his mind plotting...

"What would you say, my good Marius, if I gave him over to you? As a token of my gratitude for letting the emperor know how much I long to work in Rome."

Marius' lips parted, his mind racing... *You sly bastard....* But the chain warmed his hand, sensing that the slave was barely breathing now. He smiled. "You would do that? Give away your prized possession?"

Lucius looked at the slave and almost changed his mind, but his lust for power was stronger. "He is getting old... not that this means he's not going to be good for you for a couple of more years... but I prefer them younger." His hand caressed the young slave's back next to him, the boy's face impassive, and Marius shuddered.

"In that case, I'll gladly accept your gift."

Lucius beamed a large grin. "Let's do the paperwork quickly. I don't want to hold you back on your trip."

He called his scribe, and the ownership papers were drawn up and sealed.

The men clasped their forearms, Marius grinning at Lucius. "I will not forget this favor."

"The pleasure is all mine, my good friend."

"Where are his belongings?"

Lucius just smiled. "On him."

Marius swallowed and made sure he put an evil smile on his face. "I see... in that case, we'll be going."

"Farewell, my friend. I hope Kyle brings you just as much joy as he's brought me in these past years."

Marius smiled. "I sure hope he will. I'll recommend you to the emperor."

Lucius' eyes gleamed, and he looked at Kyle. "Behave, Kyle. Do not disappoint."

The slave answered, his voice soft. "Yes, dominus."

Lucius watched them leave, vaguely regretting, but putting his hopes into this gesture to gain Marius' support.

Marius walked the slave down to his army, stationed outside the villa's walls, and his centurion's face fell, his friend, Clavius, the older man's face dubious. "What the hell is this?" He gestured at Kyle, vaguely disgusted, and Marius shrugged.

"My new slave."

Clavius scoffed. "A fuck boy?"

Marius clenched his jaw. "He's a gift from Lucius."

Clavius laughed, loud. "What?! He gifted you his fuck boy? The famous Kyle..."

His eyes grazed over the young slave and Marius' brows furrowed. "Famous?"

Clavius clasped his shoulder. "You're so young and so innocent... of course, he's famous. Famous for his skills in bed. I am amazed Lucius let him go but then again... he might be growing old..." He laughed again and watched Marius, the thirty-year-old man all of a sudden unsure, already fed up, and Clavius bumped his shoulder with his fist. "Ok, take first this leash off him, he'll look better, less like some sort of parakeet, and dress him up for fuck's sake... he is almost naked. You want him to survive in the camp? Then hide his ass." He laughed again, leading them to the blacksmith.

The collar had been welded on the slave's neck and the blacksmith sighed, grim. "I'll have to hammer it off, but heat it first..."

Marius looked at him. "There's no other way?"

The blacksmith shook his head. "It's been put on forever, as I can tell." He pulled the tight collar from the slave's neck. "See? He has burn scars. Must have hurt like a bitch when they put it on."

Marius blanched but held tight. "Just do your best."

The blacksmith nodded and talked to Kyle. "You'll have to be very still, boy. I don't want to smash your skull in."

The slave just nodded, pale as a sheet.

They lay his head on the anvil and Marius soothed him, gently holding his arms. "Just lay still. Don't move." He could see the panic in his eyes, the blacksmith lifting the red-hot iron rod, putting it on the collar, waiting for it to heat. Then he took his hammer and struck down, a loud clank, but the collar held, Kyle's body jerking slightly. Marius held him tighter, his teeth clenched. The blacksmith heated the collar again and hit harder, the metal splitting in two, revealing the slave's neck marred by scars, the skin chaffed raw in places.

Marius hissed, jerking the slave up by his arms, not even thinking as he pulled him into an embrace, feeling him tremble. "Shhh, it's going to be fine..."Marius looked at his skin, a sudden anger flooding him. He turned to Clavius. "Get the medicine man."

Clavius nodded and left, Marius gently pulling the slave by his hand. He followed, numb, his face blank. They got to where Marius' tent had stood, but it had already been folded for the last stretch of their journey and Marius made him sit on a stump, waiting for the medicine man. The young soldier arrived and eyed the wounds, taking salve out of his bag, gently applying it all around the slave's neck.

He addressed Marius then. "The burn scars are old, those will stay, but for the others, there's a good chance they will heal and fade."

Marius nodded, grim, and looked down at Kyle, the young man just sitting, blank, maybe in shock. Marius knew what it meant for a slave to be pulled out of his usual lifestyle, even if it had been hell. New master, new rules, new life, the vast unknown. The comfort of torture gone, facing new ones maybe.

He waited until Clavius came back, carrying some clothes. "Here... make him change, or put these on top of his... gown? He can't stay barefoot either, for fuck's sake." He also handed him a pair of sandals, shaking his head slowly.

Marius nodded, handing the clothes and sandals to Kyle. "Put these on."

"Yes, dominus." Numb, his hands trembling, he dressed, and Marius sighed, his frustration rising. Of all things, he was now stuck with him.

Clavius looked at him. "Just sell him at the nearest town."

Kyle's shoulders stiffened, his breath short, but he didn't dare look up and Marius watched him, pondering his friend's words. "No... Lucius might come to Rome. I can't insult him by selling his gift straight away." He turned to Kyle. "You'll travel on the cart with my belongings. There's no way you can walk until Rome."

Rome. The word echoed in Kyle's head, this word which had meant so much hate, maybe in another life, too far, buried deep in his soul. He tried not to shake, to control his emotions, as he'd been trained, but it was all too much, the collar missing from his neck, feeling the wind on his skin, being clothed properly, and leaving...

He sighed, his breath shaky, and let Marius guide him to the cart, patting the top of his items. "Climb up and sit." He gave him then a pouch of water and some bread. "Eat and drink."

"Yes, dominus."

Marius watched him carefully, looking for signs of him caving in, knowing how fast a slave could turn into a desperate wretch of a human being, but Kyle seemed just shaken. *All the better.* He went to his horse, the army rising, leaving. Rome soon, he thought, and his mind was on his home, empty save for his father's slaves checking on it from time to time. *I need to build up a household...* He pulled a face, tired of it already. *At least, I have Kyle. Not that he would be of any use in the household, he probably spent his days in Lucius' bed or being fucked senseless...*

Marius rode to the front, leaving the cart and Kyle, and the slave watched him go, his heart clenching, his old home fading in the distance, this place he abhorred... but it had meant safety so far, routine, even if it had been torture from the start. He knew what to expect; it was ingrained in him, and now... he had no idea and Marius leaving left him anxious. He didn't dare look around and the soldier leading the cart didn't talk to him, so he watched the landscape go by, musing that he hadn't even been tied down. He could have fled, but there was nowhere to go, so he just sat on the cart, bathing in anguish.

Dusk was falling when they mounted a hill and then Rome sprawled at their feet, and Kyle's eyes grew wide.

It was huge... bigger than what he had imagined, lights being lit everywhere, stone houses and walls, the noise steadily rising. He sat very still when they entered the city walls; the army marching to their quarters and the cart veering towards hills surrounding the city, out of the larger roads. He spotted Marius' horse leading the way until they stopped in front of a wall with a large door. Marius got off and opened the door wide, leading his horse in, followed by the cart and Clavius.

Home... how he had longed to be here and now... the empty house didn't tempt him. Clavius and Marius tended to the horses. His father had kept the house stocked but hadn't left any slaves.

Kyle climbed down from the cart and looked at the huge villa, the first courtyard facing an entrance door and Marius gestured at him to follow. "Come, Kyle. This is your home now."

They walked around; the door leading to a large atrium, other doors leading to rooms, the private bath, more rooms on a top floor, a large terrace overlooking Rome, the lights bright against the dark evening sky.

He took it all in and Marius faced him, his eyes dark. "Look at me." He raised his head and Marius cupped his chin, forcing his gaze into his eyes. "That's better." He felt the slave tremble, his lower lips quivering, and Marius didn't let go. "This is difficult for you? To look at me?"

He nodded, his eyes welling up.

"Why?"

"I was not allowed to look at master Lucius..."

Marius sighed; his face clouded with anger. "Well, I am not Lucius, so you can look at me, especially when I ask you to. It might take some time..."

Kyle tried to hold his gaze, but his eyes darted away. Marius let his chin go, Kyle's head sinking straight away.

"So, rules in this house..." Marius stopped, unsure. *What are the fucking rules?* He had no idea, but he saw the slave's distress, how he floated in this unknown environment, his mind not comprehending that he was not a in constant threat, maybe even craving that well-known fear. "Rules are the following for now. I don't have household slaves, but I expect my father to bring me some tomorrow. Until then, you'll be my personal slave. I'll need to purchase other slaves soon... I expect you to help me dress, bathe, escort me to various places if needed. Once you know the city better, I will send you on errands, maybe to pick up or deliver letters, go to the market."

Kyle waited, his stomach like ice, trying to comprehend his words. *Errands? As in, leave the house?* He could not even leave Lucius' room without permission. He trembled, his legs weak, and Marius saw it, cursing himself for going too fast.

"Alright... this might be too much for you. Just tend to my needs for now."

Kyle nodded, vaguely comforted. *But what needs?* He had not shown any inclination so far to bed him.

Marius watched him carefully and sighed. "I am not too much into boys... so, for now, don't expect anything."

Kyle's mind went numb. *Don't expect anything?* He had been used to be pushed to overdrive, sometimes not even knowing how much time had passed or how many men he'd been with and now, nothing? He reeled at the thought, although deep down he'd wished for this, the complete absence of sex blew his mind and he had a hard time even imagining how it would be... Utterly shocked and drained, he sank to the floor on his knees.

Marius' lips pinched in anger, but he didn't scold him. "Come... you must be tired. Clavius will eat with us downstairs and spend the night. My father left some food, I hope."

He followed Marius downstairs, and Clavius was already plundering the kitchen. "Your good father left us food..." He looked up, watching Kyle, pale, shivering. "Your fuck boy here is a mess...."

Marius just frowned at him and gestured to sit down. Kyle instantly knelt at his feet, and he didn't object, knowing this was a safe anchor point for him, ignoring Clavius' mocking smile.

He fed him whilst eating and Clavius mocked. "Soon, he'll be sucking your cock during meals, you'll see."

Marius looked at him, his face cold with anger. "No, he won't. I don't intend to bed him at all or use him for any other purposes."

Clavius looked at him, mild. "You may not have a choice."

Marius looked up, irritation clouding his handsome features. "What on earth are you saying?"

Clavius smiled. "My gentle friend... fuck boys like him..."—he waved Marius' irritation away at the word — "... they've been trained for long months to fulfill their master's desires... and when I say trained, that's not for the light-hearted... then, they spend their youth being fucked, either by their master or whomever he wishes to give them to..." He raised an eyebrow at him, and Marius fumed. "So, you think you're doing him a favor when you say you don't want to fuck him or make him suck your cock, but he is craving it, my friend... maybe not now, but soon, when he'll get to accept you as his dominus and get to like you." Marius looked down at the kneeling slave, his mind trying to grasp his friend's words. Clavius patted his hand. "You'll make him miserable, all the while thinking you're saving him..."

Marius closed his eyes, not wanting to believe what he'd heard, but he knew Clavius was right. He trusted his friend. "Perfect..."

Clavius laughed. "Yes... you're in a great situation... I told you to sell him... any decent brothel would pay you a small fortune. I am sure half of Rome's elite have fucked him already at Lucius' parties. Ain't that so, boy?"

Kyle shivered and Marius asked him, his stomach clenched. "Answer him."

Kyle sighed, licking his lips. "Master Lucius had many guests, dominus. I didn't know their names... some came from Rome."

Clavius smiled. "Any private sessions?"

Kyle swallowed. "Not really, dominus... more in groups..."

Marius clenched his fists. "How many of them?"

Kyle shrugged slightly. "I never counted, dominus."

Marius' eyes blazed, and he looked at Clavius. "Don't tell me he'll miss these."

He shrugged. "Maybe not, but he'll miss being fucked, that's for sure."

Kyle swallowed and lowered his head, wishing he would stop, his mind too tired and freaked out to think properly.

Marius rose. "Enough of this... let's go to bed."

Clavius smiled. "I'll take one of your guest rooms."

Kyle helped Marius undress, and he headed straight to the bath, his head too full. He walked into the big pool, the water still hot, and looked at Kyle. "Undress and come in, wash me off."

Kyle took his clothes off and Marius looked at his body, so lean, the bones curving the skin, but the muscles there somewhere in the memory of his meagre flesh. He sighed in relief when he noticed he hadn't been castrated. *Nor cut.* A slight shock in him, seeing that starved body, but with the promise of what it could be once his flesh had filled up.

Kyle walked up to him and skipped the routine of oiling his skin, as Marius was already in the bath. He bathed him with soap and a soft sponge, massaging his muscles, standing close to him, utterly shameless, and Marius relished his touch. *Maybe Clavius is right...* but he couldn't bring himself to touching him, knowing also full well that Kyle would do anything the moment he'd say it.

They finished washing and stepped out, walking naked to Marius' room.

Marius folded the covers back, gesturing to Kyle. "No sleeping on the floor. That's also a rule. Once this household is running, you can have your own room... or sleep with me when you're in my room."

Kyle nodded, his throat clutched, barely understanding that years of sleeping on the cold floor were over. He bit his lip not to cry, not to fall to pieces in front of his dominus, but he was too tired, too overwhelmed, and his shoulders shook silently, his tears spilling. He knew he would be punished but didn't care anymore, maybe being beaten up potentially bringing up some of the lost comfort of his everyday life, so predictable in its horror.

Marius watched him, first not even realizing he was sobbing, then silently cursing himself. He pulled the slave close, locking him in his arms, laying down on his side, drawing the covers on them. He felt Kyle stiffen, and he held tight, his voice soothing. "Cry all you want. I am not going to hurt you. Just cry this out, you'll feel better." Marius held him as he sobbed, not holding his voice back, and Marius' heart wrenched.

Finally, after a while, Marius felt him still and relax. Kyle had cried himself to sleep and Marius let him go, sighing. *Perfect...* and they were just at the beginning. *Maybe Clavius is right about selling him...* He watched him sleep though, and his heart stirred. We'll make this work, he thought, snuggling in the blankets, making sure he didn't touch him at all.

II

Marius woke early, as usual, hearing Clavius downstairs opening the front door. Soon, his father's voice reached him, and he jumped out of bed, Kyle wide awake already, kneeling on the floor, naked.

"Get dressed!"

They put clothes on, Marius softly cursing at his father, and he had just finished when there was a knock on the door and his father entered. Kyle sank to the floor, not daring to look up, listening to the men greet each other.

Marius' father's eyes darted to the kneeling slave and his eyebrows shot up. "What's this?"

Marius looked at Kyle, slightly annoyed at his father's words. "This is a gift from Lucius..."

His father walked to Kyle, his voice cold. "Get up." Kyle obeyed and Marius watched as his father cupped the slave's chin and yanked his head up, his lips curling into a smile, turning back to Marius. "He gifted you Kyle? His prized slut?"

Marius winced at the word. "How do you know him?"

His father let Kyle go. "Kneel." The slave sunk to the floor, trembling. "I know him because I attended one of Lucius' parties..."

Marius blanched. "Did you...?"

His father laughed. "No... I am not into public fornications... but I had to watch it. There were quite a few guests who were keen on mounting him." He laughed at the memory. "Well, he's a valuable slave and I am mildly surprised you accepted him, but it gives me hope that you've changed and are ready to embrace a Roman lifestyle. Did you fuck him?"

Marius moaned. "No... not yet."

His father waved his finger in front of his face. "Wrong answer. He needs to know who's the master of this household. You know this."

Marius nodded, wishing he would stop.

"Anyway, I have bought you a couple of slaves until you expand your own household. Don't spoil them rotten, they are used to harsh discipline with me."

His gaze went back to Kyle. "Just like him. I know Lucius, he is even harsher than I am, so don't spoil him. I know how soft you are."

Marius' eyes blazed. "I am not soft."

His father mocked. "Prove it." He looked at him, his eyes cold. "Fuck your new slave. Claim him as your own." Marius swallowed, nervous, and his father pursed his lips. "I thought so..."

Marius' eyes shone; his voice clipped. "I'll do it. Leave us."

He watched his father leave and close the door, his eyes still doubting, and Marius' anger flared up. He turned and pulled Kyle to his feet, pushing him against the bed, kicking his legs apart, shoving his tunic up on his back. Marius stopped, waiting for resistance, but the slave lay very still, waiting, his back barely moving.

His father's voice seeped in from the corridor, talking to Clavius. "My soft-hearted son is supposedly claiming his new slave. I'll believe it when I hear it."

They laughed, and raw anger clouded Marius' mind. He grabbed a bottle of oil from the nightstand and poured a generous amount into his palm, rubbing it on the slave's backside, mortified in the cloud of his mind that he was aroused, and he slammed into him, making him cry out. He fucked him then, hard, not caring, fueled by his anger, his father's words, anger swelling at his own weakness, grunting, moaning.

Kyle whimpered softly, more shocked emotionally than from the pain. He was used to that, and the oil helped somewhat, but it still hurt. He squeezed his eyes shut, panting, wishing Marius would just finish. Kyle felt Marius' hips jerk harder, and Marius came inside of him, grunting.

Marius stilled, in a daze, and pulled out, letting Kyle slip to the floor, the slave's back drenched, cum seeping out of him. He sat on the floor, very still, softly panting, and Marius fought the urge to scoop him up. Instead, he pushed his anger to the front, dressing, his voice hard. "I am your dominus now."

Kyle pushed the words out, soft, his voice quivering with the shock. "Yes, dominus."

Marius whirled and left him, banging the door open, and his father clasped his shoulder, grinning. "Son! I am most impressed."

Clavius watched his friend, livid, his eyes darting to the prone slave. Marius nodded to his father, bile rising in his throat, and he hurried downstairs, followed by them, to check on the slaves his father had bought.

Later, when the slaves had been settled, and his father and Clavius had left, Marius decided to go back to his room.

Kyle had already cleaned himself and the floor up, his drained face empty of emotions, his thoughts bitter. He had thought for a fleeting moment that Marius would be different and his throat tightened. Of course, Marius was a Roman, and Kyle scolded himself for believing in his kindness.

Kyle didn't care about being sore, but his heart ached. He busied himself though and tidied the room, putting Marius' clothes away when Marius walked in and Kyle froze, dropping to his knees, his arms stretched out in front of him, palms up, his forehead pressed to the cold marble of the floor.

Marius watched him in the ultimate submissive pose of slaves and his heart wrenched, but he steeled himself and walked to him. "Get up."

Kyle did, clenching his jaw at the pain, standing as best he could, and Marius tipped his chin up, looking into his eyes. "There's a room for you in the slaves' quarters. When I need you, I'll ring you."

"Yes, dominus."

Marius wanted to ask him whether he was in pain, but his father's words rang in his ears. "Go and stay there tonight."

Kyle nodded, fighting his tears. On top of the humiliation and assault, he was now rejecting him. He left on shaky legs, fighting the urge to run, and went straight to the slaves' quarters, Marius' father's old slave showing him his room, a small space with a single bed. Kyle sat down, closing the door, first time ever alone, in his own room. He curled up, his knees in his stomach, fighting his pain, and his tears flowed.

Kyle had lunch later with the others, not talking, all of them silent, grim, and the older slave distributed their tasks. Kyle had to help with the washing, and he didn't mind, working with another slave girl who was new. She was crying a lot, sniffling, wiping her tears, but he didn't know what to tell her so just kept working, the mindless physical task a blessing to keep his mind off his thoughts and keep his body drained.

When they were done, the old slave, Sixtus, came to get him. "Dominus wants you in his room. Can you wrap a toga on?"

Kyle nodded and left, his stomach in a knot. He knocked and waited to be called in, kneeling straight away, but Marius was irritated and snapped. "Get up, for gods' sake, and put this on me!"

He gestured to the toga on the bed and Kyle rose, picking it up, expertly wrapping it around him, arranging the folds. It was exhausting after having done the washing, the material heavy, and Marius was taller than the average Roman, which made it even more difficult. Kyle clenched his jaw, though, and made sure it was perfect. He had learnt this the hard way with Lucius and mastered it to a point where he had even received a compliment from him, once.

Marius watched Kyle work in the mirror, his emotions raging inside of him, regretting what he'd done in the morning but knowing he could not apologize, ever.

Finally, Kyle stepped back, and Marius looked at his work, amazed.

He smiled, turning to the slave. "I think I've never had anybody put this on me so well. It even feels comfortable, which is a rare treat." He sighed. "I need to leave to attend the Emperor's reception and won't be back until late. Wait for me here, I'll need you when I come home."

"Yes, dominus."

"And don't wait kneeling. You can sit or just sleep a bit."

Kyle nodded, swallowing, and followed Marius out of the room.

He still had kitchen duty and then dinner. He also decided to clean the bedroom out and wash down the terrace, which had seen better days.

Busy all afternoon, he finished at sunset and went for dinner, his body and mind drained, dreading the night. He could predict Lucius after all those years. The older man had had his habits and routines despite his temper flares, but Kyle had known what to expect, consistently, even if it had been mostly unpleasant. With Marius, he was lost. Kindness one moment, then violence, his constant brewing anger, then nothing. Kyle would have preferred Marius being consistent, but he had no choice, and he didn't even know about punishments. With Lucius, it had been clear from the start. *You do this; you get this.* He had known it and had tried to avoid it as best as he could, but here... He had no idea, and it threw him in a state of vague anguish.

He waited, watching the sunset on the sparkling clean terrace, Rome below, the city beastlike, stretched between the hills. He sat down in the room on the floor, near the bed, and waited, his back to it, the night slowly stretching, his eyelids heavy.

He must have slumbered, but Kyle woke with a start when he heard footsteps, and knew Marius was back. The night was pitch black outside, possibly in the darkest hours, and he kneeled, waiting. Marius entered, his eyes darting to him, but he didn't need to talk, Kyle was on his feet, walking to him, wordlessly taking his toga down, carefully folding away the heavy material.

Marius undressed and grabbed his arm. "Bathe me first."

They walked to the bath and Kyle bathed him, anxiously noticing that he was swaying a bit, his breath smelling of wine. Back to the room, Kyle continued folding the toga and Marius collapsed on the bed, utterly drained by the party's civilities, the endless chatter, and blaring music. He also had too much to drink, and his eyes focused on Kyle's lean frame, folding the toga away, stashing it into a trunk carefully.

Marius waved him over, his voice heavy with wine. "Come here..."

Kyle edged closer to the bed, his heart beating in his throat, and he stopped, his thighs against the mattress, and waited.

Marius watched the young man, vaguely irritated at him, not even knowing why. Maybe because he had no idea what to do with him after this morning. *He's just a slave, come on, don't overthink it.* But guilt ate at him, his own behavior seeming monstrous looking back, and he extended his hand to Kyle, his voice mild. "Care to join me?"

Kyle wordlessly climbed on the bed and lay down next to him on his side, his breathing shallow, watching Marius carefully.

Marius turned to him, facing him, his eyes dark in the night. "Are you afraid of me, Kyle?"

Kyle's heart raced at the question. *How to answer this?* He was afraid, but that could anger him... yet, lying would bring punishment, or so he thought, and he let out a shaky breath. "Yes, dominus."

Marius waited a bit, pondering his words. "Why?"

Kyle couldn't look at him any longer and lowered his eyes. "Because you are unpredictable, dominus."

Marius' eyes widened. *Unpredictable?* He had never thought of this and looked at the young slave, his eyes downcast, trembling. "Unpredictable? How?"

Kyle chewed his lower lip but sighed, giving up, not caring anymore if he got punished for answering his questions. "I never know what to expect from you, dominus. One moment you are kind and gentle and the next..." He couldn't continue, his mind drifting back to the morning.

Marius looked at him, grim. "I've been more on the battlefield than dealing with a household full of people who need constant directions."

He was not even sure why he was explaining this, and Kyle looked at him. "If I may... maybe just a simple set of rules? Behaviors linked to punishment."

Marius scoffed. "Punishment? I don't intent to...", but again, his mind went to what he'd done, and he silenced. *It had not been punishment, though...* His voice hardened. "What I did this morning was not punishment."

Kyle sighed. "I know, dominus..."

"But?"

Kyle licked his lips. "I am in no position to tell you anything, dominus. What you do is always right."

Marius' eyes blazed, angry at his meekness. "Just tell me what you're thinking!"

Kyle looked at him. "You could have been a bit gentler, dominus."

He didn't reply because he knew Kyle was right, yet, that ritual was supposed to convey dominance so... His lips curled into a mocking smile. "Don't tell me you're not used to being treated this way by Lucius." Kyle stayed silent and Marius felt a wicked feeling inside of him. "Tell me how he used to treat you." He watched Kyle blanch in the dim light and his lips curled into a small smile. "So?"

The slave's voice was soft. "What do you want to know, dominus?"

"Just tell me what he did to you." *And I might not feel like shit about myself.*

Kyle licked his lips. "The daily routine was the following: he woke up and sometimes wanted to have sex or I sucked him off, depending on his mood. Then I dressed him, and he went for breakfast and his daily tasks. After lunch, he came back for a nap and maybe sex too... went on his business later and back after dinner for his bath and bedtime."

Marius frowned. "And you? What did you do all day?"

"I was chained to the bed, dominus."

He said it so matter of fact that Marius choked. "What?"

"I was chained to the bed, dominus."

Marius had a hard time processing this. "So... When did you eat? Attend to your needs?"

"When he was in the room. Feeding was when he allowed it or fed me himself. Usually twice a week, dominus." Marius' lips parted and Kyle continued. "I had been trained to be a sex slave, so this is what I was used for. By Master Lucius or his guests. Or both."

Marius looked at him, grim. "And punishment?"

Kyle winced slightly. "Anything from flogging to whips. Master liked to use a riding crop in the bedroom." The entire conversation had made him uneasy and unpleasant memories bubbled to the surface, making him shut his eyes, before he realized that this was probably not allowed, so he forced them open again, waiting for Marius to continue.

"You heard my friend, Kyle. What he said yesterday at dinner." Kyle just nodded and Marius asked. "Is it true?"

The slave pondered his response, especially in the light of the morning's event, but just sighed then. "You can do whatever you want with me, dominus."

"Even if it means I won't touch you again?"

Kyle stayed silent a bit, torn between his feelings, but just closed his eyes. "Yes, it is your right to decide what you want. So, if that's your decision, then I have to accept it, dominus."

Marius stayed silent a while, his mind fogged by the wine. "But if I decided to use you in bed... would you like that?"

Kyle looked at him. "I would accept your decision, dominus."

Marius smiled mockingly. "That's not what I've asked..."

"Yes, I would like that, dominus." Although he was not sure, having only seen the rough side of him, but he didn't want to anger him either, it was not his choice, anyway.

Marius sighed, closing his eyes. "You can leave now, Kyle. Get some sleep."

The slave looked at him, slightly puzzled, but got up and slowly left the room, Marius already asleep.

In the morning, Marius woke with a splitting headache, Kyle already next to his bed with a cup of water and he downed it eagerly, sighing. "I shouldn't drink..."

The slave didn't comment, and Marius got up to dress, Kyle holding his tunic ready with his shorts. He dressed, the sun already high, and his stomach grumbled as he sat down to eat, glancing at the slave. "Have you eaten?"

"Yes, dominus."

He nodded, content. "You should eat. You're too skinny."

Lucius liked me that way, but he kept his thoughts to himself, enjoying that he didn't have to starve anymore. "Yes, dominus. I will make sure I eat."

He waited until Marius finished and collected the platter, leaving to the kitchen. Marius went down with him, looking for Sixtus, their old family slave gifted to him by his father to run his household. "Sixtus, do we need more slaves?"

The old man thought about this, his eyes drifting to Kyle. "Depends on how you want to use Kyle, dominus. He is quite versatile, but if he'll be caught up with..."

Marius waved him away. "Not full time..."

The old man nodded. "Then in that case, we might maybe just need one more to help the cook and one more to help around the house with cleaning."

Marius nodded. "How are the new ones?"

Sixtus spread his palms. "You know how this goes... the cook is a seasoned slave. She's been in a good household and knows what she's doing. The young girl however... she can't stop crying... and she is latching on to Kyle, being of the same age..." Marius' face darkened, but he didn't comment. "So, there's also your stable slave, but he is fine, too."

There was a knock on the main door and Sixtus stepped over to answer the door, letting Clavius in.

"My good friend!", the centurion grinned, shaking Marius' arm. "Come on! I've come to take you to have some fun today. We'll go and visit the baths, have lunch, and go to enjoy some nice girls!"

He winked at him, and Marius sighed. "Maybe not end this whole day in a brothel?"

But Clavius was tugging at him, grinning. "You're exhausting yourself with your new fuck boy?"

Marius frowned. "No... of course not."

Clavius pouted. "Oh... not to your liking?"

"Leave this.... let's go."

Clavius watched him carefully, but didn't comment.

They left then and Sixtus returned to his duties, walking to the kitchen where Kyle was helping the cook. "Kyle, come with me. Lisandra can take over." The young girl was crying again, silently sniffling, and Sixtus grabbed her arm. "Stop this or dominus will have your hide! This is no way to behave here." She tried to stifle her sobs but failed and he left her, gutted. Maybe she should be sold, he thought, leading Kyle to an abandoned interior garden to the right of the atrium.

It must have been lovely once, the young slave mused, looking at the dead fountain, the overgrown roses and trumpet flowers, the purple acacias. There was a rotten pergola too, with wilted roses full of thorns, and a rectangular fish pool, dried out, dead leaves rotten to a crisp littering the bottom.

Sixtus looked at him. "Any good at gardening?"

Kyle shrugged. "No, but I can try." Long-lost memories of his childhood came back, when he had been gardening with his grandfather, or just building huts out of wood... He pushed them back, his tears welling up. *All dead now. Gone, the village on fire.*

Sixtus patted his shoulder. "Well, this is yours for the next couple of days. Make it pretty."

He nodded and took the top of his tunic down, letting it pool at his waist. *It's going to be too hot soon*, the sun scorching down in the small garden. He cleaned the fountain, methodically scrubbing away with the tools he'd found in a small shed near the stables and soon sweat was pouring down his back. He didn't mind, intent on the task, just making sure all was perfect, the white marble slowly coming out from under the grime, the dead leaves. *Sixtus would need to call somebody to repair it, maybe get some water lilies too?* He then went on to trim the rose bushes which had overgrown the pergola, threatening to break the fragile structure. *Wood would be needed and paint, maybe limestone?* He snipped at the stems, the thorns lightly scratching his arms and hands, but he didn't mind, the dull pain dimming the one he had lower below.

He stopped to drink and stand in the shade a bit, then continued until dusk when Sixtus got him for dinner, amazed already at the work he'd done. "This will look good."

Kyle nodded. "You need to have the fountain repaired and we'll need some plants and wood, too."

"I'll take care of this tomorrow. Just tell me what you need." The old man watched him fondly. He already liked him a lot, wondering how Kyle had stayed sane in Lucius' household, but then again, he didn't want to ask him anything. Memories could rip you apart.

Marius hadn't returned, and they went to bed late, leaving their doors open to hear him if he arrived in the night, but dawn rose, and he was nowhere. Still, Sixtus didn't worry. It was common practice for young men to stay out for several days. He harnessed the donkey and tied him to a small cart, heading to the market.

He turned to Kyle. "Keep an eye out while I'm gone." The young slave looked vaguely panicked, and Sixtus looked at him with a warm smile. "You have the most sense here now and I need to do the shopping. I will buy what you asked for, for the garden too."

Kyle nodded, opening the gate for him, and Sixtus left, sitting on the small cart. Kyle got to work then, back into the garden. He opted for simple shorts, the sun too hot, and worked for hours, snipping at the vegetation, piling it up. *We'll have to drag it outside or burn it*. He stopped for brief breaks, watching the garden take shape, and then continued.

Kyle was working on the trumpet bushes, trimming them, and he had to reach high, stretching his muscles to reach the higher branches, the tortuous twigs hugging the stone walls, climbing. He hadn't noticed the pair of eyes roaming his body, looking at his taut muscles, too absorbed in his work.

Marius stood with a small smirk on his face, leaning against the archway leading to the garden, watching Kyle work. He was dizzy with the wine they had had with Clavius, and his night at the brothel, his tongue thick in his mouth, his mind still hazy. He walked up to Kyle slowly and put a hand on his back, marveling at his scars. Kyle whirled and his eyes flew wide at his sight, collapsing straight to the ground on his knees at Marius' feet.

Marius sneered and pulled him up, losing his balance and shoving Kyle against the wall, his face inches from the slave's face. "So... what are you up to?"

Kyle stammered, pinned to the wall. "I... Sixtus asked me to arrange the garden... dominus..."

Marius looked around, swaying. "Looks a mess..." He turned back to Kyle, his lips slowly approaching his, whispering. "I'm sure you'll do a good job..."

His hands slid up to Kyle's face, and Marius pulled him into a kiss, his tongue pushing into his mouth. He tasted of wine, but Kyle let him, not daring to kiss him back, just opening up to him, his tongue gently meeting his tongue. Marius insisted though and Kyle swiped his tongue across his, lavish strokes which made Marius moan.

He pulled away, whispering. "You're a great kisser...", then returned to Kyle's mouth, his breath ragged, kissing him with his mouth open wide, their tongues intertwining. Marius pulled Kyle's lower lip into his mouth, gently nibbling the soft flesh, then pulled away, his eyes glazed over. "If we don't go to my room now, I'll fuck you against the wall."

Kyle's heart beat fast, but he held Marius' gaze and let him lead him out of the garden, up the stairs to his room. Memories of the previous day came into his mind, and he was still sore, but there was no way he would refuse him. Marius banged the door shut and kissed him again, pushing him towards the bed, making him crawl up on it. He tugged at Kyle's shorts and took them off, peeling his own tunic down, all the while caressing Kyle, moaning into his mouth. Kyle knew all too well where this was leading, but he was still dreading it, facing the unknown.

Marius broke their kiss to turn Kyle on his stomach, his head turned to the side, grabbing some pillows to raise his ass and he got the bottle of oil from the nightstand. He was more careful now, even if drunk, to make sure Kyle was lubed up, pushing two fingers inside of him. Kyle gasped, but the pain was manageable, and he was slightly relieved. He felt Marius on top of him then, his arms around his head and he relaxed, letting Marius push inside with almost no resistance, feeling the burn where he was still sore, but it went away quickly, just to be replaced by the fullness of Marius.

Marius moaned and started to move, slowly. *Gods, he feels divine...* He made sure to move at a languid pace, watching the slave's eyes close, his soft breaths and moans. He lent down to nibble his neck, lick it, and he felt his body react to his touch. Marius grabbed his wrists, pushing them onto the mattress. "You like this?"

Kyle could barely talk. "Yes, dominus..."

"Good..." He continued, picking up the pace, their moans filling the room as he thrust harder, feeling Kyle grip his cock deep inside and he was almost losing it already, panting into his ear. "You feel so good... I'm going to come..."

Kyle just moaned and Marius pushed his index and middle fingers into his mouth, feeling him suck them. He groaned and closed his eyes, lost in the rhythm, hard, fast, and he came, groaning loudly, his hips rocking into Kyle. A short while after, Marius rolled off him, dizzy, dazed by his experience, his consciousness drifting, and he fell asleep.

Kyle watched him, slowly recovering, getting up to pick up his shorts and sneak out. He washed quickly at the well in the wash yard, and went back to the room straight away, bringing a warm cloth to wipe Marius off. He didn't wake, and Kyle waited, not daring to go away.

Marius woke later, opening his eyes, moaning. Reality hit straight away as his mind recollected what had happened, but it was murky, mixed with his experience at the brothel.

He looked at the slave resting next to him, his eyes open, and asked, his voice raspy. "Did we...?" Kyle nodded, and he sighed, closing his eyes. "Did I hurt you?"

"No, dominus."

"Good... Oh gods, I am dying..."

He sat up, trying to stop the world from turning, and Kyle rose. "Do you want to drink?"

"Water..." Kyle went to the jug and poured a large cup, handing it to him. "I slept?"

"Yes, dominus."

Marius closed his eyes, completely lost, cursing Clavius for his ideas of fun... *What the fuck's going on with me? Bedding this slave...* He cursed softly, trying to get up, but he felt sick, not just because of the wine.... He moaned and rolled on his side, watching the sunset through the balcony columns.

"Sunset? How long... ah, never mind. Help me up."

Kyle took his hand and pulled him up, Marius' blue eyes dazed under his black hair, smiling slightly. "What the hell... I can't even see straight..." He pulled a face, swallowing his nausea, and leant on Kyle's shoulder to walk outside to the balcony, collapsing on the bed there.

The weather was warm, and he just lay there, at ease, looking in wonder at the sparkling terrace. Kyle brought a sheet to cover him, and he was just grateful, slightly ashamed, too. *I said I would not touch him... so much for this...*

"Are you hungry, dominus?"

He mused, his eyes glinting in the sun. "Yes... maybe. Bring something light. My stomach is revolting."

Kyle left then, and Marius stayed, facing the sunset, when he heard footsteps and Clavius appeared, grinning. "What's up?"

Marius grimaced, not even getting up, annoyed. "Damn you and your fun! I almost died."

Clavius laughed, lying down on the other bed. "Softy... look at this terrace and this view! Amazing." He turned his head when Kyle appeared with the food, laying it on a low table between them. Kyle had brought enough for two, having seen Clavius arrive earlier. Clavius eyed him carefully, the slave pouring him a glass of watered wine, and water for Marius who could not even look at him.

Clavius smiled and waited until Kyle left again. "So, you fucked him?"

Marius smirked. "You were there, you moron."

"Not that morning... today?" Marius blushed slightly, annoyed at his reaction, and Clavius laughed. "Cheers to that!"

Marius' irritation flamed up, his anger hammering at his painful temples. "I was drunk."

Clavius patted his hand, shoving food into his mouth. "Why are you upset? That's what he's good for. You are quite lucky in that sense; he is a fine one."

Marius closed his eyes. "I am not into boys."

Clavius laughed hard. "I think you were very much into him this afternoon." He rolled from laughter and Marius closed his eyes, pained. Kyle appeared then, bringing some fruits and cheese, waiting when he had put the plates down and Clavius spoke to him. "Your dominus would like your sweet ass for dessert." He roared with laughter.

Kyle didn't reply, just stood with his head lowered, and Marius sighed. "Stop your nonsense, will you?"

Clavius raised his glass at him. "To you and your lovely fuck boy."

Marius closed his eyes, his lips pinched. "Don't call him that."

"Oh really? What should I call him then?"

But Marius didn't reply, his eyes on the sunset.

Kyle waited until they finished, and Clavius was relating their adventures at the brothel, endlessly teasing his friend. "You might not be that much into boys, but boy, that hooker you fucked senseless, she was something. The whole brothel could hear you."

He laughed hard, and Marius fumed. "Just shut up. It is embarrassing enough as it is." But he was smiling too.

His eyes drifted to Kyle who had started putting their meal away, looking at Marius. "Anything else, dominus?" He had left the wine out and the jug of water with their cups.

"No, Kyle. Just come back here."

Kyle nodded and left, coming back a while later and he sank to his knees next to Marius, his head bowed.

Night was falling, and they sipped on the wine and water, silent, cricket songs filling the night, both men grim, watching Rome light up. Kyle had already lit the torches and candles on the terrace, bathing it in a soft glow, and Marius' hand went to Kyle's head, without thinking, petting him, absentminded, not even realizing he was doing it.

Kyle kneeled very still, his emotions raging. *What is he doing?* He said he would not touch him and now... petting his head? It felt good though, and he didn't pull away, of course, but he was confused.

Clavius smiled, looking at them. "Looks like you can't keep your hands off him after all."

Marius snapped out of his reverie, pulling his hand away as if he had touched fire. "I... I am still drunk..."

Clavius laughed, shaking his head. "Whatever... don't mind me..."

Marius looked at Kyle, the slave kneeling, not moving, his head down. He vaguely remembered them kissing... how good it felt. *Damn it.* The night air was warm, and he felt horny again a bit, longing to touch him, feel his mouth... *What the fuck's wrong with me?* He cleared his throat. "You can leave and retire for the night, Kyle."

The slave rose and bowed. "Goodnight, dominus."

He left and Marius had already regretted it, steeling himself.

Clavius smiled. "Why did you send him away?"

"It's bedtime. I can't have him kneel all night either."

His friend toasted him. "You should just let it go, Marius. He is your slave. Just fuck him when it pleases you. You're overthinking this again."

Marius' lips pinched. "Hardly... and don't say fuck."

Clavius mocked. "Make love? That would imply you have feelings for him..."

Marius sighed. "True... oh, fuck it! Fuck this shit! I should just sell him..." But he knew he could not and decided to keep away from him for a couple of days. They went to bed then, Clavius sleeping over, as was his custom.

III

In the morning, Clavius and Marius left early for a military council at the palace, and Kyle went back to the garden. Sixtus had had the fountain repaired, and Kyle worked all day fixing the pergola, painting it anew. He then planted the waterlilies in the fountain and the fishpond and trimmed the remaining trees and bushes.

By night, he was exhausted, but waited for Marius, not expecting anything at all, but knowing that the possibility was there, but when Marius came home, he just asked him to undress him and went straight to bed, dismissing him.

Marius watched him leave, and he cursed under his breath, his blue eyes blazing.

The same scenario repeated itself for the following days and Kyle buried himself into his work, vaguely shaken by Marius' attitude, anxious. Again, he could not predict what would happen and when... and how. Just hoping, guessing.

His body had not been used to being neglected for so long. With Lucius, there had always been something, day or night, every day. He had made sure of that and if he could not do it, he would have asked one of his bodyguards, soldiers, or the slave master. It hadn't mattered as long as Kyle had gotten it every day. It had been even more intense when they had had guests or had been hosting parties. Obviously, what at the beginning of his captivity had been an act that had almost taken his mind away, after his training and during all those years, it had become a necessity, something he'd even learnt to enjoy... so Marius' behavior threw him in a state of despair and need. His chest swelling, he had to retire over and over again without Marius touching him and his despair grew. Still, he worked on his tasks; the garden taking shape.

Marius held for ten days, avoiding Kyle as much as he could, seeing that melancholic look in his grey eyes, a slight twinge of despair each time Marius sent him away to his room. Marius steeled himself, though, not wanting to give in to the senseless feelings he had for Kyle. He buried himself in his new life, spending time with Clavius, going on errands and to slave markets with Sixtus. They still needed two slaves, but he couldn't find what he was looking for, and his frustration chewed at him.

One evening, though, Marius came home and went straight to the garden, wondering how it looked, and he was floored, standing in the archway. The fountain trickled, the delicate sparkling statue of a woman pouring water out of her vase, water lilies softly drifting on the pond's surface. Bushes and trees were neatly trimmed, and the paths renewed, the grass fresh, still a bit weak. Purple acacia flowers hang heavy, their scent sweet in the warm air. Torches shone on the walls, and he wandered down the path leading to the pergola, the wood new and white, the roses tamed, gently hugging the frame. There were several beds laid out, and he sighed, lying down on one of them, his eyes in the stars. *This is heaven...*

He heard footsteps and Kyle stopped next to him. "Would you like to eat your dinner here, dominus?"

Marius looked up at him and shook his head, his mood mellow, the air thick between them. The slave only wore his light tunic, the flimsy fabric gliding down on his left shoulder, and Marius' eyes roamed his body, noticing how he had filled up, the regular food and physical work sculpting his muscles, his skin tanned golden under the sun, his grey eyes shining in his face.

"I ate in town."

Kyle nodded and turned to leave, but Marius' voice snapped in the quiet garden. "No! Stay."

He stopped immediately and kneeled at his side, waiting, his heart racing.

Kyle was so close, his face within his reach, and Marius sighed, closing his eyes. *Ah! Fuck it...* He turned to Kyle from where he was laying and leant towards him, his hand gently tilting his head up, pulling him towards his lips into a soft kiss. Kyle shuddered and his lips parted, letting Marius invade his mouth, their breaths ragged in the warm night. Marius pulled him up next to him, impatient, not breaking their kiss, lying side by side, his hand roaming the slave's body, pulling his tunic up, feeling the warm, toned muscles under his palm. Kyle bathed in his touch, slightly trembling, hoping it would last before he changed his mind.

Marius breathed. "Touch me..."

Kyle's hand flew to his side, to his back, caressing him under his tunic, letting his hand stray on his abs, lower down towards his erection, which he felt pressing into his palm, a soft moan escaping Marius' lips. Kyle didn't need to think about what he was doing, but it was still different. He'd rarely been kissed after his training, or felt cared for, and this was the first time somebody was so gentle to him. It almost made him cry, but he knew better, and swallowed his tears, pushing into the kiss, all the while stroking him, Marius' breath quickening.

Kyle broke the kiss then, letting his mouth stray down the Roman's body, his lips closing around his cock, letting it slide into his mouth. Marius' eyes flew open, and his hands went to Kyle's head, but he didn't push him away, and soon, he was writhing on the bed, gripping the sides, his moans filling the night air. Marius felt that warm mouth around his flesh, Kyle's tongue stroking it up and down, bathing in his saliva, Kyle's hands caressing him, working on him, and he was lost in his pleasure.

Kyle made sure he did all he could to please him, enjoying it really for the very first time, wanting to push him over the edge. He was good, and he knew it, watching the man's face, his eyes closed, his lips parted, panting, and moaning. He smiled, knowing Marius was close, and sucked him harder, pushing him over the edge when he swallowed him whole, deep. Marius came then, growling, his warm semen spurting out in thick waves, and Kyle swallowed it all down, milking him to the last drop until he softened, sliding out of his mouth.

Marius reached for Kyle and pulled him to his chest, his hand lightly caressing his shoulder. They didn't speak at all for a while, Marius still processing what had happened, but then he turned to Kyle, smiling. "This was amazing..."

Kyle looked at him, happy. "My pleasure, dominus."

They lay quietly again. Marius didn't want to tell him anything of his struggles, after all, what for. He could live with this deal, just casual sex, nothing else, but as he lay there with Kyle in his arms, a slow feeling crept into him which he could not quite place.

Kyle lay on Marius' shoulder, his eyes on the Roman's profile, his blue eye, strong nose and jaw, his black hair, and for the first time, something stirred in him. Maybe he could learn to live with him without fearing him every day. After all, he'd treated him well until now. He had already forgotten being used that morning, his mind clouding it over as it had done it with all his memories and experiences of hours of savage fucking after which he could barely walk. They did not matter, and the sooner they were processed and walled up, the better. Marius had drifted off to sleep, and he snuggled closer to him, his eyes heavy. Soon, they were asleep in the warm night under the stars.

Next morning, Marius woke still on the garden bed, and he sat up, vaguely ashamed again. Clavius' words raced in his head. *Maybe he's right, I shouldn't complicate this too much...* His breakfast had been prepared and laid on a small table next to the bed, and he ate heartily, his thoughts drifting to last night.

Clavius walked into the garden, looking around, whistling. "Wow! I never knew you had this garden here..."

Marius looked up. "Yep. It's Kyle's work..."

"What? Your fuck boy's? I'm impressed!"

He sat down and dug into the food, winking at Marius who had clenched his jaw. "Don't call him that."

"Oh, sorry... I forgot you have an issue with it..." He was mocking him of course and Marius sighed, letting it go. Clavius looked at his drawn face. "You slept here? You look like you just got up."

Marius nodded, not elaborating further.

His friend sighed. "Anything I can help with? I am bored out of my wits."

Marius looked at him. "Yes, you can come with me to the slave market. I still need to buy two of them and could use your brain and your eyes."

Clavius grinned. "No problem! I know how much you like that place."

"Yes... and tonight, my parents are coming over... join us?"

"Yes, why not... I'll be the buffer between you and your father." They laughed, but Marius was already dreading tonight. His father had always had high ambitions for him, wanting him to join him in politics, retire from the army, marry... Marriage was going to be on the table, no doubt, and he was not looking forward to it.

Clavius watched his blue eyes cloud over, the slight dent between his brows, and he clasped his shoulder. "Thinking about marriage?"

Marius blinked, surprised. "I didn't know you could read my mind..."

Clavius laughed. "I'm older than you and have known you for years. I know how you feel about marriage."

Marius' voice tensed. "I just don't think it's the right time... I'm still in the army, will probably be sent on another mission before I am allowed to retire... Leave a wife here alone whilst I'm campaigning?"

Clavius nodded. "True, true... but wives can stay alone, no worries." He winked and Marius knew he was alluding to his own wife, Tertullia, who didn't mind where her husband was as long as she had her young bed slaves and her social status and lifestyle. Still, this was not the life he wanted...

His thoughts were interrupted by Kyle, who came to pick up the leftovers. The slave was wearing a white tunic, the material softly flowing around his tanned body, and both men watched him in silence as he put the plates and cups on the tray.

He picked it up and turned to Marius. "Would you like anything else, dominus?"

The way he'd said it, with a glint in his grey eyes, made Marius blush slightly, and he had to clear his throat before answering. "No. I'm leaving shortly with Clavius, so come to my room to help me dress."

Kyle bowed and left, his hips swaying lightly, and Clavius whistled. "My... my... look at what he's becoming..." He smiled at Marius. "You are a fool if you don't take advantage of having him."

Marius waved him away and stood. "Whatever... I need to dress."

Clavius was already in his light toga. "I'll wait for you. Don't take too long..." He had a smug smile on his face and Marius frowned, disapproving. He left to his room and Kyle was already there, ready to wrap the lighter toga on him. *It would still be hot today...*

He stood whilst Kyle's hands worked on him, lightly brushing him sometimes and he had to steel himself not to grab the slave and throw him on the bed. Kyle bowed when he was done, and Marius hurried outside. "Get Sixtus. We're going to the slave market."

Kyle went to get the old man, who pestered a bit but got ready quick

They left then and Kyle got to his tasks, keeping busy being the only way to keep him from thinking too much about Marius and this whole new situation he was in. He had walled up his emotions until now, just mindlessly working on his chores, whatever he'd been assigned to do, but this wore on him, and he started to come out of the fog he'd put himself into. Deliberately trying to ignore that Marius was a soldier... one of those generals who'd ordered his village and tribe to be destroyed... one of those who... He shut his eyes to his memories, pushing them back to the dark places of his soul, and he continued to scrub the dining hall. It needed to be spotless for dinner. His stomach turned to ice when he thought of Marius' father, the influence he had on his son. He hadn't been back at the house since that morning, and Kyle dreaded him more than anything.

Marius and Clavius arrived at the slave market on foot, the sun already hot in the sky, and Marius was already fed up. Sixtus trailed behind them, silent. The auctions had already started, and they watched, bored. Mostly prisoners of wars got sold first, young boys or men, but he was not interested in those.

Clavius nudged him. "No boys?"

He shook his head. "I have Sixtus and Kyle. The rest should be women... I can't stand males bickering all the time."

Clavius shrugged, and they waited. Women and girls came next, and they looked at them, some so frightened they could barely stand, and Marius winced each time one of them got sold. He noticed then a woman being dragged onto the block, crying, her eyes darting back to a young girl, around eleven years old, her face marred with tears. *Mother and daughter.*

Marius' heart clenched, and he gestured to Sixtus. "We'll buy her and that young girl, too." He pointed at them and Sixtus nodded, a bit surprised because he would have preferred two adults, but he didn't argue.

Clavius watched him and chirped in. "You want to buy a child?"

Marius looked at him. "So what?"

He spread his palms, grinning. "I didn't know you were into children..."

Marius frowned at him but kept his eyes on the auction block, the woman standing there naked, her eyes wide, taking in the crowd. She had a nice body, with soft curves, but would be too old for most men who were waiting for the younger girls to be brought out. A couple of brothel owners bid on her, but Sixtus outbid them all and got the woman for a fairly good price. She was dragged down the block, crying, her arms reaching for the child, but the trader swatted her with his whip and dragged her away.

Marius clenched his jaw, and they waited until the child was brought out. She stood, terrified, and obviously, many more men bid on her, and a couple of women, and the brothel owners. She was thin, her blonde hair reaching down to the middle of her back, blue eyes, and soft lips. The price kept rising, and the traders smiled mildly, seeing the competition. She was stated a virgin which raised the stakes. Sixtus looked at Marius, mildly alarmed that the child's price was already over that of a good house slave, but he just nodded at him.

Clavius took his arm. "Really? She is skinny... What will you use her for?"

Marius shrugged him off. Obviously, at the end, he was left with one other noble who had set his eyes on her, and they competed, until Marius leant down to Sixtus and gave him an outrageous amount. The old slave looked at him, his eyes wide, but he just pushed his back a bit and waited. The announced amount silenced the crowd, and the other man gave in with a slight bow, some clapping.

Clavius whispered. "Are you insane?"

But Marius didn't comment and made his way to the cages behind the auction blocks.

The trader was already there, a sly smile on his face. "Very good choice, dominus."

He didn't care and gestured to Sixtus to pay for the slaves. The woman was led out first. They had put on her a dirty tunic, and she was barefoot. She was shoved to the ground at Marius' feet on her knees, her face blank. They brought the girl out then, also in a simple tunic, barefoot, and the woman clutched at her, screaming.

The merchant raised his whip, but Marius' voice snapped. "Don't touch them!"

The papers were signed, and Marius let the woman cradle the child before Sixtus pulled her to her feet, the girl clutching at her mother's tunic, her eyes wide.

They left then, and Clavius walked next to Marius. "What was this good for? Paying a small fortune for this child?"

Marius sighed, his brows furrowed. "I couldn't stand the thought of them being separated..."

Clavius sighed. "By the gods, Marius, you can't save them all."

His friend looked at him. "I know... but at least she won't get fucked to pieces tonight, torn from her mother."

Clavius looked at him, grim, but didn't comment further.

They arrived, and Kyle opened the door, curiously eyeing the woman and the child. Sixtus made them kneel in front of Marius and he spoke to the woman. "What's your name?"

"Melissa, dominus."

"What did you do in your previous household?"

"I was a maid, dominus."

"Are you any good at cooking?"

"Yes, dominus, I also helped in the kitchen sometimes."

"Good." He looked at Sixtus and the old man nodded. Marius turned to the utterly terrified child. "What's your name, child?"

She couldn't answer, her lips trembling, and her mother reached over to squeeze her hand. Still, she kept silent, and Marius turned to Melissa. "What's your daughter's name?"

"She's called Brianna, dominus."

"How old?"

"Eleven, dominus."

"What did she do in your previous household?"

"She helped with various minor tasks, dominus, mostly gardening and cleaning."

"Who's the father?"

The woman swallowed, her eyes welling up. "He is dead, dominus. Killed when we were captured. I was pregnant with her..."

Marius' lips pinched. Still, he had to ask. "Is she a virgin, as stated?"

"Yes, dominus. Our previous owner liked boys."

"Why were you sold?"

"He got into debts and couldn't pay them..."

Marius sighed, his emotions raging, and his eyes went to Kyle, his grey eyes on the woman and the child, pale. He turned back to the woman. "Well, you're in my household now. You will help Shayla in the kitchen and your child can continue doing the various minor tasks she's done before. There are only two other male slaves, Sixtus here, and Kyle. Sixtus is in charge of running this household and making sure you're all busy. Do your tasks well and behave, that's all I ask, and you will be treated well."

"Yes, dominus, thank you."

Marius watched her, her trembling lips, her hands still clutching the child. "You have nothing to fear. Your child is safe here."

Her shoulders slouched, and she whimpered. Marius left them with Sixtus and gestured for Kyle to follow. Clavius left for his home to change and be back for dinner.

Marius noticed the gleaming corridors and his room, the floor like mirrors, and he looked at Kyle whilst he unwrapped his toga. "Your handiwork?"

"Yes, dominus."

"That young girl will need some tasks. Can you think of anything she can do? I bought her for a small fortune, so make sure she's used."

"Yes, dominus."

Marius sighed, his thoughts on tonight's dinner, not even realizing he was sharing his thoughts with Kyle, it seemed so natural. "My father is going to tease me because of that little girl... I need to make sure she's useful."

"I'll make her work, dominus."

"Good... now to take a bath because I am filthy from the streets and that market. Horrid place..."

Kyle didn't comment, and they walked to the bath, Marius asking him to join him. Kyle sat on the pool's side, his legs in the water, behind Marius who sat on the stone bench in the water, and Kyle massaged his back and neck, the tension slowly easing off him and he asked, his eyes half-mast. "Were you also sold on a market?"

Kyle's hands stopped for a split second, just to resume. His voice was heavy, almost pained. "Yes, dominus."

"Lucius bought you?"

"Yes, dominus."

"But you were not a virgin?"

"No, dominus."

"Why?"

Kyle sighed, trying to wall up his feelings. "When our village was raided, we fought, even us, young boys... but there was not much we could do... I was raped, like all the others, by the soldiers..."

Of course. "And Lucius?"

Kyle licked his lips, wishing he would stop. "Lucius bought me for his own personal pleasures, dominus."

"Tell me what happened."

Kyle's hands stilled again, but he steeled himself and continued, trying to sound neutral, but his voice was dull, dead, as he recounted his first year on the estate. "Master Lucius brought me home. I was quite wild, not accepting my fate or anything that had happened to me. I could not speak or understand Latin. He kept me tied down on a stand and spent days just taking me or giving me to his bodyguards, soldiers... I got beaten too. I gave in after a couple of days, there was nothing left to do... He kept me chained to the bed and we spent another couple of days, just him and me... I had to learn the rules, but it was difficult at first as I still couldn't understand anything. He sent me then to a training house in a city close by..." Marius stayed silent, and Kyle continued, drained. "The training house was essentially a brothel, but they also taught me basic Latin, reading and writing, household chores... And of course, training me to be a bed slave..."

"How?"

"I had to learn with the trainers and then practice on the clients. It took a while, as I was still not surrendering fully. Beatings and starving got me where they wanted me, eventually. And rows of clients... I gave up for good and just tried my best..."

"How long did you stay?"

"A year, I think, maybe more..." Kyle stopped, fearing that he might hate him now, after having had all those men, and more at Lucius' estate...

Marius turned a bit and pulled him down next to him in the water, lacing his arm around his shoulders. Kyle fought his tears, his throat clutched, the memories tearing at him. Remembering his old self didn't help either... those times when he could still do what he wanted, being the clan leader's eldest son... He shut his eyes, wishing his thoughts away, vaguely aware of Marius' hand tracing his shoulder. He opened his eyes and looked at the Roman, but Marius just rose with a sigh and took his hand.

"Come... let's dress, my mighty father will be here soon..."

He let Kyle bring him his clothes and when he was done; he grabbed the young slave by the shoulder and tipped his chin up.

This time, Kyle held his gaze and his blue eyes bore into his. "I know what you were when Lucius gave you to me. I also sort of guessed what you've been through, and it doesn't matter to me at all." Kyle's eyes welled with tears, but he held Marius' gaze, tight, not letting them flow out. Marius pulled him into a hug, his voice soft. "As long as I live, you're safe with me. I won't sell you."

Kyle's legs gave way, and he went to the floor, his hands wrapping around Marius' calves, his head pressed to his feet. "Thank you, dominus."

Marius watched, wide eyed, and pulled him up, his voice choked. "Go and change. They will be here soon."

Kyle left, his tears flowing, and changed into his festive tunic, rushing to the kitchen to check with Sixtus if all was in order. The new slave had adjusted well, and she was still silently tearful but doing her job.

He found the child sitting there and extended his hand to her, smiling. "Come with me, Brianna?"

Her mother looked up and nodded, and the little girl took his hand. She had been bathed and changed into a light blue gown, matching her eyes, her blonde hair clean, flowing down her back.

Kyle showed her to the dining room. "Tonight, you can help me here. Make sure you keep an eye on the lamps and candles and if one of them goes out, light it." She nodded, still not talking, and Kyle showed her the way to the kitchen. "I might need you to go and get some more food and plates. Can you help?" The little girl nodded, and he scooted down to her level, his hands holding her hands. "I'm Kyle. A slave like you. And you shouldn't be afraid of me."

She looked at him, her voice soft. "My best friend was called Kyle."

He smiled. "Wonderful!"

Her eyes went into his. "He's dead now."

Kyle shuddered, but squeezed her hands. "But we're not. I can be your friend if you'll have me?" She smiled timidly, and they left for the kitchen to prepare the dishes.

Clavius arrived first, knowing he should be early to ease Marius' nervousness, and he had been right; his friend was already pacing the entrance.

"Come, come... these are only your parents...", but Marius' tortured look made him shut up, and he stepped to him, grabbing his shoulders, making him stop. "Hey... you're a grown man... what could go wrong?"

He sighed. "Everything..."

They waited when there was a loud knock on the door. Marius opened it and his father stepped in, followed by his mother who straight away hugged him. "My boy! I'm so glad to see you!"

His father greeted Clavius and then turned to his son. "Marius, thank you for having us. How are you managing?"

They walked towards the dining room on the top floor. "I'm doing fine, father."

They lay on the couches, Kyle and Lisandra immediately coming to serve them. The young woman had calmed down, mainly due to Sixtus' endless scolding, and she also listened to Kyle, who helped her adjust.

Marius' father eyed them and turned to his son. "You should breed them." Marius almost choked on his wine, and his father smiled. "What's wrong? They are young and healthy, nothing better than breeding your own slaves, right? This way, you can keep them or sell them."

Marius just nodded, determined not to argue. "I will think about it, father, thank you for the idea."

Kyle came back, Brianna trailing behind him and he made her kneel further away, to monitor the lamps and candles, and Marius' father turned to him. "A slave girl? What on earth were you thinking?"

Marius replied, his voice clipped. "She came with her mother."

"Ah! I am surprised they allowed her to live at all…"

Marius knew what he was referring to. Slave girls were killed, usually after birth, and he just shrugged. "You just told me to breed them. She'll grow up here, it's very much the same."

His father looked at her. "Pretty too…"

Marius shuddered, closing his eyes. "Yes… but I don't touch children…"

His father smiled, raising his glass. "I know. Well, in a couple of years, she can have children with your precious Kyle, too."

Marius didn't reply, chewing his anger.

Clavius came to the rescue, distracting his father with some inappropriate topic, and his mother turned to him. "How are you doing, son?"

"I'm fine… it's just strange to be idle here in Rome… I like action."

His mother smiled. "I know… but you need to think about settling soon?"

He nodded, anguished at where this was going whilst dinner was served, Kyle and Lisandra putting the different meals in front of them, serving more wine. Kyle then knelt behind Marius to tend to their needs if needed. He threw a quick glance at the little girl, but she hadn't moved, carefully watching the lamps and candles. *Good.*

Gaius, Marius' father, turned to him. "Son, your mother is right. You need to settle soon, and by this, I mean your marriage, of course." Marius shut his eyes, pained, just to look then at Clavius, who just shrugged. His father continued.

"You are a grown man, Marius, you can't procrastinate this any longer. Next week, I'd like you to come and attend a dinner party at our house where I will introduce you to some ladies, all possibly quite suitable to be your wife."

He sighed. "Father... I might go on other campaigns..."

"So what? She'll stay here and wait for you. All wives do that. But I can't have my son be unwed and live the life of a bachelor, not with your status." His eyes pierced him. "Especially not now when Lucius gifted you his whore."

Marius fumed at his words but decided not to argue, very much aware of Kyle's presence behind him and he gestured to him to fill his cup. He was drinking again too much and knew he shouldn't, but his nerves were on edge. Kyle walked next to him, and their eyes locked briefly over his cup. Marius fought the urge to just reach out and touch his hand, but he knew it was not possible and drank instead deeply.

The meal continued, his father endlessly listing possible brides, and he was annoyed, wanting away from it all. *Wife... just what I need, a woman in this house whom I should bed and have children with...* The whole idea seemed horrendous, and he drank more, Clavius raising his eyebrow at him, gesturing to slow down. He shrugged, his mood dark, but stopped, knowing that he would not even be able to get up if he continued.

They were over with desserts, and his father turned to him, slightly frowning. "You drink too much."

Marius' eyes blazed, but he forced a smile. "Why, thank you for pointing it out, father. I wouldn't have noticed it myself."

The old man smiled at him. "Mocking me? Well, that's a first but I'll take it's the wine. Just make sure you don't make a habit of it."

Marius opened his mouth, his face veiled with anger, but Clavius jumped in. "Anybody fancy going to the arena tomorrow?"

Gaius turned to him. "Might be a good idea. Marius?"

He brooded, trying to kill Clavius with his stare. "Fine..."

Clavius beamed. "Excellent! Some killings, races, good fun!"

Gaius rose. "Well then, I believe it's time for us to go. Don't forget next week's dinner party. Be at your best and try not to drink too much. The ladies are all of respectable families and I expect you to have chosen your wife to be by the end of the dinner."

Marius rose, slightly swaying, his eyes dark. "Of course, father."

Gaius just smiled. "Don't bother escorting us out, your good slave can do it, he can at least walk straight."

Marius blanched but Clavius was at his side at once, grabbing his hand, which he had fisted. "It was a lovely evening, thank you."

Marius watched his parents follow Kyle, who led the way with a torch.

Clavius turned to him, gently pulling his arm. "Come on, big boy... time for bed."

He followed his friend, letting Clavius push him onto his bed. "Your fuck boy can take your clothes off."

Marius made a feeble attempt to rise, his anger plain. "I told you..."

Clavius laughed. "Yes, I know. Still, I can't help myself. You should drink more so I don't have to listen to your bullshit... ah Kyle, come, boy, your master is wasted again, and I will leave you as I don't doubt he's going to make good use of your body again." He laughed and left, watching Marius' eyes blaze in anger.

They were left alone, and Marius sank back to the pillows, his throat choked, bitter. He let Kyle undress him, pulling his clothes off and putting the cover on top of him. "Stay, Kyle..."

He kneeled on the bed, waiting, and Marius turned to him. "I don't want to get married..."

Kyle looked at him, his grey eyes silent. Not having a choice in anything was his daily existence so he could relate to Marius' struggle. Still, marriage didn't seem that bad...

"Can you imagine having a wife here, in this house? I'd have to sleep with her too..." He chuckled, the wine warming him. "That dinner party... should I take you?" Kyle's eyes widened and Marius laughed. "No, of course not, but it's tempting." He reached out and took Kyle's hand out of his lap, gently tracing his veins. "I am not going to do anything with you tonight... not when I'm drunk again..." He sighed, letting his hand go. "Go to your room... or else... I'm not sure I can stay away from you."

But he was already falling asleep, and Kyle left him, slowly closing the door.

IV

That dreaded dinner party had arrived, and Marius stood in front of his father's house with Clavius in tow, dressed in his best attire. He was already fed up and anxious too.

Clavius slapped his shoulder. "You might find that your father has chosen some fine women."

He just looked at him, already defeated, and they waited until a slave opened the door. They were led to the dining hall, the guests already there, all five families, parents with their daughters, and they silenced when Marius and Clavius entered.

Gaius rose to greet them and introduce him. "This is my son, Marius."

They greeted him, their eyes roaming his body, his face.

They took their places then, Marius looking at the young women. There was a blonde one, very young, and he had already mentally discarded her. *Almost a child...* His eyes roamed further, resting on a woman with brown curly hair, brown eyes, but she wasn't very pretty, and he looked at the next one, light brown hair, blue eyes... she seemed nice... onto the next one with black hair... *did father choose different hair colors?* She looked decent too, not too young, slightly shy... last one, then. His eyes met her eyes, and she smiled slightly, a mocking sort of smile which made his blood boil. She had dark auburn hair and deep brown eyes, her hair piled up high, letting just some curly strands loose around her neck. He could see from her father's toga that she was a senator's daughter, and he sighed inwardly. *Probably father's choice already....* She just toasted him and smiled again, her red lips full. She was quite beautiful in a strange way, and he decided to talk to her after dinner, despite her mocking smile at the beginning.

After dinner, they rose to talk and enjoy the large terrace overlooking Rome, and Marius chatted with all the girls, ending up with the auburn-haired one.

She introduced herself with a slight smile. "I'm Seraphina." He inwardly clocked the name's meaning but didn't give it too much attention, and she continued. "Looking forward to getting married?"

Marius frowned at her straightforward question. "Not really..."

He sipped his wine, taking care not to drink too much, and she laughed. "I can't say I was thrilled until I saw you."

He shifted. *Maybe it would be better to go with that shy black-haired one. At least, she seemed meek enough.*

Seraphina looked at him, searching his eyes. "So, tell me about yourself... you're a general, that much I know."

He shrugged. "There's not much to know... I live not too far from here, nice house, six slaves. I am awaiting my next assignment and will be off then." He looked at her. "My wife will be alone for a while until I retire from the army."

She arched an eyebrow. "Soon?"

"I don't know... if I live..."

He smiled, as she didn't seem to get shocked at his words. "Wives tend to be alone a lot, that much I know. My father is also very busy. The household is our task, anyway." She looked at him, slightly amused. "You only have six slaves, and they manage?"

Marius shrugged. "I am alone for now... there might be more needed if I get married..."

She smiled. "Yes, definitely. I am quite skilled in choosing and buying slaves, my father regularly takes me to the market. I am their only girl. We run a large household and I can also hold discipline.".

Marius looked at her, all of a sudden concerned. "Discipline?"

She beamed a smile at him. "Yes, of course. Beating them up and the sorts." She noticed his mildly shocked stare and smiled. "Don't be so shocked... I am quite mild, you know.... better me than my father." He smiled back at her, and they chatted for a while.

When the guests had left, Gaius walked up to Marius. "Fancy any of them?"

"I am not sure...."

"I saw you talk for quite a while with Seraphina? She's an excellent choice, very noble family, her father is a highly ranked senator."

He sighed, unsure. "Of all of them, she seems the most self-assured... I'm not sure I want to wrestle with my wife..."

His father put a hand on his shoulder. "But you like her, right? You will be her husband and she will owe you obedience."

Marius nodded but stayed silent. *And when I'm gone?*

Gaius urged him softly. "You need to decide tonight. I can't make them wait long, there are other suitors too..."

Marius walked to the terrace, replaying the conversations in his head. His mind on her smile, that she was, after all, beautiful, and seemed to like him already a bit. He sighed, looking at his father. "I'll marry Seraphina."

Gaius beamed at him. "I'm so proud of you! I knew you would not disappoint."

He hugged him, and Marius left, leaving it to his father to arrange the engagement ceremony, knowing that the marriage would not happen straight away.

He arrived home very late, but Kyle was up and let him in, walking with him to his room. Kyle helped him out of his toga and helped him with his bath, Marius unusually silent, almost grim. They walked to the terrace then, Marius laying down on his bed, facing Rome, and Kyle sank to his knees next to him.

Marius stroked Kyle's hair, his voice soft. "I chose one of them..." Kyle stayed silent, letting the Roman speak. "She's called Seraphina, and is quite a beauty, has brains too..." But something was nagging at him, something he could not quite place, and his hand trailed down to the slave's shoulder and back. "If I marry her, she'll be in charge of this household, especially if I'm gone on campaign..."

Kyle didn't react, he knew this was the way, but Lucius had never been married, so he had no idea what it was like to have a woman run the household. *Not much difference, probably.*

Marius watched the slave, his longing for him growing, more so in his anguished state and he pulled on Kyle's arm, patting the bed next to him. "Come here..."

Kyle climbed up and let Marius cradle him in his arms, pull him into a deep kiss. He was gentle but also hungry for him, Kyle could feel it, Marius' despair for his body, to quench out all his thoughts. They kissed and caressed each other for a long time and then, Marius suddenly got up and pulled him to the bedroom, pushing him face down on the bed, with his feet on the ground, the high bed putting him at the right angle, and soon, he felt Marius' fingers in him, coated with oil.

Marius stretched him for a long time, making him moan, and finally, pushed into him, growling, his teeth nibbling at Kyle's neck as he thrust, harder and harder, gripping Kyle's hips, feeling his hard muscles against his thighs. Marius moaned and grunted until he came inside of him, rocking his hips until he felt completely spent, marveling how good Kyle felt, how he liked this after all. He pulled out and climbed on the bed, pulling Kyle to him into his arms, both of them drenched in sweat.

Marius kissed him lightly, gently holding him, feeling the young man shudder with the aftermath. "Next time, you should come with me."

Kyle looked at him, wide-eyed. "That's not allowed, dominus."

Marius looked at him, slightly amused. "Not allowed? It's allowed when I tell you..."

Kyle just nodded and wondered if he could ever obey him... he had never been allowed to come during sex, and now...

Marius caressed him. "Do you have any idea what you're doing to me?" He looked down at the slave. "You're driving me crazy..." It was out, just like that, and Kyle's heart raced at his words. He was also slightly embarrassed and blushed in that room bathed in shadows, thankful for the dim light.

Marius didn't care anymore. He loved every minute of their intimacy and hoped Kyle felt the same. He turned to him. "Do you like what we have here?"

Kyle nodded, his eyes shining. "Yes, dominus."

Marius licked his lips. "Do you like me now a little bit?"

Kyle's lips parted, his heart racing, vaguely anguished. "I like you, dominus. You are a good master..."

Marius stroked Kyle's bottom lip, pushing his finger into his mouth. "That's not what I asked..."

Kyle moaned but held his gaze and he took Marius' finger out of his mouth, leaving it close. "I like you a lot, dominus..."

Marius kissed him again, more insistent this time, his hands roaming Kyle's body, and he was hard again, turning Kyle over on the bed, lying on top of him. He whispered in his ear. "I'll show you how much I like you..."

Kyle shuddered and closed his eyes.

Clavius obviously came early in the morning to check on Marius, and they went to sit in the garden, enjoying the shade and breakfast.

"So, you chose Seraphina?" Marius nodded and Clavius smiled at him. "From what I could tell, she wasn't the meekest."

Marius shrugged. "It doesn't matter. At least, she knows what she's supposed to do and is not an absolute horror to look at."

Kyle walked to them to bring some more fruit and Marius gestured for him to kneel at his side. He then dipped a piece of bread into honey and pushed it into the slave's mouth, letting his thumb linger a bit, against his tongue. His lips curled into a small smile, and he continued feeding him, all the while talking to Clavius. They were planning to work and attend some meetings at the palace and then go to the baths.

"Dinner at my place tomorrow?"

Marius looked at him. "Sure, why not?"

Kyle rose to gather the plates and left to the kitchen, Marius' eyes on him, and Clavius looked at his friend. "What's going on?"

Marius' blue eyes twinkled. "Nothing..."

"Oh, don't give me that look! I saw how you fed him."

Marius just smiled and rose. "We should be going, come on."

Clavius got up, groaning. "I'm getting old..." He clasped Marius' arm, his eyes on the younger man. "You're just screwing him, right?"

Marius looked down at him, his face blank. "Of course... what else do you think I could be doing?"

Clavius smiled. "Not doing, feeling..."

Marius laughed. "No, no! What are you thinking? I am merely following your advice, you know... Take advantage of having him, and all that crap."

They laughed, but Clavius wasn't convinced. He had seen the look in Marius' eyes, and it worried him mildly.

Marius came home before dinnertime, drained by the bath, the past days' events, the prospect of his impending engagement to that woman...

He walked upstairs, his mind on his thoughts, and slowed when he saw Kyle and Lisandra on all fours on the floor, polishing the wide corridor's marble. He stopped, out of their sight, and leant against the wall to observe them. *You should breed them.* His father's words echoing in his head... *what an absurd bullshit.* But he could not ignore the young woman's glances towards Kyle, her hand dipping her cloth in the hot wax at the same time as him, brushing it, her eyes trying to catch his eyes. If he had realized her intentions, he didn't seem to care and worked hard, sometimes stopping to wipe his forehead. She had a very low-cut dress, her breasts swaying as she worked, making sure she was facing him all the time.

Kyle stopped after a while, his body drenched, his tunic clinging to it, revealing his lean muscles, and Marius had to swallow hard. Kyle stood to pick up the bucket and pulled Lisandra up.

She pretended to lose her balance and fell against him; her face tilted upwards, her hands grabbing his arms. "Sorry...", lips parted, she waited, but Kyle gently pulled himself out of her arms, his face confused.

"Let's go... we have to get cleaned up and serve dinner soon."

She followed him, her face clouded over, and they saw then Marius approach them. Both slaves went to their knees, eyes downcast, and Marius stopped in front of Kyle. "Come straight up after you've cleaned yourself."

They got up again and made their way to their quarters, taking a quick wash in cold water before changing. Lisandra went to the kitchen and Kyle hurried upstairs to Marius' room.

The Roman was waiting for him, leaning against a pillar. The evening sun was still hot, and he turned to Kyle when he entered the room after a brief knock.

Marius gestured him over before he had a chance to kneel again. "Come here. You don't have to kneel every time we are in this room."

Kyle didn't comment. It was so ingrained that he had a hard time not doing it with Marius. He walked up to him, and Marius pulled him in an embrace, tipping his chin up to kiss him. Kyle didn't mind, wondering though where this would lead. He was not used to affection from Lucius, and Marius threw him a bit off balance.

He looked into the Roman's gleaming blue eyes and Marius smiled, his thumb grazing the slave's lower lip. "Too bad that dinner is coming up... and Clavius is coming over... I have some ideas about what I would do to your delicious body." Kyle blushed slightly and Marius arched his eyebrows, a small smile on his lips. "You blush? I thought nothing could embarrass you." Kyle lowered his eyes, but Marius forced his chin up. "Look at me..."

Kyle raised his eyes at him, but he could not talk. He was lost, not fully understanding what was going on, and Marius somehow sensed it, holding him closer to his chest, mercifully away from his disturbing blue eyes. "I am sorry... maybe this is too much for you. I don't even really know what's going on... the only thing I know is that I am attracted to you..." He was not sure either about his feelings at all, and Kyle's mind raced at his words. *Attracted?*

Marius pushed him away a bit, his arms around him, looking down into his grey eyes laced with worry. "Sleep with me tonight?"

Kyle whispered, shocked at his question. *He shouldn't ask, he should just say it...* "Yes, dominus."

Marius stroked his hair, pushing a strand out of his forehead. "This is difficult for you?"

Kyle licked his lips, vaguely panicked. "Yes, dominus... I am not sure I understand..."

Marius smiled. "You'll get used to it, not just mindlessly obeying orders... and being treated well..." He brushed his lips against the slave's, his black hair falling into his blue eyes and Kyle shivered as Marius whispered. "I like you a lot, Kyle..."

Kyle was still fighting them, these feelings he was having when he looked at the tall Roman, into his blue eyes, feelings he had in his arms, inhaling his scent, his lips like velvet. He would have pushed him away if he could have, but this was obviously not an option...

Marius let him go, a sad twinge in his eyes. "Go and prepare dinner. Clavius is going to be here soon..."

Kyle looked at him. "How soon?"

Marius smiled, shrugging. "You know Clavius... he can be unpredictable."

Kyle sank to his knees, and Marius frowned. "Why on earth are you kneeling now? I told you...", but his words got caught when the slave looked up at him, his hands going under his clothes. Marius' lips parted, and he closed his eyes, not seeing Kyle's small smile as he took him in his mouth.

Fortunately, Clavius arrived later and found Marius in the dining room, idly lying on a bed, swirling his cup of wine. He seemed content and had traded his toga for his tunic. Clavius arrived dressed similarly, wearing his military leather tunic, not to be disturbed in Rome's dangerous streets. He lay down and Kyle was immediately there to fill his cup.

Clavius toasted Marius. "To our friendship!"

Marius smiled, and they drank, the younger man warning him. "Do not dare getting me drunk again..."

Clavius grinned. "You have plans with your fuck boy?"

Marius frowned at the word but didn't object. "You can say that."

"He's grown on you quite a bit."

Marius shrugged, grinning. "Who would have thought, right? I didn't even know what to do with him at the beginning." They laughed, but Clavius was still cautious.

Dinner was served, and Marius made Kyle stay, occasionally pushing food into his mouth. Clavius noticed how the slave had filled up, his nimble, lean limbs stronger, his skin glowing, and he smiled, mocking. "You'll fatten him up, stuffing him all the time."

Marius' eyes went to the slave. "I like him with flesh, not like some sort of skeleton." His breath hitched when he pushed food into Kyle's mouth, his index finger staying in the slave's mouth, feeling his tongue stroking it. Kyle held his gaze and Marius' blue eyes darkened, his lips parting.

Clavius cleared his throat. "Do you want some privacy?"

Marius pulled his finger out, laughing. "No, what are you talking about?"

Clavius just smiled, but it didn't reach his eyes.

They ate and Kyle took the plates away, leaving them with their desserts.

Clavius thought this was the right moment to talk. "Marius, I've known you forever, right?" The younger man nodded, vaguely curious. "So, what is happening with your boy here?"

Marius' face darkened, a slight smile on his lips. "We've talked about this?"

Clavius held his gaze. "You lied... and pinching your lips in irritation is not going to make it go away, so spit it out... You're getting engaged soon?"

Marius moaned. "Don't remind me..."

"So, perhaps this is not the right time for you to become all besotted with a male slave."

Marius waved him away. "Besotted? That's a bit strong..."

Clavius arched his eyebrows. "Really?"

The blue eyes blazed. "Yes, really... and as a free man, I can well do whatever I damn want in my own house."

Clavius raised his glass. "Cheers to that... but Seraphina is not going to like it."

"Who cares? I'll marry her and do my duty, make her children... this is what she can expect."

Clavius mused. "I thought you were not into boys?"

Marius sighed. "So did I..."

There was an awkward silence, and Clavius softened a bit, seeing his friend's pained face. "And your boy? What does he think of all this?"

Marius shrugged. "I don't know... it is all too new for him..."

"I can imagine... be careful not to overwhelm him."

He smiled, downing his glass. "I'll try."

Clavius rose. "Man, I'd never thought you'd take my advice so much at heart."

Marius rose, clasping his arm. "Me neither..."

Clavius' eyes shone. "Take care, Marius. Do not burn yourself."

The younger man smiled, his eyes gleaming. "Thank you for worrying so much."

"That's what your best friend is for."

He left then, knowing the way, and Marius went to his room. He had to wait until Kyle was done but had stripped already, waiting for him in bed, Clavius' words in his head. *Ah, fuck him!*

Kyle arrived later and entered, softly closing the door. His heart was in his throat, still, but he walked to the bed, took his clothes off, and looked into Marius' blue eyes. The moon was casting a gentle glow into the room, the terrace curtains wide open, letting in the warm summer night air. He stood next to the bed, waiting.

Marius spoke, his voice soft. "If you want, you can come to bed."

Kyle's face contorted in confusion. *Want?* Since when was this his choice... He waited, not knowing what to do, and dread crept into him like plague.

Marius propped himself on one elbow, looking into Kyle's eyes, seeing the fear there. "Alright, just come here..."

Kyle climbed up and lay next to him under the covers. Marius turned to him. "I wish I knew you really wanted to be here... with me..."

Kyle looked at him, his eyes wide. "You said I should sleep with you. I'm here, dominus."

Marius smiled a sad smile. "I know... but do you really want to be here? If I told you that you could leave to your room, what would you do?"

Kyle licked his lips, his breathing faster. "Could? This is not my choice, dominus..."

Marius eyes' blazed. "I am telling you now it's your choice!"

Kyle shrank, scared to the bone by his brewing anger. He stammered. "I want to stay, dominus."

Marius watched him, his voice a mere whisper. "You're lying..."

Kyle blanched, his stomach knotting, utterly confused. He pleaded, close to tears. "Please, dominus, just tell me what you want."

"I want you to be here because you want to, not because I want you to, but apparently, this is too difficult for you to answer."

Kyle tried to understand, but he had no answer, his mind trying to adjust to this new situation. *Did he want to be here? In bed with a man?* These were not even questions he got asked before. It had become part of his life, part of who he was, and now, Marius was tearing wounds apart. His voice choked with tears, and he closed his eyes. He didn't even care if he got beaten up... He had no answer for him because he had no answer for himself.

Marius watched him, pained, and sighed. "Go then. I don't want you here if you don't want to be with me..."

Kyle's eyes flew open, wide, and he could not talk, the events of the past days flooring him, too much, *and now this...* He got up and backed from the bed, breathing hard, his tears flowing, blindly looking for the door but he could not reach it, when strong arms enveloped him, and he fought, panicked, forcing his constricted lungs to suck in air.

Somehow, Marius' voice came through the haze in the dim room. "Shhh... Calm down... Calm down... it's just me... gods... it's going to be fine; I am sorry, I am so sorry..." He wrestled the slave's arms down, locking them in his embrace, and Kyle sobbed, loud, giving up, leaning against Marius' warm chest.

Marius whispered in his ear, gently rocking him, cursing himself softly. He pulled Kyle up and brought him to bed, covering him, spooning him, holding him in his arms, making sure he could not bolt, and Kyle calmed down gradually, his breathing shallow.

Kyle felt the air clear around him, slowly winding down in Marius' strong arms, his vision coming back. He turned to face Marius, those blue eyes filled with concern, worry, sadness and Kyle disentangled himself from his arms to pull Marius down into a kiss, his hands in his raven hair.

He breathed into his mouth. "I want to be with you, dominus..." Even if he wasn't sure... this was what he felt then, feeling the man moan into his mouth, taking over, deepening their kiss, kissing away his tears, rubbing them off with his thumbs.

Marius didn't care anymore if he was lying or not. He had no doubts, and their raging emotions pushed them into a desperately intense coupling, letting their doubts and fears flow freely, letting the blinding pleasure burn them to crisps.

They lay together for ages, tangled in the sheets, their bodies drenched, the soft summer breeze cooling their skin and Marius bit down gently on Kyle's neck, licking the soft, salty skin.

"Mine..." He growled, and Kyle smiled up at him.

"I am yours, dominus..."

V

Two weeks had passed since that night and Marius and Kyle's relationship slowly evolved into a more intimate one. Marius wanted Kyle in his bedroom every night and essentially elevated him to being his bed slave. The young slave learned to adjust to this, so different from his previous life, yet very much the same.

Meanwhile, the engagement ceremony was fast approaching, and Marius' nervousness grew, his anguish making his temper flare more often.

He was getting ready for work one morning and struggled to buckle his armor, his brows furrowed, his lips pinched in frustration. Kyle walked up to him and helped with the strap, pulling it tight and Marius sighed. "Thank you... honestly, I was going crazy..."

Kyle raised his grey eyes to him and kissed him deeply, pushing his tongue into his mouth. He felt the man relax, and he bathed in Marius' scent, laced with the leathery smell of his armor.

Marius stood, slightly dazed, his anger wiped. "Oh, my... I wish I could stay."

Kyle smiled and pushed him away lightly. "You'll be late, dominus."

He rolled his eyes. "True..."

He hurried downstairs and left at a brisk pace, his worry chewing at him again.

Kyle went to get Brianna. He wanted to work with her in the garden where they had renovated the fishpond. He had planned to plant more water lilies and set to work, standing in the pond. Brianna sat on the side and fed the fish, the glittering golden and copper fish lazily swimming to her, some snatching the food out of her palms.

She spoke, her voice soft. "Dominus will get married soon..."

Kyle glanced at her, his face grim. Marriage was on their minds, and soon, a new domina and with it, the unknown. He sighed. "Yes..."

Brianna looked at him. "How is she?"

Kyle shrugged, busy with planting the white and pink flowers. "I don't know. She's called Seraphina, that's all I know." He smiled at Brianna, seeing her worried look. "Dominus chose her carefully, so let's hope she'll be fine."

But Brianna's face darkened. "And if she's not nice?"

Kyle straightened, his voice soft. "Let's not worry about this right now..."

The girl looked at him. "When she'll be here, will you still sleep with dominus?"

Kyle's words caught... he hadn't really thought about this... He frowned, trying to sound reassuring. "I suppose I'll know then..."

Brianna's eyes didn't leave him. "Does dominus hurt you?"

Kyle sighed, slightly frowning. "I am not sure young girls like you should discuss such topics."

The look in her eyes gave him the chills. "Our master liked my friend Kyle, and one day, he didn't come out of that room... they brought him out wrapped in a sheet..."

Her eyes welled with tears, and he stepped out of the pond, lacing his arms around her. "He doesn't hurt me... don't worry, Bri." She sniffed, and he rocked her gently, his mind drifting back to times when he'd also thought he'd never leave Lucius' room alive. He shivered slightly, shutting his eyes to his memories.

They went to do the laundry yard then, Lisandra already there, and she was knee-deep in the washing trough, her eyes blazing when she saw him.

Her dress was wet and plastered to her body. "About time! Where were you?"

"In the garden." Kyle took the clothes out which she had washed and went to rinse them in the large stone basin. Brianna helped him to wring them out and handed them to him to hang up.

Lisandra smiled a mocking smile. "Now that dominus keeps busy with you, we have more laundry to do..." He just shot her a look, glancing towards Brianna but Lisandra laughed. "You think she hasn't seen it all?" She stepped out of the trough and stepped up to Kyle, pushing her body against him, backing him to the wall of the small yard, her lips inches from his lips. "So... don't you think it would be healthier if we did something together? Woman and man..."

Brianna watched them silently. He glanced at her, nervous, and slowly put his hands on Lisandra's shoulders, pushing her away. "This is not a good idea..."

She pushed back, mocking. "You don't like women? Maybe you've never tried...?" She teased him, her hands on his arms, slowly pushing them off her shoulders, down to her waist, pouting. "Just one kiss? I am so lonely..."

He stood, frozen, not wanting to make a scene in front of the child, or hurt Lis, feeling her breasts push against his chest, her lips parting, closing her eyes... Sixtus' voice reached them then. "Kyle!"

He snapped out of it, pushing her away, her face a mask of anger, and Brianna hurried after him.

The old man hurried to him. "Come on, boy, I was looking for you."

Kyle stammered. "I... I was doing the laundry."

Sixtus eyed him curiously, but didn't probe further. "Dominus' father is here. I put him in the garden. He insists on waiting for him, although I told him I had no idea when he'd be back. Don't look like you've just seen a lion, boy! Bring him some refreshments, wine, and fruits. Bri can help you."

Kyle blinked, fear eating at him, but he went to the kitchen, Brianna in tow. They went to the garden then, seeing Marius' father sitting on one of the beds, eyeing the small gem that the garden had become. Kyle kneeled with the platter, his eyes down, putting it on the small table, and Brianna imitated him quickly, her small face pale.

She was more afraid than Kyle, having sensed the old man's true nature, and Gaius' eyes gleamed. "Come closer, little one.

She rose slowly and glanced quickly at Kyle, who didn't dare look up, but his breathing quickened. She walked to Gaius, her eyes down, and stood in front of him.

He reached out and pulled her in his lap, stroking her hair. "You are very beautiful, little one. What's your name?"

Her eyes were wide with fear, but she managed to reply, her voice too soft. "Brianna..."

"Brianna"—he tasted the name, all the while stroking her golden hair—"Beautiful name... for a pretty little girl." Brianna sat very still, her lips quivering, her eyes on Kyle. Gaius followed her gaze and his lips curled into a small smile. "Pour me some wine, boy... then you can leave us..."

Kyle blanched but obeyed, handing the cup to Gaius. He stood then slowly, and Brianna whimpered, her voice full of tears. "I want to go with Kyle..."

Gaius smiled at her, his eyes like ice. "You don't get to want anything, little one, you're a slave."

She cried, and Kyle had to steel himself to leave her there, his mind in a daze. He bumped straight into Marius under the archway, and relief flooded him.

Marius frowned, seeing his pale face and wide eyes. "What's wrong?"

"Your father is in the garden with Bri, dominus...."

"So?"

"She's in his lap, dominus..."

Marius looked towards the garden and strode there, gesturing to Kyle to follow, seeing his father eat with the child in his lap. Brianna was crying softly, and her blue eyes bore into Marius'.

Gaius looked up, smiling. "Ah, my son... perfect timing." He stroked Brianna's hair. "What a pretty little thing... do you want to sell her?"

Marius frowned, sitting down. "What? No..."

"Pity... Anyway, I came to discuss the engagement ceremony which is in three days. We will do it at my house, and then I would suggest you invite Seraphina and her parents and us for dinner. She can see the house and meet your slaves."

"In three days? Already..."

Gaius just looked at him, his face cold, his eyes drifting to Kyle who was kneeling at Marius' feet, his shoulder against Marius' thigh. "It's not too soon. The marriage can then wait, but don't wait too long. You might be deployed, and you don't want to leave your household unattended... Of course, I can take care of your slaves while you're gone." He smiled and Brianna sniffled softly, her blue eyes on Marius, pleading.

He called her to him, grim. "Come here, Brianna." She slid from Gaius' lap and rushed to Marius, kneeling at his feet, clutching his calf.

Gaius smirked. "Touching..."

Marius spoke to Kyle, gently touching his shoulder. "Take Brianna to the kitchen with you and bring back some bread and cheese."

"Yes, dominus."

He rose and grabbed Brianna's hand, the little girl hurrying with him, almost running out of the garden, away from the man who terrified her.

Kyle crouched down to her once they were out of hearing range. "Did he hurt you?

Brianna shook her head. "I was so scared..."

Kyle took her hand, leading her to the kitchen. "Make sure you stay away from him, stay in the kitchen until he leaves..." Bri nodded, and he gave her an apple, making her sit in a corner. He then picked up the bread and cheese and left, his stomach in a knot.

He heard Gaius' angry voice before he entered the garden, slowing down, his heart pounding. "Don't tell me nothing's going on, Marius, I am not blind! The way he leans against you, what Clavius said..."

"What did Clavius say?" Marius was angry, Kyle could hear it, and he stopped, not wanting to interrupt.

"Clavius said that he's worried about you, that you're getting too close to that slave. Is he your bed slave? Please don't tell me you went down that road! Not before your marriage!"

Kyle could almost see Marius' smile through his anger. "What I do with my slave is none of your business, it's not Clavius' either... at least, he is not a child..."

There was an icy silence and Kyle chose that moment to enter the garden, laying the plates on the table, turning to leave.

Marius grabbed his hand, his eyes on his father. "Stay."

Kyle kneeled, and Marius pulled him close, pushing his head on his thigh. Kyle just stayed there, trying not to look up, and Marius ate, all the while stroking his hair.

Gaius smiled a mocking smile. "I see... well, I should be leaving. Don't forget the ceremony."

Marius' lips curled up. "How could I forget, father?"

Gaius left then and Kyle looked up at Marius, wordless.

Marius sighed. "I know, pet... what a mess... Worried?"

He smiled a feeble smile, Kyle's grey eyes not giving anything away, his voice soft. "We are worried, dominus... about how she's going to be... here..."

Marius cupped his chin. "I am the man of the house, so as long as I'm here, she'll have to behave."

"And when you're gone?"

Marius' eyes shone sadly. "I hope she'll be fine..." He searched Kyle's eyes. "What else?"

The slave sighed. "When you'll marry her, what will happen to us?"

Marius frowned. "What do you mean? Oh..." He smiled, pulling Kyle up next to him, into his arms, kissing him deeply. "I will still have my own room and share my nights with you. Except when I need to fulfill my duties as a husband... until she gets pregnant."

Kyle's heart became lighter, but he was still unsure, dreading the day when she would move in.

Marius kissed him, his hand brushing his face. "You have nothing to fear, pet... I need to leave again, but will be back later for dinner." He nibbled his neck. "And later... after dinner... I'll make sure you don't doubt me anymore."

Kyle closed his eyes, moaning.

Three days later, Kyle was putting Marius' toga on, getting him ready for the engagement ceremony. He glanced up at the Roman's pale face, his clenched jaw, his blue eyes in the mirror, and he had to steady himself, his emotions toiling inside.

They had talked about this marriage, the fact that it didn't mean anything at all, that there was no love, just a duty to carry through, produce children, but still... in Kyle's culture, this was vastly different, and he could not help but compare in his head.

He lowered his hands. "I'm done, dominus."

Marius forced a feeble smile. "Perfect... as always..." Kyle swallowed, lowering his eyes, and Marius pulled him into an embrace, not caring about his clothes. "Come here..." He tipped his chin up and kissed him deeply. "Better?"

"Yes, dominus..."

"They are coming for dinner tomorrow. Make sure it's perfect. And don't let Bri near my father."

Kyle nodded. They had a lot to do still, prepare the house, the meals. He followed Marius to the door, letting him out, and then went to find Sixtus.

The old man was in the kitchen, talking with Shayla about the menu, food he needed to buy, and he gestured Kyle over. "Come, boy. You and Lisandra need to clean the entire house, make sure the garden is impeccable too. She's already working upstairs. No need to wax the floors. You did that last week. I'm going shopping. Tomorrow morning, we'll finalize the setup, some nice flowers here and there. Lisandra and you can do the service, and Brianna."

Kyle looked at the old man. "Dominus doesn't want her near his father."

"Fine... she can stay and help in the kitchen, then."

Kyle went to join Lisandra, the young girl was washing the terrace, and he got to work, wordlessly. Lisandra looked up and smirked. "Took you long enough..."

"I had to put the toga on dominus."

"Of course..." She was scrubbing the floor with her brush, her face mocking. "Now that he's getting married, your life will change... maybe you should be looking for a more suitable partner?"

She winked at him, and Kyle sighed, sitting on his heels. "Lisa, can you just stop this?"

She faced him, her face blank. "Stop what?"

"You know, the teasing, the constant allusions to us..."

She shrugged. "You might not have a choice, lover boy. Not if they decide to breed us."

Kyle blanched. He knew what that meant, he had seen it at Lucius' estate, slave babies born out of forced unions, the baby girls smashed against the wall, or dumped like trash... He closed his eyes. "Don't say that... you don't know what you're talking about..."

She crawled to him; her face close to his face. "I know exactly what I'm talking about."

He sighed, bitter. "I don't even know if I can be with a woman..."

Lisandra's face fell. "You've never been with one?"

"I've been, once or twice... a long time ago." He smiled a bitter smile. "Lucius didn't like women so..."

Her face softened. "I'm sorry... in that case, we can just take it slow?" She grinned, and he had to smile.

They worked hard until sunset, and Kyle was utterly exhausted, but the entire house sparkled, the garden magnificent.

His thoughts drifted to Marius, wondering how he was doing.

Kyle waited for him in the bedroom, his eyes on the stars. It was very late, and he struggled to stay awake, his drained body tugging at his eyelids. *Where was he? He was not supposed to stay overnight. Then again, parties could go on forever...* Loud voices reached him, and he got up, alarmed. He had recognized Clavius' voice and went to open the door when it was flung in, almost knocking him over.

Kyle caught the man stumbling through the opening, his aching arms holding him, clutching at his clothes, and Marius looked up into his eyes, smiling. "Kyle... thank the gods..."

Kyle reeled from the smell of wine but held tight, his eyes darting to Clavius who was standing behind Marius, his arms crossed, his face laced with anger. "I had to bring him home. As you can see, he can't walk."

Marius whirled around, almost losing his balance, but Kyle gripped his arm, holding him tight. His blue eyes blazed, his voice filled with wrath, but he was swaying on his feet. "I can walk... friend..." He slurred the word and Kyle looked at the two men, alarmed.

Clavius spread his palms. "I only want to help you, Marius. Clearly, you are not dealing with this situation well."

Marius laughed. "Why... how observant of you... I should be thankful... but you betrayed me, friend. Talking to my father behind my back?"

Clavius sighed. "You're drunk... just go to bed."

Marius smiled, his eyes gleaming. "Oh, I will..." He put his arm around Kyle's shoulders, pulling him close. "I will go to bed here with my beloved boy and there's nothing you or father can do about it."

Kyle paled, trying to understand, and Clavius' lips pinched. "Telling your future wife about your fuck boy here was not exactly very tactful today..."

Marius sneered. "Father brought it up... and why should I hide it? She has nothing else to expect from me than making her children... better make it clear from the start..."

Clavius didn't comment, and Marius' eyes glazed over, his anger wiped by his fatigue and his nerves on edge. His legs buckled a bit and Kyle backed with him towards the bed, his voice soft. "Come to bed, dominus..."

Kyle was worried sick, not sure how he could undress him if he lay down, but he managed to push Marius on the bed, making him crawl up on the mattress, collapsing, his eyes closed. Clavius watched his friend, his face grim. Marius moaned and Kyle started to take his toga off, noticing that it was probably ruined, stained with wine.

Marius turned over then, his arms pulling Kyle down on his body, his breath ragged. "Come here, you..."

Kyle whispered, embarrassed. "Your friend is still here..."

Marius looked at Clavius, and his mouth curled into a mocking smile. "You want to watch? Be my guest..."

Clavius shook his head, gently scolding. "Marius... this is not going to end well..."

"Just fuck off, will you? Go and lick my father's ass."

Kyle winced at his words, mortified, but Clavius just left, closing the door.

Marius sighed, chuckling, his voice heavy. "Good riddance... now, where were we?"

Kyle tried to free himself, gently peeling Marius' arms away. "I need to get you out of your toga first?"

Marius laughed softly and let him, helping where he could, until the heavy material was off, along with the rest of his clothes. Kyle pulled the covers on top of them, letting Marius kiss him, the taste of wine invading his mouth.

The Roman laughed softly. "I had too much to drink... again..." He stroked the slave's hair, smiling, his eyes fluttering shut. "The ceremony went well... but then during dinner... I have enough of people telling me what I should or shouldn't do..." He opened his blue eyes, his speech slow. "If I could... I would not do this to us... marry her, bring her here..."

He looked so vulnerable, a glint of fear and despair in his eyes making Kyle's heart race. He didn't know what to say to him, though, still not fully used to his confessions.

Marius closed his eyes, pulling him close. "Let's sleep... I'm sorry, I'm in no shape to do anything tonight..." His voice drifted off and Kyle's eyes closed too in his warm embrace.

Kyle was up early with the first rays of the sun, and he went to his business, knowing full well Marius would not wake until later. He had made sure the curtains were closed in his room.

He checked on him later, and Marius stirred, mumbling, his face in the pillows. "Is it morning?"

"It is lunchtime, dominus."

He moaned, turning over slowly. "Oh, gods... my head..." Kyle walked over to him, handing him a cup of water, and he slowly sat up, his back to the headboard. He drank deeply and sighed, squinting his eyes. "How did I get home?"

Kyle's eyes widened slightly. "You don't remember, dominus?"

Marius laughed. "No, I don't... so?"

"Master Clavius brought you home, dominus."

"Ah, ever the good friend...", but he'd noticed Kyle's pained face and his stomach clenched. "What happened?"

Kyle shifted on his feet, embarrassed. "You were fighting with him... over something that was said during dinner... I didn't quite get it, dominus..."

"He left then?"

"You told him to... fuck off... dominus"

Marius' eyes widened, but then he burst out laughing, his deep voice resonating in the room. "Oh, my... open those bloody curtains..." Kyle pulled them apart, and the sunlight streamed in, spearing him in his brain. "Ah! Close them... bloody hell... this is going to be something today..." He sat up, his head swimming, his black hair falling in front of his eyes. "Please don't fill my cup tonight, even if I ask you to."

"I can't disobey you, dominus. Just don't ask."

"I'll try... Help me dress and escort me to the garden... maybe some fresh air will do me some good..."

They walked to the garden, blissfully in shade under the pergola, and Marius lay down, closing his eyes. Kyle brought him some water and left him to his thoughts and vague nausea, his splitting headache throbbing dully in his skull... *And dinner tonight with those horrible people...* He wondered if he'd hurt Clavius so much he would not show up.

Marius woke much later to somebody softly shaking his shoulder, and Kyle's eyes swam into his vision. "I am sorry to wake you, dominus, but you need to get ready."

He moaned, his mouth dry, but the headache gone. "Let's go to the bath..."

Kyle pulled him up to sit and gave him some water. They walked then to the bath where he bathed Marius, making sure he got a little massage too.

Later, Marius stood in his toga on the terrace, waiting for the guests, his fiancée... *how absurd...* He shook his head lightly, still foggy with his hangover. He walked to the dining room, checking on the preparations, and noticed that everything was ready, the room brightly lit, filled with flowers which made the air sweet... *too sweet.*

He drew a big breath at the window, watching the sun set in its own blood when he felt a hand on his shoulder. Marius didn't need to turn around to know whose it was, and he clasped that hand, softly smiling. "Welcome, my friend."

He turned to face Clavius, the man's eyes shining. "How are you?"

Marius shrugged. "I feel like shit... I thought you might not come... Kyle told me that I wasn't very nice to you."

Clavius' eyes widened. "Kyle told you? You don't remember?"

He laughed. "No... not at all... my memories went sometimes during dinner."

Clavius' face went grim. "You don't remember what we fought about? This is worse than I thought."

"Why?"

Clavius sighed. "You told Seraphina about you and Kyle... I managed to soften it and pull you out of there, but she wasn't impressed... to put it mildly..."

Marius frowned, but they got interrupted by Kyle, who walked to get them. "Dominus, your guests are here..."

The men walked down to greet them, the slaves kneeling in the background, and Marius flinched at their sight, his stomach knotting. Sixtus opened the door and knelt straight away. Gaius was leading the way with his wife, followed by Seraphina and then her parents. They greeted Marius and Clavius, Seraphina eyeing her fiancé with a strange light in her eyes, her eyes drifting to the kneeling slaves.

She smiled at Marius. "Introduce me to your slaves. Soon, I will be their domina, and I would like to see what I'm dealing with."

Marius swallowed but didn't object and he led her to them. "Get up." He waited until they did, their heads bowed. "This is my future wife, Seraphina, your domina, soon." They bowed, silent, and he went down their row. "This is Shayla, she's an excellent cook and Melissa, her helper. These keep the house: Lisandra, Brianna, who's Melissa's daughter, and Kyle. Sixtus, who is near the door, is leading them and makes sure everything works smoothly."

Seraphina only half listened to him, her eyes on Kyle. Her eyes drifted to Marius, then back to the slave. She looked at Marius. "But Kyle is not only tending to your house, right?"

Marius' face was blank. "No, he is also assisting me with daily tasks."

She smiled. "You said something else yesterday but fine, maybe it was the wine talking..."

He fumed silently but didn't comment, and Seraphina turned to the slaves. "They are not going to be enough when I move in, but we can see to this later. And the little girl? What for?"

A tinge of anger crossed his face. "I decided to buy her. She's very useful."

She shrugged, looking them over again. "Kyle and that young girl... you could breed them? It would add value to your household."

She watched his face darken and hid a small smile. "I am not so much into increasing the number of slaves I have."

"Sure, but think about. It's common practice."

Kyle and Lisandra blanched, but their heads stayed down.

She addressed them then, her voice cold. "Your dominus only had praises for you, but I expect the utmost obedience from you when I move in."

She turned then, lacing her arm around Marius', his teeth gritted in anger. They all walked up to the dining hall, Sixtus urging the slaves to serve the food and wine.

Lisandra's hands were shaking, her face pale, and Kyle had to stop her, taking her hands. "Look at me... pull yourself together?"

She did, panicked. "What if she'll make us...you know... I was joking last day... I don't want to be a breeding mare..."

Her eyes welled up, and Kyle pulled her into his arms. "You won't be... just don't think about this. Dominus won't let it happen."

Lis looked at him. "He won't be here all the time... he might leave..."

He took her hand and led her to the kitchen. "Forget what she said. Just do your job. It has to be perfect tonight."

She took a deep breath and steadied herself, Melissa grabbing her arm as she was about to leave. "Ignore her, girl. She wants to get at you."

Lisa nodded and left; her face steadied into her mask of servitude.

Fortunately, Gaius was busy talking to Seraphina's father and their wives chatted too, but Seraphina lay next to Marius and Clavius, chatting away with them as food and drinks were served.

She eyed the two slaves and Clavius gestured Kyle over. "Fill our cups, boy."

Kyle went to get the pitchers, but Marius looked at him, vaguely shaking his head. He filled Clavius' cup, then went to swap the pitchers, filling Marius' up with watered wine. He had prepared it earlier and Marius took a long swig, grateful, holding it up again.

He waited until Kyle bent down to fill his cup again, and whispered. "Thank you... you'll have your reward for this later on..."

Their eyes locked in the briefest moment over the cup, a small smile on Marius' lips as he noticed Kyle's struggle to keep a straight face.

Seraphina watched them, vaguely listening to Clavius in the background, her heart burning. She turned to Marius, reaching to him to stroke his hand, her brown eyes digging into him. "I can hardly wait for our marriage..." her wet lips parted, and he fought the urge to pull his hand away, Clavius carefully watching him.

Marius forced a smile on his face, all the while wishing for this dinner to end, and brought her hand to his lips. His blue eyes shone under his dark hair. "Me too..." She gasped, blushing and Marius held her hand, his smile plastered on, looking vaguely content, but deep inside, he wanted to be in his room, with his beloved boy.

The dinner stretched on, their parents teasing them, and Kyle and Lisa swayed from fatigue, holding tight, their faces pale. Finally, the guests rose, and Marius escorted them outside with Kyle holding a torch to light the way in the dark entrance.

Gaius turned to his son. "Thank you, son, this was indeed a lovely night... too bad you hid your little gem."

Marius' face stayed a mask. "She didn't feel well."

Kyle bolted the door when they'd left, and he was flung against the wall, Marius' body pushing him into the cold plaster, the torch knocked out of his hand. His master's strong hands slid under his tunic and his tongue invaded his mouth.

Kyle could barely breathe, and Marius' voice whispered in the night, laced with lust. "I've been wanting to kiss your mouth all night... what do you think your swaying ass did to me during dinner?" Marius kissed him harder, his teeth ripping into his lower lip, and Kyle whimpered at the unexpected pain.

"Come!" Marius growled and grabbed his hand, pulling him to the bedroom where he had to wait until Kyle undid his toga with frantic hands, his blue eyes eating the slave's body.

They scrambled on the bed, lost in kisses, and Marius flipped Kyle on all fours, his hand reaching for the oil bottle, popping it open. Kyle braced his forearms on the bed, feeling him spread the oil on his butt, pushing his fingers in, but he didn't leave them long, and soon, they were replaced by his cock.

Marius pushed inside of him, his eyes closing, a soft moan escaping his mouth. "You have no idea how good you feel..."

He caressed the slave's smooth skin on his back, feeling the growing muscles ripple under his palm. He thrust harder, gripping Kyle's hips, harder and harder until they were both grunting, and Kyle's moans turned into mewls and whimpers, his hands fisted in the sheets, his mouth wide open. Sweat poured down his back and Marius felt close, his muscles straining. He reached down and closed his fingers on the slave's erection, stroking the smooth skin with the same rhythm as his thrusts and Kyle writhed against him. "That's it... cum for me, pet..." He thrust hard and deep and felt Kyle spasm under him, milking him too.

Marius collapsed on the bed, drawing Kyle against him in a tight embrace, his teeth nibbling on his neck, licking the salty sweat with languid strokes. "You're so fucking great..."

Kyle couldn't answer. He was utterly exhausted, his eyelids so heavy he was struggling to stay awake in Marius' warm arms.

Somehow, Marius felt it in that dark room and pulled him even closer, their drenched and spent bodies blending. "Sleep, pet, it's been a long day..."

Grateful, Kyle closed his eyes, his master's breath in his neck.

VI

Marius woke up the next morning in the empty bed, his eyes darting to the window, a glint of sunshine forcing its way through the curtains. He rolled on his back and put his hands behind his head, his mind drifting back to last night... There was something there that he wouldn't admit to himself, a slow feeling in him when he was with Kyle, when he held him in his arms... *Damn it!* He rang the bell and waited, impatient, his emotions roiling.

Kyle entered and walked up to him. "Good morning, dominus. Should I open the curtains?"

His blue eyes sparked with irritation. "Do you have to be this awfully ceremonial when we're alone?" Kyle's face fell, and he waited, unsure. Marius got up, waving at him. "Just open them, damn it!"

Kyle pulled the curtains apart and watched Marius stroll out to the terrace, not caring about being naked. He dreaded to ask him about breakfast now, not fully understanding where his anger came from, watching his clenched jaw under his blue eyes. Kyle fought them, his feelings for him, the way his heart fluttered when he looked at Marius... it was not right, not when he was a mere slave and he was a free Roman citizen, a man... Yet, the only thing he wanted to do was to walk up to him and kiss his anger away. *Maybe I should...* But the thought died the minute it was born, his fear greater, and Marius whirled around, walking up to him, his eyes blazing.

For a fleeting moment, Kyle thought he was going to hit him, and he closed his eyes a split second, his shoulders slightly hunching, waiting for the blow, and Marius' face blanched, his voice cold. "You think I want to hit you?"

Kyle opened his eyes filled with fear. "No, dominus... it's just..."

Marius' lips curled into a mocking smile. "It's just what?"

Kyle swallowed, trying to even his voice. "Nothing, dominus..."

Marius sneered. "Go, get my breakfast, and make it quick."

Kyle turned around and all but rushed out of the room, his eyes burning.

He came back as fast as he could and lay the tray in front of Marius on the table, pouring a cup of orange juice, standing back, his hands behind his back.

Marius looked at him, his face a mask of anger. "Kneel!"

Kyle went to his knees next to him, his face downcast, hands on his thighs, and waited, his breathing quick but shallow. He waited but nothing happened. Marius ate, and his eyes drifted to the slave, his anger growing at his own emotions, at wanting to pull him up and kiss him, get lost in his embrace, taste his body...

Marius was trying to quench his feelings out for him by masking it with anger, trying to convince himself that they were just signs of his own weakness. *And what did the slave feel?* He thought he would hit him this morning, and last night they had been so intimate, he had almost lost it, had almost told him... He slammed his palm on the table, making the plates rattle, and Kyle startled a bit, his heart lurching in his throat.

Marius got up, his hands fisted at his side. "Help me dress, then you can clear this mess."

Kyle scrambled to his feet and went to take his clothes out, handing them to him and Marius tugged them on, avoiding looking at the slave. He fed on his fear though, his anger growing, not even knowing why, and he looked at Kyle, standing, his eyes downcast.

Marius walked up to him, standing close, and grabbed his chin, yanking his head up, meeting his tortured grey eyes, his thumb on the wound he had torn last night on Kyle's lower lip, digging into it, the soft flesh giving way under his strength.

"How many times do I have to tell you not to keep your fucking head lowered?" Marius hissed.

Kyle's eyes welled up with tears. "I am sorry, dominus..."

"Don't be always fucking sorry either..."

Kyle swallowed, feeling his lip tear under Marius' thumb, the sharp pain, and the salty tinge of blood, not understanding Marius' rage, this sudden anger. He struggled not to tremble and held his gaze, his blue eyes blazing under his furrowed brows.

Marius smiled a mocking smile. "Good, at least you can keep your eyes on me..."

He let him go and walked out, banging the door open, and Kyle let out a shaky breath, his heart torn. He wished he could hate him, but he couldn't... and he went to gather the remains of the breakfast, leaving to the kitchen with a heavy heart, licking his bleeding lip.

Sixtus watched Marius storm out of the house, and slowly shook his head. He bumped into Kyle on his way to the kitchen and stopped the young man, eyeing his wound with concern. "You're bleeding?"

Kyle waved it away, his eyes filled with sadness. "It's nothing…"

He walked around the old man to go to the kitchen, but Sixtus followed him, pulling him aside, away from Melissa's and Shayla's prying glare. "Son, what's going on?" Kyle's face stayed a mask and Sixtus sighed. "Fine… not my business, I guess…"

The young man forced a small smile on his face. "Thank you for your concern, Sixtus. Don't worry, I'm a big boy…"

The old man patted him on the shoulder when there was a knock on the main door and Kyle went to answer it.

Clavius strolled in with a beaming smile, his mood light. "Where's your useless master, Kyle?" His words died when he looked at the young man, his bloodied lip, and Clavius' face darkened. He stepped up to Kyle and brushed his thumb over the wound. "Where did you get this?"

Kyle looked away. "Dominus left this morning, master Clavius. He didn't say where he was going."

Clavius smiled. "I see… playing rough, is he?" Kyle's face fell, and he lowered his eyes. Clavius turned towards the door. "Well, if he comes back, tell him I'll drop by at dinner."

The day passed quickly with mindless physical chores, but the mood was tense, a slight unease whilst they were waiting for Marius to come home.

Dusk crept in and the light dimmed, the sun slowly setting, enveloping the garden into shadows. Kyle lit the torches and lamps, his hands grazing the lush flowers. It was so peaceful here, only the soft gurgling of the fountain, the plopping sound of the goldfish feeding and snapping at the water.

He heard then Clavius' voice, and the centurion walked into the garden, his face alight. "Hey, boy! Marius is still not home?"

Kyle shook his head. "No, master Clavius. Can I bring you something to drink?"

Clavius lay down on one of the beds. "Sure! Some wine would be nice."

Kyle bowed and was starting to leave when Marius appeared in the archway, his eyes blazing, and Kyle stopped cold, unable to move. His master opened his mouth.

Marius then noticed Clavius and sighed, clenching his jaw. "Get us wine and dinner!"

Kyle hurried past him, and Marius plopped down next to Clavius' bed, his face dark, brooding.

Clavius smiled at him. "Now, now... what's eating you?

"Nothing..."—he snapped and looked away — "Why are you here?"

Clavius laughed. "Not happy to see me? Tough. I came by this morning, but your boy told me you had left already. Figured I'd catch you tonight. But I can leave if you want to brood on your own... or roughen up your fuck boy."

He smiled and Marius turned to him, his anger blazing. "I haven't roughened him up!"

Clavius spread his palms. "Sure, sure... he must have bitten his lip then to the blood on his own..."

Marius blanched. "What did he tell you?"

Clavius looked at him, concerned. "Nothing... the boy's a grave... I guessed it, you know, wisdom comes with old age, or so they say."

He silenced when Kyle came back, carrying their wine. Melissa and Shayla brought out dinner, and they waited until the slaves laid the table. Kyle stayed to pour their wine and then knelt behind Marius, his eyes on the Roman's back. At least, he could not see his face, his impossibly handsome face, and blue eyes... He sighed softly, not daring to move.

Marius and Clavius ate, the men making small talk, Clavius' worried eyes on his friend. He also glanced at the slave, his tortured face, and sad grey eyes, kneeling there like a statue.

Marius raised his cup after a while and Kyle wordlessly got up and filled it, kneeling again when he was done, and Marius' anger brew, feeling the slave's presence behind his back, fighting the urge to pull him into his arms. He couldn't even understand his own feelings, this sudden anger at Kyle, at his existence... *Madness, this is pure madness, I should have never let this happen...*

Clavius watched him and addressed Kyle. "Go, boy, stretch your legs. Your master and I have to talk."

Marius looked up, puzzled, and Kyle froze, his breathing quickening. He could not move, fearing that he would anger Marius.

What the actual fuck? Marius was seething, but then he snapped at Kyle. "You heard Clavius? Get up and get out of here!"

The slave shot to his feet and hurried out, not looking back, feeling Marius' piercing stare on his back.

Clavius sat up and looked at his friend. "Look at me and don't brood there like a wounded lion... much better. Now, what's this whole thing here? I thought you liked your fuck boy and now I'm worried you might tear him into pieces if I leave you alone..."

Marius waved him away. "Why, thanks for your concern, but it's none of your godsdamn business."

"I'm your friend, Marius? Yes?" Marius nodded, slightly defeated and Clavius dove in, sensing the man's shield lowering. "So, it is my business too, and I do care precisely because of that. I hate to see you like this. Tell me what's going on?"

Marius stayed silent, pondering if he should confide in him, after all, he'd talked to his father behind his back, but he was going crazy with his feelings and he sighed, his eyes softening, his voice tamed. "I am not sure what's going on, friend... I mean, it's hard to put the words to it."

Clavius watched him carefully. "You have feelings for your boy...?"

Marius looked at him, pained. "Maybe... I guess..."

Clavius sighed, putting a hand on his shoulder. "Well, could be more tragic..."

Marius smiled bitterly. "Yeah... still, I have no idea what to do now."

Clavius shrugged. "How does he feel?"

Marius laughed softly. "How should I know? He would not answer me straight, even if I asked..." His face darkened. "He is too scared, too obedient, his will has been wiped out and he'll tell you what you want to hear, so... there's no way of knowing how he feels... about me...us."

He swallowed, bitter, and Clavius sighed. "There's one way you could find out... make him tell you first how he feels..."

Marius looked at him. "How?"

Clavius shrugged. "Make him... put him in a situation where he has no choice but to tell you. But not with fear, that won't lead anywhere. In any case, I guess you could peel the skin off his back, it wouldn't change a thing about how he relates to you. He looked miserable this morning when I walked in, so..."

Marius looked at him. "So? He mostly looks miserable anyway..."

Clavius spread his hands. "Maybe he's also tormented like you are. If he has feelings for you, for a Roman general, it must be really hard to admit, even to himself, harder than for you. After all, his village has been wiped out by our soldiers. What does he know of Romans? Rape, murder, being fucked to pieces on Lucius' estate and during his orgies? A young boy like him, free, and ready to be a fighter possibly, raped, enslaved, and fucked in the ass for years by Romans...? How should he exactly feel, maybe falling for your gorgeous face and blue eyes, general?"

Marius' face paled. He had never thought of these, of what Kyle could feel, too obsessed with his own feelings, and Clavius continued, his voice soft. "You are allowed to love a slave, Marius, our laws allow it. Hell, he could even be your concubine if you wanted it, not that I would advise that with you being soon married, even so, the possibility is there. What's your torment then? But what is his torment? He's a slave, used for pleasure, I'd assume he had not been kissed until he met you, at least, not out of passion, and not taken out of passion either, or other... so he must be pretty conflicted himself if he has developed feelings for you. Guilt, probably thinking admitting it would be a crime, a relationship impossible. And you, in your own selfish way, are making things worse by giving him the cold shoulder and treating him like shit."

Marius closed his eyes, his emotions whirling. Clavius was right, his words making more sense than anything he had come up with so far.

Clavius continued watching the younger man. "Lastly, my friend, you have to decide what you want. Do you love this young man? If so, this has to be cleared between you and him. If you don't love him, then just continue what you've been doing so far, have a casual fuck, and dismiss him to his room. But you're muddying the waters and losing yourselves in it. Your erratic behavior must be pure torture for this boy."

Marius looked at him, wide eyed. "Erratic behavior? Torture?"

"Yes. You're kind and loving one day and then ask him to sleep with you, then the next day, your anger flares and you push him away. He doesn't know what to expect. And if he loves you, he must be in hell right now."

Marius silenced, his guilt eating at him. Clavius patted his shoulder, rising. "I should be going... think about what I've said, for what it's worth... and don't overthink this again...?"

Marius rose to clap him on the shoulder, calm. "Thank you, friend..." He watched him leave and sat down, his head in his hands, his thoughts slowly churning Clavius' words.

Kyle entered the garden then, slowly, watching his master sit with his head in his hands. He barely breathed when he gathered the plates, his whole body alert, waiting to be told off or shouted at, or shoved against the wall...

Marius watched him from under his hair, his nimble body leaning over the table. He could see Kyle was tense, alert, his muscles taut, and he cursed himself softly. He waited until he'd left to lift his head and he sighed deeply. *Make him say it... but how?* He got up and started walking to his room when Kyle stopped in front of him, breathless.

He just looked at the terrified young man, his grey eyes wide, his head up, not daring to lower it. His lip had scabbed, a dark patch marring the smooth flesh. Marius sighed, his voice soft. "Sleep in your room tonight, I need to think..."

Kyle nodded and watched him leave, his throat clutching. *I need to think... but about what?* He felt more lost than ever and hurried to his room, his tears spilling.

Marius had been away all day next day, not saying a word in the morning, leaving with his face grim.

When he came home, he looked at Kyle in the atrium, his face a mask. "Clean yourself up and bring dinner for two in my room."

Kyle nodded, swallowing. "Yes, dominus."

Marius left him, and Kyle hurried to bathe. He then picked up the platters and left for the master bedroom, his stomach clenched. The room was in shadows, the oil lamps barely flickering, the terrace bathed in a soft glow by the torches and lamps and Marius spoke to him, half-hidden in the shadows of the terrace's pillars. "Put the dinner on the terrace table, then close the door."

He obeyed and laid the dinner out, walking back to close the door.

Marius' voice flew through the shadowed room. "Bolt it."

Kyle swallowed, vaguely panicked, his hands trembling as he slid the heavy bolt in place.

They went to the terrace and Marius lay down on a bed, gesturing Kyle over, but before he could kneel, Marius grabbed his wrist. "No. We eat together tonight. Lie down on the other bed."

Kyle's eyes widened, but he didn't dare disobey and did as told, carefully eyeing the Roman, but Marius seemed calm and content.

They ate in silence, Kyle just nibbling at his food, his stomach like a block of granite. Marius glanced at him sometimes, his heart fluttering in his chest, so worried that he could barely breathe.

When they'd finished, Marius rose and took Kyle's hand, pulling him up. They walked to the terrace's edge, Rome at their feet, sparkling in the velvet night. Kyle could not speak, his throat choked with fear, utterly confused by Marius' behavior... again. Marius' face gave nothing away when he grabbed his shoulder and turned Kyle towards him.

Kyle raised his eyes to his, not wanting to be told off. He could feel the warmth of Marius' body, so close, but he felt his hand slide off his shoulder and Marius waited, not touching him at all, his blue eyes shining in the torchlight. Kyle studied his face, trying to guess his mood, but it didn't give anything away and he licked his lips, nervous.

Marius' deep voice flew softly in the night. "I am not angry at you, and I don't want to hurt you..." He watched the slave's shoulders relax a bit, a small nervous sigh escaping his lips, but he was still en guard, his grey eyes filled with worry and maybe something else. "So... I know this is not easy for you, but I'd like you to do what you want now. Just what you feel you want to do, at this very moment, here..."

Kyle watched him, his velvety lips moving as he formed the words, his handsome face glowing in the yellow light, his black hair blending with the night sky studded with stars. He knew what he wanted to do, and it hurt and terrified him. His own feelings like a betrayal to himself, to his dead loved ones... *What if this was a trap? A test... but did it matter?* He didn't care anymore, not even if he angered him. The dead drifted away in his head, his long-lost freedom, his fear at what the ghosts would say... only the Roman remained, waiting, his blue eyes calm, his broad shoulders slowly lifting with his breath.

Kyle stepped closer to him, not breaking eye contact, his chest against his chest, feeling his breathing, his warmth. He laced his arms around Marius' neck and pressed his body against his rock-hard muscles, pulling his head down into a kiss, his mouth prying the Roman's mouth open, his tongue pushing his teeth apart, teasing him, invading his hot mouth. He felt him respond, and he deepened their kiss, their teeth clashing as they devoured each other, but it was not desperate like before, and Kyle tried to pour all his feelings into that first kiss he had chosen to give him.

He broke it then, softly panting, coming up for air, and Marius' eyes shone. Kyle looked up at him, his mouth grazing his mouth, breathing the words, not caring about anything anymore. "I love you, dominus..."

Marius' eyes widened and before Kyle could pull away, he kissed him again, soothing, trying to make him understand that he had nothing to fear, his strong arms lacing around his shoulders.

Kyle moaned into the kiss, relieved, but still vaguely anxious.

Marius broke their kiss then, gently cupping his chin, looking down into his grey eyes, his blue eyes dark with lust. "I love you too..."

Kyle froze, his mind trying to comprehend the magnitude of the words... His master loved him... it was unexpected and frightening, yet, his heart beat faster and his eyes welled up with tears. Marius' thumbs brushed his cheeks as he cradled his face, kissing him again, deeper, his tongue lazily caressing him, exploring his mouth and Kyle melted in his embrace, bathing in their newly found love.

Dazed, they drifted to the bedroom, slowly peeling their clothes off, kissing, their hands gliding on their bodies.

Kyle lay down on the bed, flat on his stomach, but Marius pulled him up, making Kyle face him. "No... tonight, we make love... I want to make love to you..." He kissed Kyle's neck, his tongue drifting on his collarbone, making him moan. "I want to worship your body..." Marius' mouth grazed his skin, sliding down, and Kyle's eyes flew wide open when he felt Marius' mouth on his erection.

He sat up, pushing on Marius' shoulder. "No! Dominus... you can't..."

Marius looked up, a small smile on his lips. "I can do whatever I want..."—he rose over him and pushed Kyle back on the bed, slowly kissing him — "... and you will stop calling me dominus in this room... understood?"

Kyle was shocked, unable to utter a word, and Marius smiled down at him. "Say my name, Kyle."

He looked at him, wide eyed. "I... I can't, d..."

Marius put a finger on Kyle's mouth. "Shhh... yes, you can... say it..."

Kyle moaned, blanching. "Marius..."

His name on his lips made Marius groan and swoon in delight, and he kissed Kyle deeply, his rich voice full of lust. "Say it again, say how you love me..."

Kyle breathed, surrendering. "I love you... Marius..."

The Roman devoured his mouth then and trailed kisses down his body, licking and biting the soft flesh and hard muscles, growling. Kyle moaned and writhed but didn't dare push him away when Marius took him in his mouth, sucking him with languid strokes of his tongue.

His head tossed on the pillow and Marius watched him pant and moan, sucking harder, wanting him to lose it. "Come for me, Kyle..." He felt the rich cream explode in his mouth and he swallowed it all, sliding up to kiss Kyle deeply again, letting him taste himself. "I'm not done with you yet..."

His blue eyes twinkled, watching Kyle's grey eyes mist over, and he reached for the bottle of oil, spilling the golden liquid on his fingers. He pushed Kyle's knees apart, lifting them back, and pushed two fingers in him, all the while kissing him, making him moan in his mouth with each thrust.

He stopped, braced above the young man's glistening body. "More?"

Kyle's voice was a mere whisper. "Yes..."

Marius teased him, slowly kissing his neck. "Tell me what you want ..."

Kyle moaned. "Fuck me..."

Marius shook his head. "No..."

Kyle panted. "Make love to me... Marius... Love me..."

Marius pulled his fingers out and pushed his cock in with one long stroke, closing his eyes, Kyle's legs around his arms. He had to stop and breathe hard not to lose it straight away, moving then slowly, sliding in and out with long, lazy strokes, watching Kyle's eyes close, his face flushed with pleasure, his moans filling the room. He bent down to kiss him, nibble his neck, his teeth grazing his skin. Their moans grew louder as he thrust harder, Kyle's arms around his shoulders, pulling him close.

He whispered into the slave's neck. "Come for me... again..."

Kyle's back arched and Marius felt him clench inside, so tight, it made him come inside of him, howling, his teeth biting into Kyle's neck muscle, hard.

They panted, their bodies soaked, Kyle struggling to breathe under Marius' weight. He rolled down off him and pulled him into a kiss, his hand sliding down his side, making the young man shiver.

Marius looked down at him, his eyes glazed with lust. "I love you so fucking much... you have no idea..."

Kyle smiled. "And I love you too, d... Marius..."

They kissed again, Marius' lips brushing over the bite he'd caused on his neck, and he frowned, concerned. "I bit you..."

Kyle's hand flew to his neck. "It's nothing... I love it... it will remind me of you for days..."

Marius laughed. "Some reminder!" His eyes grew concerned. "I don't want to hurt you, ever...."

Kyle caressed his jaw, running his fingers along it. "This doesn't hurt that much... it's good pain."

Marius arched his eyebrows. "Good pain? What on earth..."

Kyle laughed. "Yes, the kind of pain that will make me think of you... that's good pain."

They snuggled into each other's arms, Kyle's mind playing back the events of the past hour, and he blushed, slightly concerned. "What we have here... is it forbidden?"

Marius moved a bit to look at him. "Forbidden? No... not by our laws, if that's what you mean."

Kyle nodded, his voice drifting in the night. "My father would have killed me..."

Marius froze at his words, wanting him to continue, as he knew nothing about the slave's past. He tried to sound casual, lazily caressing his shoulder. "Is that so? Why?"

Kyle shrugged slightly. "Relationships between men were not exactly allowed... not if you were from the ruling family, at least..."

Marius tensed, masking his voice. "Ruling family?"

"Yes, the clan leader's ..."

"Were you...?"

Kyle sighed, the memory blurred, distant. "I was his eldest son."

Marius shuddered, closing his eyes. *What the hell... the son of a Celt clan leader...* "Who knows about this?"

Kyle looked at him, alarmed by his tense voice. "You do... now..."

Marius exhaled loudly. "Gods... you can't tell that to anybody, got it? Not Clavius, the other slaves, nobody..."

"I didn't want to..."

"Good..."

"But why? What does it matter? They are all dead..."

His voice choked, and Marius held him tight. "Nobles, princes, highborn captives should not be kept as slaves... they are usually killed... sacrificed in the arena during games. Should anybody find out who you truly are... you would be taken from me and killed... And I would be punished too... possibly."

Kyle closed his eyes. "I won't tell... that part of me died anyway... Lucius thought I was a simple peasant."

He smiled bitterly at the memory, and Marius stroked his arm. "Let's leave it at that then..." His deep voice made Kyle melt inside. "You're mine, Kyle, and I love you. Nothing will happen to you. Do you understand? Not as long as I live... and if I die, I'll make sure that you're taken care of."

Kyle clutched at his thick arm, pulling it close to his chest. "You won't die..."

Marius smiled. "That's for the gods to decide. I'm a soldier. Anything's possible." Kyle stayed silent but his heart clenched, death settling in that dark room, making their souls ache. Marius kissed his neck, whispering. "Let's forget about death... I'm very much alive still..." He pushed Kyle down the mattress, kissing him deeply, his hands roaming his body and they were lost in each other again, the night sky filled with cricket songs.

VII

Next morning, Marius woke with Kyle in his arms, and he breathed in his scent, his mind drifting back to last night, a small smile on his lips. Kyle stirred, sensing him awake, and Marius bent down to kiss him lightly on the mouth, watching his grey eyes pop open.

"Good morning, dom…" Marius arched his eyebrows, and Kyle blushed. "Marius…"

"Much better… gods, I love to hear you say my name…" They kissed when a sharp knock interrupted them, and Marius looked up, frowning. "Come in!" Somebody tried to open the door, but it was bolted, and Marius laughed. "Hold on!"

Kyle had gotten up and slid his tunic on before he could even move, rushing to the door, sliding the heavy bolt back.

Sixtus peeped in, relieved to see Kyle whole and smiling. "Breakfast, dominus?"

"Yes, for two."

The old man bowed and left, leaving them, not fully understanding what had happened.

Kyle walked to the curtains, opening them wide, the lush morning air pouring in, carrying the scent of flowers.

Marius squinted in the sunlight, watching Kyle walk towards the bed. "Come here, gorgeous…" The young man slid into his arms, and he kissed him deeply. "I will make you pay for opening the curtains and blinding me with the sun."

Kyle smiled. "Really? It's late already. I should be working."

Marius shook his head. "Not today. Today, you come with me on my errands."

Kyle's eyes grew wide. He had not left the house since he was brought here and the prospect of going to town made him giddy but also scared. He swallowed, unsure. "Are you sure? I haven't really been out of any house…"

Marius stroked his shoulder. "Time to start, then. There's no way I'll spend a whole day without you…" His hand slid under the slave's tunic, but Sixtus came back with breakfast and Marius reluctantly let Kyle help him lay it on the table.

He left then and Marius got up, sliding his tunic on. "We need to bathe first and change..." They laughed and ate heartily, the glorious morning sun warming them.

After a thorough bath, they dressed, and Marius briefed him on how to behave as they crossed the atrium to the main door. "Just behave as a slave would, walk behind me, kneel next to me, and all the rest. You know this better than anyone."

Kyle nodded, still nervous.

Marius faced him in front of the door. "It'll be alright, pet, trust me? We're going to a private slave auction where I've been invited, dreadful, but there's no escaping it, it would have been rude to refuse the invitation. Clavius will join us, that should lighten the mood. Then we'll come home, and I'll fuck your brains out." His words sent shivers up Kyle's spine, and Marius kissed him, his voice heavy. "Let's go before I change my mind..."

Kyle opened the door for him and followed, steeling himself not to stop when he set foot on the street, strolling after Marius. The streets were quiet here, but they had to walk down to the city to get to another hill where the auction was and it got busier as they walked downwards from the hill, the city's stench reaching them before the crowds'. Kyle marveled at the people, the busy streets bustling with life, the shouting, and followed Marius closely, his eyes on his broad back, his worry chewing at him like a mad dog. Rome was dangerous, that much he knew from his chats with Sixtus.

They whirled towards a steep street, climbing up the hill, followed by some stairs, and he breathed hard, not having Marius' stamina. The scorching sun drenched their backs and Marius stopped on top of the stairs to catch his breath and cool down. They stood in the shade of a building, their backs to the wall, scanning the people passing by.

Marius turned to Kyle. "Tired already?"

"No... just a bit out of breath. I'm not used to walking that much."

Marius' heart clenched. "I'll make you walk with me more then. You can't stay locked up all the time in the house."

Kyle nodded, vaguely dizzy with the surrounding space, a bit overwhelmed to be out in the open again. They resumed their walk, a bit slower, and reached an enormous villa. Marius announced himself to the guard at the door. He walked then to the garden where the auction was held under the shade of trees. Several couches had been laid out, and a slave took them to the one on which Clavius was already laying. He was talking to another man on the neighboring couch, cups in their hands. They were laughing when Marius walked up to them and Clavius and the man rose to greet him.

Clavius gestured to Marius. "This noble man here is Titus Octavius Furius."

Marius clasped the other man's forearm. "Greetings, Titus Octavius, I am Marius Ulpius Lupus."

The other man grinned. "At last, I get to know you. Clavius raves about you all the time."

Marius raised an eyebrow slightly, but Clavius swatted his arm. "Come on, nothing to worry about."

Marius checked Titus out. A good height, almost as tall as him, a strong body from what he could tell, dark-brown hair and golden-brown eyes. They could have been brothers, save for the eye color, and he smiled at him. "And what is it that you do, good Titus?"

"I am an accountant, awfully boring, I'm afraid, for a soldier like you." Marius smiled and Titus' eyes drifted to Kyle, standing a bit behind Marius, his face lowered. Titus arched an eyebrow at Marius. "May I have a look at your slave?"

Marius stood aside, trying to sound casual. "Be my guest."

He watched Titus walk up to Kyle. "Lift your face, slave."

Kyle obeyed whilst Marius cleared his throat. "His name's Kyle."

Titus tasted the name. "Kyle... a Celt?"

Marius nodded and Titus turned back to Kyle, slowly looking him over, Marius barely being able to contain himself. He went back to his couch then and settled, followed by Marius and Clavius. Kyle knelt near Marius, between him and Titus, who raised his glass at Marius.

"To our encounter... I must admit, your slave is a rare beauty... you must have paid a fortune for him."

Marius shrugged. "I got him as a gift."

"Really? Quite a generous gift then..."

Marius didn't comment and his eyes locked with Clavius', a bit annoyed at the stranger now, and Clavius nudged him, whispering. "How come you've brought your fuck boy out of his den?"

Marius' lips pinched, his eyes blazing. "How many times do I have to tell you..."

"Don't call him fuck boy..." Clavius finished with a grin. "I know, I know..."

The couches were spread in a circle, facing a small stage where the auction was about to happen, and their housemaster stepped up to it, welcoming his guests. "Fine citizens of Rome, I have invited you here to sample the best of what Rome's slave markets have to offer. I hope you'll enjoy and get what you came for."

There was loud cheering, and applauses and Marius' lips pursed in disgust. *Some fun... human flesh on the block.* His stomach revolted, and he had to swallow bile rising up his throat.

Titus nudged his arm. "Not a huge fan of auctions?"

Marius shrugged, trying to sound casual. "No..." Still, this was not the horror of the common marketplace, so he settled, his eyes drifting, worried, to Kyle who was kneeling very still, his face ashen. *Oh crap! An auction... I shouldn't have brought him here...* Marius reached down and clasped his shoulder, leaning to him. "Are you alright, pet?"

Kyle nodded, slightly shivering, and Marius rose to leave when their host ambled towards them. "Marius, my good boy! I am so glad you came."

Marius forced a smile on his face and greeted the older man. "Flavius, so good to see you!"

"Yes, yes, how's your father? I am honored... I hear you're getting married to Seraphina, senator Quintus' daughter? Excellent choice!" Marius paled, but held tight. The old man clasped his shoulder. "Enjoy the auction! You will see, it's an excellent selection, although I see you have great taste already."

His eyes darted to Kyle, and Marius forced a grin. "Indeed..."

"I'll see you later, my boy."

Marius plopped down on the couch, fuming, and Titus raised his cup. "To your impending marriage. Congratulations!"

Marius toasted with him, but he felt sick, wanting away from it all. Still, it was too late, and the auction began with a young male slave brought out on the block. There was a lot of shouting and bidding, and he was sold to an older man, gone in a flash. Marius' worried eyes drifted to Kyle, the slave very still, barely breathing. Marius' hand went to his back, and he stroked it gently, his eyes on the auction block. He felt the clenched muscles relax under his touch and sighed in relief, feeling Kyle lean into his touch as the next slave was brought to the stage.

The world froze around Marius when he saw that scrawny little boy, probably not over ten years old, shivering, naked, under the men's gaze.

He sat up straighter, alert, his face blanched, and Clavius looked at him, frowning. "Marius... please don't make a scene..."

The younger man looked at him, exasperated, and gulped his wine down. Kyle sensed his hand being snatched away and looked up for a brief moment, only to lower his eyes in panic... *that young boy on the block...* Images from the day he had been sold drifted in, standing naked on the block, Lucius' face in the crowd when he'd won against a mild looking older man, his cruel smile, his hands on him when they had doused him with cold water and crudely wiped him off, him jerking away only to be hit in the face, hard, swallowing his own blood and tears... He shuddered, slightly losing his balance and he had to put his hand down next to him to steady himself.

The auctioneer called out. "Feast your eyes on this little bird, noble men. He is a fresh capture from the distant lands of Britannia and is still a virgin." Several men shouted that this was clearly untrue, but the auctioneer raised his hand. "This has been guaranteed by the general who captured their village himself." The noise of the bidding overtook the garden then, loud, frantic, and in that noise, Marius' deep commanding voice rose above the crowd with an amount that put an end to all arguments, silencing the other men.

There was a call from the auctioneer, but nobody dared bid against him any longer, knowing his rank and reputation, and Clavius' face fell in disbelief. "Marius... for fuck's sake...", he whispered, but Marius was already standing, jerking Kyle up by the arm.

"Come, Kyle, let's collect our new boy."

Kyle steadied himself, still dizzy, his mouth sour, not even fully understanding what was going on. He strolled after his master, though, behind the block where they kept the slaves.

Marius pulled his purse out and paid, Flavius ambling to him. "My dear Marius... I am so happy you found what you were looking for."

Marius smiled. "I am not sure this is what I was looking for, but with my household expanding soon, I need more slaves."

Flavius smiled a fake smile, looking Kyle over. "Of course... and you don't want to sell your beautiful boy here? He'd bring you a fortune..."

Marius waved him off, laughing. "He's worth more than his weight in gold."

They watched the young boy being taken to them, in a simple tunic, barefoot, his face marred with tears. Kyle's heart lurched for him when they shoved him on his knees in front of Marius, his master playing the game, but Kyle could see how his face was drawn, pale under his dark hair.

"I'm your dominus now, little one. What's your name?"

The slave handler jumped in. "He doesn't talk, Sir. We named him Faustus."

Marius pursed his lips, turning to Kyle. "Do you think you could talk to him?"

Kyle looked at him, not understanding at first. "Talk to him? Of course..."

Marius' gaze pierced him. "Not in Latin... in Celtic..."

Kyle froze, his lips parting with shock... *Celtic*... the forbidden language, the language they had beaten out of him, endless hours of flogging, beating, slaps until his mouth had been bleeding. Pain with each word that had slipped out. He'd learnt Latin fast and had striven to forget the other language, the only language he'd spoken before... *and now...*

He reeled, swaying on his feet, and Marius caught him, a sudden concern on his face. "What's wrong?"

Kyle looked at him, wide-eyed, fighting his tears. "I'm not sure I can... it's been too long... I was not allowed..."

He didn't need to finish, and Marius sighed, gently holding his arm. "Fine. Faustus it is then until we find out who you really are."

The boy didn't move, his face dull, and Kyle crouched down to him, trying to conjure his language, his tongue slowly churning in his mouth as the words left his lips, barely a whisper, tearing his heart apart. But he could not show it, not in front of the Romans watching, so he just pushed the words out, hoping he had gotten them right. "Thig còmhla rium, fear beag. Cha dèan am maighstir cron ort." The boy looked at him, shocked, and his tears flowed. Kyle extended his hand with a smile, trying to look reassuring. "Is mise Caol. Kyle. Thig."

The small boy flew into his arms, and Kyle wrapped his arms around him, hugging him tight. He got up, the boy in his arms, exhausted, his head on his shoulder, hiding away from the world in this stranger's neck who spoke his language.

Marius asked casually, his voice raw with emotions. "The boy's parents, family?"

The auctioneer shook his head. "All dead probably or sold somewhere else. He hid in a well, that's how he was found, or so I've been told."

Marius had to ask, his lips pinched. "Is he really a virgin?"

The auctioneer smiled a crooked smile. "So I've been told... apparently the general leading those troops wasn't into little boys. He was found after the fights, so there's a good chance."

Marius nodded and walked back to his couch, bidding farewell to Clavius and Titus.

Clavius rose, his eyes drifting to Kyle holding the little boy. "Marius..." He was conscious of them being watched, so he grinned widely. "Congratulations on your new purchase!" He toasted him, and Marius smiled.

Titus eyed the two slaves curiously. "They know each other?"

Marius shrugged. "Kyle has a way with new slaves."

Titus laughed. "So I see... well, enjoy your new purchase."

Marius fumed silently, but his face stayed still. "I'll see you soon? It was a pleasure."

"Likewise. Let's keep in touch. Clavius knows where you dwell, so..."

Marius nodded and waved goodbye, knowing full well that Clavius would be coming after him soon.

They left and Kyle carried the boy, his body featherlight in his arms, his bones poking at his muscles. Marius turned to him. "Maybe he should walk?"

Kyle shook his head. "If you don't mind, dominus, I'll carry him."

He looked, worried, at Kyle's drawn face, but nodded. "We'll go slow. Let me know if you need to rest."

They resumed walking then, and the small boy looked in silence at the streets steaming with people, blending his body into Kyle's. His voice was a mere whisper against the slave's shoulder. "Càit a bheil sinn a 'dol?"

"Gu taigh a 'mhaighstir."

"Is mise Brandan."

Kyle stopped slightly, floored by emotions, and Marius turned back, concerned. "You're tired? Should we stop?"

Kyle shook his head, his eyes full of tears. "He's name is Brandan, dominus."

Marius' eyes lit up, and he repeated the name. "Brandan."

The small boy stayed very still and clutched Kyle tighter, but he just whispered in his ear. "Chan eil eagal sam bith ort."

By the time they got home, Brandan had fallen asleep, and Kyle's arms were trembling with his dead weight. Still, he clenched his jaws and managed the remainder of the trip to their house. Sixtus eyed them curiously, concerned at the bony little boy slouched on Kyle's shoulder, a thin stream of drool sliding down on the slave's smooth skin.

Marius gestured towards the boy. "This is Brandan, I just bought him. He doesn't speak Latin for now, only Celtic... Go and get Melissa. She can take care of him too, along with her daughter."

Brianna was already there, looking up at Kyle, her eyes shining. Sixtus came back with Melissa, the woman's face concerned when she saw the sleeping little boy.

Marius turned to her. "This is Brandan. Take care of him, he'll need it. He only speaks Celtic for now."

Melissa nodded, and Marius turned to Brianna with a smile. "You can teach him Latin. I'm sure he'll learn fast."

Their talking woke the little boy up, and he didn't move, only his eyes opening wide, watching them.

Brianna tugged at his leg and his eyes drifted to her, curious. "Hi, I'm Brianna. Climb down? We can play." She beamed a smile at him, but Brandan just clutched Kyle tighter.

The young man slowly pried him off, gently soothing him, and Melissa smiled at the boy, extending her hand. "Thig còmhla rium. Tha thu a-nis aig an taigh." Brandan looked at Kyle and he nodded, letting him slip into Melissa's arms, crying again in her neck. She left then and Bri followed her, reaching up to hold Brandan's hand.

Marius watched them go and then reached for Kyle's hand, feeling the slave tremble, the emotions and physical strain of the past hours getting at him. "Come..." He tugged at him, and Kyle followed Marius to the bath, letting him strip their clothes, his mind numb. Marius pulled him in the hot water and held him against his chest, cradling him in his arms and Kyle's eyes closed, his tears softly flowing, his head resting on the Roman's shoulder.

Marius' lips brushed his cheek. "Talk to me?"

Kyle swallowed the lump in his throat, but couldn't speak.

Marius sighed, stroking his arm. "You were very brave today... I am sorry you had to live through this. I had no idea..."

Live through this... yes, you have no idea... no idea what it feels like to lose your freedom, your family, and friends, to forget who you were to become somebody else, to be shaped by fear and pain until there's nothing left but this fear, the fear of pain... your will gone to serve your people's murderers until you die... to love you when there should only be hate...

Kyle shuddered, and Marius held him tighter, worried sick that he might lose him, his mind playing back Clavius' words, somehow sensing the young man's struggle. *Fucked up world.* "You have the right to hate me, you know, or be mad at me... I would understand..."

His pained voice made Kyle turn to look at him, his sad, grey eyes meeting his tortured blue ones, his damp, black hair falling into them. Slowly, his voice found its way out, softly. "I don't hate you..." Marius waited, secretly relieved that he was talking, "... because you're good to me... there's less fear now..."

Marius' heart sank, desperation creeping into his voice. "I love you... you should not be afraid."

Kyle's smile was tainted with sadness. "Patience, dominus... fear needs time to go away when it's been part of my life for so long..." Marius' chest heaved with his anger, shadows dancing on his handsome face, a crease between his brows, but Kyle reached up to his face, gently laying his palm on his cheek. "Your anger will not make the past disappear..."

He leaned into his touch. "I know... still, I don't know exactly what they did to you, but..."

Kyle stroked his jawline. "Better this way..."

"I don't want to lose you..."

Kyle smiled bitterly. "I'm not going anywhere..."

The meaning of his words was not lost on Marius, and he paled slightly, his face contorting in pain, but before he could speak, Kyle pulled him down into a kiss. He didn't want to hear what Marius had to say. This was already too painful, and Marius' distress made him anxious. They kissed deeply, their tongues fighting a raging battle, and soon they were both out of breath, hugging so tight that it hurt.

Kyle turned to face him, wiggling out of his arms and he pulled Marius out of the water, wordlessly leading him to their room where he pushed Marius on the bed, crawling above him.

Marius watched him, his pale face, the dark circles around his eyes, and as much as his tormented being wanted him, he didn't want to love him out of despair. He reached up and pulled Kyle down, rolling him over, flinging the blanket on top of them.

He pinned the young man down with his leg over his thigh and gently brushed his face with his knuckles. "Just rest for now...you need it..."

Kyle tried to protest but his words died in Marius' mouth, the Roman caressing him with his tongue, letting his warmth invade him under the sheets. Soon, he felt sleepy and, despite his struggle, plummeted into a deep sleep. Marius watched him for a while before dozing off, his arms pinned around the slave's chest.

VIII

They woke much later, Kyle trying to push Marius off who all but lay on him, squashing him in the mattress.

The Roman moaned and rolled to the side, his voice slurred. "What time is it?"

Kyle looked outside, the sun setting, and he sat up straight. "It's late... I have to go and prepare dinner."

Marius turned over, and grabbed his arm. "No, you don't... you stay with me."

Kyle hesitated. "I should really go... Sixtus will be upset."

Marius' lips curled up into a smile. "Are you disobeying me?"

Kyle looked at him, a slight worry coursing through him. "Of course not, dominus... I'll stay."

Marius pulled him down into a kiss, his hand sliding up his side when a knock interrupted him. He sat up, annoyed. "Come in!"

Clavius strolled in, stopping short seeing them in bed, his usual smile on his face. "Am I interrupting?"

Marius hurled a pillow at him, grinning. "What do you think? Get your ass to the garden while we dress up."

Clavius saluted and left them.

They quickly put on their tunics, and Kyle rushed to the kitchen to get wine and help with the dinner.

Marius walked to the garden, rested and at ease, his mood unusually light.

Clavius looked at his friend. "I see that you're walking on clouds..."

Marius smirked, lying down, when Kyle appeared, setting the large tray on the low table between them. Kyle filled their cups, Marius' eyes eating him up when he leant over him.

He left then to get their food, and Clavius raised his cup. "Looks like you have solved your little issue?"

The younger man smiled. "Yes, you can say that..."

"Well, I'm happy for you, at least, you're not brooding... but this is a dangerous game, Marius. Your little stunt at the auction today didn't go unnoticed..."

Marius looked at him, frowning. "What are you talking about? I bought a slave, no big deal."

"You bought a child, a boy... dare I say what impression you gave? Especially with Kyle there... several of the honorable guests have recognized him from Lucius' parties..."

Marius blanched in anger. "What?!"

Clavius spread his palms. "No need to work yourself up... what did you expect with his past?"

Marius sighed in frustration. "I don't know much of his past."

Clavius raised an eyebrow. "Don't you? Or you're just fooling yourself."

He shot him an angry look. "What do you mean?"

"I mean you're in denial, Marius. He used to be a whore, basically." Clavius raised his hands in defense. "Don't be mad at me! I'm just stating the truth."

Marius closed his eyes, his rage toiling. "So, the good people of Rome are quick to judge... the very same men who fuck little boys at orgies!"

"Yes, well, what did you expect? They are quick to judge, and gossip is fast... this is not useful right before your marriage to the daughter of a renowned senator."

Marius sneered, downing his wine. "Let them think what they want. I don't give a shit. They are just pissed because they couldn't lay their dirty hands on that little boy..."

"That's rich coming from you, fucking your young slave boy."

They looked at each other, the silence thick between them.

Kyle and Lisandra arrived with their dinner, silently laying the table, Kyle's worried eyes on Marius who sat there, livid.

Clavius broke the silence after they'd left, his face grim. "You might hate me right now, but I'm the only one who'll tell you the truth, even if it hurts... You have to think about your reputation, especially in this cesspool of a city."

"Sure, father..."

"Don't mock me, my friend... one day, you'll be thankful."

Marius sighed, his anger and appetite wiped. He lay back on his couch, closing his eyes to the world.

Clavius pushed gently. "Won't you eat?"

"No... I'm not hungry."

"Nonsense!" Clavius ate then, alone, when Kyle came back to assist them, and he perked up. "Ah, at last! Come, fill my cup, boy, and make your brooding master eat."

Kyle's eyes drifted to Marius whilst he filled their cups, and he then sank to his knees next to him, brushing his shoulder.

Marius smiled, not opening his eyes. "Don't order him around... I'm not hungry."

"The hell you aren't!"

Clavius started throwing olives at him, hitting him square in the face and he sat up, his eyes wide.

"What the..."

His friend laughed. "Stop wallowing in your misery and eat."

Marius laughed, shaking his head, when there was a commotion at the entrance and they raised their heads, watching Marius' father storm into the garden, his eyes on his son. Marius rose to greet him, slightly surprised. Gaius stepped in front of him and, with the same motion, backhanded him in the face, making him almost lose his balance with the force of the blow. Marius' hand flew to his cheek, his eyes wide with anger, but Gaius was not done.

He grabbed Marius by his tunic with both hands and pulled him close, his face inches from his face, his voice raw with wrath. "What were you thinking?! I will not allow you to fill your house with whores!"

Clavius sat, shocked and Kyle tried not to breathe, kneeling at their feet, his eyes on the floor. *He hit him...*

It took a couple of moments for Marius to emerge from his shock, his mouth filling with the taste of blood where his teeth had cut his cheek.

He wrenched himself out of his father's grasp, making the old man sway on his feet, his eyes blazing with anger. "Get out of my house!"

Gaius smiled at him. "You don't order me around, not when I'm still at the head of this family!"

Marius seethed, his voice booming. "This is my house! Get out!"

His father just crossed his arms, facing him off. "No. And don't even think about raising your hand on me, Marius. I will have you locked up and take your slaves."

Marius looked at him in disbelief. "What... you can't do that..."

"I can do whatever the hell I want, son, and you know it. Now, let's get to the point. I will not tolerate you becoming the topic of gossip, not now when you are engaged. It is an embarrassment and a dishonor. So, your marriage will happen fast to wash away the gossip that you're surrounding yourself with young boys, and you need to get rid of one of them very fast... this is not an option, it's an order."

Marius laughed through his anger. "Go to hell! I'm not selling my slaves!"

Gaius slapped him, hard. "Watch your tongue!"

Marius saw red, and he grabbed his father's toga, pushing the old man back when Clavius jumped up, pulling on his shoulder. "Come, come, let him go... Marius! Please..."

He reluctantly let the old man go, his chest heaving, and Gaius' eyes shone. "At least your friend has some sense... You have until tomorrow to get rid of one of them." His eyes drifted to Kyle. "I'd suggest you sell this one here, at least, you'll get a decent price, and you won't be tempted to bed him."

Marius laughed. "No way! Get the fuck out before I change my mind and haul your ass out of here with my bare hands!"

He was shaking now, Clavius could feel it, his fear and shock overtaking his raw anger, the adrenaline coursing through him, and Gaius just smiled, readjusting his toga. "Rude on top of it all, and disrespectful... nice..." His eyes bore into Marius'. "Very well. You brought this onto yourself, Marius. You don't want to obey me? There will be other ways for me to get you where I want you to be." His cold eyes gleamed, and he left, the garden all of a sudden too quiet.

Clavius turned Marius around, that handsome face darkening with bruises. "Let me have a look at you..."

Marius swatted his hand away, his cheeks burning. "Leave it, it's nothing..." He sat down, wiped, his stomach clenched in ice, his eyes drifting to the quiet slave. He grabbed Kyle's arm and pulled him next to him, his voice choked. "Come here..." Kyle settled against him, his face on his chest, and Marius held him tight, fighting his tears with his jaw clenched. He knew his father well enough to know that his threats were never empty, and he was pissed. *How dare he?! The old bastard....*

Clavius sighed, trying to lighten the mood. "Well, I'd never thought the old guy would go this far..."

"If it hadn't been for you, he'd be dead..."

Clavius watched him, Marius' cheek darkening as the bruise spread to a light purple color. *Man, the old guy could still hit hard...* He was worried for Marius though and watched him clutch the young slave like he was a lifesaver buoy. *The old guy is going to get at him where he's weakest...*

They didn't have to wait long. A couple of days later, Marius read the invitation to the emperor's private party and his blood froze. His cheek had taken a light purple color and he stroke it lightly, his hand gliding on the tender skin. *Private party... more like private orgy... bring your delightful boy. Your father had high praises for him...* He swallowed, closing his eyes, and looked at Kyle, who was waiting patiently, vaguely anxious at his expression.

Marius read him the invitation and Kyle stood very silent, waiting for him to speak. "You know what this means, don't you?"

"Yes, I know..."

"I'm not going to take you there!"

Kyle walked up to him. "You don't have a choice..."

Marius flung the invitation through the room. "Damn it! Fuck them all, and fuck my father in particular, that son of a bitch!"

Kyle took his hands, trying to sound reassuring. "I've done many of these... parties... it will be fine..."

Marius shook his head. "This is the emperor's party, not some kind of countryside orgy..."

Kyle shrugged. "Men are men, doesn't matter if they're emperors or countryside nobles, or whatever..."

Marius moaned, his face miserable. "If they do anything to you... I'll have to watch..."

Kyle's eyes shone sadly, a small smile on his lips. "Yes, probably... just try not to hate me too much afterwards."

Marius held him tight. "Hate you? Never!"

Kyle looked up at him. "Don't promise something you can't keep, maybe... When is this 'party'?"

Marius whispered, lost. "Tomorrow..."

Kyle straightened. "We need to go shopping."

"What for?"

"I don't have any clothes that would fit a party like this..."

Marius stood, frowning. "Clothes? You can just wear one of your best tunics?"

Kyle smiled, bitter. "No... at these parties, you dress in a special way... and you need to look special..."

Marius looked at him, worried. "I hate doing this to you."

Kyle shrugged and pushed him away. "I'll go with Sixtus. He's going to town anyway to shop."

"Nice... leaving me in my misery."

"Go and ask Clavius if he's been invited? It would help to have a friend there..." He didn't finish and Marius knew what he meant, his face darkening.

Kyle left him, hurrying to catch Sixtus, who was harnessing the donkey to the cart. "I'll come with you; I have some shopping to do."

The old man raised his eyebrows. "Shopping? For what?"

Kyle blushed slightly. "Dominus has been invited to the emperor's private party and I have to go with him... so we need to go..."

Sixtus' lips pinched. "I know where I have to take you... gods, I hope you'll be fine..."

Kyle laughed lightly, trying to ease the old man. "Hey, I've been there before... no big deal..." But inwardly, he was vaguely panicked... *the Emperor of Rome, the man at the head of this horror of an empire... and tomorrow night...* he shook his head, opening the gate for Sixtus, jumping on the cart next to him. Marius watched them leave, and his heart clenched, but then he left too, hurrying to Clavius' house.

Of course, Clavius had been invited too, and he knew he'd have to work hard to keep Marius under check... he had been to one of these parties before and knew full well what would happen...

Marius stood fully dressed in his room, waiting for Kyle to get ready, his eyes on the night falling over Rome.

Kyle had asked Lisandra to help him put on his makeup. He had smeared a golden cream all over his body, dusting it with golden flakes that made him glint like a statue. Lisandra rimmed his eyes with black kohl, making sure they stood out in their startling grey color. He wore a sky-blue tunic, the material very light, almost see-through, the hem barely mid-thigh. A dab of dark red lip color, and silver sandals completed his outfit, a silver cloak that would hide his near nakedness until they arrived there. He looked at his face in the mirror, his heart beating fast. *What will Marius say...* He dreaded his reaction more than the entire night.

Lisandra's face was grim, and he smiled. "I look that bad?"

She shook her head. "Just... this is not you..."

Kyle looked at his reflection. "That's the whole point..."

He walked to their room and opened the door. Marius' eyes drifted to him, and his jaw parted in shock. He took him in, this familiar stranger who looked like he'd walked out of one of Rome's luxury brothels, and he walked up to him, grabbing his shoulders, a tortured moan escaping his mouth, looking at his sparkling skin, his grey eyes circled in black. "What the fuck... I can't believe this..."

Kyle silenced him with a kiss, his lips tasting of cherry. "It's me..."

"I can't do this... let's just stay here..."

Kyle shook his head. "You know the stakes... you can't anger the emperor..."

Marius sighed, looking him over again. "You're so fucking gorgeous."

Kyle's lips curled into a small smile. "Great... I didn't want to embarrass you."

Marius hugged him tight, but they had to leave, and they walked down the street to be taken to the palace. They stayed silent all the way through, Kyle resting in Marius' lap, the litter slowly swaying.

They had to cross corridors in that vast palace to be guided to the private party chamber, a huge room with statues, ornate columns, and the elevated couches of the emperor. Kyle had taken his cloak down and he was walking behind Marius and Clavius, his blue tunic flowing around his thighs, gliding against his body. Clavius had brought one of his wife's boys, clearly not interested in him, but this was common practice.

Several heads turned as they crossed to their place, Marius surprised to see Titus sprawled on the neighboring couch, his hand on a slave's shoulder, similarly dressed and made-up to Kyle. He had green eyes and long wavy blonde hair, a light green tunic, his face quietly studying Kyle when he'd knelt.

Titus beamed a huge smile. "Good to see you again!"

"Likewise..." Marius forced a smile on his face, vaguely panicked already.

Titus ruffled the young slave's hair. "This is Damianos, but just call him Damian, my trusted little Greek whore." Marius winced at the term but politely acknowledged with a nod. "I must admit, I had a hard time recognizing your slave. Kyle, right? He's transformed..."

Marius smiled. "Well, this is a party after all..."

"Yes, and it will be a good one." He grinned, and they toasted, a young slave boy filling their cups. "Whatever happened to your face, good Marius?"

Marius shrugged, smiling. "I bumped into a door last night... I was a bit drunk."

Titus laughed, and they waited whilst the guests drifted in, and the emperor arrived too, not announced by anybody, as this was his little private party. He walked around, his purple toga trailing behind him, and greeted his guests. He arrived at their couch, and they all rose, bowing.

The emperor walked to Marius and pulled him into a hug. "My good general... so good to see you... I see you brought your treasured little pet..."

Marius swallowed, nervous. "Yes, honored emperor. "

The old man smiled. "Come, come... we are amongst friends..."

"Yes, uncle... thank you for the invitation."

"Much better! Show me this beauty you have here..."

"Get up, Kyle, and lift your face."

He obeyed, slowly looking up into the void, not wanting to make eye contact with the emperor, and the old man looked him over, his eyes gleaming. "Your father was right... he is a rare treat... we'll see what he can do for us later, mhm?"

Marius blanched but tried to sound casual. "Sure, uncle..."

The emperor laughed, clapping him on the shoulder. "Very well... we also need to talk work, but that's for later, in a couple of days... Enjoy the party!"

Titus looked at Marius, wide eyed. "Uncle?"

Marius shrugged. *My fucking luck...*

The emperor climbed on his elevated platform where his couch was, his hands going to his slave kneeling at his side, a young man with a thin face, his eyes like a weasel's, and he greeted the guests, toasting with his cup. "Noble men of Rome... welcome. We have a long night ahead of us, I hope, full of surprises."

They cheered, and the party began, young boys gliding around them with jugs of wine. They filled their cups again and Marius handed it to Kyle. "Drink, you'll need it..."

Kyle took the cup and gingerly tasted the dark liquid, his tongue tingling, all his senses alert as the familiar sweet taste invaded his mouth.

He gently tugged on Marius' toga, making him look down, a small smile on his lips. "Hungry already?"

Kyle lifted his face to him and parted his lips, letting Marius kiss him, whispering. "The wine... it's tainted..."

Marius looked at him, alarmed, and raised the cup to his lips, the peculiar taste invading his mouth. "What the fuck is this?"

Titus smiled, toasting him. "A potent little mix... a light sedative with a good dose of aphrodisiac..."

Marius frowned. "You're an expert, I see..."

Titus laughed. "I have some of this at home... can come in handy if you need to tame your slaves..." His eyes shone and Marius felt like throwing up.

Still, he looked down at Kyle. "Do you want to drink this?"

Kyle reached for the cup, his face not giving away anything. "Yes, dominus..."

He let him down the cup, which got instantly refilled, and Clavius turned to his friend. "You should drink one too... for your nerves."

He grinned and Marius toasted him, feeling the liquid fill him up, a slight warmth invading his insides, flowing down to his groin... *Wonderful...* the lights danced a bit in the room, and he lay back, a bit more relaxed. He looked down at Kyle, his eyes glazed over, scanning the room.

His hand went to pet his head and the young man leaned into his touch. Some exotic dancers invaded the floor in front of them and food was served, but already, masters and slaves were slowly kissing, groping at each other. Marius reached down to pull Kyle up next to him, his nerves on edge.

Kyle sensed it and leant on him, pushing him into the couch, slowly kissing him, his tongue invading his mouth. He whispered to him. "Relax... let me guide you..."

Marius closed his eyes and got lost in their kiss, the tainted wine tingling on his skin, his hands gliding on Kyle's silky tunic. He could not tell when the dancers had left the stage, but the slow music remained and then, the emperor's voice above his head. He opened his eyes, pushing Kyle off to his side.

"My good nephew and my good Titus... care to assist in heating up the mood?... I had a great idea..." The young men looked at each other, then back at the old man, Marius' jaw clenched. "So... I thought your slaves could do us a little show on stage... they are both gorgeous and, as far as I know, experienced?" He ran his finger along Kyle's jaw and Marius' stomach flipped, but the slave just looked at the old man and parted his lips. "Why... what a good little slut..." He pushed his finger into Kyle's mouth and the slave moaned around it, closing his eyes.

Marius couldn't believe it, and he almost did something stupid when Titus rose, shoving his slave in the front. "It will be a pleasure, honored emperor."

The old man looked at him, pulling his finger out, a wide grin on his face. "Excellent! Let them take the stage."

Slaves had carried a stand in, to the middle of the room, carpeted like a large bed, full of pillows, and Kyle's and Damian's eyes drifted there, then they looked at each other.

Titus gave them each a cup. "Party time, boys, drink up."

They obeyed, Marius frozen, unable to move.

Clavius clasped his arm. "You knew this might happen... sit back and don't you fucking move. Your fuck boy here is a pro, he'll handle it. Right, Kyle?"

The slave turned to them, his eyes misted over, and he walked to Marius, kissing him deep, whispering. "Just don't forget... I love you... whatever happens, whatever you see..."

Marius swallowed, close to tears, and he let Kyle's hands go, watching the slaves hold hands and walk down to the staged bed. They stripped slowly to the music, and the guests shouted, obscene words flying through the air, but Kyle and Damian were lost already, both fully aware of what they had to do. They started caressing each other, their mouths close to the other's ear, and they whispered to each other, trying to quickly set some structure to their impro.

Damian's tongue ran along Kyle's jaw. "Top or bottom?"

Kyle whispered, kissing Damian's cheek. "Bottom..."

"Rough?"

"Let's see what they like..."

"Ok... make me hard first?"

Kyle nodded and looked into his eyes, his hands gliding down Damian's sides and they smiled at each other, Damian's mouth so close to his he could feel the warmth of his breath, the soft skin of his lips. "I actually quite like you..."

Kyle's tongue swept over his lips. "Yes... me too..."

They kissed then, slowly, their hands roaming each other, the taste of the drugged wine mingling in their mouths. It started kicking in and they felt warm, their skin tingling, their senses dulled to the noise around them, the shouting, the music... Kyle pushed Marius out of his mind, drawing on his training at the brothel, at Lucius' parties where he had to be on stage more than once. This was not too bad compared to what he had to do in the past, so he tried to make the most out of it, knowing what was at stake. They had to please the emperor and his guests... He sank to his knees, his eyes on Damian, licking his lips with exaggeration and the Greek slave's lips curled into a smile, his hands going to Kyle's hair, gently curling his fingers into it as he took him in his mouth. Damian threw his head back and moaned loudly, making the guests cheer around them. Kyle had to suppress a smile. Damian sure was a good actor, and he was already hard in his mouth, pushing in, to the hilt, slowly rocking his hips. Kyle had no trouble accommodating him. He was smaller than Marius, but still of a good size, and he felt his hands grip his hair, pumping harder. The shouting increased around them... *They will like it rough...*

Marius lay on his couch, watching the scene unfurl in front of his eyes, and his hands curled into fists at his side, his face white.

Clavius rose and sat next to him. "Scoot over..." He gave Marius a glass of wine, making sure he drank it all. "Now... much better, right? Relax your face and try to look like you're not dying from the inside."

Marius closed his eyes for a brief moment, swaying, his voice soft. "I can't watch this..."

Clavius' hand closed on his fist. "You have no choice... not with your divine uncle watching. You know what this is, Marius... you want to keep your lover boy? Act like he means nothing to you, otherwise, they'll find a way to take him from you."

Marius looked at him, his eyes widening as his words sank in. He looked back at the slaves, his eyes then drifting to the emperor, the old man slowly toasting him. He grinned at him, lifting his cup, and turned to Titus, who was watching the slaves with a smirk on his face. "Titus, let's toast to our little sluts."

"They're something, right? I have to admit, yours seems to have an incredibly talented mouth."

They laughed, and they drank deep, their eyes going back to the scene. Lying on the other side of him, Clavius left his hand on his fist, feeling his muscles tense. Marius pretended not to care though, but inwardly, his heart was beating fast, and bitterness settled in the back of his throat when the guests started chanting.

"Fuck him! Fuck him!"

Damian pushed Kyle off him and bent down to kiss him deeply, slowly turning him around on all fours, leaning on his back to nibble his throat, softly whispering. "They want more action... ready?"

Kyle pushed back against him. "Yes..."

A slave boy brought Damian a bottle of oil, and he made a show of coating his fingers, letting the oil trickle down Kyle's back, the slick liquid shimmering on the gold of his skin.

He then pushed his fingers in, all the while licking Kyle's neck and shoulders. "I can't stretch you for too long..."

Kyle shut his eyes, pretending to enjoy it immensely. "Doesn't matter..."

Damian settled back then and pulled his fingers out, pushing his cock right in, to the hilt with a rough thrust, and Kyle moaned loudly, slightly surprised. He braced his arms when Damian started pounding him, not leaving time for him to adjust, the shouting loud around them as men cheered and whistled. The drug had dimmed his senses to the pain, but it was still there, lingering, and he panted through his moans and mewls filling the room, sweat breaking down his back. Damian reached forward and grabbed his hair, yanking his head back, making his back arch even more, and Kyle's lips parted, dizzy with the sudden pain. The show seemed to work though, and he breathed hard, trying to shut out his feelings.

Marius' face stayed a pale mask, seemingly uncaring, but inside, he felt like he was falling apart. He had to steel himself not to rush down to the bed and yank that blonde slave off Kyle, all his willpower funneled into staying still.

Clavius glanced at him, not letting go of his hand. He sat up slightly when Kyle's head was yanked back, and Clavius leaned against him, his voice soft. "Stay put..."

Marius clenched his jaw and drank deeply, trying to calm the sudden rage swirling inside of him.

Titus smiled at him. "Worried about your pet?"

Marius looked at him with a mocking smile. "Not at all... he can handle worse than that."

Guests all around them were busy with their slaves, the show and the drugs fueling their desires and the entire room soon was filled with groans and moans, some just lazily watching whilst their slaves sucked them off. Marius felt his head swoon, and he wished for this whole thing to be over so he could grab Kyle and run with him, out of this horrid place. Clavius patted his hand, and he clutched at it, almost crushing it in his despair.

Finally, Damian came inside of Kyle with a growl, their bodies drenched, and Kyle's whole body trembled, his mind numb. He panted, sitting on his heels, his hands on his thighs while Damian collapsed next to him, looking up into his eyes.

His eyes misted over, his hand tracing Kyle's thigh. "You're a great fuck, Kyle."

He just gave him a feeble smile, too tired with the adrenaline going, trying to slow his breath. Some men clapped and cheered, but the others were mostly busy with their slaves, so they looked around for their clothes, slipping their tunics on. Two large eunuchs came to collect them, grabbing their arms, and they had to follow to a room where they could wash. The water was cold in the basin, but it soothed their burning skin and Kyle felt instantly better, washing off the sweat and semen. He downed a large cup of cool water and made sure to rinse his mouth out, too. Some of the golden paint had come off, but it didn't matter anymore. His head was clearing up, the drug weakened by their coupling, and his emotions coursed through him, his thoughts on Marius. He put his tunic back on and checked his face in the small mirror. Apart from the black kohl smeared a bit, his make-up seemed fine, so they walked back to the room.

Kyle walked up to their couch, his grey eyes on Marius, and the Roman fought the urge to pull him into his arms. Instead, he acted indifferent, turning to Titus whilst Kyle sank to his knees next to him, his head bowed, trying to even his breathing. The emperor walked down to them after a while and they rose to talk to him, Marius sensing this would be the opportune moment to get out.

The old man patted his shoulder, swaying on his feet a bit. "Well, well... I didn't regret asking you to bring your nimble pet..."

Marius grinned. "My pleasure, uncle... but we need to get going."

"So soon? You could not even enjoy him yet."

Marius shrugged, trying to sound casual. "It doesn't matter... I'll deal with him at home. *Please, please let us get the fuck out of here...*

The old man watched him carefully but then shrugged, his mind fogged by the drugged wine. "Suit yourself... I do hope you'll come next time, though." His eyes drifted to the kneeling slave. "Maybe you could then lend him to me for a private session?"

Marius paled but held his mask, his voice straight. "Of course, uncle."

"Great! I'll see you soon then. And Marius, get married fast, I have plans for you."

"Plans?"

The old man waved him off. "Not now... Come to the palace in two days and I'll fill you in."

Marius bowed and the old man left.

Clavius sounded grim. "He will send you away."

"I know..." Marius sighed and turned to Titus. "We're going... it was a pleasure... again."

"Likewise! Maybe next time you can come to my house for dinner? Bring your pet too... we could have a small party of our own."

He winked and Marius just smiled thinly. "Yes, why not... See you soon."

Clavius followed them outside, the night chilly under the stars and Kyle shivered, his body and mind drained. Still, Marius could not hold him, his uncle's spies being everywhere, and they traveled home in silence, the trip seeming painfully slow.

Finally, after what had seemed an eternity, they arrived, and Sixtus let them in. Marius wordlessly took Kyle's hand, feeling the slave shiver, and took him straight to the bath, stripping off their clothes. He pulled him into the hot water and took a sponge and some soap to scrub him clean, making sure he got all the paint off, running the soaked sponge on his face, his jaw. His hands washed away the kohl around his eyes, Kyle silent, letting him rub his skin raw.

Their eyes locked and Marius' feelings collided inside of him, anger, guilt, jealousy, disgust, mingling with his raging love for Kyle. He dropped the sponge and laced his arms around Kyle, pulling him close, but Marius could not kiss him, the images of that other slave fucking him still too vivid.

Kyle sensed this, and his heart sank. A sharp pain coursing through him made him moan and double over slightly.

Marius pushed him away, concerned. "You're hurt?"

He just nodded, slowly inhaling, trying to breathe through it, steadying himself on Marius' thick forearms. The Roman cursed softly and led him out of the water, gently drying him and leading him to their room. They had to walk slowly, Kyle's abused body sending jolts of pain with each step, like knife stabs.

At last, their bed. Kyle collapsed on it, curling up, his knees against his chest, biting his fist. Marius lay behind him, wrapping an arm around his waist, spreading his palm on his belly, warming it.

Kyle let his tears flow silently and Marius pulled the covers on top of them, holding him tighter, his body warming Kyle's back. "I'm so sorry..." His voice a mere breath against his neck, Kyle turned around in his arms to face him, Marius' face a grey mask in the dim moonlight.

His mouth was so close, tempting, but Kyle stayed put, not daring to kiss him, not after all that had happened. "It's not your fault..."

Marius sighed, his voice choking. "You have no idea what it felt like... to watch it... you..."

Kyle stroked his bruised face, and searched the Roman's eyes in the milky glow. "What happened there... it didn't mean anything to me, you know that, right? Nothing..."

He fell silent before desperation could creep into his voice and Marius' angry whisper tore into the night. "He was hurting you!"

Kyle swallowed, bitter. "Yes, but he had no choice... that's what they wanted..." His large grey eyes shone sadly, pleading. "It could have been worse... much worse..." He choked on his words, his memories tearing at him, and he had to close his eyes, shying away into the darkness from his handsome face and clenched jaw.

Marius moaned, pulling him closer. "Oh, gods... what a fucked-up mess!" He leant down and kissed Kyle then, deep, claiming his mouth. "You're so mine... I won't let anybody touch you again, ever..." Kyle moaned into his mouth, pushing against him, but Marius broke the kiss, gently pushing him away. "I won't do anything with you tonight, not when you're hurting."

Kyle shrugged, a shy smile on his lips. "It doesn't matter."

"Yes, it does matter to me. You are not an object, Kyle, you're my lover. I love you and I won't hurt you."

The young slave's eyes welled up and Marius' thumb brushed his trembling lips. "Outside of this room, we will play master and slave though, alright? No need to piss my fucking family off even more."

Kyle nodded, and they kissed again, slowly drifting into sleep.

IX

Two days later, Marius came back from the emperor's palace, his face grim, and he went straight to the garden where he could find Kyle. He slowed and stopped, watching him knee-deep in the small pond, weeding it, and arranging the waterlilies. Bri and Brandan were sitting on the ledge, feeding the golden fish, their feet in the water. Brandan could still not speak Latin, but he was picking it up fast with Bri, a shy smile on his face when she made him repeat the words: fish, flower, water, food... They laughed when the bigger fish tickled their hands with their mouth, their bulging eyes on the children.

Bri beamed at Kyle. "They are so soft, their mouths... they want to eat our hands." Kyle just glanced at them, smiling, and Bri grinned at him. "Look... there's one eating your leg!"

"There's more than one..." He gently swatted the fish away, but they came back, looking for something to nibble on.

The scene was so peaceful, sunlight reflecting on the soft waves, making their faces glow, Kyle's hands gently plucking at the weeds, his body glistening with sweat. He only had his shorts on, and his skin glowed in the pouring golden light. Marius sighed, his mind on his impending marriage and travel... *Why could things not just stay simply happy, like in this perfect little moment? Fucking family...*

He reluctantly walked forward, and the kids turned around, hearing his steps on the gravel. They flung themselves on their knees, Brandan so scared still that he put his forehead on the ground, too. Bri, though, knew him and stayed with her face up, smiling.

He sat down on the ledge, pulling her up. "Ask your friend to get up. He should not be afraid of me." Bri tugged at Brandan's arm, and he got up, his face lowered, trembling. Kyle walked to them, talking to him in Celtic, and he relaxed, lifting his eyes. Marius smiled. "Much better..."

The children left then, running, Brandan still too fearful, and Marius turned to Kyle who had gone back to weeding the pond. His lips curled into a small smile. "Are you deliberately provoking me bent down like this?"

Kyle turned his head. "No, dominus, not at all. "

But he was smiling, and Marius sighed. "Get out of there... let's go to our room?"

Kyle straightened, looking a bit concerned. "I need to finish this, but it can wait I suppose, if you don't keep me all afternoon. "

Marius grinned. "I can't promise anything..."

Back in their room, Marius stood, his face taut, leaning on one of the columns leading to the terrace. "I need to do the wedding ceremony fast..."

Kyle looked up, surprised. "Why? I thought it could wait..."

Marius couldn't look at him, his emotions raging. "My divine, fucking uncle is sending me away... on a campaign to supervise the building of a fucking fort and some roads with a small cohort."

Kyle's face fell. "When...?"

"I have to leave next month..." They looked at each other, Marius' misery plain on his face, his blue eyes blazing with anger and despair.

Kyle walked up to him, his voice barely a whisper. "For how long?"

Marius pursed his lips. "Fuck knows... it could be from six months... to a year."

The slave's eyes grew wide. "A year...?"

Marius brushed his knuckles on his cheek. "Yes, maybe... gods, even the thought of being away one day from you is killing me..."

He kissed him, his lips barely brushing his, but Kyle pulled away, worried. "What will happen to us? Your house?"

Marius tried to sound reassuring. "You will stay here, of course, all of you. I'll be married by the time I leave, so Seraphina can take care of you..."

He watched the slave pale, his face shutting down into a mask of indifference, his eyes cold. "Of course, dominus."

Marius grabbed his shoulders. "Don't play this bullshit game with me... I don't have a choice."

Kyle looked away, his voice soft. "I know..."

"But?"

He looked back at the Roman, his grey eyes calm. "But it is us who will stay behind with her... with you gone."

Marius knew what he meant, and he could only hope. "I'll leave instructions in place, and she'll know where her place is. Nothing can happen to you; I'll make sure of it."

Kyle didn't comment and his thoughts drifted to the possibilities of the future with her, this new domina who will be left alone with them. To the days he'd have to spend alone without Marius. The thought was killing him already, and he had to steel himself not to let his tears spill.

Marius pulled him into his arms, his tongue running along his neck. "Come to bed... let's make the most of the time we have left..."

Kyle closed his eyes, his throat clutched.

Two weeks flew by fast, and the wedding day had arrived. It was celebrated at Seraphina's father's house, so they had to wait all day for the newlywed couple to come home. The slaves were grim, even more so with Marius' impending leave, still, Kyle and Lisandra prepared Seraphina's bedroom where they would consummate the marriage... They arranged candles, red roses in large vases, and scattered rose petals everywhere.

The ceremonial statue of the god of fertility had been sent earlier, and Lis looked at it, a bit horrified. "This tradition... I mean... I just can't get my head around it."

Kyle glanced at the statue of the god, his wooden phallus standing proud and ready. He shrugged. "One more Roman madness..."

He was bitter, and Lis walked to him, gently laying her hand on his shoulder. "You're jealous... and sad..."

He didn't comment, too tired and strained to think straight. *Jealous? Maybe... Sad? More like devastated... not because you will fuck her tonight, but because you're leaving me...* He sighed. "Let's go, we're done here."

"When will they arrive?"

"I don't know..."

Kyle waited awake near the door and finally, after midnight, there was a knock and he opened it, kneeling straight away. Marius walked in, carrying Seraphina in his arms, the crowd outside cheering and laughing. He rose to close the door whilst Marius let Seraphina down. Kyle noticed he was drunk, but not too much.

She smiled at him; her eyes misted over. "Take me to our room..."

Marius smiled back. "With pleasure... this way."

Kyle carried a torch in front of them, and Marius watched his swaying hips, his mind already fed up with the wedding night. Still, he could not talk to him, so he tugged Seraphina along. Kyle opened the door to the room, the candles blazing, the sweet smell of flowers pouring out with the night breeze and Marius stopped, momentarily floored.

Seraphina's face lit up. "Oh, my... how beautiful..." She turned to Marius, lifting her face. "Thank you."

He smiled, vaguely embarrassed, and gestured her in. "This is your room now." She wandered inside, her hand brushing the flowers, her eyes going to the large windows leading to her terrace.

Marius turned quickly to Kyle, who was about to leave. "Sleep in our room tonight?"

The slave looked at him, struggling not to give away his emotions. "Thank you, dominus, but I'll sleep in my room."

Marius' face darkened, but Kyle just bowed and closed the door.

He almost went after him when Seraphina came back and pressed her body against his muscles. "I've been waiting for this night forever... come, make me yours."

Marius swallowed his anger and led her to the bed, slowly peeling their clothes off. She was quite beautiful on the bed, her red lips parted, her milky skin glowing in the candlelight, her auburn hair loose, falling on her shoulders in broad curls. He bent down above her to kiss her, his hands going to her breasts and her breath quickened, her head falling back on the pillows. She kissed him back and the softness of her mouth was odd, her tongue gentle, and it frustrated him, so he kissed her harder, pushing his tongue around her mouth to awaken her senses.

She pushed him back a bit, out of breath. "Wow... this is my first night with a man... take it slow?"

He forced a smile onto his face. "Sure..."

They went back to kissing slowly, Marius' hand trailing down between her legs.

She clamped them shut before he could touch her, and he broke the kiss, a bit exasperated. "What's wrong? I won't be able to do anything with you if you close your legs..."

She smiled nervously. "Well, take it slow then..."

He pursed his lips, a soft anger warming in his chest. "I hope you sort of know what's going to happen tonight?"

She smiled back, mocking. "Yes, I sort of know... but patience, tease me a bit more..."

Marius lay down next to her, then and kissed her softly, caressing her body, and he was already bored a bit, his mind drifting to Kyle, to his firm muscles and tongue, their passionate wrestling... *Fuck this shit...*

Seraphina pushed him away, sitting up. "I'm ready, I think... I need to give my virginity to the god."

She looked at the statue, nervous, and Marius' lips curled into a mocking smile. "You really want to do this stupid tradition?"

Seraphina turned to him, wide-eyed. "You will anger the gods talking like that!"

Marius lay back on the bed. "Nonsense, but be my guest... or, you can just come here and sit on me instead of that horrendous piece of wood."

He grinned, and her face darkened. "Very funny..." but her eyes went from him to the statue, and she licked her lips, nervous. "The god will open the way for you..."

Marius laughed. "I'm pretty sure I can do that myself."

She shot him an angry look and walked to the statue, scooting over it, the wooden phallus lined up with her cunt, and Marius shook his head. *She's fucking going to go all the way with this... what the fuck? Good thing I'm a bit drunk...*

He watched her breathe in deep and lower herself on it, stopping halfway, happy. "I think it's done."

Marius smiled mockingly. *Sure thing, love, that's not even half of what you can take in...* "Come here already and leave that horrid god."

She crawled on the bed and Marius pushed her down into the mattress, lying on top of her, his patience on edge. "Let's stop this nonsense... you want to become a woman tonight, or not?"

She nodded, her eyes wide, pinned down under his weight.

He grinned. "Good!" Then kissed her hard, making her writhe under him, one hand pinning her hands above her head, his mouth roaming her neck, licking her skin. She panted and moaned, trying to free her hands, or throw him off, but he was too heavy, and she panicked a bit as she felt his thighs push hers apart.

She moaned into his mouth. "No... wait...", but he kissed her words away, sealing her mouth, and pushed inside of her, breaking through her barrier, making her howl into his mouth. He moved then, fast, thrusting into her, her whole body rocking under him, her screams filling the room, slowly turning to wails and sobs as her pain mingled with pleasure, his breath in her neck.

He hooked her leg over his arm and fucked her harder, not caring about her cries, her arms pulling at his hand. She was so fucking tight. There was no way he could hold out for long, but he waited until she came through her pain, her loud wails melting into sobs. *Good girl.* He came inside of her then, hard, rocking his hips until he filled her to the brim. He let her go and rolled off her, propping himself on one elbow to look down at her face, long rivulets of black tears running down her cheeks, her make-up smudged, her hair a mess.

Her eyes blazed as she hissed. "Bastard!"

Marius smiled down at her. "Is this the way to thank your husband for your wedding night?"

She turned her head away, her tears spilling, and a pang of guilt ran through him.

He gently cupped her chin and turned her head back, wiping her tears. "Was it that bad?" *You came though...*

She looked at him, her eyes wide, bathing in anger. "Will it always be like this?"

Marius shrugged. "No, not always. We could take it slow next time... I guess I got carried away by your beauty..."

She blushed slightly at his lie, but her eyes shone with a new light, a twinge of hate mingled with her newly born womanhood.

He lay down, drained, pulling her reluctantly into his arms. "Let's sleep..."

Seraphina lay still on his chest, her hand on his muscles, her feelings fighting inside of her.

Next morning, they woke late, and Marius got up straight away, ringing for breakfast. They dressed, silent, and Seraphina walked out onto the terrace to admire the view. She was still sore from last night and a bitter feeling crept up her throat. This was what she could expect for the rest of her life with him? She watched him walk out to join her and her heart beat in her throat.

He smiled at her. "How do you feel on your first morning as a married woman?"

She smirked. "Sore."

Marius' face darkened, but he didn't comment.

Seraphina's eyes went to the city glowing in the morning light. "Is this how you will always be with me in bed?"

Marius could barely hide his irritation. "You enjoyed it though, right?"

She shrugged. "I don't know..."

Marius pursed his lips. "Well, I know..."

She turned to him. "Maybe you should have slept with more women. You would maybe not be this rough."

He blanched at her words and stepped close; his face clouded with anger. "Watch your mouth..."

Her eyes blazed, but she could not reply, the slaves bringing their breakfast in, laying it on the table in the room.

Marius held his hand out to her, his voice tamed. "Come, let's eat."

She took it, not wanting to make a scene in front of Kyle and Lisandra, the two slaves standing still, their heads bowed.

Marius did his best to hide his emotions in his voice when he talked to Kyle. "Kyle, have this room cleaned up after we've finished eating. Domina's goods will be brought over today. Make sure they are put in the right place."

"Yes, dominus."

His voice made Marius close his eyes for a few seconds. "Are the rooms ready for the new slaves in your quarters?"

"Yes, dominus. Sixtus had everything arranged."

Seraphina chirped in, her tone light. "I do hope you will not be trouble. My slaves are extremely well trained and obedient, and I won't allow them to be corrupted."

Marius shot her an angry look, but she ignored him and started eating.

Marius and Seraphina left then to her parents' house for lunch, and soon her trunks arrived, and her slaves. Sixtus welcomed them whilst Kyle made sure that her belongings were carried up to her room. She had brought her personal slave, a young Greek girl called Thais, but had made it clear that she wanted to expand the household. The new slaves were quickly put at ease by Sixtus, but Thais was afraid in her eyes when Kyle led her to her domina's bedroom.

She looked around and turned to him, lowering her green eyes. "Is dominus also sleeping here?"

He shrugged. "Not always, I think... he'll be leaving soon anyway..." His words caught, and he silenced, pushing back his tears.

"Is he kind?"

Kyle smiled. "Yes, you have nothing to fear." She sighed a shaky breath, and he turned to her, concerned. "But you look scared. Why?"

Thais looked at him. "Domina is not that nice, Kyle, you'll see..."

He paled but didn't probe further, he'd sort of guessed it anyway, but his voice was like steel. "Rules in this house have been laid down by dominus, he won't tolerate her breaking them."

She didn't comment and started packing. Kyle left her and busied himself with work until night fell.

At last, they arrived home and Marius spoke to him when he entered. "No need to serve dinner. We had to stay and eat there."

"Very well, dominus."

Marius looked at Kyle, but his eyes were lowered, and he sighed in frustration, leaving, leading her to her room. He stopped at the threshold and kissed her hand. "Goodnight. You must be tired."

She raised her eyebrows. "You're not sleeping with me tonight?"

His lips curled up. "I figured you wouldn't want me to?"

She sighed. "No, come in, I think we should be together before you leave on your campaign... you know, to make sure we make a baby?"

He froze at her words. "I am not sure this is the right moment for you to become pregnant..."

She smiled. "Why?"

"I might be gone for a year."

"So? I don't need you to be here to give birth."

He frowned, but followed her to the room. "I'll sleep with you tonight, but not every day."

"Oh... missing your boy?"

His face darkened at her words. "What...? Don't you..." He then noticed the kneeling slave girl next to the bed and his words caught, his eyes wide. "What the fuck?"

Seraphina frowned at him. "Language? This is Thais, my slave. Get up and show your face to your dominus." She obeyed and raised her head, her green eyes looking behind him. She had long honey colored hair and a slender body.

He looked at Seraphina. "What's she doing here?"

She sat down in front of her mirror and Thais went to undo her hair and comb it, shying from him. Seraphina's eyes gleamed in the mirror. "You have a slave, don't you? So what's the big deal?"

He sighed. "Nothing..."

"Good... she is an able little nymph... ouch! Watch what you're doing!" She swatted the slave's hand with her brush and the young girl didn't even flinch, though her skin had turned red.

Marius blanched. "Why did you hit her?"

"She pulled my hair." She rose, letting Thais undo her dress. "Don't be such a softy, dear. Slaves need discipline. Thais knows when she's done something wrong, right?"

"Yes, domina."

Seraphina smiled at him. "Maybe a bit of discipline wouldn't hurt your loose-mouthed slaves, either. You've spoiled them, especially your pampered little pet."

He stepped to her, his face dark with anger. "Watch your mouth, wife."

She smirked but kept her mouth shut and dismissed Thais, who flew out of the room. She looked up at him, mocking. "So, husband, should we do our duty?"

He looked at her like he was seeing her for the first time... *who is this woman?* His anger bathed him like a warm flame, but he just smiled. "Of course, my dear."

She gritted her teeth against the pain when he entered her, even if he had tried to be gentler at first.

He searched her eyes. "Is it better?"

She pulled a face. "Just be done with it..."

Marius' heart sank, and for a split second, he thought of stopping altogether, but then his rage took over, and he fucked her hard, spilling into her. *Fuck her and her duty!*

He got up, slipping his tunic on, his eyes blazing. "Was it fast enough?"

Seraphina looked at him, her eyes shining with tears. "Where are you going?"

Marius laughed through his anger. "The fuck do you care?"

She pouted. "I thought you'd stay with me for our first week together, at least?"

Marius pointed a finger at her. "You, you don't want to be with me... this... this whole duty thing... what the actual hell?!"

She widened her eyes, all of a sudden seeming very innocent, and he wavered, her voice thin. "This is all new to me and you're not very gentle..." She lowered her eyes and tears spilled down her cheeks.

Oh, fuck me... He sat on the bed, pulling her into his arms. "You want me to stay?" She nodded into his chest, and he sighed, his mind on Kyle and another night apart.

A week had passed, and Marius could not leave her alone. She was always crying and begging him to stay, even though during the day she was a real pest, constantly teasing and making comments.

Kyle watched Marius' gaunt face at dinner, pushing the food around his plate, barely touching it. They had scarcely talked since the wedding, and Kyle suffered quietly, not daring to go close to him with her there.

She chirped away, very much aware of the slaves around her. "If I become pregnant, it will be a great honor, a new addition to the imperial family."

Marius smirked but didn't comment, his eyes drifting to Kyle's still form.

Her lips curled into a small smile. "Which reminds me.... it would be good to have a wet nurse ready, just in case..."

He looked back at her, frowning. "Wet nurse?"

"Yes, dear. One of the slaves? If she gave birth close to me, she could feed my child too, in case I don't have any milk."

"And how do you plan on achieving this?"

She shrugged. "Breeding, of course."

Marius blanched with anger. "No! Not here, not in this house!"

"Why?"

"Because I will not be an accomplice to breeding more of these miserable beings!"

Seraphina raised her eyebrows. "What miserable beings? They're clothed, fed, some even educated, saved from their barbarian cultures and life... I would not call that being miserable. If we bred them, their child would be a slave, true, but with all the advantages of a Roman life in our household..."

Kyle and Lis listened, breathless, not daring to raise their heads, and Marius banged his palm on the table, making her jump. "No! And don't you dare do anything in my absence! "

He had risen, and she looked at him, calm. "What are you going to do about it, dear?"

He stood above her, seething. "If you disobey my ground rules, and I find it out when I come back, I'll divorce you... child or no child."

She paled, disbelieving, but the look in his eyes made her shut up. *Careful...* "Of course, I won't disobey you, dear."

Lying cunt... He felt dizzy and turned to leave. "I'm going to my room. Don't wait for me tonight."

He left then, his steps heavy, leaving her alone with the slaves. They stood, frozen, and she turned to them. "You can take the dinner away."

They hurried over to the table and started piling up the plates. She watched their pale faces and smiled inwardly, but her eyes stayed on Kyle, on the young man's smooth skin and muscles, his hair falling into his grey eyes. She could not help picturing him with Marius and her blood boiled. *And tonight...* She got up abruptly and left them; her face a mask of anger.

Lis looked after her, trembling. "Kyle..."

"I know..."

They went to the kitchen, then to the slaves' bath to clean up.

Sixtus grabbed Kyle's arm when he'd finished. "Dominus wants you in his room."

His heart fluttered, and he hurried upstairs, his stomach filled with butterflies. As soon as Kyle had opened the door, he was pulled inside, Marius' mouth on his mouth, pushing into him.

They slammed the door shut with their bodies colliding, and Marius breathed into his mouth. "Fuck, pet, how I've missed you..."

Naked, they scrambled on the bed, eating each other up, Marius biting his way down Kyle's body, making him moan and writhe.

Marius popped the bottle of oil with trembling hands and slid inside of Kyle, their eyes locking, wide. "Oh, fuck..." It felt so good that Marius felt like crying, steadying himself not to come inside of him straight away.

Kyle laced his arms around him, gently kissing his jaw, his neck and he was lost, slowly picking up the pace, their strong bodies blending.

They kissed and hugged for a while, fucking slowly.

Then Marius pulled out and flipped Kyle on all fours, biting down on his shoulder when he pushed in with one hard thrust. "I love you..." He moaned and fucked him hard, making him cry out and moan, loud. "That's right... sing for me..." Kyle was mewling, his breath ragged, lost in their passion, and Marius reached down to pump him, licking his throat. "Come on... come for me..." Kyle jerked in his hand and Marius thrust harder, his hips jerking as he came inside of him.

They collapsed on the side, panting, out of breath, Kyle on the verge of tears, his breath hitching.

Marius stroked his hair. "Shhh... I'm here... I'm sorry, I shouldn't' have left you alone for so long..."

Kyle kissed his hand, and they snuggled, the night softly darkening around them.

Marius turned on his back after a while, his arms behind his head and Kyle lay on his shoulder, looking up at his grim face, waiting.

He spoke after a while, his voice soft, tainted with anger and disappointment. "She's not what I thought she would be... even bedding her is a nightmare..." Kyle looked at him and he smiled. "Yes, would you believe this? She could be a gorgeous woman, but her temper... she's getting on my nerves." Kyle stayed silent. He had nothing to say, but dread crept into him, especially after that conversation during dinner.

Marius looked at him. "You're awfully silent."

"You're gone in a week..."

Marius sighed. "Yes, I know... I'll make sure she knows what she has to do... but I can't guarantee she won't hurt you..." His words turned to ash in his mouth and Kyle took pity on him, seeing his pained face.

He smiled thinly, trying to lighten his mood. "She can't be worse than Lucius."

"Let's hope so..." Marius hugged him tight. "I'm staying with you until I leave... stay in this room and wait for me... even if I have to fuck her out of duty, I'll come to you."

Kyle kissed him, swallowing his tears

X

The dreaded day of Marius' departure arrived. He stood in the rising sun's feeble rays, facing the terrace, and Rome, whilst Kyle buckled his armor, pulling the leather straps tight, his face like ash. They had made love almost all night, blending pleasure into pain, his body marred by Marius' bites. They throbbed with a dull ache, but he didn't mind, clutching on the painful reminders of his lover. He buckled the last strap and went to fling the red cape over his shoulders.

He was ready, and Kyle handed him his helmet, crested with horsehair. Marius looked at him and pulled him on his breastplate, the cold metal biting into his skin. They kissed passionately, drowning in sorrow, and Marius had to break it off, close to losing it.

He buckled on his helmet and his blue eyes shone. "I'll be back soon..."

Kyle just nodded, his eyes welling up.

Marius steeled himself and they went down to the courtyard, his horse ready. Kyle opened the gate for him, and he swung himself up to the saddle, leaning down one last time to kiss him on his head, whispering. "Be good, pet. I love you."

He spurred his horse down the road and Kyle closed the gate, sliding down against it, sobbing.

Thais ran down to the kitchen later, out of breath. "Domina wants her breakfast..."

Shayla and Melissa looked up, they were already preparing lunch. "Breakfast is ready over there. Lis will bring it up."

Thais paled. "She wants Kyle..."

The women looked at each other, and Shayla bellowed. "Kyle!"

The young man appeared from the pantry where he was putting away the shopping. "Yes?"

"Domina wants you to bring her breakfast up." She rolled her eyes, and he blanched, knowing full well this would hurt.

He wordlessly picked up the tray though, and walked up to her room, knocking politely.

"Come in!"

He stepped inside, carefully bowing, and set the tray on her table. She rose from her bed, her robe half-open, and he lowered his head not to look at her.

She smirked. "You don't like women? Pour me a drink."

He handed her a cup of grape juice, and she sat down, looking at his drawn face. *Miserable little pet... missing your master already...* "Do you hate me, Kyle?"

"No, domina..."

His stomach had turned to ice at her words, and she smiled inwardly at his fear. "Good. Because we will need to live together for a long time. My husband might fuck you, but I'm his wife, and you're just his slave, do you understand?"

"Yes, domina."

Her eyes locked on a purple bite mark on his shoulder, and she blanched, picturing Marius' mouth roaming the young man's body. *Horror.* She smiled though cruelly. "Well, in any case, he's gone for a while, so that's not an issue for now. I have invited our parents over tonight to celebrate his mission, make sure all is perfect. Lock down my husband's room, and clean it once a week. That should be enough. Go and send Sixtus up. I have instructions for him."

She dismissed him with a wave of her hand, and he went straight to get Sixtus.

Kyle then spent an hour cleaning Marius' room, taking the sheets off, almost still warm. He cast one last glance at the empty room and locked it, putting the key back to the master cupboard. Marius had only been gone for a couple of hours, and it already seemed like an eternity.

The parents arrived later, and the dining hall had been set up, Kyle and Lis serving the food. Seraphina had also invited Clavius' wife, and Tertullia lightened the night with her good mood and dimpled laughter. "Oh, my... you will see, my dear, you will get used to his absences... just keep busy, go out, do plenty of parties."

Seraphina's father barely tolerated the jovial centurion's wife, his smile still polite, and Gaius looked at him, rolling his eyes. "That woman is something... not sure she's the best influence on your daughter."

"Seraphina is not influenceable. She can take care of herself. I do hope she's pregnant, it would seal this marriage."

Gaius raised his eyebrows. "You're concerned?"

Quintus' face didn't give anything away. "Yes, a bit... your son has a volatile temper, and though he's an able soldier and has made a career, he also has a taste for boys..."

Gaius waved it away. "He'll grow out of it now that he's married."

Quintus eyed Kyle. "You're sure? You know what the rumor is after his latest purchase..."

Gaius' lips pinched. "Rumor is rumor, but let's find out, shall we?" He waved Kyle over and the slave kneeled at their feet. The women were busy talking, so Gaius was pretty sure they could get the answers they wanted. Gaius's voice was smooth like a knife. "Lift your face, slave." He did and looked at him, his face blank.

Quintus eyed him curiously. "He's your son's...?"

"Yes. Our good friend Lucius had the wonderful idea of gifting him to Marius on his way home. I wish it had never happened, but here we are... Kyle, you will answer my questions, boy, understood? If you lie, I'll beat the skin off your back."

Kyle swallowed, but nodded. "Yes, dominus, I'll tell the truth."

Gaius smiled. "Good boy... now, my son bought a slave a couple of weeks ago, a young boy."

"Yes, dominus."

"That boy, who is he?"

"He's a Celt, dominus, captured when his village was raided."

"I need to know why my son bought him."

Kyle swallowed, unsure if he knew the answer at all. "I don't know for sure, dominus... he just bought him, and we brought him home."

Gaius leant in, watching his face. "Did my son fuck this boy?"

Kyle blanched, his eyes wide. "What... no, dominus, he didn't."

Quintus looked at the slave, his voice smooth. "How can you be so sure?"

Kyle looked at him. "Dominus doesn't bed children."

"But he fucks you?"

Kyle blushed slightly, his voice soft. "I am not a child, dominus."

Gaius grabbed his chin, making him look at him. "True... my imperial brother told me of your little show at his party... let me quote him: impressive little slut with a fucking talented mouth."

The two men looked at him like snakes, and Kyle felt vaguely panicked and ashamed.

Gaius turned to Quintus. "So, you see, rumors are not true."

The senator nodded, toasting him. "Indeed..."

They talked about politics then and Gaius sent Kyle away, the young man's soul burning, and Tertullia noticed his pale face and miserable eyes. She waved him over, the other women thankfully busy with some gossip.

Her chubby face gleamed with mischief and joy. "Come here, Kyle, and fill my cup. I've heard a lot about you from Clavius." Kyle looked at her, silently kneeling near her couch, and she ruffled his hair. "Poor puppy... you must be lonely without that handsome devil..." Kyle's heart clenched, and his eyes welled up, wishing she would stop talking about him. "You are very pretty, Clavius was right. He likes you a lot, you know? Says you've changed his friend to the better... He loves you, right? He has never loved anybody before." Kyle's eyes widened at her words, and she stroked his hair. "That's right, precious. Cherish this in the moments when you miss him. He'll come back to you. Just keep this in your mind and you can endure anything..."

She quieted, and Kyle just kneeled, his heart racing.

Weeks later, Marius and Clavius had arrived at the fort, and they quickly took their quarters.

There was a small bath fortunately, and they were soaking in it, Marius brooding as usual, and Clavius splashed him. "Quit brooding, you big twat... I am sure your fuck boy is doing fine." Marius shot him a toxic look, and he raised his hands. "Ok, ok... so what is the news from home?"

He shrugged. "Nothing... Seraphina is late, just my fucking luck..."

Clavius grinned. "Hey, you're a potent man, scoring on the first shot, maybe? That's good blood and seed." Marius pursed his lips, but Clavius insisted. "Look, this is good news. I mean, if she's pregnant... you did your duty, secured your lineage and she will have her hands full with the child." He wiggled his eyebrows. "You'll have more time for your fuck boy." Marius smiled, but it was empty and Clavius sighed. "You're awful company... a child is not a tragedy, Marius. I wish I could have one, you know, but hey, the gods are tricky."

Marius regretted his behavior and looked mildly at his friend. "You and Tertullia could be his uncle and aunt, you know, if you accept..."

Clavius looked at him, floored. "Are you serious...?"

"Yes."

"Son of a bitch! I love you!" They laughed and hugged, Clavius clasping his back. "You have no idea what this means... I have to write to my wife."

"Yes, yes... do so. I won't change my mind."

Clavius beamed, but the shadows on Marius' face lingered, and he asked. "How's Kyle?"

Marius looked away. "Seraphina refuses to let me know... I've asked, though, I even wrote to him..."

They silenced, their eyes on the grey sky. Fall was near, and their mission was stretching endlessly ahead.

In Rome, weeks were dragging along too towards fall, in fear, Seraphina's temper setting a rhythm to their days. She had become restless with her bleeding being late, but there was no way of knowing yet if she was pregnant, and she lashed out at the slaves, her impatience searing her.

In the early days, Marius' lingering presence had kept her in check, but she had realized that he was too far, and she made sure that they knew who was in charge, walking around the house with a small whip. Her hand was quick and unpredictable, so much so, that the children preferred to dwell in the far corners of the villa, making sure to run and hide when they heard her. She sent Kyle to look for them and he always came back empty-handed, pretending he could not find them. He got five lashes then to his back, but he didn't care anymore. Kyle had endured far worse at Lucius' house, so he just stood still, braced against the wall until she beat him, out of anger and hatred, large red welts forming on his skin where the whip had landed. Kyle had taken beatings for them all, and she laughed, howling that she didn't care as long as one of them got it, but still, single lashes landed on all of them, streaking their arms, legs, and backs, whatever she could hit in the spur of the moment.

One night, she called Kyle to her room, pushing him against the wall, the whip inches from his face, her face full of hatred as she hissed. "Get the doctor. I need to know if I'm pregnant!"

"Yes, domina."

He ran to the doctor's house and the old man followed him, watching the slave's streaked shoulders.

He stopped him gently in the entrance. "Let me have a look, son." Kyle swallowed and lowered his tunic from his back. The old man hissed, gently running his hand on the welts. "Have you seen a doctor?"

"No, dominus."

The old man shook his head and handed him a pot of cream from his bag. "You need to have this rubbed on them. It will disinfect, and help with the healing. Just come to my house when you run out."

Kyle nodded, his throat clutched, and led him to Seraphina's room. He waited then, leaning against the cool wall, his back burning.

It took a long while, but eventually the old family doctor came out, and he smiled at him, walking down the stairs. "Your domina is with child."

Kyle swayed, dizzy, his thoughts on Marius. *He's going to be a father...*

Seraphina's and Marius' parents came over the next day, and she raved about the news, sitting in the garden, with her whip across her lap.

They were nibbling fruits and drinking a light wine, chatting, when Seraphina waved Kyle over. "Where are those useless children? My guests would like to have a look at them."

Kyle's face stayed calm. "I'll look for them, domina."

She looked at him, her eyes blazing. "You know what will happen if you don't find them."

"Yes, domina."

He left then, and of course, came back empty-handed. She shot to her feet, brandishing the whip. "Take off your tunic and face the wall."

He obeyed and braced his hands against the wall, slowly exhaling.

Gaius rose then, prying the whip out of her hand. "Allow me, dear, you should not do this in your condition."

Kyle's heart sank, but he held tight.

Gaius ran his hand down his back. "Impressive collection... he's giving you grief?"

Seraphina shrugged. "He's been spoiled, but he's learning."

Gaius pursed his lips and swung the whip. He hit way harder than Seraphina and Kyle's skin broke, his blood flowing down his back. He moaned against the searing pain but stood all the way until all five lashes fell and tore his back apart.

Seraphina watched, slightly concerned, and Gaius flung the whip at Kyle's feet. "Bring this back clean."

He picked it up with trembling hands, and Gaius smiled at Seraphina. "This is how you beat up slaves, dear, but I know you don't have my strength."

They laughed, and Kyle left the garden, his hand barely holding the whip slippery with blood, when the world turned and Sixtus caught him before he blanked out, the world dark.

Kyle woke in his room, his back covered in a thin gauze, a single oil lamp burning next to him, and he sat up, panicked.

Lis was there, her voice filled with concern. "Hey... calm down..."

"What happened?"

"You passed out..."

Her tears flowed, and he struggled to stay still. "How long?"

"A couple of hours... Domina knows, Sixtus told them. I think she's concerned that you'll scar even more..."

He swallowed, vaguely nauseous, the pain making him shiver.

"Lie down, Kyle, please..."

He reluctantly did so, his eyes shutting. She cried, and he had to soothe her. "This is nothing, Lis... leave it."

"Nothing? Look at your back..."

What to tell her? That a single whip could not do the damage that one could do with tiny claws of metal? That he'd howled for three days on end when Lucius had beaten the skin off his back? That sometimes he could not walk after days of being raped over and over again?

He just reached for her hand. "Just stay out of trouble... alright?"

She smiled feebly and stroked his hand. He fell asleep then, his dreams churning like dark masses.

Marius got the news weeks later when the mail arrived, and he wordlessly handed the letter to Clavius.

"Oh, my! I'll be an uncle!"

Marius smiled. "I guess congratulations are in order..."

"For you, you stud!"

They laughed and went to supervise the roadworks, the fall chill biting into their cloaks.

Foul weather had settled over Rome too, and they had to heat, the chill biting into the walls. They had bought a couple of low-class slaves to feed the fires and warm the baths, Sixtus still making sure they were well fed and cared for, even if Seraphina didn't care at all.

Kyle's back had healed, but scars remained, the already weakened skin struggling to heal. Seraphina avoided hitting him on the back, but he still got lashes everywhere else when her temper flared. Her belly had started growing, and she lived an ample social life to make sure that everybody knew she was pregnant. The emperor was delighted, of course, as well as the rest of the family, and she prayed every day to the gods to give her a son.

She read Marius' letter by the fireplace; the flames crackling with a warm glow, a cruel smile on her face at the last lines. *How are my slaves? Please let me know, Seraphina. Could you give the other letter to Kyle, please?* She looked at the sealed letter addressed to the slave and threw it into the fire, just as she had done with the others. She then sat down to write her reply, not mentioning the slaves once.

Kyle held tight, thinking of Tertullia's words, but Marius' absence and lack of communication wore on him. Winter had settled, the weather bitter, and they stayed closed in as much as they could, Seraphina's presence wearing at their nerves. She worried constantly about the child and Kyle had to go and fetch the doctor more than once, shivering in the cold streets.

Snow had blanketed the landscape and building the road was held up. *Just our fucking luck...* Marius held his wife's letter in his hands, looking at the landscape. No news of his slaves again, nothing from Kyle... Maybe he had forgotten about him. After all, it had been months. Images of Lisandra's body floated in his mind, the girl looking at Kyle... he clenched his fist, crumpling the letter... *Why would he wait for me? He had been a whore after all...* He was deeply fed up and frustrated, his jealousy eating at him. *Maybe I should just fuck a camp whore...*

The idea was tempting, but then there was a knock on his door and Clavius appeared, holding a letter. "Any news from Seraphina?"

Marius threw the crumpled letter to the floor. "Yes, of course.... meaningless shit... how she prays to the gods for a son, her parties, our parents..."

"I see... well, my wife has been to your house last week, and she has a few words for you."

Marius' eyes widened and Clavius handed him the letter. Marius read her lines, his vision blurring.

My dear Marius,
I know you're dying to hear from your lovely boy, so allow me to fill you in, as I know that Seraphina has been sparse with giving you news of him. I met him last week at your wife's little hen party and, as usual, he was his delightful self. He is doing better than expected, Marius, but your wife is a feisty creature, and she leads

your household with an iron hand. She is also quite quick with her whip, but fear not. Your lovely pet told me he had had it worse before. Rest also assured that he is faithful to you, the poor little pup, despite the girls being all over him now that they're locked up in this foul winter weather. I could not talk to him at length, but he misses you like crazy, of course, even more so that you're not giving any news of yourself. Anyway, I hope this letter finds you well and my good husband is not getting on your nerves too much. I told your good boy I would write to you that he loves you still very much.

See you soon, Tertullia

Marius' hands trembled, his emotions raging. "She's beating them up..." He moaned, and the letter slipped from his hands. He had to sit down, feeling sick. *He loves me still... he has not received news of him for months now... Faithful...* "I have to throw up..."

Clavius clasped his shoulder. "Now, now... I hope you can survive some news?"

Marius sat in a daze, his mind racing, anger boiling up like freed lava. "Fuck that bitch!"

He hurled a chair through the room, almost breaking the window, and Clavius had to grab his shoulders. "Calm down? There's nothing you can do from here."

He sighed, his voice faltering. "I want to go home..."

Clavius grinned. "Whine like the spoiled brat that you are, general, soon-to-be father?"

Marius' shame washed over him, and he quieted, and went to stand at the window, his eyes on the landscape, watching the gentle snow fall endlessly.

Snow drifted down from the grey sky, the night slowly falling, and Kyle went to his room, drained by the day's chores. They had to renovate a whole section of the house for the baby, get the birthing stool, the furniture, everything needed for giving birth, and then welcoming the little being... *Marius' child...* He was vaguely curious to find out if Seraphina's prayers had worked, and it was indeed a boy. In his culture, it didn't matter. Women were also fierce warriors, but it seemed that Romans only had eyes for boys.

Kyle lay down, finally, feeling his joints and muscles ache, and he longed for the warmth of Marius' body. He had not been back to their room, save for cleaning sometimes, and his thin blanket didn't provide enough warmth. He curled up, wishing for sleep, when there was a knock on his door.

His voice was already thick with sleep. "Who is it? "

"Lis..."

He sighed. "Come in..."

She slipped inside, her eyes wide in the dark.

"What do you want, Lis?"

"Can I sleep with you?"

Kyle sat up, wide awake. "What? No!"

She pleaded, sitting down next to him. "Please, please, I'm so cold..."

He frowned. "Go, sleep with Shayla then, or Thais..."

She looked at him, her lips parted. "I'm not into women..."

Kyle smiled bitterly. "Me neither..."

Lis' face fell. "Oh... so you're not going to..."

"No."

"Why? You're stupid if you think your master is not banging every camp whore he can find... soldiers get very lonely..."

Kyle swallowed but held tight. "I don't care... get out of here, please?"

She got up, blazing. "Fine! I won't ask again."

She banged the door shut, and he lay back, sighing, his mind on her words.

Winter passed slowly with endless chores, Seraphina wanting everything repaired, repainted, rebuilt, new mosaics laid on the floors.

The crude physical work had thickened Kyle's muscles, and his boyish looks started wearing off as he aged, his jaw more chiseled, his face taking on the looks of a handsome young man. Seraphina had calmed down a bit, her belly growing, making it increasingly difficult for her to whack them around.

She walked down one of the corridors and spotted Kyle sitting on the floor, working on a mosaic, his brows furrowed with concentration. Half of it had been done already, intricate patterns weaved in the stones with vivid colors.

He was following a drawing she had had made, working on Hercules fighting the lion, carefully selecting, and hammering the tiny stones. It was backbreaking, and he wiped his brow, unaware that she had walked up to him.

"It's going to be very nice."

He jerked his head up, alert, waiting for her to go into one of her fits, but the sarcasm was missing from her voice, her hand on her growing belly. She almost looked tame, but he stayed on his guard. He knew her too well to let it down.

Seraphina looked at him, her dark eyes scanning his body. His hands had become stronger too, and she watched them move over the colorful stones, rubbing them, his muscled fingers coated with dust. She smiled to herself. *You want your boy back, my dear? But I'll give you back a man...*

When the weather warmed a bit, the promise of spring in the air, she made Kyle go to the market with Sixtus, making sure he always had plenty to load onto the cart, then she sent him on errands, to deliver useless letters, buy things she wanted, making him climb all over Rome's hills and streets. He had gotten lost more than once but managed to find his way, and he knew now the city by heart, his stamina growing, not breathless anymore when he'd climbed a hill to one of her friends' villas. And of course, the renovation and decoration works remained, keeping them busy.

Sixtus made sure Kyle was fed more, worried at his workload, but the slave didn't complain, mindlessly obeying Seraphina in everything. She often pushed him to the brink, making him work until he shook from exhaustion, getting up at dawn to go to a market further away just to make him stay up late again with some kind of dinner party she'd organized.

And of course, she still managed to whip him around, lashes which didn't even register anymore, not even if he took them in the face. His grey eyes remained calm, his fear wiped, the constant beatings becoming a part of his life, the pain just another part of his exhausting days.

He didn't miss sex anymore, either. It had been torture at first, restless, sleepless nights tossing in bed, dreaming of Marius' body hovering over him, his mouth eating him up. This was gone now, a vague souvenir of the pleasure still there, but Marius' face had blurred in his mind, and he struggled to remember his features sometimes. His body had switched that drive off, concentrating on other tasks which required his whole being.

Spring slowly crept through the winter sky, and Marius had just arrived back from an exhausting ride down that damned road when a messenger arrived in full galop, handing a letter to him in the fort's yard.

"General, a letter from the emperor."

He raised his eyebrows, unfurling the scroll, and his heart beat faster. He called one of the soldiers over. "Get centurion Clavius."

He ran, and Marius waited, inhaling the crisp mountain air.

Clavius arrived, worried. "What's up?"

He grinned at him. "We're going home!"

Clavius' face lit up. "What?"

"Yes, my fucking imperial uncle is graciously allowing me to be present for my child's birth." He could barely believe it, *almost a year...*

They rushed packing to leave the next day. He dispatched a letter home, although he suspected that Seraphina already knew. It didn't matter. He was going home to Kyle.

Seraphina knew, of course, and she smiled thinly, walking down to the atrium, the early spring air flowing through the house. Her belly had become huge, making it difficult for her to be everywhere, but she still managed to walk around to check on the works.

She stopped Sixtus, the old man getting ready to go to the market. "Dominus is coming home soon, Sixtus. Make sure his room is ready in a couple checking of weeks, his clothes refreshed."

The old man's eyes widened with joy. "Domina... this is good news!"

She pursed her lips. "Yes, good news for you because you won't feel my whip so much."

Although she had seldom hit the old man, out of pity maybe. Her eyes turned to the yard where Kyle was getting the cart ready. She walked to him, lightly swatting his back with her whip, and he turned around, dropping to his knees.

She hooked the whip under his jaw and tipped his head up. His grey eyes bore into hers. She smiled. "Your dominus is coming home soon..." He breathed a bit harder, but his face stayed a mask. "Aren't you happy?"

"I am, domina..."

She pursed her lips, sounding disappointed. "You're a hard worker, Kyle. Too bad I'll have to let you back into the sheets soon..."

He blanched, and he watched her leave, his chest heaving.

Sixtus walked up to him. "Why are you kneeling? We should leave. Dominus will be home in a few weeks."

They sat on the cart, slowly driving to the market, and Kyle's stomach was a block of ice. Marius was coming home. And he could not decide how he felt about it.

The next few weeks were spent getting the house ready, and Seraphina rested more, her belly growing. The child was already moving a lot, kicking her, and she grew restless, worried at the prospect of giving birth. Reluctantly, she talked to Melissa, and the slave explained to her how it would be, but it was still frightening, something she could barely comprehend.

Their mothers and Tertullia also came to visit her to make the time pass faster, and they were chatting away in the dining hall one day, waiting for the slaves to bring some snacks. Kyle and Lis walked in, and Tertullia's words froze in her mouth. She could barely recognize the doe-eyed young boy she had first met almost a year ago.

The young man leaned down to her to fill her cup, and she clutched his arm, squeezing his muscles. "My, my... how you've grown..."

Seraphina grinned at her. "Noble ladies shouldn't grope slaves."

Tertullia waved her away. "I am not noble... but... this is something... what have you done to this boy?"

Seraphina's eyes shone. "He doesn't lazy around in the sheets anymore, right, Kyle?"

"Yes, domina."

"Come here."

He obeyed, kneeling next to her. "A year of good solid work will do that to a slave. That, and discipline. You should use my methods, my good Tertullia."

The older woman waved her off. "No way... but it's tempting though, if my boys could be half as handsome and well-built as your boy here..."

She chuckled and Seraphina looked down at Kyle. "He doesn't mind getting the whip either, right?"

"No, domina."

Tertullia laughed. "Don't tell me he doesn't mind!"

Seraphina lashed the whip across Kyle's face, a red welt forming straight away, running down his left cheek to his jawline.

He flinched but didn't yelp or move, and Tertullia blanched. "My dear... I don't think you should..."

Seraphina's eyes didn't leave Kyle's. He knew what she wanted to hear. "Thank you, domina..."

"Good boy. Now go and make yourself useful."

He rose and left, Tertullia barely believing what she had seen, worried sick.

His house at last... Marius rode his horse up the hill, impatient, the crisp spring air feeling warm after the winter cold. The sun was setting, but it was still early. His heart pounded faster and he jumped off his horse and banged on the gate. A few moments of waiting and the gate opened, Sixtus hurrying to him, the stable slave taking his horse.

The old man had started kneeling, but Marius caught his arm. "No, please..."

His eyes darted further away, but he could not see Kyle. He looked back at the tearful old man.

"So good that you're back, dominus..."

Marius' lips parted to ask a question when Seraphina appeared, and he stepped to her, looking at her huge belly.

She opened her arms to him. "My husband... welcome home." She beamed at him and pulled his hand to her bump, a small kick making him jump. "Oh, yes... our child is fierce... I pray it's a boy."

He looked at her; the moment seeming surreal. She had barely been his wife when he had left, and now she was about to give birth. He looked around and noticed the fresh paint, the new tiles and mosaics, and he frowned. "You redecorated the house?"

She smiled. "Well, at least you're back for sure... not even a kiss and a 'how you're doing my dear wife'?"

He blushed and kissed her lightly, worried that Kyle was still nowhere, but he swallowed the question.

She smiled at his misery. "You should get rid of your armor and get a bath; you must be tired and starving. I'll send Kyle to your room." She said it so casually, he froze, but didn't object and went straight to his room, waiting, his heart in his throat.

Kyle stood in front of the door, his hand on the handle. Marius was in the room... He breathed in deep and pushed the door in, his eyes scanning the room.

Marius looked up when he heard the door open and for a split second, his mind didn't recognize the young man walking in... until he locked eyes with his grey eyes... and his face fell, his lips parting. *What the fuck...*

Kyle's heart skipped a beat when Marius' blue eyes bore into his and his doubts evaporated. But, he also saw Marius' shock, and he slowed, hesitating, his voice barely making it past his lips.

"Dominus..."

Marius walked up to him, looking him over. He had waited an eternity for this moment, and now... He looked into Kyle's eyes, looking for him there, his hand reaching up to stroke the welt on his face, his face darkening with anger.

Kyle felt his heat, the familiar shape of his lips so close, his hand on his skin, his blazing blue eyes, and he felt his love swell. He didn't dare touch him though, worried sick that he might not love him anymore. He asked softly, his hands going to his armor's straps. "May I?"

Marius nodded, dazed, and he watched the muscled arms and hands effortlessly unbuckle them, lifting the heavy breastplate off, shedding his leather armor. Only his tunic remained, and Kyle lifted his eyes to him, standing very close, only the thin fabric of their clothes between them.

"Bath?"

Marius' eyes darkened with lust. "Fuck that...", he whispered and pulled Kyle into a kiss.

Kyle melted into him, his hands flying to his neck and face, caressing him, opening his mouth wide to his invading tongue. It had been so long, and he had not been sure, but the kiss burst his insecurities apart.

They tore at each other's clothes, Marius' hands awakening Kyle's senses, his hands stroking the Roman's skin, making him moan. He was much stronger, Marius noticed, but it thrilled him.

They stumbled on the bed and Marius pinned him down, his hair falling into his eyes. "You are so strong, pet... I can fuck your brains out now for hours and you won't tire."

Lust and need coursed through Kyle's body at his words, barely believing that Marius was there, on top of him. Kyle had doubted he could make love to him again, but the feeling had been wiped. It was just the two of them, again, nothing else mattered.

They kissed hard, and Marius felt how Kyle's body had filled up, all muscles and rock-hard angles. It made him hard, just touching that rippling flesh.

He frowned at the red welts marring his skin, but Kyle kissed him. "Leave it... just love me... fuck me..."

Marius smiled. "Ordering me around?"

"Please..."

"Please, who?"

Kyle looked into his eyes, panting. "Please, Marius..."

The Roman reached over to grab the bottle of oil, coating his fingers, and pushed one, then two in, feeling how tight the young man had become, closing his eyes. "Fuck... I don't want to hurt you..."

Kyle pushed against his hand. "It doesn't matter... just take me, please..."

Marius pulled his fingers out and slowly pushed inside of him, stretching him. "Fuck you're tight..."

Kyle breathed hard, the pain just temporary, feeling Marius burry himself to the hilt, and he could have sobbed, it felt so good.

He felt him thrust, slowly picking up the pace, their mouths wide open, panting. "I won't last long..."

Marius moaned, and Kyle looked at him. "Me neither..."

He fucked him harder, Kyle's cock trapped between them, and Kyle arched his back.

"Yes... come for me..."

He spilled between their bodies and Marius came inside of him, hard, their tongues melting into each other's mouth, slowly exploring, tasting.

Marius pulled out and lay next to him, caressing Kyle's rippling abs. "Fucking hell, you look like a god, pet..."

Kyle laughed, embarrassed, vaguely anxious. "I thought you wouldn't like it..."

Marius smiled at him. "Are you crazy? I love every bit of you..." He kissed him again, pulling him close. "I missed you like crazy... and this was way too fast, but after our bath and dinner, we'll take it slow."

Kyle looked at him. "I... I haven't slept in here since you left and domina will want you tonight..."

Marius smirked. "She can wait... she's bloated like a whale, not much we could do..." A slight fear crossed Kyle's face and Marius stroked it away, his fingers grazing the welt on his face. "I'm the man of the house here... she can't lay a hand on you anymore." Kyle's defenses came down slowly, feeling safe again, and Marius kissed him deeply. "I love you so fucking much..."

"I love you too, Marius..."

They got up a bit later and went to the bath, the dying sun tinting the windows, a golden-red light pouring in. Marius sighed in the hot water, relaxing, and watched Kyle take off his tunic and join him.

His body made his mouth water, and he pulled him close, whispering. "Turn around... let me wash your back..." Kyle obeyed and Marius' eyes grew wide, his voice a breath. "What the fuck..." His hand glided on the scars marring his back, his voice eerily calm. "Did Seraphina do this?" Kyle shook his head and Marius turned him around, his eyes cold with anger. "Then who?"

Kyle swallowed, his voice soft. "Your father..." Marius' jaw clenched, but Kyle's hands cradled his face, his lips brushing his lips. "It doesn't matter..."

Marius kissed him lightly and then pushed him back a bit, tracing the welts on his skin with his fingers. "And this.... this.... this..." He traced the one on his cheek, his eyes boring into Kyle's. "This?"

Kyle sighed. "Those are domina's..."

"Fucking bitch..."

Kyle shrugged. "It could have been worse..."

Marius' lips pinched. "It could always be worse... she had no right to hit you... or the others?"

Kyle looked away, and Marius cupped his chin, making him look at him. "The children too?"

Kyle shook his head, a small smile on his lips. "They hid and I could never find them."

Marius smiled. "I bet that worked her up."

"Yes... you can see it on my back..."

Marius blanched. "This stops now."

Kyle looked at him and wordlessly reached for the sponge and soap, lathering it up and washing his strong shoulders, his neck, the milky foam gliding down on his chest, floating on the water. "Turn around..."

Marius obeyed, and he felt the sponge glide on his shoulders, shoulder blades, down his back. He moaned when Kyle's hands massaged his head, washing his hair, his strong hands gliding down to knead his tired muscles. "If you keep doing that, I'll have to fuck you again..."

Kyle smiled. "We'll be late for dinner."

Marius turned around, kissing him hard. "Do you think I fucking care?"

His hands slid up Kyle's back, pressing their bodies against each other, pushing him towards the edge of the pool in a passionate kiss, their mouths wide open, when they heard somebody clear his throat. *For fuck's sake...*

Marius broke the kiss, his eyes on Sixtus who was standing by the pool, trying not to look at them. "Khm... Domina sent me to tell you that dinner is served, and she's waiting for you..."

Marius pursed his lips. "Fucking perfect... she can wait."

He turned back to Kyle, but the young man pushed him away gently. "Don't anger her... please?"

He sighed, his eyes mild. "How could I refuse you?" He bent closer, running his tongue along Kyle's neck, whispering. "But... I'll have you pay for this later..." He let him go then with a wicked smile and got out, Kyle following. "Tell your domina that I'll join her soon, Sixtus." The old man hurried outside, and Kyle helped him dress. "Come, let's go and join my beloved wife."

Seraphina watched them enter, their hair still wet, Marius' eyes on her with his usual sarcastic smile, and her blood boiled.

Her voice quivered with anger. "You're late."

Marius shrugged. "For my own dinner? Hardly." He lay down and gestured for Kyle to kneel next to him.

He dug into the food, eating like a lion, and Seraphina's eyes flew to Kyle, her voice clipped. "Go to the kitchen, Kyle. You can clear the table later."

He started rising out of instinct, but Marius clasped his wrist, his eyes on Seraphina. "No. Stay." Kyle knelt back, his face down, worried sick. Marius smiled lightly. "You don't order him around anymore. I'm back home."

Seraphina's eyes narrowed. "I see... well, yes, you're definitely back, for sure... undermining my authority in front of our slaves."

Marius' eyes gleamed coldly. "What authority? Oh... the one you won with your whip? Beating them around is not having authority."

She pursed her lips. "Of course... not in your book... but they obey to the letter now."

Marius wiped his mouth, looking into her eyes. "You won't touch them again, understood?"

Seraphina grinned, her eyes blazing. "Is that a threat?"

Marius smiled coldly. "No. A fact."

She sneered and toasted him. "To your return, dear husband." Her eyes drifted to Kyle, her voice dripping with sarcasm. "I hope you like how your boy is shaping up to become a man."

Marius smiled at her and looked down at Kyle. "I love it..."

Seraphina's brows furrowed, and she watched him carefully, unsure if he had meant it or was being sarcastic.

Stupid bitch. Marius had had enough, and he got up and walked over to her. "Goodnight, dear. It's been a long day."

He took and kissed her hand, smiling at her, and Seraphina's face fell. "You're not sleeping with me?"

Marius shook his head. "No. You need all the rest you can get with the baby soon here."

She frowned, her anger building. "You could still sleep with me."

"I'm afraid your enticing body would make me do something stupid... and I really should not do anything with you in your condition."

He smiled at her, and she seethed.

She watched him walk to the door, turning back. "Come, Kyle."

The slave rose and went to stand next to him, Marius' hand gliding to the small of his back. His lips curled into a smile, and they left, Seraphina breathing hard, her hand on her belly. She got up and went to her room, her anger raging.

Back in their room, Marius gently peeled their clothes off, and they went to bed, kissing softly, their hands roaming their bodies.

He breathed into Kyle's mouth. "I'll love you all night, pet... we've been apart too long..."

Kyle moaned and let Marius turn him on his belly, his whole body covering him, slowly licking his neck, biting his shoulders.

He pushed against him, whimpering, and Marius groaned. "Not yet..."

Marius felt Kyle surrender, his body giving in, and he continued teasing him, bathing him in his kisses, licks and caresses until Kyle felt like he was floating. He didn't even know when Marius had found the bottle of oil but felt his fingers push into him, fucking him with languid, slow strokes and he moaned harder, panting, wanting more.

Marius' voice pushed into his ear, his tongue swirling on it. "Such a good little pet..."

"Please..."

"Soon..."

Kyle got lost in time. Only the pleasure remained, his skin burning, tingling, his nerves raw. Marius pulled his fingers out slowly and pushed his cock inside with one long stroke, slowly moving in and out, making Kyle mewl and writhe under him, his back coated with a thin sheen of sweat. He pushed himself up on his arms, fucking him a bit harder, watching their bodies connect, Kyle's glistening skin taut on his rock-hard muscles. He felt hot and tight around him, and Marius had to breathe hard not to lose it.

He went down on his elbows, slowing down again, his head bent down to nibble on Kyle's neck.

"Your ass feels so fucking great..." Kyle moved against him, rocking his hips, fucking him back, and Marius grinned. "Nice... but you'll need to wait..." A soft whimper escaped Kyle's lips and Marius smiled in the dark room, brushing his damp hair back. "Patience..."

He kept the pace, his body coated in sweat too, their bodies gliding together, their moans and ragged breath filling the night.

Marius whispered in his ear after a while. "As much as I'd like to keep this up, I need to come inside of you..."

He pulled Kyle up on his knees and fucked him hard, gripping his hips. The blinding pleasure washed through Kyle, and his mouth flew open. Marius reached down to pump him, and he had barely closed his fingers around his girth, Kyle came jerking, clenching down on him. Marius groaned and slammed into him, exploding inside, his spasming walls milking him dry. His hands slid on Kyle's drenched back, his rippling muscles. Finally, Marius slid out of him and rolled to the mattress, utterly spent, soaked in sweat.

Kyle lay on his stomach, unable to move.

Marius propped himself on his elbow, drawing lazy patterns on the slave's shoulder blades. "Amazing is an understatement..."

Kyle just looked at him, feebly smiling. Marius pulled the covers on top of them, and Kyle crawled into his arms, resting his head on his heaving chest.

Overwhelmed, his tears spilled on his skin and Marius stroked him, his eyes welling up. "Sshhh... it's ok, I'm here, love..."

They drifted into a deep sleep, the night quiet around them, a soft glow on the ink black sky's edge.

XI

It was still dark with a promise of light on the horizon when Kyle woke up and quietly slid from the bed. He dressed quickly, pulling his tunic on when Marius woke, moaning. "Where do you think you're going?"

"I have to work."

"No, you don't." He rolled over in the bed, his hand catching Kyle's arm, pulling at it. "Come back here..."

Kyle leant over, kissing him softly, prying his hand off. "I need to go to the markets with Sixtus. You have guests for dinner."

"The old man can go on his own..."

"No, he can't. He can't lift heavy things and we have a lot to shop for tonight..."

Marius sighed, letting him go. "Who the fuck is coming tonight?"

"Your parents, all of them, master Clavius and his wife."

"Fuck... Thank the gods Clavius is coming..." His eyes shone in the dark, amusement in his voice. "Can you walk?"

Kyle smiled. "I'll manage..."

Marius shut his eyes, his voice sleepy. "Come back quick..."

"Just go back to sleep. I'll be back before breakfast."

Marius grinned. "Breakfast in bed?"

"As you wish, dominus."

The sun was already up when he came back to their room, Marius waking, his black hair a tousled mess.

He ran his hand through it, yawning. "Where's breakfast?"

Kyle looked at him, mildly pained. "Domina wants you to join her in the dining hall."

Marius rolled his eyes. "This bitch... she's not going to leave me alone."

Kyle held his tunic, matter of fact. "She's your wife?"

Marius got up, smirking. "Some wife!"

He dressed though and followed Kyle to the dining hall where Seraphina was already eating.

She gestured him over. "Lie next to me, dear?"

Marius was too tired to argue, and he even made an effort to kiss her hand. "How are you?"

Seraphina's lips pursed. "Are you genuinely interested, or you're asking out of politeness?"

Marius swallowed his irritation, determined to keep calm. "I'm genuinely interested, dear."

Seraphina eyed him, but he just ate, waiting for her answer. "I'm fine... it's just becoming difficult to sleep with the baby kicking all the time in my huge belly."

He smiled. "It is certainly impressive."

Seraphina stroked his arm, her large eyes welling up with tears. "I wish you would spend more time with me... you've been away for a long time and..."

Marius sighed, annoyed. "I am with you now?"

"I meant just the two of us... I missed you."

Yeah, right.... He looked into her eyes, and she seemed genuine, her malicious smirk gone, her lips trembling. He shifted, a bit thrown, and her large teary eyes lifted to him, her voice soft. "I love you, Marius... I always have... even if you don't..." Fat tears rolled down her cheeks, and he sat up, shocked.

What?! His shock quickly turned to a mild anguish, and he patted her hand. "Now, now... you're just too emotional in your state... Maybe it's a too early to talk about love? We barely know each other."

Her face sank. "I knew it! I knew you didn't love me..."

Marius sighed, his brows furrowing in irritation, his voice clipped. "Just what did you expect, Seraphina? We didn't marry out of love!"

She shrugged, pouting. "Maybe you didn't... I fell in love with you the first night I saw you."

He scoffed. "Yeah, right!"

She remained calm. "Yes, exactly."

His eyes widened. "You can't be serious..."

Seraphina sat up, her eyes blazing. "Why? You don't believe me? I am your wife and I carry your child. What other proof do you need?"

"That's not proof of love..."

Her face darkened. "Oh... I see... so what is?" Marius didn't reply, and she hissed in his face. "What is proof, then, for you?"

He got up, trying to tame his rising anger. "Stop this... you should not work yourself up."

She stood to face him, her belly pressed against his stomach, her voice rising. "Oh... of course... ever the considerate one... but you don't really care about me, do you? Do you?!"

His face darkened. "Stop this, you'll make yourself sick..."

Her tears spilled, but she shook with anger as she shouted in his face. "What do you care? You left me alone last night to fuck your whore!"

Something snapped in Marius, and his hand rose, a vicious back-handed blow, Seraphina's eyes growing wide, time slowing in that split second when the blow fell as she was pushed back, shielded. Kyle took it square on his face, his teeth ripping his flesh. He felt dizzy, blood gushing into his mouth from his torn lip, but he held tight, just closing his eyes against the pain.

Marius blanched, grabbing him by the shoulders. "What the fuck?!"

Kyle's eyes flew to him, warning that she was still there, and he collapsed to his knees, letting Marius step to Seraphina. "I am sorry..."

She looked at him wide-eyed, wordless, and then her eyes drifted to Kyle, her thoughts churning, fear eating at her. *This could have been me on the floor...*

She felt Marius' hand on her arm, and she shook him off, swatting his arm away. "Don't touch me!" Heaving, her hand on her belly, she clutched Lis' arm who had stepped over to her, her face blanched. "Take me to my room, Lisandra."

"Yes, domina..."

They left, leaving Marius standing above Kyle. He leant down and pulled him up, cupping his chin. The bruise on his face was darkening already, his lower lip torn, blood flowing on his chin.

Marius' eyes welled up. "Oh, pet... I'm so sorry... what were you thinking?"

Kyle looked at him, calm. "She's with child..."

Marius sighed deeply; his anger wiped by his shame. *That blow... it would have sent her to the ground...*

Kyle turned to leave, and Marius caught his arm. "Thank you."

He gently pulled his arm out. "I need to wash and clear the breakfast."

Marius swallowed. "You're mad at me..."

His grey eyes shone, mild, and he stepped to Marius, lightly kissing him on the lips. "No... but I have work to do."

Marius gestured at his face. "And this? How will you explain this?"

He shrugged. "Lisandra saw it, so I'll need to talk to her. Just tell the truth, sort of... that you hit me."

Marius smiled, bitter. "Who would believe that?"

"It doesn't matter, does it? Better to say this than confess that you meant the blow for your wife."

Marius paled, and Kyle left him, walking to the well to wash the blood of his face. His cheek burned, a dull pain in the bones and in his jaw. He stroked it, the cold water helping somewhat, then he went to the kitchen to get the trays.

Lis was already there, and she flew into him, almost knocking him over, her arms around him. "Kyle!"

He sighed, prying her off. "Lis, you have to stop this, I'm fine..."

She looked at his face. "Sure you are! Look at you..."

He grabbed her by the shoulders, his face stern. "I'm fine. And what you saw there never happened. Dominus got angry and hit me. That's all..."

She shook her head. "That's not true..."

"Yes, it is."

They faced each other off and she got it, her heart sinking. She lowered her head and nodded quietly, following him to clear the breakfast.

They busied themselves all day to prepare the dinner, Kyle's face taking on a light purple color, darker on his jaw and cheekbone. His lip had scabbed, the dark blood caked in the corner of his mouth. Seraphina had stayed in her room and Marius was in his study, writing letters, keeping his mind busy.

Night arrived, and the guests, chatting away as they were led to the dining hall, brightly lit by oil lamps in large brass stands.

Clavius eyed Kyle's face and took him aside, whilst the others were laying down. "What's up with your face?"

Kyle's face stayed a mask. "I got hit, master Clavius"

He pursed his lips. "That much I gathered... my brooding friend did this to you?" Kyle nodded and Clavius sighed. "This is hard to believe." The slave stayed silent and Clavius went to lie down, pensive.

Marius and Seraphina appeared then, their faces grim, though she was on his arm. He gently helped her lie down near her mother and went to lie next to Clavius, close to the men.

His friend toasted him. "Congratulations on your newest prowess..."

Marius smirked. "Shut up... You know nothing."

"I know maybe enough... Marius, you have to control your temper, this is not going to end well."

Marius rolled his eyes. "Please... could you not be my father tonight? He's right here."

Talking of the devil, his father turned to him. "Your slave boy has an impressive bruise on his lovely face. I can only hope you caused it?"

Marius smiled mockingly. "Yes, I did, father. Proud?"

His father smiled. "Yes. Finally, maybe you got some sense in you."

Marius' face darkened and his lips parted when he saw Kyle's face.

Clavius smirked. "Yeah, you should be really fucking proud of yourself..."

Marius opened his mouth to comment when dinner was served and they started eating, the women happily chatting away. He reluctantly listened to Clavius, Gaius and Quintus discussing politics, his eyes on Kyle, who had been called over by Seraphina. Marius froze when Kyle kneeled next to her, her fingers cupping his chin.

Kyle looked at her, letting her hand graze over his bruise. Her mother and Marius' frowned, Tertullia mortified. "Poor boy... this must hurt."

Seraphina's voice was soft. "Does it hurt, Kyle?"

"Yes, domina."

"A lot?"

He shrugged, lying. "No, domina."

But Quintus' wife wasn't convinced. "You must be of steel, boy, because that cheekbone doesn't look good at all. I've seen it on my husband when he came back from war once. Come here." Kyle moved closer to her, and she grabbed his jaw, pushing her thumb onto his cheekbone. A sharp pain made him yelp and jerk his head away.

He straight away lowered it. "I am sorry, domina..."

She smiled. "It's fine... I hurt you. Yes, so it's badly bruised, maybe cracked... it must hurt now. Don't lie again."

He nodded, his eyes welled up, and Seraphina paled. "Cracked?"

Her mother shrugged. "It's not life-threatening."

Seraphina quieted, her hand on Kyle's shoulder. She gazed at Marius and their eyes locked.

Her mother followed her gaze. "Good thing too that he takes his temper out on his slave."

Tertullia's eyes grew wide. "Marius did this? Unbelievable..."

Seraphina didn't comment, but her stomach clenched, and her fingers dug into Kyle's shoulder. He lifted her eyes to her, and she looked at him, her large brown eyes soft. "You should retire, Kyle. Let somebody else do your job tonight."

He shook his head. "Thank you, domina, but I'll be fine." He rose then and left them to walk over to the men to assist them, Lis taking over with the women.

Quintus looked at Kyle and waved him over. "So, my good wife has been playing the doctor? Let me have a look at your face." Kyle kneeled next to him, his face pale, but Quintus was surprisingly gentle, just probing the bone lightly with his fingers. "Good, it's not broken, just a bad bruise." He looked at Marius. "Impressive blow, though. It is fortunate that this sturdy guy got it and not one of the females."

Marius sighed, irritated. "Can we just get over this?"

Gaius smiled. "Sure... we're just mildly reassured that you have your priorities straight."

"Meaning?"

"Meaning that you're maybe finally over your fuck toy here now that you're married and have a lovely wife."

His words fell loud into the silent room and the women looked at them, slightly mortified.

Marius downed his cup, squeezing it hard, and his blue eyes didn't give anything away, a small smile on his lips. "Sure, father."

Gaius was a bit thrown, and they resumed eating, Marius making sure he didn't touch Kyle at all. He glanced at him though and noticed how pale he was, his breathing shallow, his face an expressionless mask. *Fuck this...*

After desserts, Marius got up and went to the terrace to clear his head. He had too much to drink again, but was not utterly drunk, and he wished them all away to hell.

Clavius silently followed him, laying a hand on his shoulder. "Spill."

Marius sighed but couldn't lie to him, his voice soft. "I almost hit her today."

"Hit who?"

"Seraphina..."

Clavius turned to him, making him face him. "What?"

Marius smiled bitterly. "Yes... she got on my nerves... said something which just made me blow up. About me fucking my whore and not sleeping with her..."

Clavius' face fell. "Is that true?"

"Yes..."

"And?"

"And Kyle got the blow. He stepped in front of her."

"Marius..."

He looked at Clavius, bitter. "Yeah, I know... She loves me, or so she says, but I don't..."

Clavius squeezed his shoulder. "Well, at least your boy saved you from a lot of trouble... I won't comment on you raising your hand to your pregnant wife, no matter what she said."

Marius nodded, giving in, his shoulders sagging. "She'll never leave me alone..."

"That's a wife for you."

They chuckled, and Clavius sighed, turning dead serious. "You have to make sure this never happens again, ever. You can't beat her around, that's not you."

Marius nodded. "I know..."

He ruffled Marius' hair. "You're a twat. A huge one. Apologize to her tonight. Hell, even sleep with her." Marius pulled a face, but Clavius jabbed him in the ribs. "That's the least you can do."

"Maybe she doesn't want to see me..."

"In that case, you'll deserve that, too."

"Thanks for your support..."

"Any time." Clavius toasted him and left him alone, facing the night.

After the guests had left, Marius stood, torn. He wanted to take Kyle to bed and make up for that horrific blow, but Clavius' words rang in his head. *Fuck, fuck, fuck...* He went to Seraphina's room and knocked on the door. Thais opened it and she sank to her knees straight away.

He stepped in, stopping short. "May I come in?"

Seraphina was in bed, her enormous belly under the covers, and she gestured him in. "You're already in..."

He walked next to the bed, looking down at her, taking her hand. "I'd like to apologize... for today. I should have never raised my hand to you."

Seraphina watched him, her mind racing. "Are you staying with me tonight?"

Marius sighed. "If you want me to, yes."

She smiled at him. "Yes, I'd like that."

Marius' eyes went to the door, hesitating. "I'll change in my room, I'll come back..."

She smiled a small smile. "Sure, dear. I'll be waiting."

He left and went straight to look for Kyle. He was in the kitchen, doing mountains of washing up with Shayla and Melissa. They almost kneeled when he waved it off, gently pulling him outside. "How are you?"

Kyle's face was drawn, white. He was in a lot of pain, his skull throbbing, but he just swallowed, trying to sound light. "I'm fine."

Marius looked clearly embarrassed. "I have to sleep with Seraphina tonight... I was sort of a jerk to her today." Kyle just nodded, too tired, and Marius cupped his face, kissing him. "You should go to bed. Sleep in our room."

Kyle smiled thinly. "I still have a mountain of work...". Marius' heart sank, but Kyle just nudged him gently. "... and you're making me run late... just go to your wife." Marius smiled and left, his eyes drifting back to the slave going back to the kitchen.

He went back to his room, changed into a light tunic, and went to Seraphina's room, not bothering to knock. The room was dimly lit, but Seraphina was still awake. He lay down next to her and pulled her in his arms, his hand drifting to her belly. He could not see her content little smile, her eyes gleaming like a snake's.

Kyle finished very late, almost in the small hours of dawn, his throat parched, a vague nausea lingering. He lay down, exhausted, in his room, not even being able to drag himself upstairs. He pressed a cloth soaked in cold water to his face and gritted his teeth against the pain, the dull throbbing somewhat eased. His mind churned the day's events, the words said, and he wondered if they were right. Maybe he had no right to take Marius' mind off his family... He'd always been called a whore, so was he one now? Yet, he loved him so much; it hurt... He turned to his side, trying to find sleep.

Next morning, Marius walked to his room just to find it empty, and he sighed and put his clothes on, wandering down to the garden. It was still early, but the air was milder. He sat down on a couch, just lying back, watching the sprouting green leaves.

Kyle walked to the garden to feed the fish, and he froze when he saw Marius, just to gather his wits then and walk up to him.

Marius patted the couch. "Sit." He did, and the Roman laced his arms around him, pulling him to his chest. "I missed you..."

Kyle sighed, facing him, his grey eyes pools of worry. "Marius... am I in the way?"

He watched as his face fall, his blue eyes widening. "What? What are you talking about?"

"You know... as in the way of your happiness, your family life..."

Marius brushed his knuckles on his cheek, making sure he didn't push the tender skin. "What's this nonsense? I love you; my life is only complete with you."

Kyle blushed, but he pushed. "I seem to cause grief... to your wife, your parents, her parents..."

Marius waved him off, irritated. "Fuck them. Who cares...", but a bitter feeling settled in his throat and their eyes locked. "Do you love me, pet?"

Kyle's throat clutched. "Yes..."

"So, stop talking fucking nonsense." Marius kissed him deep, pushing his tongue into his mouth, whispering when he broke the kiss. "I don't care what people think. I love you and I want to be with you."

"I know... but will they let you?"

A glint of fear crossed Marius' face, but he just stroked Kyle's face. "We just have to be careful..."

"Your wife is jealous..."

Marius sighed. "Yes... she is. But she'll have her baby soon and that should keep her busy, or so I hope."

They quieted and Kyle wasn't sure that Seraphina would just give up. If she really loved him, she could go all the way and become dangerous.

Marius studied his grim face and nudged him. "Hey... I won't let anything happen to you."

Kyle rose, picking up the bucket of fish food. "I need to work. Breakfast should be served soon."

Their eyes flew to the archway, the children running in, Brandan chasing Bri, laughing. They stopped short when they saw Marius, but then Bri smiled and tugged Brandan along. They kneeled next to his couch, holding hands, chuckling.

Marius had not seen them since his return and he sat up, smiling. "Get up and show me how you've grown."

They did, smiling shyly, but Bri couldn't contain her happiness and flew into his arms. "You're back, dominus!"

Marius laughed, almost thrown backwards on the couch. "Yes...", he pushed her away, looking her over, noticing how she had grown. She was turning twelve soon, and her face had become sharper, her body slenderer, shedding the soft curves of childhood.

His eyes drifted to Brandan, who stood still, but fearless. He had filled up, but his body was still lean, almost athletic, and Marius gestured him closer, the boy not losing eye contact with him, a small smile on his lips. He reached for Bri's hand, and they faced him, glowing.

"How is your Latin, Brandan?"

The boy smiled. "I think almost as good as my Celtic."

He spoke with a flawless accent, and Marius smirked. "You have a smart mouth."

Brandan just bowed, and Marius could not decide whether he was being respectful or mocking him.

"So, kids, what are you up to?"

Bri beamed. "We came to feed the fish with Kyle. Then, we'll help weed the garden and do the laundry, and maybe help in the kitchen."

"Always together?"

Bri looked at Brandan. "Yes, always, dominus."

"Like a good brother and sister."

Brandan looked at him. "More like a good couple."

Marius froze, his words caught, and Kyle playfully ruffled Brandan's hair. "You have to grow a bit for that."

He smiled at him. "Bri and I want to be together when we grow up." They faced each other and Marius' heart wrenched.

Kyle shoved the bucket into their hands. "Come on, lovebirds, time to feed the fish."

They left, laughing and Marius rose, bitter. "So much for not wanting to breed slaves."

Kyle shrugged. "They're kids... they'll grow out of it... or not... and they can't 'breed', yet." Frankly, what did you expect? They are locked up here. There's not much choice, you know..."

Marius looked at him. "I heard the girls were on your back too?"

Kyle pulled a face. "They still are... Lis more than Thais. She's shy and almost always with domina."

"Have you ever been with a woman?"

The question was out before he could think about it, and a shadow crossed Kyle's face. "Yes... not too many times, though."

"When?"

"During my training..."—he sighed, knowing that Marius would want more — "I had to learn how to please women, it was part of the package, though Lucius didn't like them at all... so, it was just during my time there that I had to bed them..."

"Had to?"

Kyle smiled bitterly. "Well, yes... it's not exactly like you have a choice."

"How can you even...?"

"Get it up? There are drugs to get you there... if you can't perform, very similar to the one we drank at that party, remember? But stronger. There are others which will keep you awake and on edge too, constantly wanting more..." Memories surfaced of those nights and days at the brothel, and he swayed a bit, trying to wall them back up. He shook his head gently, feeling faint. "You should not ask me about those days... please..."

Marius squeezed his hand, mortified. "I won't."

The kids came back, and Kyle left with them to the kitchen, Marius watching as they tugged on his tunic on both sides, pushing and pulling him, laughing.

He turned to walk up to the dining room, Seraphina already waiting for him. "Up early, dear?"

He walked over to her and kissed her hand. "You too..."

She shrugged. "I can't sleep with my belly. It's soon now. I went to pray to the gods."

Marius smirked but didn't comment. His faith in the gods had been long gone, left on the bloody battlefields where enemy and friends alike writhed in their own blood and entrails, praying to their gods in their languages. *What good did it do? What kind of gods are these, allowing some men to live a life of luxury whilst others have to serve them like animals?* He watched his slaves carry in their breakfast, his love... He steeled himself not to give any of his feelings away, very conscious of Seraphina's eyes on him.

Kyle had no difficulty playing the game, hiding his feelings and emotions had been a part of him for years, and Marius suffered quietly, thinking of the long years stretching ahead in this impossible life. *And a child soon.* He had pushed this away subconsciously to the far corner of his mind, but the reality of it hit him now, watching Seraphina's huge bump, which seemed to have appeared of nowhere, as he had been away of it all.

The food turned in his mouth and he swallowed, a vague panic creeping up on him in the stuffy room, his appetite wiped, a thin sheen of cold sweat breaking down his back. *I have to get out of here...*

He rose quickly, and Seraphina watched him, concerned. "Where are you going?"

"I have a meeting... I need to leave now..."

She wanted to object, but he had already left, rushing to his room, stumbling out to the terrace, out of breath. He braced his arms on the ledge, heaving, focusing his eyes on the city, gulping in the warming air. *Impossible fucking trap...*

He turned around and changed, throwing his drenched clothes on the floor, and then hurried down to the atrium, out the front door. He had no idea where he wanted to go, just away from this place, from her, his long strides taking him down to the city.

Without consciously thinking about it, his legs took him to Clavius' home, and he stood in front of the door, his chest heaving from the climb to the hill. He knocked, and after a short while, Clavius' old slave opened the door. He knew him and led him straight to his master. Clavius and Tertullia were having breakfast, her laughter booming through the house.

She got up when she saw him; her face alight. "Marius! What a lovely surprise!" Her soft body was around him in an instant, hugging his tall frame as best as she could. It felt so good, he had to fight his tears. She pulled at his hand, pushing him down on one of the couches. "Come, come, you must join us..."

Clavius smirked. "Modesty, woman, this is no noble way to greet our guest."

"Oh, sod off, you big boar. The boy needed a hug, any decent woman can see that. Now, drinks." She gestured a slave over and made him fill Marius' cup with watered wine. She also pushed honey and bread in front of him. "Eat, eat...you look like you've seen a ghost..."

He drank and put his cup down, a vague nausea still lingering.

Clavius watched him carefully. "What's wrong?"

"Nothing..."

"You wouldn't be here then, looking white as a sheet." Marius opened his mouth to protest, but Clavius just smiled. "Marius, I know you... so stop it and don't make me eat your lies."

He sighed, giving up. "I... I don't know how I can carry on living like this..."

Clavius raised his eyebrows, and Tertullia listened carefully. "Living like what?"

"I'm going to be a father...", he moaned, and Clavius grinned.

"Well, it's about fucking time you realized!"

Marius closed his eyes. "Seraphina is jealous of Kyle so... we have to pretend that there's nothing happening, we just fuck... and now even that is becoming complicated... and soon, the child..." Clavius didn't comment, letting him speak, his eyes darting to his wife. Marius' face was ashen. "What if they take him away from me?"

"They?"

"My fucking family! I don't know how long we can pretend this... how long I can... It's killing me... I love him..." The last words were a mere whisper in a shaking breath, Marius falling silent, his blue eyes laced with pain.

Clavius knew what he had in mind. His uncle could just take Kyle away any day. You couldn't oppose the emperor, and Marius' father was no fool. The old man had been hurt and it would only be a matter of time that Seraphina found out their true feelings. He sighed, grim. "This is a real shithole of a situation..." Marius just nodded; his eyes lost.

Tertullia looked at him, her voice soft. "So what you're saying is that he's not safe there in your home?"

Marius nodded; his voice pained. "No, he's not... not from my fucking father and my fucking imperial uncle... not to mention that cunt of a wife."

Clavius frowned. "Watch your language, though?"

Tertullia reached over to take his hand. "Maybe he should be somewhere else then..."

Marius looked at her, his eyes widening. "Where?"

She looked into his eyes, stroking his hand. "Maybe he should be here, with us."

Clavius sat up, alarmed, and Marius' face fell. "What?!"

Tertullia smiled mildly. "Think about it, dear. Taking your slave from you would be a family matter for your imperial uncle, long live the emperor! But... he would not be interested in taking him from a modest centurion's home... that would be an embarrassment, really..."

Clavius frowned. "Hey!"

She quieted him, all the while holding Marius' hand, his face ash-white, her words racing in his head.

She smiled at him. "You could sell him to us and when the waves have quieted down, we'll just sell him back to you. Easy-peasy...you know we'd take good care of him, and you could come and visit, away from prying eyes..." Clavius turned his finger around his temple, but she swatted him off, smiling.

Marius' guts filled with ice. Yet, he knew, she was maybe right, the only sane person in this madness... *but how... how to do this to Kyle? Would he understand? Would he forgive him, ever?*

He rose, his face drawn, his voice soft. "No... I won't sell him to you..." Clavius sighed but Marius turned to her, clinging to her warm, brown eyes and friendly smile as he pushed out the words. "I'll gift him to you..."

Tertullia nodded, in tears, rising to clasp him in her arms, squeezing tight, and he sobbed, clutching at her.

XII

Marius arrived home late and Sixtus rushed to him in the atrium. "Dominus, at last! The baby... the baby is on the way."

He stood, dumbstruck, his emotions raging, and he let the old man lead him upstairs to the dining hall, her cries filling the house. He stopped, unable to move. Kyle hurried to him, a cup of wine in his hand, and Marius downed it, flinging the cup to the floor, clutching at him, holding him in an iron embrace.

Kyle moaned. "You're crushing me..."

Marius let him go, bracing at his shoulders. "When...."

"It started hours ago. The doctor is in there with Melissa and Thais. It should be over soon..."

They listened to her screams, and Marius paced the room, livid, his eyes darting to Kyle. *I should tell him, but how now...*

They waited for what seemed like hours, Kyle watching Marius exhaust himself, pale, pacing the large room back and forth.

He got up and walked to him, stopping him mid-stride. "Stop, please? Just come and sit down. You'll need your strength." Marius obeyed, in a daze, and sat holding his hands, squeezing them.

Kyle looked at him, worried. "You were gone a long time..."

"I was at Clavius' house."

He relaxed, a small smile on his face. "In that case, you were at least safe."

Yes, safe... Marius looked at him. "What do you think of Clavius?"

Kyle shrugged. "He is a nice man, and he clearly likes you."

"And his wife?"

Kyle smiled. "She helped me a lot when you were away. I think she has a kind soul and heart. She cares, you know?"

Marius' lips parted, but then Melissa arrived, her hair plastered to her face. "Dominus... your child is born..."

He shot to his feet and followed her to Seraphina's room, slowing at the entrance, the smell of blood overpowering. Seraphina lay on the bed, her pale face framed by her wet hair, a small bundle in her arms. She smiled feebly at him, and he walked next to her, dazed.

Her eyes shone sadly, and her smile turned bitter. "It's a girl..."

Marius looked at the small being and gingerly stroked her face, the skin soft under his finger.

Seraphina barked at Melissa. "Put her in her father's arms!"

She obeyed, gently laying the baby in Marius' arms, and he held her, his whole being warming, feeling her featherlight weight on his muscles, her soft breath against his cheek. He bent down to kiss her, and she cooed, making his heart melt. "She's beautiful..."

Seraphina's eyes blazed. "She is a girl! The gods are cruel..."

He looked at her, shocked. "She's healthy and alive. What more do you want?"

She pulled a face. "I wanted to give you a boy."

Marius smiled down at the baby, not even registering her disappointment. "She's perfect."

She smirked, tired and irritated, her grief for her boy choking her.

Melissa gently lay a hand on her arm. "You will need to feed her, domina."

She pulled a face but shrugged. "Alright, I guess I have no choice now that she's here."

Melissa took the baby away from Marius, and Thais left the room too. Melissa put the baby on Seraphina's breast, the tiny being trying to latch on it, clumsily searching for her nipple.

She looked at her, irritated. "What's she doing?"

Melissa patiently guided her, and she suckled hard, making Seraphina yelp. "Ouch! This hurts!"

She hissed, her face clouding, and Melissa soothed her. "It hurts the first few days, but your breasts will get used to it. I had a cream prepared for you if you're too sore, domina."

Seraphina pinched her lips, her angry eyes flying to Marius. "See what I have to endure as a woman? Watch and learn next time you have a fit about your miserable life."

He felt slightly ashamed in that dim room, the soiled sheets laying on the floor next to the birthing stool, caked with blood, but her behavior set off alarms, the concern plain on Melissa's face.

Seraphina looked at him, her voice like venom. "You can go now and join your fuck toy. Have fun!"

He shook his head. "What are you talking about? I'll stay with you..."

"No! I don't need you here. Send your useless whore in here to clean up first. Then you can fuck him to pieces." Her words choked, and he blanched, Melissa very quiet, trying not to look at them, her eyes on the feeding baby.

He backed out and went to Kyle and Thais, silently waiting on the corridor. "Go and clean up that room. Kyle, come to my room when you're done."

He nodded, silent, and they went in to clean up, Seraphina's voice shrill in the night. "Finally! Get this junk out of the room. I gather your master has told you to join him, Kyle? You know what? Take Thais with you. She's a great fuck, or so I've heard..."

Marius almost stepped back but then thought better of it and left, his anger swelling, his heart in pieces.

Kyle came to their room much later, his face drawn. Seraphina had not stopped, and by the time they had finished, Thais had been sobbing. He had to hold her to calm her down and then had told her to go to her room in the slaves' quarter, but her eyes had grown wide.

"I have to go with you. She said so. If I disobey, she'll beat the skin off my back."

Kyle shook his head. "Dominus won't let her. Just go to your room."

She chewed her lips, worried sick, but then obeyed, and he made his way to their room.

Marius turned to him. "At last... she gave you grief?"

He shrugged, too tired to even think. "No... more to Thais..."

Marius nodded, not probing further. "I have a baby girl..."

Kyle smiled. "Yes, congratulations, dominus."

He looked at him, mildly scolding. "Not in this room?"

"Of course..."

Marius turned to him, taking his hands. "I have to tell you something..."

Kyle cocked his head. "Yes?"

His blue eyes bore into his. "You know that my uncle is the emperor... and that I angered father... remember when he hit me?" Kyle nodded, unsure where this was going. "Seraphina is jealous, and she could any time find out what we have here... she might have done so already..." Kyle nodded, and Marius continued, bleeding every word. "My imperial uncle could... he could just take you away, claim you, you know?" Kyle paled, his heart racing, but he didn't interrupt him. "So... you're not safe here... I don't know how long we can pretend that we're only just fucking casually... I think Seraphina will not buy it for long... so..." He struggled, taking a deep breath. "So maybe the best would be that you went somewhere safe until we figure something out."

Kyle stood, Marius' hands warming his hands, not fully understanding. "Went somewhere else? But where? This is my home, here..."

His words died and his face fell, his eyes wide, and Marius' fingers closed on his hands, feeling them tremble. "It would be temporary only... until my fucking family forgets about us, about you..."

Kyle stammered, in shock. "But... where? Where would I go?"

"Clavius' house."

His lips parted, and Marius felt his hands go limp, his voice choked. "You sold me to your friend?"

Marius held his hands tighter, desperate, his blue eyes filled with love. "No! No... I didn't sell you..." Kyle relaxed, sighing, when Marius drove the knife through his heart. "I gifted you away..."

There was a dead silence following his words, Kyle's face going from relief to grief, a bitter sadness at Marius' words, even if his reason was screaming at him, his heart shattered into a million pieces, the shards biting into his very core. He doubled over slowly, moaning, and his legs couldn't hold him. He wrenched his hands out, Marius' hands burning him, his throat choked by tears, slowly sinking to his knees, looking for comfort in the only position he knew would maybe bring some mercy from his tormentors.

Marius watched him sink back into his submissive self, surrendering his will to him, his body screaming mercy, and he couldn't stand it. He tugged at him, his voice full of tears. "Get up, please, just get up, talk to me..."

But Kyle was gone, and he lowered his forehead to the cool floor, oblivious to his desperate lover's attempts to make him rise.

Marius whispered, frantic. "Get up... oh gods... Kyle, please, please, love..." He covered his back, squeezing his shoulders, his whole body rocked by sobs. "Please... I am sorry... I won't do it... I'm not letting you go..."

Kyle rocked his body, gently moaning, his face on the cold floor. *It feels so good... just away from this madness... away from him...* Darkness fell, soothing, a black void which enveloped him like a mother's arms.

Kyle woke with the morning light in their bed, alone, and he could not move, his eyes on the terrace, the spring breeze gently ruffling the curtains.

Clavius and Tertullia stood in front of the door, looking at the wreaths. Her eyes grew wide. "The baby is here?"

He sighed. "Fucking perfect timing..." He knocked then and Sixtus opened. He gestured them in and went to get Marius.

He was with Seraphina and the child, the tiny girl cradled in her arms. She seemed more at peace, but her face was grim, still mourning the boy she had prayed for. Marius sat next to the bed, his mind numb, when Sixtus knocked and poked his head in. "Dominus, master Clavius and his wife are here..."

Seraphina shot an angry look at him. "Now? What got into them?"

Marius sighed. "They could not know... let me deal with them."

Clavius watched Marius approach, his face ashen, dark circles under his eyes. He patted his back. "Congratulations, I see you can't sleep already..."

His eyes were so tortured that Clavius had to shut up, and Tertullia hesitated. "We can take him away another day?"

Marius wavered when there was another knock, and Sixtus opened the door to let their parents in.

Gaius stormed to his son, clasping him in an embrace. "Son! Where's my grandchild?"

He gestured towards the stairs. "Upstairs... Sixtus will take you..." He had forgotten that Brandan ran to their house yesterday to tell them the good news. He watched them hurry upstairs and turned to Clavius and Tertullia. "He... didn't take it very well... blacked out... I put him in bed in our room... he might be awake..."

He couldn't finish, and Clavius held his arm. "Let my good wife deal with this. Come, let's sit and talk."

Tertullia smiled and walked upstairs. The men sat in the garden; this garden Kyle had built with his bare hands. He was not here to feed the fish, and they plopped noisily, their bulging eyes searching for him. Marius collapsed on a bench, his eyes staring into emptiness.

Clavius sat facing him, trying to catch his eyes. "Tertullia will pick his pieces up, don't worry..."

His voice swam in sadness. "How did you find such a great wife?"

Clavius shrugged. "You know how it is... nobody wanted her... too plump, too dimpled, too loud and funny... Me? I saw her and I couldn't give a shit that she didn't have the body of a goddess or the haughty, aristocratic prim face... She had life and her eyes... like velvet. She made me laugh... the rest is history." He smiled mildly at his memories and Marius' tears flew. Clavius grabbed his hand, searching his eyes. "I am sorry for you, I truly am, but you can't give away how you feel, not with those vultures in the house. Marius, look at me. Pull yourself together, soldier. Onwards and upwards."

His words reached the core of Marius' being, his training kicking in, and he wiped at his tears, his face taut into a mask of military discipline.

Clavius smiled. "That's my boy."

In the meantime, Tertullia had found their room, and she stepped in cautiously, her eyes on the slave's still form in the bed. Kyle's eyes drifted to her, and he knew he should get up and kneel, but he couldn't move. She rushed there, sitting next to him, gently stroking his hair. He closed his eyes, her soft hands making him well up. He cried silently, tears rolling down his cheeks, soaking the sheets.

Tertullia spoke softly, stroking him. "I know this must be very hard for you, pup... I know... but trust me, he wants the best for you, to protect you. We'll take care of you; you know us by now? My silly husband and me." She smiled, and he looked up at her, clinging to her kindness and warmth. "I like you, pup, a lot, but you know that. We'll have fun, you'll see. And then, you can come back in no time."

She quieted, the conversations of the grandparents seeping in from the corridor, and he froze. She lay a hand on him. "We should go. Those vultures are here, circling. Gather your stuff? Can you manage?" He nodded, his stomach in such a knot that he thought he would throw up, and she knew, smiling down at him. "Come, pup, let's get this over with." She rose and held her hands out to help him sit. He steadied himself, drawing on the last bit of his mental strength, clinging to her, breathing in deep. "Good boy... nice and steady."

Kyle straightened, smoothing down his tunic, standing. He let go of her hands and walked on shaky legs to the door, Tertullia following him downstairs where he went to his room. He didn't have much to pack, just his clothes, shoes, and he shoved everything in a bag. Tertullia stroked his back, making him stop. "Say then goodbye to your friends. We need to be out of here fast, pup. Alright?"

He nodded, his voice soft. "Yes, domina..." Her eyes welled up and she stroke his face, leaving him.

Kyle packed in his bag, mindlessly, not thinking.

They met their parents in the atrium, Tertullia walking in and they stood, facing each other, Marius and Clavius on one side, the happy grandparents and Tertullia towards the kitchen. Polite smiles were exchanged and Tertullia looked at Marius, noticing his masklike face, his eyes cold. *Good.* They talked about the baby then, excited, all happiness and sunshine.

Kyle held Lis tight, the girl in a complete shock, and the children clung to him too, crying. He looked at Melissa, pained, his voice gone. "Take them off me..."

She pulled them off, and they cried in her arms, Lis going into a fit of rage. "Why? Why you? Why is he giving you away?!"

Kyle choked, unable to answer, and Sixtus stepped to him, grim. "Take care, son... I will miss you."

He just nodded, gripping the old man's hand. Shayla pulled him in an embrace, and he then looked at the children. "Don't forget to feed the fish..."

Brandan faced him, his face white. "I won't forget what you did for me, ever."

He swayed, but then clutched his bag and left to join Tertullia, Melissa holding Lis back.

Gaius turned to his son, holding a letter. "I almost forgot, Marius. I have a message for you from my dear brother."

Marius took it away, his eyes flying to Clavius, but he opened it, pulling on his discipline.

My dear nephew, I hope your return is full of joy and you are happy with your little family. I have also not forgotten your delicious little pet and much as I hate to do this to you, I'd like to request that you give ownership of him to me. You see, I would like to explore his talents...

His hands shook, but his lips curled up into a smile. "Dare I say you know what's in this letter, father?"

Gaius smiled, glancing at Quintus. "Let's just say that I just might..."

Kyle stepped into the atrium at this very moment, stopping short next to Tertullia, his face pale as a sheet. Their eyes locked with Marius for a brief moment, before Kyle lowered his head fast, kneeling next to his bag.

Marius swallowed, pushing his training to the front. He rolled the letter up and handed it back to his father, Gaius' lips parted in shock. Marius looked him in the eyes. "As much as I would like to, I can't honor my uncle's noble request. You see, I no longer own that slave."

Gaius scoffed, his anger rising. "Don't play me, Marius!"

But his son just looked at him, his blue eyes like steel. "I'm not playing you, father. I gifted him away yesterday to Clavius." He grinned and clasped Clavius on the back.

The centurion shrugged, embarrassed. "And I can't thank you enough, my friend."

Gaius and Quintus exchanged a quick glance as Tertullia stepped to them, playing the utterly embarrassed lower-class woman. "My, my... well, I don't think his honored highness would want a slave from us, a humble soldier and his wife, khm... Khm.."

Gaius looked at her, horrified. "Of course not... this... well, I'll tell my brother myself... he'll be disappointed, no doubt..."

Tertullia fussed around, waving at Clavius. "Lets' go then, husband; we don't want to disturb your family gathering. Much joy with your new baby!"

She walked over to Marius and kissed him on the cheek, her eyes boring into his. "We'll see you soon? And thank you again for your precious gift."

He just nodded; his whole being funneled into not collapsing. *Please look at me, pet...*

His eyes went to Kyle, but he didn't look up and Clavius walked over to the kneeling man, gently touching his shoulder. "Come, Kyle, let's go home."

Kyle rose, turning after him, swinging his bag on his shoulder, and they left, the door shutting, making Marius close his eyes for a split second.

His father was all over him, smiling widely. "Well, at last, you came to your senses. Well done, son. And now, let's talk about the reception at the emperor's palace to present your baby...."

They walked to the garden, Marius vaguely listening, his mind reeling.

They arrived at the modest villa later, and Clavius walked Kyle around. It was much smaller than Marius' but still had a small garden in the back, no balconies, but hanging corridors on the yard. There was only the old slave who was half-retired, the cook, a large African slave woman with a wide grin, another young boy named Simeon and a young girl called Nikhe. They all welcomed him warmly and Clavius showed him his room. It was smaller than the previous one but had a small window and it was a blessing to have light and some fresh air.

Kyle put his clothes into a trunk under his bed and changed, walking to find them sitting in the dining room, the large windows open. He kneeled, his face lowered, and Tertullia cupped his chin, lifting his face, smiling at him. "You don't have to kneel all the time here. Not with us. When we have guests only. So, other rules and timings..."

She told him in detail how the household worked, and he listened carefully, trying to remember everything, his mind on his new duties and home, still shocked, his breathing shallow.

Clavius had to leave, and she waited until he was gone, her voice soft. "Marius might not be able to come straight away, pup."

His eyes were like pools of still water. "It doesn't matter..."

"You're mad at him?"

Kyle swallowed, empty, and couldn't answer. He whispered. "I need time..."

She stroked his face. "You escaped by a hair width; you know that? He did the right thing, even if you hate him now..."

He looked away, unable to think.

She sighed, softly nudging him. "Go to the kitchen and eat something... and I know you're not hungry, but you are... so just go... Tabia will give you food, her cooking is divine."

He rose and walked to the kitchen, slightly lost but following the scent of food drifting out. Tabia eyed him and gestured with her huge ladle towards the crude wooden table. "Sit down, new boy, you have to eat." She had a rich voice and a healthy laughter. She scooped a huge bowl of thick broth and pushed it in front of him with a spoon. "This is magic... it will give you strength. Not that foul Roman food, this is from my homeland, taste it. Eat, skinny boy."

His stomach flipped, but the broth's delicious smell made his head swoon and he gingerly tasted it. It was very rich in taste and he sighed, eating effortlessly.

She grinned at him. "Good boy! I love a healthy appetite. You're hurt, I can see that, but Mama Tabia's cooking will heal you."

She busied herself, and he ate, feeling much better.

She took his bowl away when he had finished and cupped his jaw. "Your face is beaten up..."—she shook her head, hissing — "Animals..."

Kyle swallowed, and rose. "Thank you. It was delicious."

She grinned at him. "Any time. You're hungry? Just come, and I'll stuff you, like this brat here!"

She swatted Simeon on the backside, making the young boy yelp.

"Hey!" He turned to Kyle, beaming a large smile. "Welcome!" His face grew all concerned, and he gently reached up to stroke his face. "Wow... does it hurt?"

Kyle nodded. "Not too much anymore..."

Tabia swatted Simeon's head. "Take your hands off him... Watch out, this young Greek god has a soft spot for pretty boys..."

Simeon rubbed his head, shy. "So what?"

Tabia shrugged. "Nothing... just keep your hands to yourself."

Simeon took Kyle's hand. "Come, work with me."

They went to gather cleaning supplies, and Kyle had to teach Simeon. He was a terrible cleaner, and the house looked a tip.

He had made him work hard, and by night-time, the floors sparkled, all the torches and lamps refreshed and polished. Simeon sweated profusely, smiling at Kyle when they were done, half-naked, their bodies glistening in the golden lamplight.

Tertullia walked in, her jaw dropping. "My... what have you done, boys?"

They smiled at her, Simeon walking close to her. "Like it, domina?"

Kyle watched a bit uneasily how close he stood to her, and she stroked his arm. "Yes, pet... I love it." Her eyes drifted to Kyle. "Thank you. I think Simeon needs a teacher."

He shifted at her tone but cleared his throat. "Sure, domina..."

Simeon skipped to him. "Let's go and wash. Dinner needs to be served."

He took him to the slave's bath, a small room with a small pool. He stripped, utterly shameless, and Kyle followed him.

They washed, and Simeon eyed him. "You have a nice body."

Kyle blushed. "Thanks... I guess."

He laughed. "Domina likes you already. Will you sleep with us?"

Kyle froze, his eyes wide. "What...?"

Simeon didn't notice, too busy washing his hair. "Yes, you know, as in her bed?"

He winked at him and Kyle swayed, vaguely dizzy. "I... I don't think so...", he moaned and tried to shut the pictures out of his mind.

Simeon walked up to him, patting his back. "Too fresh? You're new. I forgot you just arrived this morning." He grinned, and they went to serve dinner.

Kyle went straight to his room when it was time to retire, his heart heavy, his body thankfully exhausted, but the new place didn't bring any sleep and his aching heart didn't help either. He hugged his blanket tight, his tears flowing, his throbbing cheekbone reminding him of Marius. He cried himself to sleep eventually, the moon softly shining through the small window.

Marius looked at that large moon overlooking the terrace, its shape swaying. He was so drunk he could not move, so he just lay on his couch, shivering in the spring night, his tears spilling down his cheeks.

He chuckled, taking a large swig straight from the jug, his face dark, his blue eyes unfocused pools of sadness. "I miss you so much, pet... please don't hate me..."

His whisper flew into the night, the moon's face mocking him, and he threw the empty jug at it, the clay shuttering on the white marble.

I should go to bed... He tried to turn around but failed, his eyes drifting back to the moon... *I'll just sleep here then...*

But sleep would not come in the cold night and he steeled himself and got up, going to his room, staggering, barely making it to the bed. He collapsed on it, face down, Kyle's scent invading his senses and he clutched at the pillows, soaking in his smell. He could almost taste him on his tongue, and he cried, his face buried in the sheets.

XIII

S everal weeks had passed since that day when Kyle had moved out and Marius could not go to Clavius' house, his family still doubtful, the city full of spies and Seraphina being her usual demanding self.

Marius busied himself with his child then, the little girl growing despite her mother still struggling to bond with her. He loved her and filled his emptiness with spending time with her, cradling her. Marius also went to the market with Sixtus to replace Kyle, and he left it to the old man to choose a gentle, middle-aged slave with a simple peasant mind somebody had named Paulus. He worked hard and made small wooden toys for the children, making them laugh. Marius buried himself into work too, but his eyes had grown dull, that fiery spark dead, his face dark under his black hair.

Kyle had adjusted well and Clavius and Tertullia had to admit he was a rare treasure. He had transformed their garden and kept the house sparkling. They had repainted with Simeon and cleaned the kitchen, earning an enormous bowl of broth and sloppy kisses from Tabia. They had not talked again about Kyle joining Simeon and Tertullia in bed, but he knew he was spending some nights with her when Clavius was out on his errands. He knew, of course, and couldn't care less. But Clavius and Tertullia could also see how Kyle was fading away, his torn heart bleeding him dry, his grey eyes shining dully with that melancholic look on his face.

One day, Clavius walked up to Kyle, smiling. "I'm going to meet my huge brooding friend... any message for him?"

Kyle blanched, his heart clenching. He squared his jaw, though, closing his eyes. "No."

Clavius clasped his shoulder. "Kyle... don't torture yourself."

The young man just turned and left him, his eyes burning.

They met on the training grounds, Marius buckling his leather armor, waiting for him, his eyes asking.

Clavius smiled, tense. "So, let's start this little training before our fat flows out."

Marius laughed softly. "What fat?"

Clavius noticed that indeed he did not have an ounce of excess fat, if anything, he was leaner... He shrugged. "You lost weight. That doesn't count. I have an African cook."

Marius swirled his gladius, looking at him. "Too bad for you."

But his banter was forced, and Clavius walked up to him, clasping his shoulder. "I'm sorry, but I have nothing for you..."

He nodded, grim, and his shoulders sagged.

Clavius searched his eyes. "Give him more time... he's still hurting..."

Marius sighed. "Me too... every fucking day... tell him I love him. Just tell him. I don't care if he hates me..." His voice choked, and he pushed his helmet on his head, gesturing to him. "Come on, fat boy, show me what you're made of."

But a couple of weeks later, Marius had been due for dinner at Clavius' house, and he was waiting in the small garden, noticing how tidy it was. The old slave had led him there and had asked him to wait, the masters being busy dressing. Marius frowned as he was not early, but waited anyway, silently fuming. He had given up meeting Kyle, his mind trying to blank him out of existence, but he was in a miserable state, his nerves eating at his body. He had lost weight again, and he felt his tunic too loose. Marius didn't care though, leaning against a small cherry tree, his eyes on the flowers in the leaves.

Kyle walked in, carrying a tray with drinks, not knowing whom the guest was he had to serve, and he froze, seeing him standing there like a ghost. Their eyes locked, and the tray cluttered to the floor, the jug and cups shattering. Kyle stood there, heaving, in shock, ready to fly, and Marius didn't dare move, his eyes silently pleading him. Kyle noticed how gaunt he had become, the dark shadows on his face, those blue eyes drowning in sorrow. Marius' lips parted, and he sighed, lowering his head, defeated, and Kyle's heart lurched in his throat.

He rushed to him, knocking Marius against the tree, his hands fisting his black hair, pulling his head back, slamming his mouth on his mouth, feeling how cold his lips were. Kyle pushed his mouth open with his jaw, pushing his tongue in, Marius' taste invading him, his love mingling with his anger at him, his teeth bruising the tender flesh of his lips. He pushed against him, not letting him breathe, pinning him against the tree, tearing at his hair and Marius whimpered, crying softly from relief and pain.

His arms went around Kyle's waist, but he didn't try to take over. Marius let Kyle eat him up, just feeling his body against him, his teeth and lips bruising him, choking the air out of his lungs. Marius would not push him away though, and Kyle sensed it, feeling him fight for air. He broke the kiss, heaving, his hands not letting go of his hair, his body crushing him into the tree's hard bark. He looked up into his tortured blue eyes, his lips red from his teeth, panting.

Kyle tugged at his hair; his grey eyes filled with wrath. "I am still fucking pissed at you..."

Marius nodded, dazed. "I know..." His arms fell to his sides, his whole body relaxing, giving in to him, and Kyle watched him, mildly thrilled, not seeing his usual sarcastic, superior smile.

His grey eyes turned darker and Marius waited, his breath caught, a soft moan escaping his mouth when Kyle twisted his fist in his hair. "You'd deserve so much more pain..."

He panted, his eyes darkening. "Yes... I am so sorry, pet..." Kyle closed his eyes at his pleading and Marius thought he had lost him again. Without thinking, he sank to his knees, and Kyle's eyes flew open, his hand still in his hair, looking down into his blue eyes. "I am sorry..."

Kyle breathed. "Are you begging?"

Marius nodded; his lips parted. "Yes... please forgive me."

Kyle knelt in front of him, mildly dazed, his hand unfurling in his hair, caressing the pain away. He kissed him deep, his hands on the back of his head and on his neck, his tongue warmly stroking his mouth, his tongue, his teeth. "I forgive you..." Marius cried softly, and Kyle cradled his face, kissing his tears away, shutting his eyes to the unbearable pain of seeing him so vulnerable, on the ground. He got up, pulling him up, his eyes dark with lust, whispering against Marius' mouth. "Masters should not kneel..."

"I'd do anything for you..."

Kyle smiled. "Watch what you're asking for..." He took his hands, slowly pulling him to his room.

They barely fit, Marius' huge frame filling that tiny room, but he didn't mind, his hands trembling as he held himself back, letting Kyle lead their dance, and the slave peeled their tunics off, all the while looking into his eyes.

Marius felt it, how fragile this was, and he had to close his eyes when Kyle's hand grazed his erection, his breath shuddering. "Look at me." His eyes flew open and Kyle smiled thinly. "Don't close your eyes... I want to see you..." Kyle could barely contain himself either, fighting the urge to surrender to Marius or continue toying with him.

Marius swallowed, sinking to his knees again, his eyes not leaving Kyle's, his lips parting. Kyle's breathed hitched when he took him in his mouth and he swayed, Marius' hands cupping his bottom, kneading the flesh. Kyle moaned, letting him suck him, their moans filling the room, and he pulled out, not wanting to lose it. He shoved Marius on the shoulders, and he crawled on the narrow bed, Kyle climbing between his thighs, swallowing his cock whole. His back arched, and he growled, not daring to touch Kyle's head.

Kyle watched him writhe and moan, bringing him close and then pulling off, kissing him wide. "Not yet..."

Marius sighed but waited, panting. Kyle straddled him and lowered himself on him, pushing in his rock-hard cock coated in his saliva. Marius eyes rolled back as he rode him, pushing him in to the hilt, grinding his hips.

Kyle leant over him, cupping his jaw. "Look at me..."

Their eyes locked, and he rode him hard, both panting and moaning, their eyes wide open, Kyle's arms braced on his shoulders as he pushed back, fucking him back with the same force.

Kyle kissed him, his tongue pushing in. "Come for me..." Marius lost it at that moment, coming deep inside of him, feeling Kyle's warm cum coat their abs. Kyle scooped a good dose up, licking it off his fingers, leaning down to kiss him, making him taste him, pushing his juice into Marius' mouth, still trapped under his body, not breaking the kiss until he'd swallowed it all. Marius was drenched, dizzy, madly in love, but he stayed quiet, the words on his tongue.

Kyle watched him, mildly amused. "Such a good little cum slut."

Marius' eyes gleamed, mildly shocked. "That's not a way to address your dominus..."

Kyle smirked, his eyes not giving anything away. "You're not my dominus."

"Ouch..."

Marius barely breathed, sliding out of him, the slave still straddling him, his arms folded on his chest. "Do you love me, Marius?"

He breathed, almost whispering. "Yes, I do. I love you..."

"Good boy..." Marius closed his eyes and let Kyle's tongue roam his body.

Clavius and Tertullia were waiting in the dining room, nibbling on some snacks. They had noticed earlier that Marius had disappeared from the garden and Tertullia was thrilled that her plan had worked.

Clavius looked at her. "Where are they?"

She smiled. "It's not like they have too much choice? Probably in Kyle's room."

Clavius scoffed. "Marius is sleeping in the slaves' quarters? I'll tease him until his deathbed."

He laughed, and his wife toasted him. "I do hope that they're not sleeping, dear. I do hope they're at it like rabbits."

Clavius grinned and drank with her, watching still with awe, her eyes shining with mischief, her dimpled cheeks framed by her bouncy curls. "You are a good woman, Tertullia."

She waved him off, chuckling. "Don't flatter me, you wild boar." But her cheeks were flushed, and she secretly loved him to bits in her heart.

They lay in each other's arms, the bed so narrow that Kyle had to lie almost on top of Marius, wedged against the wall. He propped himself up, gently tracing lazy patterns on Marius' skin. "You need to go for dinner."

Marius sighed, his eyes clouding over. "I know...", but he didn't move, the silence thick between them, his eyes roaming the room, the bare, cracked walls, the bed's hard wood digging into his back through the thin mattress. He shifted, his arm numb under Kyle's weight. "How can you sleep on this?"

Kyle smiled. "It's better than the floor."

Marius moaned. "I should just keep my mouth shut."

Kyle looked at him, his grey eyes calm. "Yes, you should sometimes."

"Are you still mad at me?"

He mused, tracing his collarbone, sending shivers down Marius' spine. "Not that much... I get why you did it... but it still hurts. I don't think you fully understand what it means to a slave to belong to his master... and I love you, it makes it all the more painful." Marius' heart raced at his words, but he was still unsure whether he had not pushed him too far. Kyle pushed himself off him, getting up and he pulled him up too. "Let's get dressed. You shouldn't make them wait too long."

He reluctantly obeyed, and Kyle tied his belt, trailing his hand down to his waist. "You've lost a lot of weight." His eyes watched him, playful. "I prefer you with more flesh."

He had to smile at his allusion. "I'll eat more, I promise."

"Great..."—he opened the door, gesturing him out — "Start now? You know the way..."

Marius stopped, hesitating. "You're not coming?"

Kyle pursed his lips. "Somebody has to serve the food?" Marius' face fell and Kyle stepped to him, lacing his arms around his neck. "I know you don't want to leave me but you don't belong here..." The narrow, dim corridor served a range of doors, the ceiling so low that Marius could almost reach it. Kyle brushed his lips against his. "Go upstairs. I'll be there soon."

He nodded, his throat choked, and Kyle let him go, gently shoving him.

Marius walked upstairs, his mind fogged, but his heart beating warmly again, and Clavius rose to greet him, clasping his back. "Come here, big boy! I hope you managed to 'talk' through your issues with your love boy?"

He wiggled his eyebrows, and Marius blushed slightly.

Tertullia gestured for him to lie down. "Come, Marius, don't listen to this brute. He has no manners."

"What have I said wrong?"

Tertullia just waved him off, Simeon handing a large cup of wine to Marius, curiously eyeing him. "Simeon, be a dear pet, go and help Kyle bring up the food." He left quickly, and she turned to Marius, apologetic. "Simeon has no proper manners; he is a Greek peasant boy. He will stare at you, utterly unashamed."

Clavius laughed. "He's only good at looking good and frolicking in the sheets." Marius' eyes grew wide and Clavius scoffed. "Not with me, dimwit, with my excellent wife here."

Tertullia blushed slightly, but her eyes shone. "Well, there's no harm in having a bit of fun, especially when you're away and I'm all lonely."

"Cheers, my dear."

They toasted and Marius shifted, not wanting to comment.

Fortunately, Kyle and Simeon brought the food and they busied themselves serving them, Kyle piling a huge amount on Marius' plate. He watched him do it, a small smile on his lips, and Clavius eagerly rubbed his hands.

"Let's dig in... my good Tabia has worked wonders again."

The food was indeed divine, and they ate heartily, all the while making small talk, Marius telling them about the baby, how she was growing and lighting up their days.

Tertullia carefully wiped her mouth whilst the slaves cleared the table and brought up dessert. "And your wife?"

Marius' face went grim. "She is better now with her... I think she got over it, that she didn't have a boy." He quieted, not wanting to tell them anything about the nightmare he was living with her, not with Kyle kneeling behind them.

Her eyes flew to Clavius, but she didn't comment, knowing how fragile Marius was. At *least, he has eaten... that's a start.*

They nibbled some fruits and Clavius turned to him. "I heard rumors of barbarian rebels giving some grief to our troops up north?"

Marius nodded. "Yes, I've heard it too... random attacks on patrols, but they don't come close to the forts for now."

"What does your imperial uncle say?"

Marius shrugged. "He's fuming, but for now, he wants the generals there to deal with the situation."

"For now?"

"Yes..."

Their eyes locked, and Tertullia blanched. "You're not going to be sent there... are you?"

Marius didn't comment, knowing what she meant, that Clavius was close to retirement. Going to supervise roadworks on peaceful territory was not the same as going to try and tame rebel barbarians.

Clavius sighed. "Just our fucking luck..."

Marius tried to sound light. "Hey... he hasn't said anything yet. He might also send somebody else..."

Clavius pursed his lips, downing his wine. "Thanks, but I'm not buying your bullshit. You know it as much as I do that you're his favorite."

There was nothing much left to say, and Marius rose reluctantly. "I have to go. Thank you for this lovely dinner." His eyes shone, and he kissed Tertullia's hand, their eyes locking.

She patted his hand. "I'm glad you enjoyed it. Come back soon? Kyle, be a dear and escort our good guest out."

He rose and Marius followed him to the entrance, his heart already in pieces, when Kyle turned around and pulled him into a deep kiss, pouring all his love and grief into it. They hugged then and Kyle steeled himself to let him go, holding the door open. They couldn't speak and he watched him leave, leaning against the door to close it, his chest heaving.

They didn't have to wait too long for the emperor's missive and Clavius was packing, fuming. "I knew it... bastard!"

Tertullia watched him, her heart in her throat, but she was trying to sound reassuring. "Come, come... it will be over fast. You're not going alone."

He shot her a look. "Why, thank you, wife, I know... but it is still bloody tricky." He sighed, stopping to think. "I don't want to die in a northern shithole, choking on my own blood... not when technically I should be enjoying my retirement."

She walked over to him and pulled him into her arms. "I know, dear... but you won't die, you're a tough little boar."

"Yeah... sure..." His eyes darted to the slaves, packing his clothes. "Kyle! Pack your stuff, I'm taking you with me."

They all froze, and Tertullia grabbed his arm. "What? You're not serious."

"Of course I am. I'll need a sturdy slave there..."—his lips curled into a mischievous smile — "And so does my brooding general."

Tertullia understood then, and she turned to Kyle. "You heard the man... pack up, pup."

He left in a hurry, his mind numb. They were leaving Rome for the northern borders, unknown dangers lurking in those hostile lands... and Marius... he hadn't seen him for three weeks...

They left the next day, very early, the sun barely rising, and Clavius rode next to his cart, Kyle silently sitting on the bench, driving the mules.

Clavius spoke to him, his face grim under his crested helmet. "You know why I'm taking you with me?"

"You need me, dominus?"

Clavius pursed his lips. "You are very useful, don't be mistaken on that, but I need you to first and foremost take care of Marius. He can't be efficient with his bleeding heart, and we all need him to be sharp and ready. Our lives are at stake..." Kyle nodded, a warm feeling invading him, but Clavius was cautious, eyeing his blank face. "Understood?"

"Yes, dominus."

"That's my boy!"

A small smile played on Clavius' face as he thought about the document in his satchel stacked on the cart.

Marius was supervising the last preparations at the barracks, a young recruit holding his horse, the nervous animal chewing on his bit.

At last, Clavius arrived, and he looked down at him. "Not on your horse, general?"

"I was waiting for you." His voice was clipped and Clavius noticed the dark circles under his eyes, his face drawn, pale under his helmet. Clavius hadn't seen him since that dinner, too busy with court matters, and his worried eyes flew to Marius' hands, shaking as he read a last missive from the emperor. He tucked it in his saddlebag and got on his horse, the black stallion pawing the ground.

They were riding with several centuries and all the carts were lined in the back, so Marius could not see Kyle, and Clavius held his mouth, not wanting to deconcentrate him. He went to shout orders, and Marius took the lead, at least two long weeks of journey lying ahead. Still, he didn't mind, mercifully away from Seraphina and that miserable existence without his lover. He only regretted leaving the child behind, not knowing when he could hold her again, this little bundle of joy which meant everything to him.

Fortunately, the children loved her and played with her a lot, babysitting her, her senses awakening, and Seraphina let them, not interested anymore in her daughter, leaving her to the slaves. She had insisted that he bedded her before he left, but Marius had refused, pushing her into a fit of rage. He had retired to his room then, drinking himself into oblivion.

He shook his head, leaving Rome, the streets still quiet in the early dawn. They had to keep a good pace and he could already hear Clavius riding down their lines, scolding. Marius smiled, but he was worried for his friend, knowing full well the dangers lying ahead. The barbarians had managed to kill the general at one of the forts and that was where they were headed now, for gods knew how long. His bitter thoughts flew back to Rome, to Kyle, wondering what he was doing. *I couldn't even say goodbye, love...*

They set camp for the night, the men settling, guards taking their places, although there was nothing to fear here.

Marius was tired, his nerves frayed, and he examined the maps of their journey in his tent, carefully tracing the roads. His armor weighed a ton on his exhausted body, but he didn't care.

Camp slaves carried in a bathtub and started filling it with hot water when Clavius walked in. "My butt is sore from all this riding."

Marius smiled, not lifting his head. "I missed you and your whining."

"Ha! Well, you will be happy to have me now for months, until we smoke out those shitheads from their accursed woods. Anyway... why do you still have your armor on?"

Marius shrugged. "I was busy..." He gestured a slave over from the bathtub and the slave unbuckled his straps, taking it off, helping him out of his leather tunic.

He let him do it and Clavius' face fell when he saw Marius' linen tunic loose around his gaunt frame. "Marius... what the fuck..."

He shrugged, his eyes dull. "It's no big deal..."

"You're wasting away."

He sighed, determined not to give in to his emotions, his voice soft. "You're not helping..."

"Oh... maybe I can help, actually... I have something for you."

Marius pursed his lips and waited; his arms folded.

Clavius walked up to him, putting his hand on his shoulder. "I wanted to surprise you when we arrived but, looking at you, I think this is a better time if I want you to make it there alive." He walked to the tent's entrance and folded the lapel back. "Come in."

Kyle pushed past him and stopped short, his eyes on Marius.

The Roman's face fell, his lips parting in shock, his voice a breath. "Kyle?"

Marius could not believe it, blinking, fear invading him he might be hallucinating but Kyle walked to him and cupped his face. "Yes..."

His hands on his skin made Marius swoon, and he grabbed his shoulders not to fall, Kyle's arms going around him, alarmed at how much weight he'd lost again. They hugged, Marius closing his eyes in shock.

Finally, they parted, Marius looking at Clavius, clenching Kyle's hand. "I... I don't know what to say..."

"Then shut up." He took a scroll out of his tunic. "Here. This is also for you."

Marius raised his eyebrows. "A letter?"

"Just open it, you giant twithead."

He unfurled it and read the lines written in neat black ink and his eyes closed, his hands trembling, looking at him. "This is for real?"

"Yes, twat. I'm gifting your precious one back to you. We had a deal, or so I seem to remember."

Marius couldn't speak, and Kyle went to his knees, whispering. "Thank you, dominus..."

"My pleasure. Now, enough of this nonsense, boys. We are up early tomorrow. See you fresh and ready at dawn's early lights."

Marius stepped to him, his voice almost gone. "Clavius, I...."

Clavius grabbed his shoulders. "Save it and do me a favor: fuck that depressed, drowning- in-sorrow look off your face and feed properly. You can't ride into that fort looking like your own grandfather."

He left before Marius could react and he turned to Kyle, kneeling next to him, pulling him into a kiss. They tumbled on the carpeted floor of the tent, their mouths wide open, panting, Marius crushing Kyle against his chest and the young man sobbed, his tears flowing down Marius' neck.

They stayed there for a while, just hugging, crying softly, then Kyle sat up, pulling him up. "Come..."

Kyle pulled him to the bath and peeled his tunic off, pushing him into the tub. He left then to get more hot water and came back with two full buckets, carefully emptying them in the tub. Kyle stripped and climbed in behind Marius, soaping his back, washing his hair.

He was much leaner, and Kyle spoke softly, gently tugging at his mane. "You promised you would eat..."

"I am sorry... I tried..."

He didn't comment and climbed in front of him, facing him, kneeling, rubbing the soap on his abs, his eyes meeting his eyes, his hands gliding to Marius' cock, making him lean his head back and moan.

Kyle's lips pursed. "Let's eat first."

Marius looked at him, his eyes wide. "Are you serious?"

"Yes, come." He helped him out and threw a sheet on him, walking to the low table where the slaves had laid out the food, some meat and bread with fruits.

Kyle watered the wine up and offered Marius a cup, making him sit and he watched him eat, his grey eyes shining when he stopped. "More."

Marius shook his head. "I can't."

"You promised..."

Kyle got up and stood above him, picking up a piece of meat from the plate and pushing it in his mouth, his finger lingering on the roof of his mouth. Marius' blue eyes sparkled, but he didn't push him away, and Kyle fed him slowly, his finger teasing him until a point where Marius could not take it anymore and he suddenly got up, grabbing his wrist, his eyes dark with desire.

"You're such a tease, pet..." He kissed him hard and Kyle mewled, melting into his mouth.

Marius pulled him to the bed, almost throwing him on it, and Kyle pretended to resist him, trying to free his hands from his grasp.

Marius pinned him down, both wrists shoved into the mattress, and looked into Kyle's eyes, full of defiance, a small smile on his lips. "You're mine, pet, stop fighting..." Kyle tugged again at his hands, arching his back, trying to push him off, knowing full well he was working him up, that sad misery gone from his face as his dominant side took over, his eyes shining. "You're disobeying me?"

Kyle just shot back. "Get off me!"

He laughed. "No!" He pinned his arms above his head, holding them in an iron grip with one hand and the other grazed Kyle's lips. "Disobedient little pets get what they deserve..."

Kyle's eyes darkened at his words, and Marius grazed his fingers along his jawline. "Open your mouth..." He obeyed, his lips parting, and Marius pushed two fingers in, deep, making him almost choke, sliding them in and out. "Good boy..."

Kyle sucked them, saliva dripping from his mouth in a thin stream, the taste of Marius' skin making his mouth water.

Marius pulled his fingers out then and pushed them deep inside of Kyle, making him cry out and writhe under him as he fucked him hard, kissing his cries away. "Turn around..."

He let his hands go and watched him get on all fours. Kyle knew this was going to hurt, but he didn't care, whimpering when he felt Marius leave the bed to walk to the bathtub. He picked up the bottle of oil and went back to him, caressing his back and sides, pouring the oil on Kyle's hole and down his shaft, slowly pushing in.

Kyle pushed back on him, moaning hard when he bottomed out, and Marius closed his eyes, his chest heaving. "Oh, gods... Kyle..."

"Fuck me... please..."

Marius drew out, slowly pushing back in, picking up the pace gradually to let him adjust, thrusting harder when he heard him moan and cry out, his own pleasure building, gripping Kyle's hips tight.

They came together, collapsing on the bed, Marius pulling him close, dizzy, out of breath. "I love you... I'll never let you go again..."

Kyle's eyes closed, and he clung to him, burying his face into Marius' side, into his scent. They fell asleep, their skins glowing.

XIV

They drifted in and out of sleep in that dark night, groping for each other, for the other's warmth.

Marius woke shortly before dawn, looking at Kyle sleep in his arms and his chest swelled. There was no way he would let him go again, not ever, and the prospect of being on a mission with Kyle thrilled him, far from Rome, his wife, and his meddling family, even if it was dangerous. The camp stirred around them, men groaning, their sleep parched throats making them cough.

Marius stirred, and Kyle's eyes flew open, for a moment not even believing he was next to him.

Marius smiled and kissed him, his voice full of regret. "Time to get going."

"Already?"

"That's military life for you."

Kyle rose then, quickly dressing. "I'll get your breakfast."

Marius pulled a face, the air too cold in the tent after the warmth of the sheets. "I'm not hungry..."

"Yes, you are."

He could not object as Kyle had already left, so he dressed, waiting for him to put on his armor. He took a large swig of water, feeling already better, but the past months had worn him out, and he sat, vaguely dizzy. He had drunk too much too, and it had been taking its toll.

Kyle came back quickly, carrying a basket of food, bread, honey, and some dates, which he laid out on the small table. "Eat."

Marius' lips curled up. "Bossing me around?"

He kneeled next to him, looking up into his eyes. "Your breakfast is served, dominus."

"Are you playing with me? Why are you kneeling?"

But Kyle didn't comment, and Marius sighed, playing along, and he ate and fed him at the same time, like in the old days. Each time he'd push food into Kyle's mouth, he had to lick his fingers, which led him to eating more, and before he'd realized it, he'd cleared the table.

Kyle rose then and helped him put on his armor, buckling the straps tight.

Marius watched him, feeling so full he thought he'd be sick. "I'll pay you back for this breakfast..."

Kyle just smiled mockingly at him, playfully wiping a crumb off his lip. "Yes? I can hardly wait."

Marius' eyes darkened, but then Clavius stormed in. "Oh... am I interrupting?"

Kyle left him, smiling, and started packing. Marius turned to Clavius. "No..."

"Good! Let's go and have a meeting before we set off."

He eyed Marius as they walked through the still dark camp, Marius' strides a bit more secure, his face a bit less pasty. "Had a good night?"

His lips curled into a smile. "You can say that, yes." He stopped, and Clavius turned to him. "Clavius... I..."

"Shut it, I don't need your pathetic thanking. Just make sure we survive this shit." He grinned and strode off, Marius following.

They marched all next day and set the camp up again for the night.

Marius turned to Clavius in front of his tent. "Dine with me tonight?"

"Don't you want some privacy?"

Marius smiled. "I'll have that later. Just come and eat with us."

"Sure, sure... let me shed my armor and I'm all yours."

Kyle was already in his tent, waiting for him, rearranging the last bits of furniture.

He turned when Marius entered and walked to him to take off his armor. "Your bath is ready."

"Great..." He felt drained, his body screaming from hours of riding. Truth was he had neglected his training during weeks, let alone riding his horse. Marius lowered himself into the tub and hissed at the scalding water. "You want to burn my skin off?" Kyle didn't comment and handed a cup to him. He drank deeply and grimaced. "Water?"

The slave raised his eyebrows. "You'd prefer that awful beverage your soldiers drink?"

Marius laughed. "It's called posca and is quite potent."

Kyle shrugged. "Do you want some?"

"How about wine?"

"I don't think you should drink wine."

They looked at each other, and Kyle's heart beat faster, but he kept his face still.

"I don't think that's your decision to make." Marius' voice was clipped, on the verge of anger, but Kyle didn't want to give up.

"You will get drunk...." He walked closer to him and pushed him forward, starting to soap his back, his hands gliding on his muscles. "... and you're not nice when you're drunk..."

Marius closed his eyes, his anger dwindling. "I won't get drunk...", but he was not sure, knowing how much he'd drunk the last couple of months.

Kyle leant down to run his tongue along his neck. "... and if you get drunk, you can't make me pay for breakfast..."

Marius moaned, reaching up to pull him in the tub when Clavius entered. "I'm here! Haul your ass out of the tub, Commander, and let's eat!"

Kyle helped him out and disappeared to get their dinner, Marius slipping on a light tunic.

Clavius shook his head. "You look like shit..."

"Thanks..."

"Anytime. So, what are we drinking?"

Marius sat down, and Kyle came back, setting their food on the table.

Marius pursed his lips. "Apparently, I'm off wine, so you have the choice between water or posca."

Clavius raised his eyebrows. "Off wine? That's a first for you."

He shrugged, but his eyes were following Kyle. "Let's drink then some of that potent little posca". Kyle pulled a face but served it anyway, and they toasted. "To our gruesome fucking march."

Clavius dug into the food and sighed. "I will miss Tabia's cooking..."

"It will do good to your growing belly."

"Hey!" They laughed and Clavius noticed, relieved, that Marius was in a better mood, his face smoother, but still just a shadow of his former self. Clavius mused, drinking. "Hey, remember when you were just a new recruit? First time we met?"

"Yes... you were bossing everybody around."

"And you were an arrogant patrician prick. I could have torn your throat out. Come to think of it, you still are."

They spent the rest of the dinner mildly teasing each other and remembering the old days, Kyle wordlessly changing the plates, making sure that Marius ate as much as he could, pushing the food in front of him whilst he talked.

Clavius left then, and Marius sat in silence, swirling his drink. He didn't feel the usual fog that he had felt during his wine induced meals when he had drunk between each bite to force the food down whilst Seraphina had been spewing venom. Thankful, he reached for Kyle's hand when he walked past. "Are you done?"

He nodded, and Marius rose, pulling him into a kiss.

Kyle grimaced. "That drink is still in your mouth..."

"So?"—Marius made him kiss him again, wide — "That's your punishment for not serving me wine..."

Kyle smirked, gently pushing at his chest. "I don't like wine either..."

"Oh... so what do you like, my little, picky pet?"

Kyle wordlessly sank to his knees and took him in his mouth, running his tongue down his length, taking him in deep, all the way. Marius moaned, his hands going to his head, his fingers gently gripping his hair. He started thrusting slowly, Kyle matching his moves, pushing in deeper. His gag reflex had long been gone and he let Marius fuck his mouth, relishing in his taste. Kyle felt him tense, his moves faster, erratic, and he took him in deep, holding him tight by his hips, feeling his warm cream spurt out in waves. He swallowed it as it ran down his throat, licking him dry. He pulled off, slightly out of breath, his eyes dark, and looked at him, licking his lips. Marius pulled him up with shaking hands and kissed him wide, his own taste invading his mouth.

He moaned, and Kyle pulled back. "Delicious, isn't it?"

Marius hugged him tight, laughing, vaguely embarrassed, but thrilled at the same time.

The same routine continued for weeks, the air crisper, pine forests everywhere, and the soldiers marched nervously among the huge trees dripping water as rain had been falling for days, making their march a mild torture. So many places for the enemy to hide, even if those rebel troops had been spotted further up. They were on edge, their eyes darting towards the trees, the depth of the forest.

Marius rode in the front, his cloak soaked, the rain finding a way in through his armor, soaking his clothes and body. His horse was drenched too, gentle whisps of vapor seeping from the animal's coat. *Fuck this shit...* He could hardly wait to arrive, knowing they were thankfully close, possibly arriving before sunset. He was determined to push forward, even if the roads were muddy here, the men slipping, struggling to maintain their balance with their heavy loads.

Marius had regained his strength though, his mind cleared from days and nights of drinking for months, as Kyle had steadfastly forbidden him to drink anything stronger than posca, which he had mastered to flavor differently, despite his own revulsion for the drink. Marius had also gained weight, the endless hours of riding building his muscles, his meals being soaked up by his hungry flesh. His eyes shone with a new light, nights spent in his lover's arms, carefree, far from their enemies in Rome and his bloodsucking wife.

His eyes drifted to Clavius, who had ridden up to him, his white horse's flanks spattered with mud. "Fucked up shithole of a mud-shit northern country... Are we stopping to set camp?"

"No, we're pushing ahead. I want to be at the fort."

"Yeah, makes sense... these woods are giving me the creeps... the men are on edge too."

Marius nodded. "All the more important we're safe tonight. How's the back doing?"

Clavius spat, fed up with the rain. "They are struggling. The carts are getting stuck all the time. Shitty mud. I can't believe these savages can live here in this dirt hole."

They rode then in silence, the light dimming, and Marius thankfully saw the clearing with the fort in the misty dusk. Clavius turned his horse and rode down their line, the horns blowing, and the fort answered.

Marius stood in front of the gate, announcing his titles, and they opened the gates wide, the men marching in, impatient. Clavius went to settle them and Marius joined the officers in charge, the men grim.

"Greetings, Commander, I am Julius Septus Quintus, centurion in charge since the death of our general."

"Greetings, Julius. How are things?"

The men looked at each other, and Julius cleared his throat. "We have a bit of an unrest amongst our men. Hopefully, this will cease with your arrival."

Marius shot him a look but decided not to comment. "And the rebels?"

"They've been quiet lately. We have a couple of villages nearby, but the inhabitants keep away. We don't know for sure if they are in contact with the rebels."

"Fine. We'll convene tomorrow morning to address the troops. I want everybody in the main yard, ready, at dawn. Centurion Clavius is in charge now as second in command." The other centurions mumbled, but Marius silenced them. "There's no room for unruly behavior, not from your men, and not from you." His blue eyes bore into them and they fell silent, saluting and leaving.

Julius turned to him. "Your quarters are ready. There's a small bath linked to it. Do you need a slave?"

Marius shook his head. "I have my personal slave with me... somewhere..." He wondered where Kyle was, vaguely anxious. Julius nodded and shifted on his feet, the younger man embarrassed, smoothing his blonde hair back, and Marius raised his eyebrows. "What is it?"

"Our Commander had a whore... a personal one... so I mean... would you like to have her?"

Marius just stood, blinking. "What? No. No, I don't need her. Who is she?"

"She got offered to him a year ago by one of the village leaders, she's his daughter, actually. You know, to seal the peace."

Marius turned to him. "You've just said she is a whore."

Julius shrugged. "Well, she is one now."

Fucking perfect.... Marius sighed, pondering. "Would her family take her back?"

"I highly doubt it. They know what's going on between these walls. I mean, we have more of them..."

Julius shut up, a bit anxious at seeing him so concerned, and Marius steeled his face. "Fine. Just keep her with the others. I don't need her."

Julius nodded when the door opened and Clavius strode in, followed by Kyle. He was so covered in mud that Marius had a hard time recognizing the slave.

Clavius pestered. "Those damned carts... they had to be pulled out again... but they're finally here..."

Kyle breathed quietly, his whole body trembling from the effort, a thin stream of blood flowing down his arm, blending into the dark mud. He could not feel the wound, covered in mud, chilled to the bone by the icy rain.

Marius spoke to Julius, walking to Kyle. "Take me to my room."

Kyle and Clavius followed him, and Julius left them alone. He closed the door and Kyle collapsed on the floor, his head dizzy, the pain flowing down his arm.

Marius kneeled down, concerned. "What's wrong?"

Kyle's eyes flew to his shaking arm, the adrenaline rush dying down, the pain biting into his flesh.

Clavius noticed the wound first. "He's hurt... look."

Blood was oozing through the muddy paste on Kyle's arm, the clay-like earth dark red, gently trickling down to his fingers, spattering on the floor.

"Fuck..." Marius helped Kyle up, pulling him to the small bath. He sat him down, taking his clothes off, Kyle numb, shaking. "Come on, pet, in you go."

He slid him in the hot pool, Kyle's head resting on the side, his eyes closed. Marius and Clavius took their armors off, helping each other, and went into the pool, Marius pulling Kyle against him, washing the mud off his arm, his face. Blood flowed softly, swirling in the steaming water. It was heaven after that drenched icy ride, just to lie there. Kyle came out of the haze, the pain bearable. He looked at his wound, a large cut on his arm, less vicious though than what he'd thought. Something had cut it whilst he had been struggling to free the cart.

Kyle relaxed in Marius' broad arms, his head laying on his chest, his eyes closed, and Marius just stroked him, grazing his knuckles on his face, his black hair falling into his eyes. Clavius watched them, warmed by how caring Marius looked, a side which he rarely showed, hiding behind that brooding, angry look most of the time.

Clavius washed his hair and climbed out, drying himself off. "I'll go and find some food in this shithole."

Marius looked up at him. "Find some salve and bandages too."

He nodded and left, leaving them alone.

Kyle opened his eyes and turned to face Marius, straddling him, his hands sliding to the back of his neck, stroking him, leaning into a deep kiss, their mouths parting slowly, their tongues meeting, swirling gently, tasting, sliding on their teeth.

Marius hands slid down Kyle's back, holding his hips. "Clavius will be back..."

"I know..."

They laughed softly and climbed out, drying each other off, their hands straying. Marius growled, his arms lacing around Kyle, pulling him close. "If you keep teasing me, I'll have to fuck you..."

He smirked, pushing him away. "Your friend will be back soon..."

Marius caught him from behind, biting down gently on his neck. "Yes... maybe he could join us?" Kyle stiffened and Marius swore gently to himself, hugging him tighter. "I'm sorry, pet, I didn't mean it..."

Kyle turned to face him, looking into his eyes. "You want to share me?"

Marius smiled, vaguely embarrassed. "No, it just slipped out... a joke? Forget it."

Kyle watched him carefully and kissed him lightly. "Your call."

Marius' face fell. "What...?"

"I wouldn't mind... if that's what you want."

He shook his head, grinning. "I don't think Clavius is into boys."

Kyle cocked his eyebrow. "Maybe he's never been with one."

"Oh, he has... early days..."

"So?"

"So nothing. You're mine."

He kissed him harder when Clavius came back.

"Gods... dress the fuck up!"

They slipped their tunics on and Kyle took the basket of food from him, setting the table. There was an awkward silence as Marius processed Kyle's words, looking at his friend. Clavius handed him the bandage and salve and Marius took care of Kyle's wound, gently wrapping it. Kyle poured watered wine for them, as there was nothing else, and Marius still pulled a slight face at the taste, drinking only out of thirst.

They ate heartily, though the food was cold, meat and some vegetables with a cold sauce, bread, olives, and fruit.

Clavius rose then, dead tired. "'m retiring to my room, it's close down the corridor. See you tomorrow. And don't spend the entire night fooling around. It's late already."

But he knew his words fell on deaf ears, seeing Marius' eyes fill with lust when he looked at Kyle, a small smile on his lips. The slave kneeled next to Marius' leg, his hand around his calf, his face pressed against his thigh and Marius watched Clavius, amused, his eyes gleaming. "Goodnight, my friend."

He scoffed. "It's gonna be a good night for you, that's for sure. Have fun!"

He left, and Marius looked down at Kyle. "What are you doing?" But Kyle just kissed his way up his body, pushing his tunic off, pushing him towards the bed. "Are you sure? You're hurt..." His words died when Kyle landed on top of him on the bed, pushing his tongue into his mouth.

They made love for hours, until, exhausted; they fell asleep in each other's arms.

Next morning, Marius watched silently the troops gathering, his helmet strapped tight on his head, a small smile on his lips.

Clavius looked up at him. "You have the smug look of somebody who's fucked all night."

Marius' eyes didn't leave the troops as he answered with a small smile. "I didn't fuck."

Clavius scoffed. "Yeah, right! So, what did you do?"

"I made love."

He addressed the troops in his usual stern tone, setting ground rules and expectations. The legionaries had expected some spoiled, patrician young man from Rome, and they listened, white-faced, to that tall man, his blue eyes piercing them.

The briefing was over, and they were sent to training. Marius and the officers joined them, spending most of the morning with the men.

In the meantime, Kyle busied himself with household tasks and baking bread. Fortunately, he had spent a lot of time in the kitchens and had learned to cook with Shayla and Tabia. This came in very handy now, and he decided to cook something for dinner.

He had taken some spices and ingredients from Tabia's kitchen and went to the supply rooms to get meat and vegetables. There were not a lot of slaves in the camp and he stood out a bit, the men eyeing him curiously. He also spent most of the day just walking around and getting to know the large camp, marveling at how the Romans were capable of building complete castles out of nothing.

The fort brought back unexpectedly painful memories of his capture though and his breathing quickened whilst cooking, his heart hammering in his chest, soldiers around him making their own meals, baking their bread. They were bantering and laughing, not paying too much attention to him, but they were close, and he had to brace himself against the stove, dizzy, trying to focus on the food rather than the men around him and their conversations inevitably drifting towards whores, captured women.

"Hey, I still remember that day when the general received that cute girl from the village chief?"

The other men laughed. "Yeah... she was something... didn't want to have anything to do with the boss..."

"Yeah, we had to hold her down..."

"... and suck her breasts whilst the general fucked her with his fingers... said she would love it, though she had no idea yet..."

They laughed. "Oh, yeah... she cried, but she got sooo wet..."

"Couldn't help it..."

"He fucked her hard. By the end, she wanted more!"

They howled and Kyle closed his eyes, his hands trembling as he stirred the pot, his vision blurring with tears... *Animals...* He could hardly wait to get out of there, listening to them relating their nights with camp whores and new recruits.

Finally, the food was ready, and Kyle packed the iron pot, bread, and fruits into his basket, turning to leave.

He came face to face with one of the soldiers, looking him over. "Who are you? I haven't seen you before."

One of the men turned to him. "You're a slave, right?"

Kyle nodded, frozen, the soldier too close, and he stepped back, waiting.

His lips curled into a small smile. "You're scared? What's your name, slave?"

He pushed the word out, his throat clutched. "Kyle..."

Another soldier looked up from his baking. "Oh, a Celt!"

There was laughter, and the soldier stepped closer. "Don't move... so, a Celt? What's a Celt doing here?"

"We love Celts, don't we?" Laughter again, and Kyle blanched, his memories flooding in.

The soldier mocked him. "Look at you... all white and trembling..."

Another soldier stepped next to him. "Hey, he's new, so he probably came with the general... we should leave him alone."

"Yeah, maybe..." A slight unease settled in the group and they cleared the way for him. "Off you go, slave boy."

Kyle hurried past them, carrying his basket, his legs barely holding him, his mind on that awful day when his life had been thrown upside down...

The smell of burning wood and flesh, screams of agony, the stench of blood, seeping into the slippery soil, crying, his father's glassed over eyes as they cut him open, his eyes on him, strong hands holding his shoulders, his voice gone in his throat from howling and screaming. Shut him the fuck up... A hand clasped over his mouth and he bit it, hard, the taste of blood invading his mouth. Howling. The hand torn away, a huge slap that sent him to the ground, dizzy, blood flowing into his eyes, his mouth full of dust. Yanked up again and dragged away, his legs kicking, fighting, shoved face down on a table they used for outdoor meals... Voices above him, two soldiers holding his hands down, his legs kicked apart, his pants cut open. He fought, his voice raw, almost gone... somebody slammed his head into the table and he felt his strength dwindle, swallowed by the blinding pain... through the haze a horse's prancing legs... tire him out, boys, you know how... laughter... a sharp, agonizing pain... somebody panting in his ear... you're so tight, boy, we'll fuck you for hours...

He stopped, unable to go further, and leaned against a wall, heaving, throwing up bile, his back drenched. His whole body trembled with the violence of his memories, and he cried softly, sitting against the wall, his head on his knees.

Marius and Clavius arrived back at his room in a good mood. They had trained hard with the men and had meetings then, discussing how they would proceed with the neighboring tribes and villages. Rebels were nowhere in sight and this mission started to look less threatening. They stepped in and Marius noticed, surprised, that the room was empty.

Clavius sat down, his eyebrows arched. "Your lover boy?"

"I have no idea... he probably left to get something to eat."

"Talking of which, I am starving..."

As on cue, Kyle entered and momentarily froze when he saw them, but then, he quickly composed himself and put the basket down to lay the table. Marius was too lost, replaying the various scenarios in his head, to notice how pale Kyle was, his hands slightly shaking.

"Maybe we should meet with the village leaders first?"

Clavius smiled, drinking a deep gulp of watered wine. "What a success it's going to be, especially now that one of them has his daughter working as a camp whore."

Marius shrugged. "She was the general's cherished favorite for a while, or so they say, decent first night and all the rest of it... I am not sure that's a bad thing?"

Kyle's head swooned at his words. *You have no idea...*

"Well, yes...in that case, maybe. It will not hurt, provided they cooperate..." Kyle served the food and Clavius sat up straighter. "Is this Tabia's cooking I smell? Boy, don't tell me you can cook like her..."

Marius smiled at Kyle. "Hidden talents?" He took his hand, but Kyle slipped it out, refilling their drinks, and it made Marius frown, his blue eyes following the slave.

Clavius raved. "This is excellent! I can't believe you learnt how to cook her stuff... if anything, this is going to make us survive this shithole place!"

Marius didn't comment, his annoyance growing each time Kyle evaded his touch. His anger flared, and he looked at him, his voice like ice. "Come here and kneel." He pointed at the floor next to him and Kyle swallowed, obeying the command automatically, not thinking.

Clavius raised his head. "What the fuck are you two playing?"

Marius didn't answer and looked down at the slave, his bowed head and heaving shoulders. He put his hand on Kyle's back and felt him shrink away. Marius' face darkened, but he went back to eating, leaving him kneeling.

A while later, Marius gently tipped Kyle's head up. "Food?"

Kyle shook his head and lowered it again. He had seen the glint of anger in Marius' eyes, the hurt, and his heart beat faster when realization hit him that this was now his life and that Marius had been the only solid anchor point so far, the only one who really cared. *And I'm treating him like the others... like those soldiers...* His head swam with his torn wounds, long buried memories and emotions washing over him like crashing waves. Marius loved him and was the only one left to protect him... He felt the Roman's heat radiating from his skin, his bare thigh close to him as he kneeled, Marius having resumed eating and ignoring him. Overcome with remorse and drained, Kyle rested his head on Marius' bare thigh, the familiar warmth of his body comforting, his scent. He closed his eyes, close to tears.

Marius blinked down in surprise when he felt Kyle's head on his thigh, watching him close his eyes. He momentarily stopped chewing, slowly swallowing, his brows furrowed in confusion. He noticed then how pale Kyle was, and his hand went to caress his hair, his strong fingers gently stroking, soothing, almost anticipating him pulling away.

Kyle felt Marius' hand in his hair, his fingers gliding into it, massaging his scalp, and he sighed softly, pressing his face closer to his skin.

Clavius looked at them, slightly concerned. "I don't even know what kind of fucked up shit this is..."

Marius' face stayed calm. "Something's off..."

Clavius rose. "I'll leave you to it."

Marius just nodded and waited until he'd left, slowly continuing his caresses, Kyle's tears flowing down his leg. He stopped and tried to pull him up, but he couldn't move him, so he had to cup his chin and force Kyle's head up, Marius' blue eyes mildly alarmed. "What's wrong?"

Kyle's eyes swam in tears. "We are in a fort..." He stopped and looked into Marius' eyes... *Please understand, please, please...*

He watched as Marius' lips fell loose, his eyes widening. "Oh, fuck..." He rose then, his strong arms pulling him up, dragging him to the bed. He lay Kyle down gently, lying next to him, spooning him, his arms locking him in place. Kyle sighed, slightly unnerved, wanting to move away but he couldn't, not from him...

"Talk to me...?"

Kyle sighed. "No... it's too painful..."

Marius made him face him, turning him around, his brows furrowed. "What happened? You were hurt?"

Kyle shook his head. "Not now... but this place, the soldiers, they brought back memories of that day... when I was captured..."

Marius stroked his face. "You can tell me..."

Can I, love? Kyle looked at him, hesitating, his eyes pools of sadness. "It's not a pretty story..."

Marius smiled, bitter. "Those never are."

"Alright..."

He told him then; the words spilling out like dark ooze, Marius very still, his face blanching, but he listened all the while, realizing maybe for the first time how damaged Kyle was. Nothing he hadn't guessed, but coming out of his mouth, it took a different color, a foul taste, and he swallowed, vaguely ashamed.

Kyle stopped, utterly drained, fearful of how he would react, and Marius spoke softly. "How can you love me...?"

Indeed... but even now that he had recounted it, that life didn't make any sense anymore. If his father had been alive, he wouldn't have let him tear him from Marius. Kyle whispered. "I just do... I'm safe with you."

Marius pulled him closer, his lips grazing his lips. "You have no idea how much..."

They kissed softly, Kyle's eyes boring into his. "I could ask the same... how can you love me? I'm just a whore..."

Marius' face flinched slightly, and he grazed his thumb on Kyle's lower lip. "Is that what you think you are?"

Kyle exhaled a shaky breath. "That's what I've been made into..."

"Those times are over."

"We still fuck..."

Marius pulled a face, lightly stroking Kyle's face, his eyes locking with his eyes. "We don't fuck."

Kyle raised his eyebrows, his lips parting. "So, what are we doing...?"

He bathed in Marius' blue eyes, his lips close, his breath a whisper. "We make love..."

Kyle closed his eyes and let Marius kiss him deep, letting him run his tongue along his mouth, stroking, pushing in, tasting him with lavish strokes, his hands cupping his jaws. He whimpered when he pushed him back into the mattress, hovering over him, not breaking their kiss, and Kyle gave in, his body relaxing. He belonged to Marius, and the Roman felt him surrender and bathe in his love.

Marius whispered in his mouth. "I'll love you all night..."

And Kyle closed his eyes, letting his tears flow.

XV

M onths had passed, spring turning into summer, no sign of the rebels, and they gradually relaxed, running negotiations with the neighboring villages and tribes. Life at the fort continued as usual, with the same disciplined daily routine, and Kyle had adjusted to the soldiers' presence. Marius had made him stand behind him at one of the briefings, and since then, they avoided him like the plague, knowing whom he belonged to.

He cooked for Marius and Clavius every night, and dinners together had become a routine, a warm moment when the two men's friendship deepened, exchanging news from home, although Marius couldn't care less about his wife's letters depicting her social life. If anything, Tertullia wrote more about his daughter, and his thoughts were bittersweet. She was growing nicely, but he was missing out on it, and he poured all his affection onto Kyle, their love even stronger than before, their nights pure bliss, their passion busting his brooding, angry mood to pieces.

As summer dwindled to its end, chillier nights settling in with light rains, they received an invitation from one of the tribal chiefs to meet for a banquet to celebrate their pact. Marius was cautious though, his brows furrowed when he read the letter, the other officers waiting.

He glanced at Clavius. "What do you think?"

"Could be tricky... but again, this is the guy who already gave away his daughter, so? Maybe he can be trusted. It's just a dinner, after all."

"We can't offend him by refusing, but we won't go without an escort. We'll take twenty of your men, armed."

"Mhm... you want to go to a banquet with armed soldiers?"

Marius smiled. "It's on my terms or we're not going."

Clavius raised his hands and left to gather his men.

Julius stepped to Marius. "The envoy is going to come back with us."

"Sure. You're coming too. Have a cart prepared with some gifts, that will not hurt. I'll have my slave drive it."

Julius saluted and left to prepare.

Marius rose and went to his room, looking for Kyle. He was cleaning, washing the floor on all fours, and Marius watched him, leaning against the door.

Kyle turned his head around. "Back already?"

"Don't mind me. I'm admiring your ass."

Kyle rose and stepped to him, wiping his hands on his tunic. "I'm dirty..."

Marius kissed him. "I know... but, as much as I would like to fuck you to pieces, we need to leave."

Kyle arched his eyebrows. "Leave? Where?"

"We've been invited to a banquet by one of the savage chiefs, the father of that whore girl, of all things." He rolled his eyes and watched Kyle get ready, washing quickly and changing his clothes, putting on a pair of pants and a shirt.

Marius smirked. "You are even sexier like this..."

Kyle pulled his tongue at him, making Marius growl and catch him from behind, his strong arms lacing around his chest, pinning his arms down. "Don't provoke me..." Kyle's breath quickened when he felt Marius' mouth on his neck, his teeth biting down softly. "Mhm... you taste delicious..." He smacked his ass, letting him go. "Enough... we'll be late. Come, I need you to drive the mule cart."

They left to join the party, waiting on the main street of the camp, facing the gate. Kyle climbed on the cart and they rode off, the huge double gates wide open. He was thrilled to leave but also vaguely anxious, and they rode next to the wild river flowing behind the camp, its current strong, white frothy waves running like mad horses.

They followed the envoy on his stocky brown horse, the mood light, discussing how they would get the supplies for the upcoming winter. Kyle watched the pine tree forest around them, the river still wildly flowing to their left, the narrow path dwindling, following its curves. The dark woods made him uneasy, and he wondered how the officers' mood could be so light, Marius' booming laughter echoing in the forest.

They had been riding for a good hour, maybe more, when a clearing appeared in front of them, letting some sunshine in. It looked idyllic, with the wild river, the strong hush of the waters somersaulting on black rocks and the whispers of the pine trees. Marius marveled at its beauty, when a piercing cry made his blood froze, Clavius' head whipping up, their wide eyes locking, their hands flying to their swords.

Kyle watched in shock as the barbarians poured out into the clearing from the woods, their bloodcurdling war cries echoing, slamming into the Romans like a hammer. Marius shouting orders above the chaos, his sword already out, slashing at them as they surrounded them. The mules reared, and Kyle jumped, tumbling off the cart. Thankfully, they didn't care about him and he ran towards the chaos along the river, frantic to get at Marius.

Marius fought, shouting all the while to his officers, his eyes darting towards the soldiers who were struggling to fight back, but Roman discipline and fearfulness got the best of the barbarians who were superior in numbers but lacked fighting and defense skills. Still, they were fierce, and they fought hard, blows raining on their armors, making Marius pant in pain each time when he had to then retaliate. The clearing was too small, and the river didn't allow any escape. They could only hope that there were not more of them.

Marius' rage was plain, slashing the warriors to pieces with his sword, his face lashed with their blood. He whirled with his horse when time stopped. He watched in slow motion, in utter shock, as Clavius fought a barbarian, not seeing the other one raise his sword. Marius shouted, or so he thought, and for the briefest moment their eyes locked when the blow fell on Clavius' face, blood spurting from the horrid wound. His horse reared, and the centurion fell into the swarming river, his body swallowed by the hungry tides.

Marius' throat dried out from howling, spurring his horse forward, and his eyes grew wide when he saw a swift shadow run on the riverbank and then a lean muscled body, bareback, plunge into the hurling tides headfirst. He knew that muscled back too well and his world froze as he watched it disappear in the grey and white tides. *Kyle.*

The world froze as Marius watched the two men who meant the world to him disappear into the frothing waves.

A blow to his back made him whirl, slash out with his sword to split the barbarian's head in half, his shock still too plain to be able to fight properly, and his arm trembled from the next blow. Then, the barbarian in front of him fell, his eyes wide, pierced by a sword, and Julius appeared, the young centurion's eyes wide, pulling at Marius' horse's rein.

"We have to go. Now!"

Marius stammered. "They... they might be alive..."

Julius looked at his shocked face and yelled, yanking at his rein. "Maybe... but we have to go now! Come!"

He spurred his horse, not letting Marius' rein go, and his horse flew after Julius', the surviving officers behind them, fleeing before other enemy reappeared.

The journey home had been a blur, Marius replaying the scene in his head, disbelieving, knowing full well that even if he'd survived that wound, Clavius could not have survived in full armor in that wild river. *And Kyle...* He closed his eyes, nausea invading his senses as his horse ran. He clutched the mane, the fort finally in sight, the foaming horses almost dying of exhaustion. Julius shouted the password, and the gates opened, letting them in.

Marius jumped off mid-stride and threw up, his hands on his knees, the shock washing everything out of him. His hands shaking as he was trying to recompose himself, a concerned, blanched Julius' hand on his back.

"Commander..."

He sighed, knowing he could not be weak now, his mind reeling from grief. "I'm fine..." He panted, straightening. "Thank you, Julius..." The young man nodded, and Marius pushed the words out, his voice stronger. "Assess the damages. I want a full report. Meeting room, now..."

He sat with his officers in the meeting room later, his eyes on Clavius' empty chair, and his heart constricted, painful, almost knocking the breath out of him. *My friend, forgive me...* Julius handed him the report.

Human losses: 12 soldiers, Centurion Clavius

Material damage: 2 mules, 1 cart, 20 jugs of wine, 10 loaves of bread, vegetables, fruits, vinegar, 1 slave

Marius closed his eyes. *Material damage...*

He had to swallow hard, bile rising in his throat, his blue eyes darkening with anger. He looked up at Julius. "Thank you, centurion. Now, for the course of action... Send a messenger to this swine of a chief and let him know that his insolence will cost him his village if he doesn't explain himself."

Julius shifted, uneasy. "He might not have anything to do with it..."

Marius pursed his lips, his grief fueling his anger. "I don't give a fuck at this point... they think I'm nice? I'm anything but..." He breathed in deep. "I have a dead officer, an excellent one... there's no amount of explanation that will save that barbarian's ass."

Julius frowned. "With all due respect, we can't erase a village and a tribe out of revenge."

Marius raised his eyes on him, the glint in them making Julius shiver. "Oh... but we can... and we will... soon."

Kyle ran and saw Clavius plummet into the water, and he didn't think, yanking his shirt off, plunging where he had seen him disappear, the cold water biting into his skin, the strong current sucking at his body.

Kyle didn't care though, his hands frantically darting around in the swirls, his fingers locking onto metal, gripping tight, not letting go, as the current dragged them along. He stayed as best as he could towards the bottom, the heavy armor dragging them down anyway and his hands found the straps which he undid, his eyes wide open, struggling to see in the froth. Kyle let the armor slip out of his hand, holding on to the limp body by his leather armor, swimming hard with his legs to find the surface, his lungs close to exploding. As they got closer to the surface, the current got stronger, making them whirl, but he held tight, memories of his childhood and youth pouring in when this was a game, swimming with his friends in the icy rivers of his homeland, having major fun. His body remembered too, locked into survival mode, his mind only on getting up for air, out to the bank.

Kyle's head emerged finally, breathing in hard, pulling Clavius' head up, holding him in a choke hold, his face white as a sheet, with the oozing blood of that horrid wound on the side of his face. *He might be dead...* but he chased the idea out of his mind, watching the shore from the running tides, swimming on his back, dragging the dead weight of the centurion. The river was larger here, but still tricky, jagged rocks rushing towards them, and it was a struggle to evade them in that treacherous tide. Kyle also unbuckled the straps of the leather armor, letting it go, and the helmet. It was easier this way, just the tunic on Clavius, and his pants.

Fortunately, the river was not too cold, warmed by the summer sun, but still wild, bouncing them around as they slid fast, a rock appearing in the front, making Kyle try to swim around it. It hit his right shoulder, making him grind his teeth in pain, but it was not too serious, just a cut and a bruise, the pain still white-hot. He cursed softly, praying that the river calmed a bit, and somehow the gods listened, because it was tamer now, the current still strong but less frothy, the rocks disappearing.

Kyle was too tired, he could feel it, the water invading his mouth as Clavius' body dragged at him. *Let him go...* a small voice in his head... *you'll die with him...* His grip loosened when Clavius coughed, making him jolt and hold him tighter. *He's alive...* His heart fluttered, and with an ultimate effort, he swam towards an enormous tree trunk drifting down the river. He managed to grip a branch, letting them float with the current, watching the shores in the distance. The farther the better from the place of the attack, but he gathered they were already quite far. Clavius moaned, coughing more water out, and Kyle held him gently, letting him drift on his back, his thoughts going to Marius. *He thinks we're dead...* his heart constricted, but he held tight, letting the trunk carry them far.

Dusk was setting in when they finally slowed down, and Kyle felt a bit more rested. He let go of the tree, and swam towards the shore, reaching the pebbled bank, dragging Clavius out. He collapsed then, out of breath, his shoulder killing him, but he steeled himself, rolling Clavius on his right side, listening to him breathe softly, watching in horror that wound running down the left side of his face, the cheekbone visible under that wide cut. It had stopped bleeding though, and he gently probed it, his mind racing. It would have needed a doctor, but obviously, this was not an option here in the wild. He searched for a jagged rock and tore half of his pants off, binding the wound as best as he could with it. *Now, food...*

His eyes went to the river, lazy here, but huge fish were swimming close to the shore in the shallow river, and he stepped in, softly, waiting, poised. One came too close, and he slammed his hands down, gripping its slippery body, flinging it out to the shore like a bear, going back then for more. He managed to fish three out, and went to gather firewood and dry moss to light it. It was exhausting, but he was rewarded with brightly lit flames soon. Content, he ripped the fish open with his teeth, gutting it with his bare hands, and soon they were roasting on the dancing flames. Kyle sat, warming his soaked body, watching Clavius' face. *He will need to wake soon...*

When the fish was almost ready, Kyle sat down next to him, the sun almost gone, and gently nudged his shoulder. "Dominus... wake up..." Clavius moaned, but his eyes stayed shut, so Kyle nudged a bit harder, wanting him to be conscious, just to be safe.

Finally, Clavius' eyes fluttered open, his unfocused, shocked eyes locking on Kyle, the pain invading his senses. He gasped; his voice caught in his throat. "K... Ky..."

"Shhh... yes, it's me. Don't worry, we are out of the water, but you got badly hurt, your face. Just rest, but stay awake?"

Clavius nodded, his eyes shutting to the pain, but he was alive, he could barely believe it, his eyes opening to the vision of the flames, the roasting fish, the half-naked slave leaning above them, taking them off the fire. *He saved my life... this boy...* His thoughts drifted to Marius, and Tertullia. *They think I'm dead... oh gods... and I might still be soon...* The pain was harsh, and his hand went to his face, feeling the bandage.

Kyle was there in an instant. "I can't do anything better, sorry. You should eat?"

He presented the fish to him on a large leaf, tearing a piece off and pushing it in his mouth, but Clavius couldn't chew it, each movement of his jaw a nightmare.

He moaned, gently shaking his head, and Kyle understood. He took the morsel out of Clavius' mouth and chewed it to bits, mixing it with a gulp of water.

He gestured to Clavius to get on his back and open his mouth. *What the fuck...?* He did it though, and Kyle gently leant over him, over his open mouth, hooking a finger in his jaw so that he wouldn't close it, letting the mushed flesh slide into his mouth from his mouth. Clavius was too shocked to protest, feeling the young man's soft lips on his, the warm food sliding down his throat.

It felt divine, and Kyle smiled. "More?"

Clavius nodded feebly, and they repeated the routine until he signaled he'd had enough. Kyle ate then the rest, and made him drink the same way he had fed him. "Now, let's rest. Tomorrow, we'll have to walk if you can manage." He had gathered a bunch of branches with leaves and made a make-shift place to sleep, rolling Clavius on it, covering him with more leafy branches. "Should be better than nothing?"

Clavius nodded, grateful, his eyes closing, warming next to the radiating fire, and Kyle curled up close on the pebbles. He didn't care, used to sleeping years on the cold, hard marble floor naked, and went to sleep straight away.

Marius went to his room, his eyes roaming the empty space, the table where they should have been having dinner, having their usual banters, his lover next to him, teasing him... His blue eyes shone in the dark, a vivid pain searing his inside, making him slouch down into his chair, his head going in his hands.

There was a soft knock on the door, and a young camp slave sneaked his head in, carrying a basket. "Your dinner, dominus." He quickly laid the food on the table, Marius' eyes not leaving him, and he looked at him. "Should I stay, dominus?"

"No..." He watched him leave and eyed the food, the large jug of wine... *Fuck this shit...* He couldn't eat, his stomach like iron, but he drank, downing the whole jug of wine until he could barely see, his eyes drifting to the empty bed. *Why, pet? Why did you jump?* But there was no answer, and his anger rose, born out of a grief so deep he thought it would choke him. Marius howled then, rising to his feet, his vision blurring with tears of rage and pain, and he hurled the furniture in his room, breaking them with his bare hands, sending everything flying into the walls until he collapsed, panting, out of his mind.

Morning rose on the riverbank, with soft pink lights and birds in the sky. Clavius blinked in the light, slowly emerging, the pain still strong.

Kyle's face swam into his vision. "Good morning, dominus. Slept well?"

He nodded, unable to speak, and the slave gently pulled him up. "Can you sit?" He steeled himself and sat, vaguely dizzy, but he showed the thumbs up. Kyle put some mushed berries in his hands on a leaf. "Lick it. I don't have anything better." Clavius did, painfully so, but it felt good. "So, we should go, walk up the river and we should get to the fort ... after a while..." He seemed unsure, worry chewing at him at the prospect of being in this foreign land with the enemy close.

He looked at Clavius. "We can't give away that you're a Roman officer... we need to pretend that you're just a nobody, a commoner." Clavius nodded, grim, and Kyle thought hard. "A commoner and his slave. Traveling."

Kyle smiled. "At least you're more or less decently dressed in your tunic and sandals." He looked down at himself and grinned. "And I am fine for a slave."

Clavius looked at Kyle's torn trousers, jagged above the knee, and his sandals. He smiled despite the pain.

"Ok, let's go? Do you think you can walk?" He pulled Clavius up, the centurion swaying, and he clutched his waist. "Lean on me. That's better. Let's go. They might have spotted the fire..."

They started walking then, each step torture, following the river upwards.

Marius woke to the sound of knocking. He had not washed and was still in his armor, on the floor, on top of the pile of rubble he had created. He got up, swaying, anger invading him, a slow, steady burn. "Come in..."

Julius stepped in and froze, looking into Marius' eyes, those blue eyes burning with a demonic flame. Marius smirked, seeing his face. "I made a mess. Have it cleaned up."

"Yes, Commander... khm... We are about to dispatch the letters to the families of the deceased... any messages from you?"

Reality hit Marius hard, but he swallowed, his pain quickly engulfed by his wrath. "Yes... come with me."

He went straight to the meeting room and wrote to Tertullia, the bold letters flowing in black ink, his eyes burning with a new light. It chilled Julius, and he waited, silent. "Here... have it dispatched with the rest..."

"Yes, Commander."

"I'll clean myself up and then we meet in half an hour here. Gather the officers."

Julius saluted and left.

Marius blue eyes filled with wrath and grief. *You'll see... I'll make the world burn for you...*

Kyle stopped in the afternoon, unable to carry him further, feeling Clavius lose that small strength he still had left. The shores had become more unfriendly. Soon, they'd have to leave them and walk deeper into the woods.

"Let's camp here..." Clavius moaned, lying down, his eyes shut. "I need to have a look at your wound, but first, let me gather some herbs and food. I'll be back..."

Clavius watched him disappear in the undergrowth, and his heart clenched. *What if he left him? After all, he could just escape now... get his freedom back. Britannia wasn't very far, maybe a couple of weeks of travel... He could just go...* Unable to stay awake any longer, he went into a deep sleep.

When he woke, it was getting dark, and the fire was burning next to him, the air chillier, the smell of roast meat in the air.

Kyle was crouching next to the fire, watching the rabbit in the flames, his eyes drifting to the stirring man. "We can eat soon..."

He had come back... Relief flooded Clavius and shame... He looked at Kyle, his wound a throbbing torture under the bandage. "Thank you...", it was a mere whisper, but Kyle had heard it, relieved that he talked.

He smiled. "I'm most happy you can talk, dominus. Now, let me have a look at that wound. I found something which might help..." He crawled next to him and gently removed the bandage, putting it in the fire. Kyle then washed the wound out carefully, Clavius' face blanched, gritting his teeth against the pain. "So, now, I'll put some honey and clay into it... I found some close..." Clavius watched the bee stings on his body, and Kyle shrugged. "Yeah, they were not happy that I stole their honey..." He laughed and smeared the wild honey into the wound. "This is how we cured our many cuts and scratches when we were kids... after having gotten our asses whooped by our mothers..."

Kyle quieted, painful memories choking his throat... *Mother...* she was so gone in time, her face a blur... He shook his head, concentrating on the wound, and Clavius watched the lingering pain on his face.

He then smeared clay onto the wound, making sure to wait a bit until it dried on the surface. He tore his trousers further, the hem higher than mid-thigh, and he chuckled. "I hope we can find some civilization soon or I'll be forced to walk around naked."

Clavius laughed softly at the image, and Kyle bandaged his head. The pain was slightly less, and he sighed. "Much better..."

"Good! Now to food. Can you chew?"

He pulled a mischievous smiled at him and Clavius felt all warm inside. "Yes, I think so..."

"We'll see..."

Kyle pulled the soft meat off the bones and made Clavius sit up, handing him the food. He chewed slowly, and Kyle sighed. *Maybe he would live after all...*

They ate in silence, watching the sunset, the river bathed in blood.

"Bring me the girl." Marius' voice was soft in the semi-dark room, but a shiver ran down Julius' spine.

He didn't dare disobey though and went to get the chief's daughter from the camp prostitutes' quarters. "The commander wants to see you."

She followed him, shivering, because she had heard of what had happened. Her large, blue eyes welled up with tears, her long, blonde hair trailing behind her, her dress a mere piece of flimsy, white linen sticking to her body.

Julius knocked and pushed her inside. "Here she is, Commander."

"Leave us."

He did, closing the door, exhaling loudly, and leaving as fast as he could.

She watched the man's broad back, standing, facing the window, his arms folded, and waited, clasping her hands in the front. He turned then and her legs quivered, seeing the cold hate in his blue eyes, his black hair falling into them, his handsome face which didn't belong with those eyes filled with darkness.

His voice was soft as he approached her, but she trembled, that voice seemingly coming out of a grave, cold, dark. "Do you know why you're here?"

She backed to the door and stood there, braced against the wood, her eyes wide. "No..."

He looked her over, standing very close, his hand tracing her face, her shoulders, her hips, his mouth curling into a small smile. "You don't know..."

She shook her head, her eyes welling up.

His eyes bore into her. "Your father made a grave mistake... and I intend to make him pay for it..." She breathed faster but held his gaze. "So, you, little dove... you're going to help me..."

Her voice was a breath. "How...?"

He stroked her face. "You know your settlement better than anybody here... so, you're going to help us map it, so we can strike with the biggest efficiency..."

"But... but you'll kill him..."

He grinned. "Yes, so? What does it matter to you?"

"He's my father..."

His eyes shone with an evil light as he cupped her chin. "Some father... giving his daughter away to become a whore..."

Her tears spilled. "He didn't know... he thought I would be married to that man..."

Marius laughed then, not letting go of her chin. "Married to a Roman, you?"

She could not lower her eyes, so she just let her tears spill, shame washing over her.

He pushed closer, pressing her against the door, and her body reacted to his heat, despite her will to hate him. She cursed it then, this treacherous body which had been conditioned to respond to men, her skin tingling, her nipples becoming erect under the flimsy fabric of her gown.

Marius smiled, his lips inches from hers. "Such a slut..."

His hand trailed down her side and she felt it glide up between her legs to her core, trailing the wetness there, his smile mocking. She gasped when he shoved two fingers inside her, almost lifting her off the ground, pushing her into the door. "Is this what you like, little slut?"

She whimpered. "No..."

"Mhm... your body is telling a different story..." She panted when he started fucking her, shoving his fingers inside, hard. "A very different story..."

He pulled his fingers out and dragged her to the bed, shoving her face down on the mattress, her legs on the floor.

She felt her gown pushed up on her waist and she screamed when he pushed inside of her, rock-hard, his hand fisting her hair, yanking her head back. "You don't want to help us? Maybe I can make you change your mind..." Her lips parted in shock when she felt him slam inside of her, fucking her hard, his anger fueling him, oblivious to her cries. If anything, it made him crueler, leaning on her, his breath in her ear. "So... will... you... help... us?" She cried, shaking her head, and he fucked her harder.

Finally, he had enough and pulled out, turning her around, yanking her up by her gown, holding her inches from his face, her eyes glazed over, her face marred by tears. "You can go through this each night? Or... I have a better idea. If you don't help, I'll make you be the cheapest whore in this camp and I'll have you fucked to pieces by the lowest level grunts, hell, I'll even pay the whole cohort the first round..." She listened to him, her eyes widening, disbelieving, and he smiled a cruel smile. "Oh... you don't believe me?"

Marius let her go, and she slid to the floor, watching him stride to the door and ask a guard to get Julius.

The centurion arrived minutes later, his eyes flying to the prone woman on the floor, but he stood at attention to Marius, the commander's eyes wild blue flames in his face. "Take this whore back to their quarters and fix her price to the lowest possible."

Julius blanched. "How low, Commander?"

"As low as you can go... and then inform the men. I'll pay the first round for everybody."

She screamed then, giving up. "Noooo! No..."

Marius turned, his eyes like a snake's. "What is it, dove?"

She looked at him, pleading. "I'll do it. I'll help you."

"Good girl..." He turned to a livid Julius. "Our priced dove here will help us kill her father and destroy their village. Make sure she gets out of the whorehouse and she's cared for."

"Yes, Commander..."

"She needs to cooperate fully, giving us the plans, routines, everything we need to know about those filthy savages. If she doesn't, the first deal goes." He looked back at her. "Understood?"

She nodded, unable to talk.

Marius gestured towards her. "You may take her away."

Julius walked to her and gently pulled her up. Her legs trembled, and she clutched at his arm, not looking at Marius who just watched them leave, smiling.

Kyle and Clavius continued their slow march for two weeks, his wound healing faster than expected with Kyle's remedies, honey, and clay. He had to wash out the bandages every night and left the wound under the layer of clay in the open air.

Nights had become chillier, the scent of fall in the air, and one night, they were sitting next to each other, shivering under the stars. Clavius lay down, trembling, the pain making him weaker, a slight fever coursing through his body. Kyle watched him and, after a split second of hesitation, spooned him, his arms going around him, warming his back.

Clavius froze, but then the gentle warmth radiating from the slave's near naked body made him smile. "Just don't tell Marius when we get back, he'll skin me alive."

Kyle smiled. "I don't think so..."

"Yeah, right..."

Kyle kept quiet, and they drifted off to sleep.

"There's a military envoy at the door, domina."

Tertullia rose, her face blanched, and she reached for Simeon, the young man confused at her alarmed face. "What's going on?"

She took his hand and walked down to the door, the military envoy grim, handing her two letters. "I am sorry, lady Tertullia."

Her head swooned, and she knew, her hand clutching Simeon's hand not to collapse. Her old slave closed the door, and she opened the official letter with trembling hands, reading the lines, her vision blurring, a sob escaping her throat as her hand clasped her mouth. The slaves knew then, and they paled, Simeon holding her up. The letter slipped to the floor and her eyes flew to the other one, Marius' bold black letters running on it. She opened it; her heart torn.

Dearest Tertullia,

You know now that I couldn't keep my promise to you, to protect your dear husband, my dearest friend, in this world. He died fighting, but his body fell into a river and I can't send him back to you. This is also my failure. You must also know that my faithful love jumped after him in a vain attempt to save his life and disappeared in the flow. They are both dead and it is unbearable. I pray that one day you can forgive me for failing you. I must have my revenge now and then will hopefully join them fast.

Yours ever, Marius

Tertullia stood very still, her heart racing, her tears flowing. Clavius was gone, so was Kyle, but Marius... Marius was still alive, although barely, she knew. Her thoughts flew to Marius' daughter, the darling six months old who needed him with her crazy mother, completely oblivious of her...

She looked at Simeon, the boy in tears. "We are leaving, Simeon. Pack up, pup."

The boy looked at her, bewildered. "But... where?"

"To the fort."

His eyes grew huge. "But domina, this is dangerous... a Roman lady like you, traveling alone?"

She smiled, her eyes shining. "Not a Roman lady, but a peasant woman, with her only son." She pinched his cheeks. "And her African cook... Prepare the mule cart and get me some peasant woman's clothing, same for you." She hastily dressed, prepared to leave. "Nikhe, come with me to my sister, you too, old man.

I'll leave the house to her cares. Pup, when I'm back, you're ready to go. Wait for me, and then we'll leave at night, away from prying eyes."

"But domina..."—he wriggled his hands, mortified — "Dominus is dead... why are we going?"

She stroked his cheek. "Your looks outgrow your wits, Simeon, but this is why I like you so much... We can't do anything for Clavius anymore, but we can still save Marius... now, pack, and stop asking questions."

She came back much later, carrying also a precious little item, and she changed quickly, Tabia and Simeon ready, her pots, herbs, and spices on the cart, along with their clothes and food. She climbed up, Simeon at the reins, Tabia in the back.

She turned to the faithful cook. "Tabia, your magic will be needed. I hope we won't be too late."

Tabia grinned, her teeth gleaming in the night. "Do not worry, domina, I am ready."

Nobody paid any attention to the poor peasant woman and her son leaving Rome on their mule cart, their African slave in the back, singing her mournful songs from her homeland, grieving her master.

XVI

The plans to raid the settlement had continued as the early fall chill settled in, the chief's daughter helping them as best as she could, scared to the bone from Marius, that horrid night still vivid in her memory.

Unexpectedly, she also grew quite fond of Julius, the young centurion spending more time with her, as he had been put in charge of making sure that she was cared for. He also realized, not without shame, that his feelings for her had changed, and he was looking at her with fresh eyes.

Marius had noticed it, of course, and it warmed him. This gave him another way to force her to do what he wanted if she wavered.

His thirst for revenge overrode his reason, his broken heart hardening, not letting any of his softer emotions to the surface, and he grew cold, almost verging on cruelty. The soldiers feared him like the devil as he had become ruthless with the slightest misstep, his punishments harsh. Nobody could reason him, and a slow underlying terror had settled between the fort's walls.

Reluctantly, Kyle and Clavius turned away from the river, the banks giving way to jagged rock cliffs, impossible to climb.

"We have to go and find a road."

Clavius nodded, and they both knew this meant civilization, other humans. Clavius' wound had healed, an impressive scar running down his face. He caressed it sometimes, softly laughing. "This is my retirement present..." He was still weak, though, and their progress was slower than expected.

Trudging through a thick forest, they arrived on a dirt road in the woods. Clavius sighed. "We have no choice but to follow it." They could not hear the river anymore and it unnerved them. Still, they walked, looking off in the landscape, Clavius in his tunic and sandals, and Kyle in his impossibly short trousers which barely covered his ass.

After a while, they stumbled on a few men camping near the road, and the men looked at them, rising from near the fire. Clavius looked nervously at Kyle. There were five of them, probably some sort of merchants, all sturdy looking men, seemingly unarmed. They waved them over and Clavius stood facing them, making sure they saw his scar. One of the men came closer, a tall man with a rugged face, short, brown hair, brown eyes, a small smile on his lips. He looked in his forties, his hair greying at the temples, a huge hunting knife strapped to his thigh.

The leader probably, Clavius thought, and the man gestured towards his scar. "Wow! Impressive... you got it in a fight?"

"Yes, against some bandits."

"Who are you?"

"I am but a humble merchant."

"And the boy?"

Clavius didn't like the man's smile. "He's my slave."

The leader eyed them. "You have nothing?"

"No, those bandits took everything we had. We barely survived."

"So... you could use some money, stuff?"

Clavius nodded, and Kyle's eyes didn't leave the leader, watching him carefully.

He grinned. "Ok, let's make a deal. Your slave's sweet ass for some money and clothes? You might need them, it's getting cold."

Clavius frowned, swallowing his anger. "I am not selling him to you."

The men roared with laughter. Their leader grinned. "We don't want to buy him... just fuck him."

They laughed, and Clavius blanched, looking at Kyle who slowly nodded to him. His eyes grew wide, mouthing 'no' but Kyle spoke before he could change his mind. "Half up front, and half after, and you give the clothes to my dominus now."

The leader grinned. "Mouthy, aren't you?"

Kyle's lips parted, and he licked them. "You want to see just how much? Pay."

The leader's eyes darkened, and the others laughed. He grinned, tossing a purse to Clavius. "Count it. You'll get the other half when we're done. Here are the clothes too."

Clavius' hands shook mildly, but he counted the coins, and checked the clothes. "Fine..."

"Deal!" The leader grabbed Kyle's hand, and they disappeared, with the other men following, into the undergrowth.

Clavius collapsed on the ground, trying his best to ignore the grunting and moans coming from the bushes, sweat trickling down his back, hoping that they would not kill them later. *What the fuck was Kyle thinking... then again, we would have not escaped... fuck, fuck, fuck...*

They finally came out, Kyle's hair tousled, his whole body glistening with sweat, and the leader tossed another purse to Clavius, who had scrambled to his feet.

"Thanks for this... he's a real treat... you would earn a fortune making him work as a whore."

Clavius smirked. "I might take your expert advice."

They dressed then quickly, and the leader walked up to Kyle, slipping a gold coin into his hand. "This is for your talented mouth."

Kyle just smiled at him and pocketed it.

They left then, Clavius feeling sick. He could not even talk to him for a while, just watching Kyle's blanched face. They came across a small stream, a bridge running over it, and Kyle stopped, stooping down on the bank, shoving his fingers down his throat. He threw up and then drank long gulps, washing his mouth out.

Clavius walked to him, putting his hand on his back. "You sure you had to do this?"

He wiped his mouth, straightening. "They would have killed you, and do it anyway if we refused, so, yes, I am pretty sure we're better off."

He smiled feebly and Clavius' face softened. "I... I don't know how I will ever be able to repay this to you."

"You don't have to... let's go."

They continued, Kyle busy walling up the memories of the past events, like countless times before when he'd worked in that brothel.

Dusk settled, and they spotted an inn on the side of the road.

Kyle's face beamed. "We have money now, so let's get a decent night's sleep, finally... and a well-cooked meal..."

Clavius grinned. "Though your wild cooking wasn't bad either."

They went inside, cautious, but as they were properly dressed, nobody paid any particular attention to them.

Clavius walked to the innkeeper. "A room for me and my slave."

The older man looked at Kyle. "He can sleep in the stables."

Clavius laced his arm around Kyle's shoulder, pulling him close. "He sleeps with me."

The innkeeper grinned and gave him the key. "Sit down and have some food?"

Clavius nodded, and they sat down to a tabel, Kyle's eyes shining with amusement. "You're a good actor."

Clavius smiled, embarrassed. "I hope you didn't mind."

Kyle looked at him. "Would you like to?"

"What?"

"Sleep with me."

Clavius went bright red. "What? No... I am not so much into boys... and Marius would kill me."

Kyle pursed his lips. "Maybe not... but it's your call, you know."

They ate silently when the food arrived, listening to the surrounding conversations.

Clavius had enough of the local language to understand and he leant to Kyle. "There's a city apparently a few days' walk from here. We could find some work and gain enough money to get a cart and a mule to get home faster... I honestly don't think I can walk all the way, not if the weather turns..."

He was tired, all his energy fueled into healing his wound, that scar still painful, throbbing sometimes. Kyle nodded, his mind racing.

They went to bed then, sleeping in the same bed, but Clavius made sure he was nowhere near Kyle, and the slave looked at the ceiling, his thoughts on Marius... *How are you doing, love? We're coming home, you know... Forgive me...*

Marius was sitting in his room, utterly drunk. This had become a habit at nights when he was finally alone with his ghosts and shadows in that too empty room. Drinking himself to oblivion, the vile wine making him nasty, even more than usual.

His thirst for revenge burnt in him, burning him alive, his soul a dark pit of grief. There was nobody to soothe that ache, to love the hatred out of him, to tame his restless, wounded spirit. That monster lurking in the depths of his soul, the spawn of a loveless childhood and a harsh father, had finally been set free, and it bathed in his sorrow, sucking up his suffering like a leech, making his blue eyes shine with cruelty.

The small mule cart proceeded towards north, undisturbed, the jovial peasant woman leading it, or her son, that stunning boy with his green eyes and curly dark hair.

The town, finally, after days of walking under the falling rain. This was Roman territory already, but they didn't dare disclose Clavius' identity as he had no papers on him, and soldiers and officers were quick to kill, and slow to trust.

They entered by the city gates and Clavius stopped on a small forum, sitting on a bench, utterly exhausted with a splitting headache. "So.. let's think... we need to get back there soon before the weather turns too bad. So, we need jobs..."

Kyle looked at him. "What are your skills?"

Clavius grinned. "I can fight."

"Very useful..."

"Hey, don't mock me... ok, I admit, I know nothing but hacking and slashing... so..."

Kyle's eyes were already drifting towards a side street branching out. Colorful clothes hung between the narrow walls, drifting bodies in and out of the doors.

He smiled, looking back at Clavius. "We could earn money faster... good money. See, I also have skills..."

Clavius blanched. "No way!"

Kyle put a hand on his arm. "Listen, see that street? That's a whore street. You rent a small two-story flat and then you make your whore work whilst you live upstairs... good money and fast." He winked.

Clavius pulled his arm out, outraged. "I won't pimp you out!"

Kyle sighed, his eyes large. "You won't have a choice... I need you to make this work..."

"You're insane!"

He shrugged, his eyes clouding with sadness. "I wish this wasn't the only option... but considering our set of skills..."

Clavius fumed. "You could cook or clean."

"Yes... but we need money fast, right? Those jobs are done by slaves, so we would struggle to find a demand for it... and even if we did, it's not paid well..."

Clavius sighed, his eyes drifting to that street. "Fuck my life..."

Kyle rose. "Mine too.... let's go."

They walked to the street, straight to a red door, and Clavius knocked.

They waited until a tall eunuch opened up, his lips tainted red, a long red and gold robe wrought around his frame. "Yes?"

Clavius cleared his throat. "I would like to rent one of your flats."

The eunuch's eyes drifted to Kyle, eyeing him up. "Pretty... a bit too old, but you'll have costumers who prefer that. Come in."

They settled on the soft couches, the light dim in the carpeted room, the walls covered in green velvet with golden flowers. "Rent upfront for a week. And a tenth of your earnings."

Kyle squeezed Clavius' hand to signal it was alright, so he paid with some of the money they had left, sick to his stomach.

The eunuch led them to their flat then and opened the door, his long hand sweeping around in the bottom room, addressing Kyle. "Here's where you work, and your master can live upstairs. You stay as long as you pay the rent."

They nodded, and he left them.

Clavius collapsed on the red velvet bed, his face a picture of misery. "I can't do this..."

Kyle smiled, eyeing the room, the red carpeted walls, the small stand with a golden-framed mirror. It was a bit tattered, the red carpet frayed at the edges, the gold peeling off the mirror's and bed's frames, but at least it was clean.

"That's right...you can't... but I can." Kyle grinned and pulled him up. "Let's go shopping with what we have left. I need clothes and make-up."

Clavius followed, sick, and they asked for directions to a small shop where Kyle found what he wanted. They then went back, and he sent Clavius upstairs to get settled.

Kyle changed into the skimpy tunic he had purchased, the blue material almost see-through, and applied kohl around his eyes, his body lightly dusted with bronze flakes, his lips red.

He knocked them on the ceiling with a pole and Clavius walked down, floored. "What the actual fuck..."

Kyle smiled. "So, I got to get to work. Make sure you sort of pay attention to what's happening... I might need your fighting skills if a customer doesn't behave."

"Fucking perfect..." Clavius moaned and their eyes locked, Kyle's grey eyes burning.

"We'll have that money in no time. Just think happy thoughts. I'm good at this, trust me?"

Clavius swallowed hard, his thoughts on Marius. *Man, he will kill us...*

The following days went by with Kyle working almost from dusk till dawn and then sleeping, collapsed on the bed, for most of the day. They went to the bath every afternoon and then he got ready; the clients giving each other the door as his reputation spread, Clavius trying hard to ignore the sounds drifting up from the ground floor. He counted their money in disbelief. At this rate, they could buy the cart and the mule at the end of the week. Worry chewed at him though, despite Kyle reassuring him that he was fine.

The small mule cart arrived at the fort one chilly evening, one day before the planned raid of the settlement, and it stopped, the jovial peasant woman shouting up at the guards.

"Tell your general that we need shelter for the night!"

"Who are you?"

"I come from Rome. I am a simple peasant woman and need shelter. I have some excellent goods, so I can pay you."

"The general doesn't give a fuck about peasants. Fuck off!"

Tertullia's lips pinched. "Just bring me to him. I have a great cook. I'm sure he can use some decent food."

One of the guards chuckled. "He might be more interested in your boy there." They laughed at Tertullia, who stayed calm, waiting. "Fine! Wait here."

Julius went to talk to Marius, the only one who still dared to disturb him in his room.

"Come in, Julius... what do you want?"

He swallowed, looking at the sitting figure in the shadows. "Commander, there's a peasant woman in front of the gates. She wants shelter. She said to tell you that she has a superb cook with her and that you might use a decent meal..."

Marius' eyes gleamed, cold. "You come here to talk to me about a peasant woman?"

Julius shuffled his feet. "She also has a young boy with her..."

Marius stayed silent for a split second, then his laughter boomed through the room. "What the hell... let her in and bring her here... if she doesn't deliver on her promises, I'll cut her up alive..."

"Very well, Commander."

He left, running, and the gates opened, the small cart trotting inside.

Julius welcomed her; the young man's face bleached. "You need to come with me. The general wants to see you... I must warn you though, good woman, commander Marius is.... restless and with a quick temper... beware... just mind your words and your actions."

Her eyes shone, but she didn't comment, and they all walked to his room, following Julius.

He knocked and opened the door. "Commander, the peasant woman and her..."

"Just let them in and fuck off."

Julius gestured them in and closed the door, his chest heaving.

Tertullia had a hard time adjusting in the semi-dark room, spotting Marius' still form in the chair, a cup in his hand. Tabia and Simeon stood against the door, terrified.

Marius spoke then, his voice soft, sending chills down their spines. "So... good woman... what brings you here? I must warn you I have no patience for bullshit..." He could not recognize her in the dim light, his vision blurred by the wine, her shawl on her head.

Tertullia then stepped forward, fearless, pushing her shawl down to her shoulders, her bouncy curls freed, tumbling down her back. Her motherly voice pierced the dark, stabbing Marius into the heart. "You don't recognize me, Marius, dear?"

The cup fell to the floor, Marius' eyes wide, his shock knocking the breath out of him.

She hurried to him, looking down into his blue eyes, filled with ghosts, mad, and she hugged his head against her soft tummy. "I'm here now..." She felt his arms go around her waist, letting go, his demons shattered by her scent, her warmth. He sobbed into her gown, his body rocking in her arms, long howls of grief piercing her heart. "Sh... sh... I'm here, love, I'm here..."

She made Simeon light the brass lamps, the room slowly coming out of the gloom, Marius slouched in his chair, his hair a mess, his cheeks streaked with tears. He hadn't shaved for days, a dark beard sprouting on his face. His eyes followed Tertullia around the room, the plump woman clearing the mess with Tabia.

She walked to him, cupping his chin, lifting his hazy eyes to her. "Bathe, please? Simeon will wash you and shave off this scruff. He is an able little pup. I need somebody to show me where Tabia can cook. She will prepare our meal."

He nodded, dazed, but got up and walked to the door to talk to the guard. "Go and show this slave where she can cook, and then escort her back."

The guard watched him wide-eyed, not used to this soft tone, but obeyed, and led Tabia away with her pots, pans, and bags.

Marius walked back to his room, slowly peeling out of his clothes, numb. He could not look at Tertullia, and walked to the bath, lowering himself in the hot water, sighing when it enveloped his body. Simeon was next to him in an instant, utterly shameless, soaping him up methodically, and he let him, not even paying attention to what he was doing. He remembered Kyle's hands on his body and his tears flowed, thankfully invisible, on his wet face. Simeon soaped his face up then and carefully shaved him, making sure that his skin was smooth and perfect, his hands sliding all over it, rubbing some oil in after he'd finished. Tertullia watched them and busied herself with clearing the table and the broken jugs and cups all over the floor, alarmed at their number.

She waited for him to get out, still swaying, slipping a tunic on. Marius collapsed into his chair and she handed a cup of water to him. "I think this would be better for you now..."

He didn't comment, still not fully believing she was here, his voice a whisper. "I couldn't save him... I just..."

She stopped him, watching his crazed eyes carefully in his drawn features. "It's not your fault. Clavius was a soldier. He knew the risks. We all knew... but you... your letter?"

He shrugged. "We are raiding them tomorrow... those bastards..."

"You might be rushing to your death."

Marius smiled, bitter. "Yes, all the better... to end this..."

Her face steeled. "You should be ashamed." His face fell, paling, and she continued. "You think nobody needs you? That you're the most miserable now?"

He blushed, vaguely ashamed, and she reached into her gown, pulling a small square of wood out. "You want to die, Marius? Have a good, hard look at what you're leaving behind..."

She handed him the piece of wood and he looked at the painting on it, the portrait of a six months old baby, her large dark eyes framed with jet-black curls, smiling.

Marius' heart burst in his chest because he knew what she had brought him. His daughter. His daughter he had forgotten in his insane grief and mad hate.

She watched his face decompose, his eyes filled with tears, gently caressing the painting, and she spoke. "She needs you, Marius. Your wife doesn't care about her. Fortunately, she has Thais and Melissa and the children... and Paulus, to take care of her when her mother is always out, socializing. But she needs a father, somebody who cares for her, who will protect her. You... that is, if you are willing to stay alive?"

He looked at her, ashamed, his emotions washing his hate and lust for death out like a tide. He kissed her painting, putting it against his chest, sighing deep. "Let me do something..." He walked to the door and told the guard to get Julius.

The young centurion arrived shortly, seeing, surprised, the room lit up, the peasant woman sitting at the commander's table.

Marius gestured him in, his face pale, but a new light in his eyes. "Call off the raid tomorrow. I need to reach out to that chief and talk to him. Make sure he knows." Julius tried very hard not to show his relief and joy, not fully understanding what was going on. "Oh... and have Clavius' room prepared for his widow."

Tertullia waved to Julius, smiling, and the young man thought he'd gone insane. He left, his head reeling.

Tabia arrived then and set the table, putting her huge pot of broth in the middle.

She served a copious amount to Marius, and he sighed. "I don't think I can eat all this..."

Tertullia chuckled. "Just start eating. You won't be able to stop."

He shrugged and dug in; the taste bursting in his mouth, making it water. He ate without thinking and Tabia smiled. She then poured a pale-yellow liquid out from a jar, its perfume pervading the room. Her thick voice filled the space. "This will get rid of the wine, dominus, and your heavy head."

He sniffed at it, but Tertullia toasted him, bringing her cup to her lips. "Cheers to us, dear."

Marius drank deeply and the cool, sweet taste washed down his throat. He finished his bowl, slightly amazed that he'd eaten it all, the spicy food making his body tingle. He also felt all of a sudden incredibly sleepy, his nerves soothed, and he yawned, vaguely embarrassed. "I'm sorry... I never feel so sleepy usually..."

Tertullia smiled, putting her full cup down. "It's the shock, dear, of my humble appearance. Sleep then. I'll see you tomorrow."

She helped him up and walked him to his bed, tucking him in, watching his blue eyes roll up, and he was knocked out in seconds.

Tertullia turned to Tabia. "Just how much valerian did you put in that drink?"

She grinned. "Enough to knock out a rhino, domina."

They laughed softly and left him, his soft snores filling the room.

"The week is up, and we have already enough money to get out of this shithole!" Clavius was grinning, putting the coins into purses, Kyle silent, exhausted, watching the soft rain fall outside.

It was late afternoon and their last day in the city. Clavius had already informed the eunuch that they were not staying, much to his dismay. He had offered an insolent amount of money for Kyle, but Clavius had, of course, refused it, already sick of this whole affair.

He gently touched Kyle, making him face him. "You're alright?" Kyle nodded, too tired to talk. "Let's go... we need to buy that cart, the mule and supplies, and get the fuck out of here."

They walked to the market, Kyle still vaguely made-up, an entire week of it making it difficult to wash it off, but nobody seemed to care. They struck a deal fast and shopped enough food to last for their journey. The fort was a week's ride away, at last, and they set off, not wanting to lose time, Kyle awfully quiet, leaning against Clavius driving the cart.

The weather was turning foul, icy rain falling from the cold sky, the mud churning on the road and Clavius cursed softly each time the cart or the mule slid in it.

They traveled uninterrupted, crossing other travelers, but Clavius' impressive scar made other folks shy away, even rogue barbarians, their eyes just fleetingly glancing it over, mumbling, riding forward.

He grinned at Kyle. "This scar is scaring the bastards. I guess I should be thankful to the barbarian scum who did this." They laughed, but Clavius could not ignore Kyle's grey eyes swimming in sadness and fear. "Marius eating at you?"

The young man closed his eyes. "Yes... a bit."

"I'll talk to him. I owe my life to you and your able ass... he has to shut up and shove it." He grinned, but Kyle wasn't so sure.

Finally, the fort came into view in the dusk through the curtain of rain and their hearts raced.

"Now... we don't have the password, but if we're lucky, they'll let us close enough so that one of my guys recognizes me... or so I hope..."

They approached slowly, stopping short in front of the gates, and Clavius' voice boomed. "Anybody from the fourth century on duty?"

A soldier answered. "What's that to you, peasant? Fuck off quickly before we shoot your ass full of arrows."

They laughed on the wall, and Clavius grinned. "Balthus, you son of a bitch, if you don't open up, I think you'll hear of the general and myself."

There was a long silence, and the soldier poked his head out, his voice choked. "Centurion Clavius?"

"Not his ghost, that's for sure..."

"We buried you yesterday..."

"Well, I'm back. Open the goddamn door before I freeze my ass off in this rain."

The gates opened, and they were let in, his soldiers around Clavius, clasping his back, hugging, grinning.

Kyle sat on the cart, his heart racing.

Clavius grabbed his hand. "Come, let's surprise my brooding friend. I am sure he is in a wine induced coma, wallowing in self-pity over our untimely deaths."

He pulled him to Marius' room, knocking hard, his voice drifting through the wood. "Come in."

Kyle felt like suffocating, his heart in his throat, and Clavius' smiled at him, full of mischief. "Lets' go..."

Marius watched the door open from where he was standing near the window, expecting one of the slaves, or Julius, watching the two men walk in holding hands, and for a split second, he couldn't recognize them, his mind having buried them, the ceremony still fresh from the previous day where he had made peace with his loss, clutching Tertullia's hand.

Clavius grinned. "Speechless, my good friend? That's unlike you..."

His voice knocked the breath out of Marius, the shock too big, the blood draining from his face. *Clavius.* But his parted mouth couldn't form his name, watching in a haze as he approached, tugging somebody behind him, grey eyes lifting to meet his. *Kyle.*

His world darkened, and they caught him before he would black out, heaving, clutching him into their arms, kneeling on the floor as they could not hold him up.

"Hey, big boy... don't faint on me!"

His voice dragged Marius back, their warm arms around his body, Kyle's scent invading him, feeling his neck under his mouth. "Oh, gods... oh gods...", he could only moan, a cold sweat breaking down his back as he was struggling to remain conscious.

Clavius grew alarmed, disentangling himself, gently shaking his shoulder. "Hey... come on, I'm sorry, maybe we should have asked somebody to come in and tell you... hey..."

Marius raised his glazed eyes at him, trying to focus on his face, his features sharper, that huge scar marring the left side. Marius' hand flew to it, the flesh warm under his touch, his voice a mere breath.

"You're alive..."

"No shit... Thanks to your love boy here..."

Marius' eyes flew to Kyle, his love bursting him apart, he clutched at him, pulling his body close, slamming his mouth on his mouth and Kyle opened up to him, hungry for him, their tongues meeting in their warm pool, the feeling overwhelming, making them cry softly as they kissed, out of breath. Clavius watched them with a small smile, waiting until they parted, panting, their eyes locked, clutching at each other, Marius' voice a mere whisper. "My love... oh gods..."

They hugged, and Clavius rose. "I should leave you alone."

Marius looked up at him. "Don't you dare...don't you dare disappear..."

He raised his hands. "Ok, ok... besides burying me, did you also reallocate my room?"

Marius sighed, his eyes twinkling. "I'm afraid so.... your good wife has moved in there..."

Clavius blanched. "Tertullia is here?! Why didn't you say so?"

He whirled when the door opened and she stood there, struck, her eyes wide, taking in the scene of Clavius standing over Marius and Kyle kneeling into each other's arms.

She couldn't speak and her hand flew to her mouth, tears spilling. They rushed into each other's arms, Tertullia collapsing onto Clavius' chest.

A little while later, they were all sitting in Marius' room, Tertullia on Clavius' knees, and Kyle leaning against Marius, the Roman's arm around him.

Tertullia turned to Clavius, stroking his face. "You have to tell us everything... I still can't believe it..."

Clavius gestured towards Kyle. "They boy knows more... I woke up to the smell of grilled fish."

Kyle blushed when he felt Marius tighten his arm around him. "Tell us, love..."

He sighed, recounting what had happened, Tertullia's eyes wide.

"You can swim?"

Kyle shrugged. "Yes, we swam a lot when I was a kid...", he shut up, and she understood, Marius gently holding him.

"And then?"

They talked further, taking over from each other when they arrived at the part when they had met the merchants, and Clavius shut up, his face grim, watching Kyle.

Marius frowned. "What happened?"

There was silence, and Clavius cleared his throat. "Well... we had little choice, barely dressed and unarmed... so... we agreed to their deal... it was that or we were dead... again..."

Marius' blood ran cold. "What deal?"

Kyle spoke then very softly, his voice neutral, carefully choosing his words in front of Tertullia. "They wanted to spend time with me in exchange for money and clothes so..." He felt Marius stiffen, his body taut with his rising anger.

He didn't need to continue, and Clavius looked at his friend. "You're pissed? In that moment, I was pissed too, but we had no choice, really..."

Marius quieted but his anger brew under the surface and his arm loosened around Kyle, the young man hurt to the core at the unfairness of it all.

They recounted their arrival to the city, their struggle to figure out what to do on hostile land, and Kyle saw how much Clavius was embarrassed, not knowing how to continue, fearful of Marius' reaction.

Kyle pushed Marius' hands off him, slightly facing him, his anger boiling. "I'm sparing you the effort of taking your hands off me once you find out what we had to do in order to make it back here on time, alive."

Marius' face fell. "Kyle..."

"No, let me finish. We rented a whorehouse and sold my body out for a week to gather enough coins to make it back to you." He shut up but faced him off, his eyes welled with tears, not lowering them. "And now, you can hate me all you want."

Marius' shock was plain, his face contorting in pain at his words, knowing he should understand but his jealousy burst into flames in his chest, clashing with the joy of his love being alive, and an impossible anger rose in him, those demons still very much present, waiting, lurking.

He rose, his eyes not leaving the slave, but he spoke to Clavius and Tertullia. "I think you should retire... this has been a long day..."

Clavius stood, his hand going to his arm. "Marius..."

He shrugged him off. "Go... now. I'll see you tomorrow."

Clavius and Tertullia left then, worried sick, holding hands.

Marius watched him and Kyle didn't lower his eyes, defiant, his anger too plain, the events of the last weeks tearing at him.

Marius' eyes blazed, his voice seething. "How many?"

Kyle blinked, thrown. "What?"

Marius grabbed his tunic, pulling him up, his face inches from Kyle's face. "How many men?"

Kyle swallowed, breathing hard, trying to free himself. "It doesn't matter... they don't matter... let me go!"

Marius grabbed him harder, the fabric biting into his throat, making it a struggle to breathe, Kyle's eyes going wide. *He's going to kill me....*

"How... many..."

He tried to remember, panicked, pushing out the words from his airless lungs. "I don't know... thirty... maybe..."

He clawed at Marius' hands, struggling to free himself, and Marius let him go just before he would black out, heaving, collapsing on the floor, his hand flying to his throat. Kyle only had one idea. *Flee. Out of this room, away from him.* He shot to his feet, but he was dizzy and Marius caught him, flinging him against the wall, the shock so painful he moaned.

Marius stood in front of him, close, his face a mask of anger, his hands fisted at his side. "Just where do you think you're going?"

Kyle watched him, panting, out of breath, his anger wiped by his fear coated in his love. Utterly exhausted, he gave up. *Because I still love you... despite everything... and I can't bear to lose you.* He slid down the wall, to his knees, his forehead going to the floor, his hands reaching for Marius' legs, enveloping his calves.

His voice flew softly. "Just do what you want with me... I'm yours, dominus."

His words burst through the haze of Marius' mind, his eyes growing wide at Kyle's sight and his words. His love for him battling with his hate, his revulsion at what he'd told him, what he'd done, even if he had had no choice... Days ago he'd mourned him, and now he'd almost killed him...

He breathed in deep, his hands going under Kyle's armpits, pulling him up. "Get up." Kyle did, his face lowered, in a daze. "You know what I'm going to do to you?"

Kyle shook his head.

Marius cupped his chin, forcing his eyes into his eyes. "I'm going to fuck the memory of those men out of you."

Kyle's eyes welled up, his heart beating fast, but he said nothing. There was nothing left to say. He had given it all up.

Marius let him go. "Bend over on the bed, feet on the floor. And don't you dare fucking move."

He obeyed, waiting, his tears streaming into the sheets and Marius watched him, his anger slowly dwindling. *What the fuck am I doing?* He watched Kyle's back move up and down as he breathed, quietly, then walked up to him, standing between his parted legs, slowly caressing his back.

"Missed me...?" There was no answer, and he stopped. "Answer me."

A soft sigh. "Yes..."

He continued his caresses, pushing his demons back, watching Kyle's eyes close, his tears spilling silently, and a twinge of pity raced through his heart. *This is your love, asshole... what are you doing? He saved your best friend's life...* Marius' eyes drifted to his daughter's painting on the bedside table and his face fell, his hate shattered by his love, and he looked down at Kyle with new eyes, that red cloud of raw anger lifted off, shame washing over him.

Marius crawled up on the bed and pulled Kyle up into his arms. "Come here... come here... oh gods, what an asshole I've been, love..."

Kyle froze against him, but Marius just stroked him, his side, his back, his hands roaming Kyle, cradling his face, slowly warming him up. "Look at me... I am sorry... forgive me, pet..."

Marius kissed him deep, his tongue stroking Kyle's mouth, his teeth, his tongue, and Kyle melted at his words, relief flooding him like a tidal wave.

He kissed him back, pushing his tongue against his, slowly, making him moan, Marius close to tears. "I missed you so much... thought you died... I'm so fucking jealous... I love you..."

Kyle just kissed him, unable to talk, overwhelmed by his kindness and love.

Marius smoothed his palm along his cheek, kissing him between words. "Forget fucking... I'll love you to pieces..."

XVII

They lay quietly, Marius behind him, his head propped on his arm, his other arm around Kyle, listening to the rain spattering the window.

Kyle's eyes went to the portrait on the bedside table. "Your baby?"

He felt Marius nod, feeling him smile through his words. "Yes... she's grown a lot, right?"

There was a twinge of sadness in his words, and Kyle held his arm tighter, trying to comfort him. It was still warm under the sheets, but a vague chill radiated off the walls now. They would have to heat soon.

Kyle felt Marius' lips graze his neck, and he turned his head to look at him, a small smile on his lips. "More?"

"No, love... I just can't believe you're here... I thought I'd lost you forever."

That wild, mad light flicked through his eyes, and Kyle reached up to touch his face. "You were in a lot of pain..."

It wasn't a question, and he didn't need to answer, Marius' eyes lost in the distance of his memories. "I guess I lost it a bit... you and Clavius... it was too much... I almost raided that settlement we were going to? It would have been suicide, but I didn't care at that point... I wanted to die, and join you." He shivered, realizing now that if Tertullia hadn't come, he would have run to his death, not knowing they were alive... and his daughter would have been an orphan. "I was selfish, as ever."

Kyle frowned. "You are anything but."

Marius sighed. "You are too kind, pet... I don't even deserve you."

Kyle turned to face him, searching his eyes. "Are you serious?"

"Yes..." He quieted a bit, his hand tracing the slave's back, his eyes softly glowing in the dim light. "I should free you for saving Clavius' life."

His words chilled Kyle, his lips parting in utter shock. *Free. Freedom.* A long-forgotten word, something he had banned from his life, accepting fully what he had become, belonging to Marius being probably the best thing that could have happened in this existence, and now, he wanted to end it? He knew about freedmen, free but somehow still belonging to the extended family of their dominus, but as freedmen, they could work, build their own business, have a family, but a relationship would be impossible with Marius... a life with him, in his home...

And free to do what? Move back to his homeland? His village and family gone, wiped out, the land invaded by Romans, roaming an unknown world which suddenly seemed too big, too dangerous.

His eyes grew wide, his panic-stricken voice barely making it past his lips. "I don't want to be freed..."

Marius looked at him, puzzled. "You don't? But... that would be the only suitable reward for what you've done, hell, it's not even enough...I thought this was your dream...you could go home, it's not far from here you know?" He felt so much pain, but he was determined to carry it through, out of his love for him.

"No!" He grasped Marius' shoulder, his fingers digging into his flesh. "Promise me! Promise me you won't do it."

"Kyle..."

"Just promise... please..." His eyes begged him, full of tears.

"I can't make such a promise... it would be foolish. Circumstances change and I might need to free you..."

"No... please..."

Marius sighed, looking at him. *He is truly desperate... what the...* He stroked his face. "Alright.... Can I at least put it in my will that if I die, you are to be freed? I don't want you to end up in a bad place."

"Yes... maybe?"

Marius smiled, trying to reassure him. "Then I promise not to free you whilst I'm alive. Happy?"

Kyle relaxed a bit, breathing out. "Yes...", but his eyes were still full of fear and Marius pulled him into his chest.

"I would have hated to be without you, but I thought I'd make you happy..."

"I'm happy with you. The rest doesn't matter..." He pushed his head into Marius' chest, feeling his warmth, inhaling his scent, his mouth on his skin, his salty taste on his tongue.

He licked Marius' skin, planting soft kisses on, it and he felt him shudder, goose bumps rising under his lips.

Marius' voice, amused. "If you don't stop, we won't sleep..."

Kyle didn't stop, and licked his way down Marius' body, making him moan and roll his eyes back.

The camp doctor examined Clavius' scar, gently probing it. "Impressive healing... I couldn't have done any better... well, maybe sewing it together would have minimized the size of it, but the tissues healed nicely. Any pain?"

"Yes, sometimes, in the bone." Clavius rubbed his face, grinning. "But I don't give a shit, I'm alive. Thanks, doctor."

He strode back to the officer's building, knocking on Marius' door, waiting to be called in. He poked his head in. "Interrupting?"

Marius looked at him, amused. "No... I already did a morning briefing, remember?"

"How could I forget? Your mighty commanding look with those dark circles around your eyes..." Marius smirked but didn't comment. "Where's your love boy?"

"He went to get breakfast."

Clavius walked to him. "Sit down. So... the men are shit scared of you. Rumor says that you've been possessed by some demons and have lost your mind." Marius remained quiet, his blue eyes not giving anything away. "So?"

"So... maybe there's some truth in that... I wasn't myself."

Clavius sighed. "It will take a lot of work to make this right."

"I know..."

"You have to behave like a real commander and control your temper..."

"Yes..."

"Quit drinking..."

Marius waved his hand. "I got it."

"Really? I hope so. That young centurion did a damn good job of keeping your reputation up."

"I know..."

Clavius quieted, watching him, not really knowing how to broach the subject. "So... yesterday... after we'd left..."

A shadow crossed Marius' face. "I wasn't very nice to him... but then, I realized what a jerk I was and... let's just say we worked it out."

Clavius sighed. "I'm mildly relieved. I owe my life to your boy. Whatever he did, he did it to save my ass. You should be worshipping him instead of being your usual angry self."

"Yes... let's not talk about this anymore...? I'm trying really hard to forget what happened."

"Sure.... but rumor says you were not without fault either..."

Marius blanched slightly, knowing what he was referring to, his voice hard. "I wasn't myself."

"Frankly, I don't think that's an excuse."

"She was a whore, no big deal..."

They looked up when Kyle entered, shutting up, but he knew them too well to know that something was up, their faces too composed, Marius too pale.

He laid out the breakfast. "Master Clavius, are you eating?"

Clavius rose, patting him on the back. "No, I've eaten with my wife." He looked at Marius. "Tell him."

Marius watched him leave, a flicker of anger in his eyes, spinning into a mild fear.

Kyle turned to him. "What should you tell me?"

Marius shifted, waving towards a chair. "Sit down..." Kyle watched his blue eyes fill with misery. "I did something whilst I thought you were gone forever, and I'm not proud of it, especially after the way I treated you yesterday..." Kyle waited and he continued, mildly resigned. "I wanted that barbarian girl to help us, you know, the one who's been given away by her father, so... I asked Julius to bring her to my room and..."

He stopped, unsure how to word it, and Kyle spoke softly. "You raped her."

Marius' head whipped up. "What? No... I mean, I wouldn't call it rape... she was a prostitute after all..." But he wasn't sure anymore, squirming in his seat under his grey eyes. "In any case... I threatened her... that if she doesn't cooperate with us, I'll have the whole cohort go through her..." His own words made him sick and a vague nausea swept through his body, making him close his eyes.

Kyle watched him, pity, and anger coursing through him, revolted more by his threat than the fact that he'd forced her. "Would you have carried it through? Your threat?"

His heart beat fast and Marius looked at him, pained. "Probably... I was mad, completely crazy..."

Kyle pulled a slight face. "Why are you telling me this?"

"Because you deserve to know... and now, you can hate me all you want."

Kyle hid a smile, listening to him using his own words. He poured a cup of posca and handed it to him, his face calm. "Nothing can be done about what you did, so you'll just have to live with it. I could sulk and push you away, but I know who you are." Marius' face fell, but Kyle raised his hand. "And I love you, anyway... I guess that in our own ways, we're both damaged... just differently."

Marius' heart raced. "You're the best thing in my life."

"And you in mine... just don't forget this if things ever get rough."

Fall settled in, a slow chill in the damp air, the rain wearing at them, the constant fog sitting on the landscape. Their negotiations with the ruling tribe went slowly, the rebel tribes gone again, or so it seemed.

One rainless day, they decided to go hunting. With winter near, they needed to stock up the supplies and Marius was quietly thrilled, the idle diplomatic meetings and sitting in the fort getting on his restless nerves. Clavius decided not to join them, his scar giving him grief, the weather throbbing in his cheekbone and head, so Marius set off with a couple of officers and soldiers, the hunting master, and Kyle on a cart which they hoped to fill with game.

They were progressing slowly on horseback, going deeper into the forest, but not too far from the fort, alert, but not worried. There hadn't been any signs of the rebels so far, and the neighboring tribes had all signed a peace treaty. The hunt master spotted some deer tracks, and they quieted, slowly progressing, spotting the animal among the trees. Marius looked at Kyle and gestured to him to stay behind, so he stopped the cart and sat, watching them gallop away, chasing the beautiful animal which had shot off into the woods.

Kyle settled in for a long wait, hearing them shout, their voices dwindling. A slight unease settled in him, the forest quiet around him, too quiet, the pine leaves softly whistling in the fall breeze. He pulled his shirt tighter, and hugged himself, a slow chill creeping in him.

Kyle waited for what seemed like hours until the sun seemed high up into the sky and he fidgeted, nervous. Where were they? His eyes darted back to where they had come from, in the direction of the fort. Should he leave and get help? *But maybe they just rode too far...* One of the mules' ears perked up, and his heart fluttered. Maybe they were riding back? He listened, and there was the distant sound of hooves, slowly approaching.

At last... relief flooded him as men became visible in the woods, but something was off.... the lead horse not being Marius' black stallion... tall men clad in animal skin, their faces covered with beards. His blood froze, and Kyle jumped off the cart, running as best as he could into the woods, those hooves too close, hammering the ground. He was knocked off his feet and crashed into a tree; the world going black.

Kyle woke slowly, a dull throb on his forehead. He opened his eyes carefully, his heart hammering in his chest, hearing foreign voices around him in a guttural language he could not understand. He moved his hands and realized, surprised, that he had not been tied down. He looked around carefully. A large village, probably, huts and burning fires, women cooking on them, warriors walking around. He felt the ground under his body and shifted his eyes to the man sitting next to him, waiting, his eyes lost in the flames of the fire in front of him. *How long have I been knocked out? Where am I? Where's Marius...* His hand went to his head, and he felt a cut on his forehead, already scabbing. *Nothing too bad.*

The man sitting next to him spotted him move and turned around, a large grin on his face. He had a long scruffy blonde beard and long hair, all dressed in skin and fur. "Awake last?" His Latin was crude, and Kyle just nodded, not wanting to talk.

The man got up and pulled him up, dragging him to a large hut in the middle of the village, shoving him in. Kyle landed on his knees and decided to stay there; the position bringing a mild comfort in his panicked state.

He looked up, straight into the steely grey eyes of their leaders, his rich brown beard and long hair, his amused face. "You're a fast runner. My men had a hard time catching you on horseback."

He spoke Latin well, and Kyle just watched him, breathing hard.

The chief watched him carefully. "You are not a Roman."

Kyle decided it was probably better to speak at this stage, his mind racing. "No, I'm not.... I'm a Celt."

The chief raised his eyebrows. "A Celt? Interesting... but you work for the Romans."

"I don't work for them. I'm a slave."

"Whose slave?"

Kyle's guard went up. *Careful.* "Just a camp slave."

"Your name?"

"Kyle."

The chief tasted his name. "Kyle... nice name. I knew many Celts and tribe leaders when I still traveled there."

Kyle shrugged. "I was a simple peasant boy, nothing more."

He nodded, eyeing him curiously. "Well, Kyle, as you can see, we kept you alive. My men sort of figured that you must be a captive. But those days are over. You are free now."

Kyle blanched, looking at him. "What...? But..."

"Is there a problem?"

His chilled tone made Kyle lower his eyes. "No... I mean, I ought to thank you."

"Start by getting up. You don't have to kneel to me." Kyle got up, on shaky legs, standing in front of him. "I am Adelbrand, and I lead this tribe. I think you might have heard of me."

Kyle knew who he was. The father of that girl, their supposed ally, but he just shrugged. "I am a simple camp slave, I don't know much."

Adelbrand smiled. "Yes, of course... so, you look like an able young man, strong, but I gather you have no fighting skills?" Kyle nodded. "Not an issue. You can learn with us and fight with us. Take revenge on those savage Romans who took years of your life... and maybe more?" Kyle swallowed, shame washing over him. Adelbrand smiled wryly. "I figured... So, my offer is up, boy? What's your decision? You can also leave and try to make it to Britannia, but the roads are tricky and full of Roman soldiers..."

Kyle swayed a bit, steeling himself after a few moments. He had no choice, again, his thoughts flying to Marius. *Forgive me, love.* "I'll stay with you, Adelbrand."

"Excellent! Now, just stay, as this might be a glorious moment for you too and your vengeful little heart." Kyle stood next to him, a few other fighters walking in, and Adelbrand boomed. "Bring in the prisoner."

A half-naked man was dragged in then, his hands bound behind his back, and he was shoved down to his knees in front of Adelbrand.

That muscled back.... the jet-black hair... Kyle felt the air being knocked out of him as his stomach became a pit of ice. A warrior yanked the prisoner's head up by his hair, his blue eyes wild, a gag pulled tight into his mouth. Their eyes locked and Marius' face fell momentarily in shock, just to be slowly replaced by a burning hate.

Adelbrand looked at Kyle, his smile mocking. "Isn't that a glorious feeling, the mighty Roman general Marius kneeling at our feet?" The others laughed, but Kyle couldn't, too shocked, his mind numb. "I see you're in shock, boy, but he can't hurt you. He can't hurt anybody."

The fighter next to Marius kicked him in the belly, and he howled, doubling over. It took every ounce of Kyle's self-control not to lurch forward and protect him. *Do not give yourself away. Think. Think.*

The fighter pulled Marius' head up again, making him look at Adelbrand with his eyes filled with pain. "See... this is what happens when you mock me and think that your pathetic peace treaties mean anything to me... I have the upper hand now, having you at my feet. You will stay with us and I'll negotiate your life with the emperor. I know who you are. He will probably not let you down. Then again, you are all dogs and you would eat your own child if it meant winning a war..." He turned to Kyle. "Did this Roman dog cause you grief?"

Kyle nodded, making sure his voice didn't falter. "Yes."

"Beat you up, raped you? Treated you like shit?"

"Yes."

Adelbrand's lips curled into a cruel smile. "It's payback time then... but we can't really damage our priced negotiation good here, can we?"

He paused, thinking, and Kyle spoke, trying to put all his hate and hurt into his voice. "I would love to take care of him, if you don't mind, just to make sure he suffers the way he made all of us suffer... without damaging him too much, of course..."

Adelbrand watched him with an icy smile. "Tempting... but I don't know if I can trust you, you served them after all."

"I had no choice... they have ways to get you there..." His face was so miserable that the old man bought it, seeing his tears pool into his grey eyes.

Somehow, he reminded him of his dead son and his heart clenched at the young slave's suffering. "Fine, fine... let's do this." He turned to the fighter standing next to Marius. "Chain him and cage him up on the cart. He can stay the way he is. Oh, and make sure he gets a good beating before you stash him away. He deserves it... not too rough though, he needs to live."

The fighters left, grinning, dragging Marius out. Kyle watched them, his heart bursting, his face impassive, cold.

Adelbrand turned to Kyle. "We are moving North soon in the mountains for our winter settlement. They can't reach us there, these bastards!" He waved a tall fighter over. "Lothar, give the boy clothes and show him around. He'll also be in charge of this animal of a Roman here. He has a lot to make him pay back."

Kyle smiled at Adelbrand. "Yes, I do..."

"Very well! Go with Lothar and then you can watch over this beast. In a couple of days, you can drive the cart with the convoy." Adelbrand clasped his shoulder. "You remind me of my son... he died fighting these bastards... but I am glad we saved you. If the emperor doesn't give a shit about this general, you can kill him the way you want. Torture him for hours... anything you want."

Kyle smiled back at him, his eyes gleaming. "Thank you..."

Back at the fort, Clavius and Julius watched the forest, dusk settling, a light rain falling from the grey sky.

"They should have been back by now... let's send the cavalry to search for them."

Julius nodded when a black stallion galloped out of the woods, wild. Clavius' blood froze, seeing the riderless mount. "Marius' horse...open the gates!"

They did, and the animal flew in, soldiers catching the reins. Clavius and Julius ran down from the ramparts, trying to calm the wild animal, his eyes darting around in their orbits. Clavius soothed him and his eyes went to the saddle, Marius' cape on it.

He took it off, alarmed at the bloodstains, and Julius took the scroll wedged between the saddles leather flaps. "Look..."

He opened it and wordlessly handed it to Clavius.

We have your general. Inform the emperor that he is alive, and he needs to negotiate if he wants his beloved nephew back in one piece. Your letters can be left in that big oak tree near the river. Just follow it, you can't miss it. If you don't obey and try to come with an army, he dies. Adelbrand

Clavius' hands shook. "A messenger, quick! Get ready to deliver this to Rome..." *Rome, weeks away...* He looked at Julius, their faces ashen, Clavius smoothing his hair back. "Fuck! Fuck! Fuck!"

"You're in charge now, Clavius."

"I fucking know it... let's write a response to these shits..." *And Kyle? Where was the boy? Probably killed...* "A response and then we're patrolling. Let's try to find survivors and see where they got caught. Prepare two centuries." *My friend... I hope you're not too bad off...*

Kyle followed Lothar, trying as best as he could to ignore the desperate groans and cries coming from behind the huts, the dull thud of blows raining on human flesh.

The tall fighter brought him to a supply room and gave him clothes. He also showed him where they had stashed the food and ingredients. "You will need a cooking pot, here. Make sure that Roman animal is fed, but not too much. He can't die, but we won't make him feel full either." He grinned, and Kyle gathered what he needed. Lothar then gave him a large knife. "Here, you'll need this. If he gives you grief, just poke him enough to draw blood? That should shut him up!"

Lothar laughed and Kyle smiled, a strange feeling overcoming him, the knife familiar in his hands. He knew how to fight, of course, but kept his mouth shut. He had to wait and play the game, praying that Marius would somehow understand.

They strolled around the village, and Kyle realized it was bigger than he'd thought, memories of his village pouring in, this long-lost feeling of just doing what he wanted.

Lothar glanced at him. "You're awfully silent?"

Kyle swallowed, not even having to fake how moved he was. "It's just... this village... it's very similar to mine... how mine was... brings back memories."

Lothar stopped; his eyes filled with sympathy. "You're free now and you belong with us. Even if you're a Celt, we fight for the same cause. Freedom from these oppressors, these monsters... I do hope the emperor won't negotiate; I want to be there when we kill that son of a bitch of a general." He spat and clasped Kyle on the shoulder. "Talking of which... here he is... I'll leave you with him, have fun. This small hut next to the cage is yours. You can sleep in there until we leave."

Kyle nodded, his eyes on the still, huddled form in the cage put on a big cart. He approached carefully, not showing any emotions, his training kicking in when he had to fake all the time and keep his face still.

He couldn't help drawing in a sharp breath though when he saw Marius' bloodied body, his hands and feet in shackles, a large iron collar on his neck. The shackles were bound by chains, but he could not see how long they were. Marius curled up into a fetal position, knocked out cold, his lips parted, blood seeping out of his mouth on the cage's dark wooden floor. His body was full of dark bruises, his ribs slowly rising. They had left his pants on, but that was all the clothing he had, and Kyle shivered, the chilly air getting at him despite being fully clothed. His hands went to the cold iron grate of the cage, testing the bolts. It was strong, and they hadn't left him a key, of course. He sighed, going into the small hut to put his stuff down, and then he went to gather some firewood.

He lit a good fire in front of the hut, close to the cage, hoping that some warmth might seep up to it, and he proceeded to cook oatmeal, a large pot, waiting for Marius to regain his senses.

Kyle had to wait until night fell. The air chilled, and he stoked the fire up when Marius stirred, moaning. Kyle was on his feet in an instant, going to the cage, looking around to make sure that there was nobody near.

Marius sat up, his blurred vision slowly clearing, an agonizing pain coursing through his body. He tried to move his hands, but they felt heavy, a sudden chill running down his skin as he realized he had been shackled, his hand painfully rising to his throat, feeling the cold iron collar against his skin. He looked up, the cage's ceiling too close, and a vague panicked seized him when he realized he could not get up fully, not with his height... if he could even get up, every move a torture, his bruises stabs. *Broken ribs... probably more than one...* His lips cut, his stomach so painful he felt like throwing up whatever was in there, the metallic taste of blood rich in his mouth. He moaned, bathing in pain, the chill of the night biting his bare skin.

Marius caught a movement out of the corner of his vision and moved his head to the side, his eyes locking with Kyle's, those grey pools silent. Marius' blood warmed, a slow anger rising in him, and he watched Kyle's lips part, just to shut again when Lothar stepped up near the cage.

"Awake? Good... we don't want you to die... yet!" He laughed, putting his arm around Kyle's shoulders. "Must feel real good seeing this beast all tied down and locked up?"

Kyle's eyes bore into Marius'. "Yes, things got really rough for him..." A slight spark lit up Marius' blue eyes at his words, and Kyle's heart raced. *Please, love, please understand...*

Lothar patted his back. "I'll leave you to it. Make sure he feels like shit."

Marius watched him leave, his eyes drifting back to Kyle, silent, but the hate was gone from them, his handsome face streaked with dark bruises, and Kyle stepped closer to the cage, his lips very close to the cold bars, his voice a mere whisper. "We are being watched..." Marius blinked slowly once, and Kyle got it, smiling slightly. "I'll get you some food and water."

He went back to the fire, and Marius hugged his knees to his chest, the cold chains lacing around him. He shut his eyes against the pain, the bitter cold, his mind racing. *Can I trust him? Should I? But his words...* his words made him cling to the only hope he had, that he loved him more than freedom, the possibility of a new life. Marius watched him come back and push a bowl of oatmeal in, the soft mush gently fuming in the cold air. Marius reached for it, unsure if he could eat anything at all, his stomach a block of pain, but he forced it down anyway with trembling hands, the hot paste feeling divine in the cold.

He leant back; the bowl sliding from his hand, tumbling towards the grates where Kyle pulled it out.

"Drink." He pushed in a water pouch and watched as Marius drank, the water spilling from the corner of his mouth, carving a path in the dried blood on his muscled neck.

Kyle swallowed, steeling himself to hide his emotions, when Marius went back to hugging his knees, his forehead resting on them. The collar bit into his throat and he had to shift his head upwards, realizing maybe for the very first time what slaves had to endure when they were captured. He swallowed, the food and water somersaulting in his bloodied stomach.

His hand went to the collar, trying to loosen it obviously to no avail, and Kyle spoke to him, gently. "Don't give in to panic, just accept it... if you tug at it, it will chaff your skin raw and make you lose your mind..."

Marius looked at him, his eyes wide, but he let go of the collar, slowly exhaling.

"Good... I can't keep talking to you... they might hear it... just play the part, act like I'm driving you crazy..."

Marius nodded, his eyes closed, and Kyle left him, shivering, knowing he could not give him anything warm for now. He stoked up the fire, and some warmth drifted into the cage, making Marius sigh. Kyle watched as his large body slid to the side and collapsed in utter exhaustion on the floor of the cage.

The day rose, bleak, the air filled with moisture and the promise of winter. Kyle had cooked oatmeal again, but he had also secretly put honey in it, watching Marius gobble it down. Marius pulled a face, though, to make sure that onlookers thought it tasted foul. Kyle then quickly washed the bowl out, getting rid of the evidence. He was also busy packing, Adelbrand having decided to leave earlier, fearing that the weather would turn before they could reach the mountain passes and roads.

Lothar walked up to the cage. "How is our beast doing?"

Kyle pulled a face. "Being his usual Roman self... even caged up, he thinks he's the king of the world."

Lothar took his sword out, poking Marius in his side, making him scramble back into the cage, yelping at the sharp pain. A small drop of blood appeared where the sword had broken flesh. "See? Just poke him with your knife when he's being an asshole."

He laughed, and Kyle grinned at him, playing the part when he was dying inside. Marius pushed his hand on the wound, grinding his teeth, his eyes shut tight.

"Get ready to leave in a couple of hours. Your cart can will be in the middle of the convoy. We don't want our precious cargo unguarded. The road is long and treacherous, but just follow the riders. They know the paths well. In a couple of days, we'll be walled up into the mountains, partying." He winked at Kyle. "There are some girls who are dying to get to know you... And this one here...", he gestured at Marius "... can rot in a nice cozy cave we have carved in the rock... a bit cold, but not enough to kill him." He laughed and left, swinging his sword.

Kyle breathed deep, his eyes going to Marius, those blue eyes burning into Lothar's back. He went to pack the cart, stashing it on the right on the driver's bench. Two sturdy horses were led to him by a young boy and he helped Kyle hook them to the cart, the large draft animals peaceably waiting.

Lothar rode up to him. "Let's go."

Kyle got on the cart, his back wedged against the cage, and followed Lothar's horse, driving the cart into the flow of horses, pedestrians, carts leaving the village towards the distant mountains. His heart was heavy and his mind busy... *What to do now?* They were effectively trapped...

They stopped at night to camp and Kyle raised a small tent to sleep next to the cart, busy then with cooking, but Lothar walked up to him. "Come, eat with us."

Kyle glanced at Marius, sitting, quietly shivering, his eyes lost in the distance. "I need to feed him first."

Lothar laughed. "You don't have to feed him every day... Were you always fed?" Kyle shook his head, an icy feeling inside of him. "So, the fuck do you care?"

He looked up at Lothar, an evil grin on his face. "You're right... let's go."

They left, and Marius watched them go, drawing on his training to bear the hunger and the cold. His whole body ached from being cramped up in the cage, jostled all day on uneven roads, the unyielding iron wheels bouncing on every rock and into every hole.

Kyle came back much later in the night, his heart clenched, just to find Marius collapsed on the hard, wooden floor, his body having given up out of exhaustion.

Next morning, they left, and Kyle hadn't fed Marius at all nor given him water, wary of Lothar's prying eyes, smiling at him with satisfaction when he noticed Marius' parched lips.

He rode next to the cart, grinning. "I see you got a taste of making him suffer? Good. He should too." He spat square into Marius' face, the Roman just wiping it off, not caring.

The sputtering mud from the road and horses had covered Marius' body, his muscles clenched against the chilly weather, and in the afternoon, a torrential rain poured down on them. The top of the cage was made of wooden planks, but the rain filtered through the cracks and the wind blew it inside, drenching him. Marius pressed his knees into his chest, hugging them, the water streaming down his uncontrollably shivering body, his bruises aching with every move. His shackles had rubbed his skin raw, and the water bit into them, making him even more sore, the burning pain constant. He whimpered, slowly losing it, not knowing how he could hold any further, but he licked his arms, the small rivulets of water somewhat quenching his thirst.

Kyle turned back at the sound, worried sick, watching alarmed, Marius hug his knees, his face buried in his arms, his whole body shaking. He gestured Lothar over. "I know he needs to suffer, but if we don't do something, he'll freeze to death before we arrive, or worse, become sick and die on us..."

Lothar watched the shivering wretch, and his lips curled into a smile. "Yes, I see...you're right. Do you have your horses' blankets?" Kyle nodded. The crude blankets were under his seat, stacked with the rest of the supplies. "Let's throw one on him. That should keep him alive, hopefully."

Kyle reached down and pulled the blanket out, the rain thankfully stopping. They stopped to allow Lothar to open the cage, and he threw the blanket on him. "Here, Roman scum... don't you die on us!" He laughed and banged the cage shut, Kyle starting the cart again.

With his strength dwindling and his hands a bunch of pain, Marius managed to pull the blanket around his shoulders. It felt divine, even if he was still cold, his body was at least sheltered somewhat from the wind. He rested his head on his arms and fell asleep, exhausted, his hunger and thirst burning in him.

Marius and Kyle could not speak, the riders too close on the roads winding towards the mountains. Pain and cold had become Marius' companions, his mind numbed to them, as well as hunger and thirst.

Whenever they camped, the kids came and poked him with long sticks, making him move around the cage, laughing, and Kyle had to let them until they got bored with it. Sometimes, it was the warriors who, drunk, made fun of him, rattling the cage with their swords, not letting him sleep, and they provoked him to lose it and bang his body into the grates, just to collapse, heaving, in tears.

He'd been locked up for a week and hadn't been able to stand at all, wrapped most of the time in that filthy blanket, his eyes dull, lost in some distant space.

Finally, they arrived at the mountains, the single path slowly rising, and they had to ride in a single file, the path narrow, barely allowing the cart to fit, winding upwards into the woods.

Marius sat in the cage, his back to Kyle, oblivious to the jolts of the cart on the uneven path. His hunger tore at him, slow tears forming in his eyes at the pain, when he felt a small poke in his back, the gentle jab of an elbow. He slowly slid his hand down, moving it against the cold bars, stretching his fingers, and he felt Kyle's warm fingers locking around them, gently squeezing. He shut his eyes, overcome with emotions, their intertwined fingers hidden by Kyle's back and cloak.

Kyle felt how icy Marius' fingers were, a shadow of concern on his face, and he tried to convene some warmth and comfort through their skins touching, his heart beating fast. Slowly, he pulled his hand out and heard Marius whimper, but he then pushed his fingers back, a piece of bread in them. Marius took it and brought it to his mouth, his face hidden in the blanket. The riders could not see what was happening, riding in front and behind the cart, and Kyle fed him bit by bit, until he ran out of bread. Kyle held Marius' fingers then, gently stroking through the icy grates, not caring that his fingers froze too, their backs inches from each other.

XVIII

News of Marius' capture had reached Rome fast, the messengers riding like crazy, straight to the imperial palace.

The emperor read it, and his face clouded in anger. "How dare they?! Get my brother and inform Marius' wife too..." His advisors watched him, their faces alarmed, as he paced the room. "These bastards! They think they can blackmail me?" But this was Marius, his nephew... he wavered, his hands flying to his balding head.

He paced for hours, debating with his council, when finally, Gaius arrived out of breath. "My son..."

"I know... shit, shit, shit!"

"What are you going to do?"

"I don't know what they want... I have to leave them a message in a shithole tree..." He clasped Gaius' shoulder. "I will not let them kill him. He's my nephew."

"What if they ask you for their lands back?"

The emperor quieted. "We'll see... I don't know until they tell me what they want..."

Gaius felt dizzy and sat down, drained, his mind on his only son. *Marius...*

Seraphina listened to the messenger, her face white, her dark eyes widening at the news. "He's dead?"

"No, My Lady, just taken prisoner."

Thais' hands flew to her mouth, and Seraphina slapped her in the face. "Stop it! So, the noble emperor will get him out of there, right?" She smiled, rising. "Nothing to worry about. I have a party to attend, so if you will excuse me..."

The messenger saluted and left, Seraphina crossing the dining hall to go to her room. "Thais, come and help me get ready..." She bumped into Melissa carrying her daughter. "Oh... here you are. Listen, your dominus was taken prisoner in the North by some barbarians... the gods know when he'll be back... anyway, I am going out, make sure she's fed and put her to bed on time."

Melissa blanched, clutching the child. "Yes, domina..."

Seraphina stroked the child's chubby face. "Your daddy is not ready to come home yet..." She laughed. "She doesn't even know what he looks like." Bitter, she left in a whirl, her mind on the party and a pair of warm, brown eyes.

The gruesome journey continued in the mountains, the path winding up into the rock, the sheer walls to their right and a dizzying void to their left, the cart barely fitting, but the sturdy horses knew the way and continued, placid, not losing their footing or shying from the void.

Kyle and Marius held hands as best as they could, but Marius' strength was dwindling with every passing day, his exhausted, starved body giving in to the cold, that single blanket not offering enough protection against the crisp, cold air pouring down from the mountains.

Lothar shouted from the back of the cage. "We can't stop on this path, so just carry on. We should be at the end of it by night."

Kyle signaled that he'd heard it, raising his whip, but his mind raced, looking down into the void, rocky slopes, and at the bottom, a thin stream surrounded by pebbled shores, snaking through the valley. A falcon appeared above them, screeching, something attached to its legs, and it flew to the front.

Lothar laughed. "At last, your bastard uncle has sent a message. You might die tonight, Roman, if he lets you go. I'll make sure you don't go easily. It will take hours!"

Kyle felt Marius' fingers clench around his, and he squeezed reassuringly, his heart in his throat. Slowly, he squeezed harder, turning his head, meeting Marius' eyes through the grates, gesturing with his eyes towards the void.

Marius followed his stare and blanched, but his mind had given up already, resigned to whatever fate the gods had in store for him.

A sharp light shone in Kyle's eyes as he took his knife out and, swift as lightning, jabbed it into the right horse's rump, the animal rearing at the sudden pain, shying from it. He watched in slow motion as the horse pushed his companion over the edge of the path, the animals screaming, their bodies sliding into the void, pulling the cart with them. Kyle held on to the grates of the cage, their eyes locking with Marius, their fingers intertwined through the bars. *I love you*, Kyle mouthed, and let go, his body disappearing as Marius' world was thrown upside down, the cage tumbling down the steep hill, freed from the cart and the screaming horses. Marius lost consciousness at the third bounce, hitting his head violently into the cage's bottom, blacking out.

There was a commotion in the ranks, Lothar watching, howling, the cart disappear, then slide down on its side, the horses a tangled mess of flesh and tack, their rippling bodies sliding down the steep slope. He could not see in the distance and the dust Kyle clutching one of the horse's mane, laying on his body, sliding on it, the animal's flesh ripped to shreds by the stones. Kyle's mind was on Marius, praying to whatever gods that he survived the fall. The cage tumbled violently down the slope, bouncing and rattling, until it came to a stop near the stream, its side torn open.

There was an eerie silence as the barbarians struggled to see what was going on with the dust settling. The horses seemed dead, laying near the stream, and there was no movement from the cage either. Lothar couldn't ride to the front, but they passed the message on. There was no way they could go down here, but farther away, where the path ended, it was possible, and they decided to ride on and come back through the valley to see what was left of them.

Kyle heard them move, hiding behind the horses' bodies, watching them go. He waited, his eyes on the cage, on Marius' still form, white as a sheet, barely visible through the mangled grates. *Please, please, gods....* He waited some more and when the last one of the barbarians had disappeared, he got up and ran to the cage. The side was torn up, and he climbed in, crouching down to Marius' prone body, blood streaming from his head, his black hair full of it, his chalk-white face still.

Kyle shook his shoulders, his voice a whisper. "Wake up, love, please..." He put his head on Marius' chest and was rewarded with a light thud, his heart still beating.

He ran to the stream and scooped the icy water up in his hands, going back to him, pouring it in his face. He slapped him then, hard, and Marius jolted, drawing in a big breath. Kyle slapped him again and this time, his eyes flew open, glazed over with shock. His eyes locked on Kyle, a thin stream of blood escaping his mouth.

"Come on! Get up!"

Kyle tried to pull him up, but Marius couldn't move, bruised, and battered by his fall, his head swimming. His breath flew. "Run, Kyle, leave me..."

These were his first words since his capture, and they made Kyle die inside. "No... I won't leave you."

Marius closed his eyes, another gush of blood leaving his mouth. "Just go... please..."

"No! No! Get up! Get the fuck up, soldier!" Kyle was yelling now, not caring if the sound traveled in that treacherous ravine, pulling at his shoulders. "Get up, soldier! Move!"

His words hit something deep within Marius, and he sat up, his hands flying to Kyle, clutching at him for support and, in an extreme effort, Kyle pulled him up, making him scramble out of the cage on all fours. He was heaving, crying, but he could not give up, not now.

Kyle tugged at his armpit. "Get up! Let's go!"

Marius held on to him, slowly rising, his legs barely bearing his weight. The icy air bit into him, and he shivered, the fog slowly clearing.

"That's it... come on, we have to move. Lean on me..."

They moved then, slowly; the shackles making it very difficult to progress. But slowly, shuffling, trailing blood, they managed to disappear into the woods of the valley.

Kyle sat him down against a tree, pulling his cloak off and putting it around Marius' shoulders. "Stay here, I'm going back to that cart to gather some supplies. They won't be here until dusk..."

Marius closed his eyes, unable to talk, but Kyle leant over to him, his lips on his bloodied lips, making him moan, that single warm kiss sending electric waves up his spine and into his core.

"I'll be back..."

Darkness, pain... I'm here, open your eyes, please, love... No, leave me alone... it's good here... peaceful... Come on! Wake up! No... Light streaming in, his eyes opening, Kyle's face so close... Marius raised his hand, trying to touch his face, but his shackles weighed them down, the unforgiving metal sliding on his bloodied skin.

Kyle watched his hand fall as Marius whimpered.

"We have to take these off... I found the keys." He undid them quickly, the collar making Marius choke as he wrenched it off. He coughed, crying against the sudden freedom, rubbing his wrist.

"Stop... you'll make it worse..." Kyle's gentle touch, his grey eyes filled with love. He was carrying a big satchel and reached down to him. "Let's go, get up!" With an ultimate will, Marius rose, leaning on Kyle's shoulder. "We'll follow the stream upwards not to leave prints... come on!"

He led Marius in the water, the icy stream freezing their feet off but soothing his pain. They walked then, slowly. *Too slow,* Kyle's eyes darting back to the cart, disappearing with the valley turning. He had no idea where they were, probably in barbarian lands, far from everything.

They had walked for hours in the icy flow, until they could walk no more, their legs numb, and Kyle led Marius towards the woods again, making him sit against a tree.

"Here... eat."

He pulled some raw horse meat out of his bag and pushed it towards Marius, the dripping meat feeling divine after three days of starving. Marius moaned, the blood flowing down his chin, the chewy meat sliding down his throat.

"Drink." Kyle pushed the pouch's neck into his mouth, the icy stream of water washing down his throat. He gulped it down, his tears flowing. Kyle stroked his face. "My poor love..." Marius just cried softly; his eyes closed. Kyle looked around, nervous. "Feeling better?"

Marius nodded, his voice weak. "Yes..."

"Alright, put these on. They might be a bit small as they are my size."

He handed him his spare clothes and boots, helping him dress, not caring about his blood tainting them. It felt so good after weeks of being almost naked that Marius almost lost it again, his mind reeling.

Kyle clutched his hand. "Let's go... you'll have time to cry later."

Marius grinned, despite his pain, but got up, feeling better. He was still dizzy though, his head splitting, and leant on Kyle to continue walking. They went into the woods, walking on the soft leaves, trying not to leave prints. The forest gently sloped here, and they walked upwards, panting, Marius drawing on his military training and discipline to keep going, his jaw clenched.

Kyle panted, holding him by the waist. "We need to be as far away as possible. If they come down to the valley, we need to be out of it...." His eyes scanned the landscape, the trees, remembering what he'd learnt in the woods of his childhood. "Come, let's climb. See the light amongst the trees? That's where we're going..."

Marius focused on that light, pushing his body to the brink.

At last, they emerged above the woods on a large field, the mountain peaks huge around them, utterly and completely lost...

Kyle sighed. "Let's continue... far from where they were heading."

Marius slouched on him. "I'm not sure I can..."

Kyle looked at his livid face caked with blood; his hair matted around the large cut in on his scalp. "Just a bit more... please?"

His blue eyes shone dull. "I'll try..."

They resumed their painful walk, step by step, crossing that huge mountain field to a stony field.

Kyle hurried on. "We won't leave any prints here on the rock. Come on, just a bit further."

He felt Marius' arm tighten around his shoulders, breathing hard, and they plowed on, their jaw clenched, the bare landscape hugging the mountainside, gently sloping upwards.

Kyle went around boulders and there, wedged a bit higher up, he spotted a cave. "There... just to there and we stop."

Marius steeled himself, and they crawled up there, collapsing onto the hard stone, heaving.

Lothar rode his party down to the valley. The sun was already setting, and they arrived at the horses' gruesome remains almost at dusk, shadows crawling out of the woods. They inspected the remains and cursed softly.

"They escaped?"

"Are you crazy? That slave boy could hardly wait to get his hands on that Roman..."

"Maybe the Roman has him? After all, he could have survived in that cage..."

Lothar rode his horse down the stream, looking for prints, but there were just a few leading to the woods. He then rode back, following them to the stream. *Clever... If he survived, why didn't he just kill that slave? Why not? And his shackles? He's roaming the woods chained up?* Something was off, but he could not quite place it, and he swore under his breath. "Let's camp... we'll hunt them down tomorrow." Adelbrand had been furious... he had received favorable news from the emperor and they had to find Marius alive...

Kyle rose from the ground, leaning over Marius. "I have to go and gather some things. Just rest." Marius looked at him, nodding, unable to get up, despite the cold stone chilling him to the bone.

Kyle left then, hurrying before darkness fell, gathering large pine branches with his knife, finding herbs, moss, tall grass. He then found a spring and filled all their pouches to the brim, washing his face. Berries. Some eggs in a nest. He headed back, hurrying, worried about Marius, and found him unconscious, sleeping on the cold floor. He lay the pine branches down, making a thick bedding, laying some moss and grass on it. Kyle then gently nudged him, making him moan.

"Nooo..."

"Yes, love, just a tiny bit..."

Marius' eyes flew open, looking lost, mildly panicked, and Kyle clutched at his hand in the darkening cave. "Roll over..." He helped him, and Marius sighed, feeling the soft bedding under his body. After weeks of sleeping on the hard wood of the cage, it felt like heaven and he cried, letting his sobs overcome his mind.

Kyle stroked his arm. "Can you stay awake a bit?"

He nodded, his face in his hands, trying to catch his breath.

"Alright, a fire is not an option, but I have found some eggs and berries and we still have that raw horsemeat. We should eat it fast. Here, drink first."

Marius sat up, his lips quivering. They ate the meat, berries, and eggs, then night fell, dark around them. Kyle munched the herbs with some water, spitting a thick paste out in a bowl.

"Here, let me rub this into your wounds..."

He applied the warm paste gently on his feet, wrists and neck, Marius' eyes lost in space, watching the stars being born in the night sky.

His voice was soft in the velvet night. "Was it like this for you? When you were caught?"

Kyle's hand stopped, and he wiped it on his trousers, sitting next to him. "Yes, it was similar... but we were several in a cage... and I couldn't keep my pants... and... at night, we were taken out and they had their fun with us..."

Marius closed his eyes. "I'm sorry..."

"What for? You were not there."

"But I'm a Roman..."

Kyle quieted, his thoughts on his words. *Did it matter now? No... not anymore. Not to him.* "So what? First and foremost, you are Marius... and I love you." Their eyes locked and Kyle pushed him down, locking him in an embrace, trying to give some of his warmth to his tortured body.

Marius sighed. "You could have gone with them..."

His grey eyes shone in the darkness of the cave. "I don't know what it will take to make you understand that I'm not going to leave you, not ever...?" He mused. "You have a hard time accepting love..."

Marius' throat choked, his tears welling up. "I have not been loved a lot..."

Kyle leant down to him, kissing him, pushing his lips apart, the taste of blood invading his mouth as his tongue snaked into his mouth, roaming it, lavish strokes which made Marius moan, his aching body hungry for him.

"So... I'll just have to love you even more... just kissing for tonight... and caresses... you can't do anything in your state..."

They kissed until Marius fell asleep in his arms, Kyle watching the night stars, Marius' arm on his chest, his head on his shoulder.

They were up at dawn, before the sun was fully up, the sky still dark, hurrying as best as they could, Marius walking on his own but limping with his wounds and stiff muscles. He still put himself in a military march, and Kyle followed next to him, both breathing hard, determined to get away from the barbarians, the mountain air cold around them.

Lothar also got his chasing party to rise early, and they followed the river, riding fast, until they found their prints darting in the forest. It was all easy until they reached the rocky landing and Lothar cursed softly, his eyes on the mountains.

His friend rode next to him. "So?"

He smiled. "So... they are probably lost and have no idea what's coming..." They eyed the grey clouds close to the summits. "Snow, and soon... they will freeze to death... still, let's ride a bit further and then wait. Without a fire, they are as good as dead..."

Kyle and Marius had been walking almost all morning, a sudden chill in the air making them shiver, Kyle's worried eyes on Marius' pale face.

They sat down on some rocks, shivering, rubbing their hands. "We have to get down from here... somehow..." The mountain landscape stretched endlessly between the peaks, not a valley in sight for now. Kyle breathed into his hands. "If we light a fire, they'll see it. I gather they are after us..."

Though they had made sure to walk on rock mainly, climbing sometimes, trying to take paths where horses could not follow. Kyle sat silently and then shot to his feet and gathered some wood from the nearby trees.

Marius followed him with his eyes. "What are you up to?"

"Lighting a fire..."

"But..."

Kyle did it, fast, with a flintstone, and the branches crackled loudly.

Marius' eyes grew wide. "Are you insane?"

"Come! Let's go!" They darted off in the opposite direction, watching the thin smoke rise into the air, and Marius got it, walking faster, away from that fire.

Lothar spotted it, the thin column of smoke, and smiled. "There they are! Let's go, boys!"

They set off, their horses galloping, just to find that they could not reach that ledge. He cursed, and they got off, climbing, and walking fast, their swords drawn. Finally, the fire, but there were no fugitives in sight. He whirled, understanding, but his eyes darted to no avail around...

"Fuuuuck!!" His howl echoed in the empty landscape and his men shifted. He lowered his sword. "Ok, let's get back to the horses and cut them off...", though he had no idea where they were, and two pairs of eyes watched them from the trees as they stroll off.

They waited until they disappeared and climbed down, walking in the opposite direction from them.

"If they are on horseback, we have to stay on uneven terrain and climb..."

Marius nodded, exhausted already.

They climbed higher up, hoping that they would see some way of getting down from the mountain, but the peaks stretched ahead, unforgiving, the weather turning foul, dark clouds hanging in the sky, a mild wind blowing steadily. Kyle was shivering, but he was in good health, and used to being cold and starved when he'd been with Lucius, his will overriding his body's signals.

Marius was a different affair. Weak, battered, his head throbbing with his wound, he stopped, unable to continue, his eyes glazed over.

Kyle stepped to him, immediately holding him up. "Don't sit... if you sit down, you're as good as dead."

Marius panted, his breath thick in the cold air. "I can't..."

Kyle put his arm around his shoulder, his eyes darting around the landscape, finding a crack between the rocks, maybe enough to fit their bodies, facing a grassy field gently sloping. "Look, just until there, come on..." Kyle dragged him painfully, his legs almost giving way, but they managed to get there, and he made him sit down, sheltered from the wind.

Marius leant back against the rock, his eyes closing, his face strikingly white in the frame of his black hair and sprouting black beard. Dark purple and black bruises blotched his skin, and Kyle's heart clenched, unsure whether he would survive.

He gently crouched down to face him. "I need to go and find food."

Marius just nodded; his eyes closed.

"Look at me... stay awake..."

Marius opened his eyes, but he was struggling, sleep pulling at him like a warm dark blanket. "I am not sure I can..."

Kyle clutched his shoulder. "You have to..."

He sighed, sitting up straighter, watching Kyle leave, walk out on that grassy field when he stopped, his body taut, his hand flying to his knife.

Marius tensed, watching him stand, immobile, drawing the knife. *The barbarians?*

Suddenly, Kyle sprinted, his legs propelling him forward, knife in hand, and Marius watched him chase a rabbit, the animal fleeing wildly. It was too late though, taking a sharp turn, and Kyle was on him, turning his muscled body, his face tense, fixed on the animal. He leapt then and slammed the knife down, tumbling and rolling, the rabbit stuck on the large blade, writhing. Kyle sat, wringing the rabbit's neck with one swift motion of his strong hands, panting, his eyes ablaze, a small smile on his lips.

Marius' heart wrenched at his sight, in awe of his hunting skills, his mind on what he could have become if he'd stayed free. He watched him walk back, the rabbit dangling from his hand, blood dripping to the ground.

Kyle grinned at him. "That went better than expected. We can't cook it, so I hope you like raw meat." He sat down and skinned the animal, laying the fur carefully aside, and cut steaming pieces off, handing them to Marius.

He took them and ate slowly. "You should eat too..."

Kyle shrugged, nibbling on the bones. "I can manage, but you're too weak. Eat and don't argue. I'll find more, don't worry."

"You're a good hunter..."

Kyle pulled a face, his emotions racing. "Decent, maybe..." He refused to talk further, the memories too painful, and picked up the soft fur, rolling it between his fingers. "Mhm... this is too small, but we'll keep it." He stretched it on a rock, weighing it down with smaller stones. "It's small, but it's fur... and we'll need more."

Marius looked at him, drained, but the meat warming him somewhat. He hugged his knees, his lips quivering.

Kyle shot him a sympathetic look. "I'm sorry, we can't have a fire just yet, now with those assholes still around..."

"You're already outdoing yourself... Kyle... I'd be dead without you."

Kyle looked at him, getting up. "You'll be dead if I don't hunt... I'll be back. Don't sleep?"

Marius nodded and watched him leave, his eyelids heavy. He struggled to stay awake, but the cold helped somewhat, his body shivering.

Kyle roamed the fields for hours, making sure to leave some small clues to find his way back. He ate berries and hunted small rodents, filling his bag with them. Looking up, he spotted a brown patch under a rocky cliff and walked cautiously closer.

The huge bear lay on its side. It had been probably dead for days, the pungent smell of rotting meat invading his nostrils. He still approached it cautiously, his eyes darting around for other predators, but there were none. Exhaling softly, he walked next to the animal, his eyes gleaming, and proceeded to cut its skin off.

He was exhausted by the time he'd finished, dusk settling in, dangerously quickly and he bundled the stinking skin up, tucking it under his arm. He left swiftly then, following his clues in the dim light, the wind stronger, chilling his bones.

Marius startled when Kyle's form filled the crack's entrance, the overpowering smell of rotten meat making his stomach flip. He breathed through his mouth, his eyes wide. "What the f..."

Kyle grinned, tossing the skin, some firewood and his bag down. "I found a dead bear."

Marius moaned, livid. "Great..."

He watched Kyle stretch the skin out on the sheer rock, same as the rabbit fur, and he scrapped at it with a rock, working methodically, sweating despite the biting cold. Kyle then added all the salt he had in his bag to it, making sure it was well covered, and then busied himself with taking the dead rodents out of his bag, skinning and gutting them.

His eyes darted to the dark sky filled with stars. "They won't see the fire up here, not the smoke either. The night is too dark and there's fog now settling below."

Kyle lit the fire, the warm flames slowly seeping into their flesh and bones. Marius sighed, closing his eyes, but Kyle swatted his thigh. "No sleeping yet."

His eyes flew open, a small smile on his lips. "You're being a real bossy little twat..."

Kyle's eyes gleamed. "Your teasing temper is back? Maybe there's hope." He put the rodents on sticks and roasted them on the crackling fire, the smell of the rotting, drying fur everywhere.

Marius pulled a face. "This smell... horrid."

Kyle grinned. "Your spoiled Roman ass can't handle a bit of stink?"

His face darkened, his eyes lighting up. "Watch your mouth..."

Kyle smirked. "Or else...?"

Marius lunged at him, pinning him to the ground, panting, their faces close. "Or else..."

Kyle wriggled his nose. "You stink too... don't blame the bear..." They laughed and kissed deeply, but Marius was too weak still, and Kyle rolled him off. "You're useless... sit and eat."

They ate the rodents, the scorching flesh divine in the bitter cold, and then lay close to the fire. Kyle spooned Marius as he needed the warmth more, his body still shivering despite the fire's radiating heat. Kyle stroked his shoulders and side, sending more shivers down his body. Marius' eyes closed, and he dosed off at last.

Days had passed, their progress steady, their worried eyes glancing behind and around them. The landscape seemed deserted though, and they were progressing on rocky land. Kyle had bundled Marius into the bear's fur after two days, and he felt much better, less cold, but worry chewed at him, watching Kyle in his plain leather clothes, his breath billowing in the air with every step. A couple of flakes drifted from the sky and Kyle stopped, watching them fall, holding his palm out to watch them melt on his skin, the tiny ice crystals landing on his face, tingling, his face turning upwards as more and more flakes fell.

He sighed, a vague happiness glowing inside, and Marius watched him, amused. "Surely this is not the first time you see snow?"

Kyle smiled; his eyes lost in his memories. "No... but the first time in years that I can enjoy it..." He looked at the intricate pattern of the flakes on his sleeve. "I was not allowed to leave the house with Lucius..." Marius' face contorted, and he embraced him, just holding him as the snow fell. Kyle sighed, pushing him away. "Nice... but we need to go... Look, there seems to be a cave further that way..."

It seemed very far, in the rock, a small opening and Marius steeled himself to continue walking.

It took them hours to get there, Marius' tired body screaming at him, every step a torture in the heavily falling snow, Kyle's eyes on that single dark hole in the rock which seemed to drift further with every step. Still, they had no other option but to reach it, hoping that it was empty and large enough.

When they arrived, it seemed even smaller than from afar, barely allowing them to crouch in, following the damp walls with their hands, Kyle's voice echoing in the narrow corridor.

"It might become larger, hopefully..."

The distant sound of water, gentle drips and Kyle hurried a bit more, feeling a gentle warmth invade the air, a soft glow in the distance. The narrow tunnel ended, and he found himself in a big room, the ceiling stretching endlessly towards a hole high up, letting the light in. His eyes fell on a large pool in the cave, gently fuming, the smell of sulfur strong in the air and his heart fluttered.

Marius joined him, panting, and his eyes grew wide. "Is that what I think it is?"

They looked at each other, relief flooding their senses. They strode to the water and Kyle tested it, carefully lowering his hand in. It was hot but bearable. His eyes darted around, spotting another underground spring, and he ran there, tasting the cold water.

He looked at Marius, who just stood there, floored. "We have a hot and a cold spring. I think we can stay here for a while... rest a bit."

He made a fire with the wood they had gathered, watching the smoke snake its way to the opening in the domed vault. Kyle's eyes sparked. "Time for a bath, dominus."

Marius snapped out of his trance at the word, frowning gently. "You don't have to call me like that, ever..."

Kyle smirked, taking the fur off him and tugging at his clothes. "When we're back in Rome, I'll have to... besides..."—his eyes lifted to him, a small smile on his lips — "I'd like to... sometimes..." He kissed Marius but didn't let him do anything, peeling his clothes off. "I'll need to wash these too... a bath will do you good..."

Marius hadn't washed since his capture, and he just stood there, letting Kyle take his clothes off, the young man silent when he looked at his body, black and dark purple bruises everywhere, raw wounds were the shackles had rubbed his skin off, covered in grime, and he swallowed, his tears welling up, his voice soft. "Come... in you go..." He helped Marius into the gently sloping pool and let him lie there, his eyes closing, a quivering breath escaping his mouth. His tears flew and Kyle stroked his face, washing it off, gently scrubbing with his fingers, careful with his hair full of dried blood where his wound was.

Marius looked at him. "Join me?"

Kyle quickly undressed and lowered himself into the scalding water, but it felt out of this world after their bitter cold journey, and he couldn't believe their luck. He continued washing Marius' hair out, revealing the wide cut on his scalp.

He pulled a face, and Marius hissed in pain. "Ouch... it burns."

"Yes... not pretty, but your head could have split in half, so you're lucky, in a sense. It's going to be a nasty scar, thankfully under your hair..." Kyle's hand glided down his face, washing the grime and blood off, the rest of Marius' body soaking in the warm water. "It could have been on your pretty face..."

"Pretty?"

Marius' eyes gleamed with amusement and Kyle smiled. "Yes, pretty... even with this beard."

Marius' hand went to it, rubbing his chin. Used to being shaved clean all his life, it irritated the hell out of him. He sighed, exasperated. "Just shave it off with that able hunting knife? I can't stand it..."

Kyle's lips parted, his fingers stroking the dark strands. "You're sure? It's very soft..."

Marius scoffed. "Yeah, I'm sure... you can keep yours and stroke it all you want."

Kyle looked at him wordlessly, reaching for his knife. "Hold still..."

He put the sharp blade to Marius' throat, the arteries gently pulsing under his skin, and he watched him swallow, a vague nervousness and thrill in Marius as he felt the cool metal on his skin. Kyle scraped the knife upwards, cutting the hair like butter, and Marius closed his eyes, feeling the cold, metallic blade glide on his moist skin, the cool air biting into it as his beard disappeared.

Kyle smirked. "You'll be cold."

"I don't care. Id' rather be cold than have all that fur on my face."

Kyle finished and lay the knife aside, washing the rest of the hair off, gently massaging the pink skin. "There... all done."

Marius opened his eyes, a small smile on his lips. "And you'll keep yours?"

Kyle leant close. "Yes... for obvious purposes, against the cold... and you can tell me later how it feels when I'll have my mouth wrapped around your cock..."

Marius' eyes widened at his unexpected comment. Unable to retaliate, he just lay back in the pool. "Some things you say...."

"Let me wash you properly." Kyle scraped the softened grime and blood off his skin, his nails gently scraping, grazing, his hands rubbing his skin, and Marius was aroused, despite his body being a block of pain. Kyle smiled. "You're sure you're up for it? You look a mess..."

Marius' eyes were dark. "My body has a life of its own... or so it seems..."

Kyle smirked, straddling him carefully, leaning in to kiss him, doubt in his eyes. "Not sure we can fuck...you're in pain."

Marius put a finger on his lips. "We don't fuck...?"

Kyle rolled his eyes. "Fine..." His eyes drifted to the fire, burning heartily, and he got up, leaving the pool, laying the bearskin down next to it. He went back and held his hands out to Marius. "Come out...you're clean now."

He helped him out, holding his numb body up and walked him to the bearskin, laying him down near the raging pyre, lying next to him, propped on his elbow, tracing his bruises. "Now... feeling better?"

Marius nodded, swallowing, madly in love, and Kyle leant down, his mouth roaming his body, kissing his pain away. He glided it down to Marius' erection, slowly pushing him into his mouth, making him gasp and close his eyes. He sucked him slowly, to the hilt, licking his way up. "So... how does it feel?"

Marius grinned, breathing hard. "Divine..."

"Good..."

He continued until he felt him tense, his moans louder, feeling him lose it and fill his mouth, sobbing at the blinding pleasure and Kyle swallowed it all, gently licking him off, sliding up his body.

"I think you should sleep now, and I'll wash our clothes and cook."

Marius didn't object, and he closed his eyes, soon sound asleep.

The cave was warm around the pool and the fire, so Kyle washed their clothes out, laying them out to dry near the flames. He proceeded to roast the rodents he had caught earlier in the morning, his eyes in the flames, sitting close to Marius' head, the Roman's face peaceful at last, his lips parted, those familiar features Kyle loved and had dreaded at the same time.

His fingers just gently traced his silky black hair, not wanting to wake him, musing on how close they had been to his death. The thought was unbearable to Kyle, and he swore to get him home safe, even if he knew that they were utterly lost in these savage lands, chased probably... a soft quiet settled in the semi-dark cave, the sun probably setting and he gathered the rodents' fat in his iron pot, waiting for them to cook. That fat would be useful soon to make lamps, or so he hoped.

Maybe they could camp the winter out here, after all, they were deep into the mountains, probably too far from those barbarians already. He thought of hiding the entrance to the cave, his mind racing, maybe walling it up if there would be enough snow. The meat sizzled on the sticks and his mouth watered. He was hungry but hadn't realized it, having walled it up, feeding Marius first to the brim, eating what he'd left... sometimes just scraps. Marius needed it more though, his body still too weak and his mind... Kyle's eyes drifted to his face again. *They hadn't broken him completely, but it had been close... so close...*

Marius' eyes fluttered open, and Kyle smiled down at him. "Hungry?"

Marius' head swam. The water had sapped his strength away, his aching muscles healing, but he nodded, feeling incredibly weak. Kyle pushed him up to sit, holding him until he found his balance.

"I'm fine..."

They huddled near the fire on the bearskin, and Kyle turned their clothes over. He took the rodents off the flames and handed a stick full of them to Marius, taking the other one. They ate heartily; the meat burning their mouths and tongues.

"We'll camp here for a while... maybe until the weather is better?"

Marius nodded, the mere thought of moving making dizzy.

Kyle handed him the water pouch. "I'll hunt until you feel strong enough to join me and then we'll leave. When you are healed, find our way back home."

Marius watched him with mild eyes. "You sound awfully confident..."

Kyle shrugged, smiling. "We are lost... I'm just trying to be optimistic." He looked around, his eyes shining. "I still can't believe our luck..."

His boyish enthusiasm warmed Marius' heart, and he reached for him, pulling him down on the bearskin, just holding him, his black hair falling into his eyes, framing his face, untamed. It had grown and Kyle's hands snaked into the silky strands, pulling him into a kiss, minding his wound.

XIX

They had settled well in the cave, Kyle gathering supplies and hunting, killing sleeping bears in their caves for their fur.

A thick snow had covered the landscape after a few weeks, and they were undisturbed, walled up sometimes for days. It didn't matter, safe in the warm cave, the entrance covered in snow; they were invisible, staying in each other's arms for days sometimes, making love, Marius strength coming back slowly.

Kyle pushed Marius' limits sometimes, making him wrestle him, slowly pushing him around mentally, making him feel stronger, making him want to dominate. He was worried as he had become mellow, a slow fear in Marius to hurt him, and Kyle craved the darker side of him, a stronger man who took what he wanted. Marius was still tearful sometimes, waking from nightmares when Kyle soothed him, knowing all too well those dark hours of the night when he had also woken in cold sweat, screaming... but there was nobody to help him then, if anything, he got beaten into silence.

One day he came back from hunting, flunking a small deer down, out of breath, when Marius laced his arms around him from behind, his mouth on his neck. "I missed you..."

Shivers ran down Kyle's spine, but he pretended to not be in the mood, and pushed at him. "Let me go... I need to skin this deer..."

Marius held him tighter, growling. "It can wait..."

It thrilled Kyle that he would not let him go straight away, and he pushed further, wriggling in Marius' arms. "Let me go, you big bully..."

Marius spun him around, clutching him to his chest. Kyle felt how strong he had become again, and his heart beat faster, looking up into his blue eyes, his jet-black hair flowing around his face, his lips curled into a small smile.

"Bully? That's new." He kissed him firmly, pushing his tongue in, but Kyle yanked his mouth away, and Marius' eyes darkened, his lips parting.

He grabbed Kyle's neck and held tight, his hand in his hair, pushing his lips apart. Kyle mewled in his mouth, still fighting, but he gave in when he felt he would not let go.

Marius broke their kiss, out of breath, pulling Kyle's head back. It was almost painful, but not quite, and Kyle's eyes darkened, his chest heaving with lust. "Stop fighting, pet... I'll so fuck you now you won't be able to walk."

Kyle smirked. "Prove it... you're all mouth..."

Marius flung him down on all fours, tugging at his pants, and Kyle fought back, just enough to make it difficult, and make Marius grab his hips, smearing a good dose of spit all over his hole.

Kyle squirmed, whimpering, and hissed when Marius buried himself to the hilt. "Bastard..."

The pain was gone in an instant, but Marius stopped, concern washing over him. "I hurt you?"

Kyle looked back, his eyes blazing. "Don't you dare fucking stop now..."

Marius grinned down at him and fucked him hard, gripping his hips, their moans filling the cave. They came together after a while, collapsing, Kyle looking down into Marius' eyes, their bodies glistening with sweat. "I missed this..."

Marius grinned. "Me too..."

Meanwhile, at the fort, they had no news of Marius, thinking he was still a prisoner somewhere in the mountains. Clavius had let the emperor know they had found the settlement empty, the barbarians' traces leading to the mountains, possibly for the whole of the winter. There was no way they could reach them, and they walled themselves up in the fort, grim, Clavius clinging to some hope when everybody around him had already buried the general.

It was the same in Rome, his father and the emperor agreeing that Marius would not survive the winter as a captive and that if the barbarians didn't communicate, it probably meant he was dead. Still, officially, he was just missing, and the emperor bid his time to declare him gone for good. Seraphina made peace with the thought of him never coming back, not caring, as she was busy with her social life.

The weather got milder after a few weeks and they decided to move before the snow cleared completely, reluctant, as they loved the cave with all its comfort. Still, there was a long journey ahead, and they packed up, bundling their supplies and fur on their backs. Kyle had made new clothes for them out of animal skin and fur and they were warm, ready to walk in the cold. One last glance at their haven and they crawled out into the blinding sunlight, the air crisp around them, the snow glistening like diamonds.

They headed off towards the other peaks, vaguely hoping that they were walking in the right direction, towards the south. Marius had healed completely, the scar on his head just barely visible in his shoulder-long hair. He had insisted on being shaved but didn't mind the hair, and Kyle loved it, those silky strands flowing around his gorgeous face and blue eyes.

They were walking fast, used to the mountain terrain after months of roaming them, hunting, and gathering. Their mood was light in the warm sun, and from afar, they just looked like two barbarians on a stroll.

After a couple of days, they found a path snaking through the peaks, and it led towards a valley, a distant village's smoking huts visible down below.

Kyle sat down, pensive. "We can't go near that village, not for now... not until we find out where we are..."

Marius nodded, grim. "Let's continue up here, following the valley. We might be lucky finding a road... or some travelers who know where we are."

Kyle looked at him. "We need also to lie about who we are... until we find a safe place."

"We could be two barbarians just traveling?"

Kyle smiled. "You don't look like one."

"And with a beard?"

"You look like a Roman with a beard."

Marius laughed. "So, what do you suggest?"

"I am a barbarian, sort of..." Marius nodded, looking at his long hair, and beard. Clad in fur, he looked the piece of the Celtic warrior on a journey. Kyle continued, watching him carefully. "I could be the traveling Celt, and you, my Roman slave, fallen from grace..."

Marius' lips parted, his eyes wide. "What the fuck? Slave?" Kyle nodded, dead serious, and Marius laughed, his heart like ice. "Who would believe this? I have a patrician face..."

Kyle smiled. "You could be a Roman's bastard, maybe born out of rape. Black hair and blue eyes are not common? It fits."

Marius fell silent. Kyle had a point... a very valid one. He sighed. "How the fuck do you expect me to play the slave?"

Kyle shrugged. "You've seen me enough... just do the same. Be meek, submissive... and you need a new name. You can't be Marius when the whole barbarian world might be after you."

"What the fuck..." Marius whispered, trying to still his racing heart.

"So? Any preference?"

He laughed. "I have no clue..."

"How about Marcellus? It is almost like your name now."

He sighed, giving in. "Fine."

Kyle beamed. "And I'm Brian, the Celtic warrior on a quest to find his long-lost brother."

They continued their journey then, staying away from the valley and the villages, stumbling on small man-roamed paths in the woods just to stray away. At one point, though, they took one, winding down into the valley, their hearts in their throats. It led to a larger road, traces of wheels, and they followed it, Marius walking behind Kyle. Soon, they spotted a village on the right, but they walked farther, not wanting to stop.

A man was coming down the road, maybe in his fifties, tall, his light brown beard and hair blending, walking a donkey, its back full of bags. He slowed, careful, but not hostile, and stopped in front of them, greeting them in his language, but Kyle looked embarrassed, answering in Celtic.

The man smiled, switching to Latin. "A Celt here? Unusual."

Kyle shrugged, trying to sound casual. "I'm roaming the Empire, looking for my brother."

The man looked at Marius, who did his best to lower his eyes. "And your friend?"

"He is not my friend. He's my slave."

The man looked puzzled but didn't comment. "Come with me to my village. I can put you up for the night. We rarely get visitors." Kyle hesitated, but the man just grabbed his arm. "Come, come... I see you need persuasion, but a good meal near the fire will change your mind, good man."

Kyle sighed and followed him, swiftly glancing at Marius who played his part.

They followed the man to the village, to one of the bigger huts, and he gestured them in. "Sit down and wait for me. I won't be long. There's wine on the table. Your slave can serve you."

Kyle walked into the sparsely furnished main room, a hearty fire in the fireplace, a table, and a jug of wine with some cups. They took their fur coats off and Kyle sat down, looking at Marius. "I'm afraid you'll have to kneel."

He pursed his lips. "Fucking perfect." Marius did it though, a strange feeling coursing through him being at eye level with Kyle's hips in this position.

The man came in then, looking them over, sitting down in front of Kyle. "So, you're looking for your brother..."

"Yes... he was captured years ago by the Romans. I barely escaped. He could be anywhere..."

The man nodded. "You'll have to move further south; this is not so much a territory Romans control... I mean, they think they do." They laughed, Kyle playing the part, and the man's eyes drifted to Marius. "And this one here? He looks like a Roman..."

Kyle smiled. "He's a bastard. A Roman's bastard, or so I've been told when I bought him."

The man nodded. "Such a huge man and you can control him."

Kyle smiled, his eyes dark. "Yes... let's just say that he might be big, but he's been trained to be a slut."

Marius' face flushed red, thankfully keeping his eyes down, his fingers digging into his thighs. *What. The. Fuck.*

The man looked at him, incredulous, but then burst out laughing. "No way!"

Kyle smiled. "Well, it's difficult to believe, but that's how it is..." He hooked his finger under Marius' jaw, tipping his head up, his blue eyes boring into his, making Kyle shiver. *He's pissed... but he can't do anything now...* He looked down at him, cupping his chin, his thumb under his mouth. "Aren't you a good little slut, pet?"

Marius' voice was like ice. "I am, dominus..."

Kyle smiled, grazing his lower lip, pushing his thumb into his mouth. "Suck."

He did, holding his gaze all the while and Kyle pulled out his thumb, fisting his hair. "Good boy..."

Marius lowered his head again, his heart burning from shame, desire? He could not tell and kneeled silently.

The man shook his head. "My, my... that's uncanny, but then again, why not? Better than shagging goats, I guess."

They laughed again and talked whilst eating, the man telling him how to get to the nearest town, how to avoid Romans and get further south. "All roads lead to Rome if this is your last destination. With a good pace every day, you'll be there by springtime."

Kyle blanched. *They were far...* Marius tensed, and Kyle just put his hand on his back, soothing.

Their host rose. "Come, I'll show you your room."

They followed him, and he left them, Marius pushing Kyle into the wall, his eyes blazing, whispering. "What the actual fuck..."

Kyle laughed softly. "I had to make up something credible..." He kissed him deep, kissing his anger away. "Besides... you looked incredibly sexy on your knees..."

Marius laughed, embarrassed. "Just don't get used to it."

Their hands roamed their bodies, and they tumbled onto the bed.

Next day, they set off early, eager to continue. They crossed the nearest town, blending into the crowd, exiting through the main gate and the road stretched towards the distance, paved. A soft sigh escaped their lips as they looked into the setting sun. Rome at the end of the road. Weeks away...

They were walking at a good pace, determined to get there, despite the dangers lurking everywhere. They crossed several villages, towns, travelers, and Kyle managed to trade his furs for coins and food. It was still not enough for horses, and his mind was on other possibilities when they stopped to camp one night.

They were increasingly into Roman territory, but still had to be cautious, as with Clavius, so they played their parts. But Kyle knew they needed more money than what they could get for furs.

He looked at Marius and sighed. "We should get horses to finish this journey faster..."

Marius looked at him, frowning. "That's a lot of money, even if they are older animals."

Kyle sighed, his eyes not leaving him. "Yes, but... soon, we'll be on Roman territory, where we can switch our roles back... I mean, you could be more like a Roman bastard merchant type of guy..."

Marius smiled. "What's the merchandise? We don't really own anything."

"Me."

Marius froze, slowly understanding, and he rose, grabbing Kyle by his shirt. "No fucking way!"

Kyle squirmed, his hands flying to Marius' hands, his eyes calm. "We don't have a choice. If you want to get home, walking is dangerous and too slow..."

Marius growled. "No fucking way... No, no, no..."

Kyle peeled his hands off, sensing him wavering, as his mind raced, desperate. "I did it for Clavius and I'll do it for you. Hell, I'll do it ten times."

Marius' face fell, paling. "No, love... I can't bear it..."

Kyle cradled his face. "Yes, you can... and you know I'm right."

Marius' eyes glazed over with sorrow as he breathed. "Fuck."

He sat down near the fire and held Kyle against his chest, bitter, knowing that he was right but not wanting to admit it, to give in to it.

Kyle turned his face towards him. "You could watch me at that party... now, you won't even have to watch... it's easier."

"I had no choice."

"You don't have a choice now either."

A few days later, they stopped at a barbers' shop in the nearest town, and Kyle had his beard shaved off. He kept his long hair because it suited his purpose, Marius watching his face appear from under all that fur, his light-brown hair framing his features, brushing his shoulders, his full lips, and his heart wrenched. *Fuck, he is beautiful...*

Marius stepped to him and brushed his hair back, grazing his knuckles on his face. "You're so fucking beautiful..."

"Good."

Marius closed his eyes. "You're sure?"

"Yes. Let's find a place where we can sell my able body. But first, trade in our clothes. You look like a savage."

Marius blanched but followed him. They found a small shop who took in their fur clothes and all the fur they had left, and soon, they walked out wearing Roman clothes.

"And now... let's see where the good citizens enjoy themselves..."

They roamed the city, looking for whores, brothels and soon enough, they found the district.

Kyle's face lit up. "This place, they will let you rent me out... I can stay here and leave a portion of my earnings. Easier for you, as you won't need to be involved."

Marius looked at the door, holding Kyle's arm in an iron grip, his voice soft. "No..."

"What? But..."

Marius took his hand and strolled out of that street, not letting Kyle's hand go, and they burst out on a small square, near a fountain. Marius whirled around and held him tight. "No fucking way. It's not happening, love. You are not a whore."

Kyle's emotions raced at his words, a warm feeling inside of him but also vague panic. "But... we need that money."

Marius stroked his face. "No, we don't. We'll manage, we'll walk all the way... I don't care when we get there, but I'm not selling you out to other men... no way."

Kyle gave in, his heart melting, and they kissed, Marius hugging him tight.

Their long journey began then, a slow progress made, but their hearts were at ease, hunting again, trading, buying weapons, hunting some more. They were dressed like rogues, in leather pants, tunics and boots, their hair brushing their shoulders, traveling together almost like brothers, as the weather got milder, the promise of spring in the air, and the roads becoming busier as they approached the heart of the empire.

Rome. Rome, at last, after weeks of walking and trading. They stopped, looking down at the prowling city, hugging in the setting sun's rays.

"We made it, pet."

Kyle just nuzzled his neck, disbelieving. It seemed surreal...

Marius grinned. "Come! Let's surprise my wife!"

Kyle looked at him, puzzled. "Are you sure? Maybe go, and see your parents first."

"No. I want to go home... see my daughter."

Marius' heart raced at the thought and he hurried, Kyle strolling behind him, setting their bodies on a swift jogging pace which had become routine.

Soon they were at the gates and took to the hill where his villa was in long strides, the streets so familiar. Kyle's heart raced in his chest. He had left a year ago... it seemed unreal to be back, walking on the warm paved streets. But he focused on Marius' broad back, his raven hair floating behind him.

They stopped in front of the villa's door, panting, radiant smiles on their faces. Marius knocked, and they waited, holding their breaths slightly, their stomachs filled with butterflies.

Slowly, the door opened and Sixtus peeked out, the old man not recognizing them straight away in their clothes and with their long hair. "We don't want to buy..."

"Sixtus!" Marius' voice boomed, amused. "Don't you recognize me?"

The old man's eyes grew wide, and he wavered, almost fainting when Kyle caught him, mildly chiding Marius with his eyes.

"Dominus... dominus...", the old man tearful, his voice quivering, "We thought you died..."

"Well, I am very much alive. Where is my wife?"

A strange expression crossed Sixtus' face and his eyes closed. "In her room..."

"Excellent!"

Marius whirled and left before Sixtus could stop him, and he clutched at Kyle. "Go after him, boy."

Kyle frowned, but first he gently sat Sixtus down and went to the kitchen to get some water where Shayla and Lis screamed their hearts out seeing him, hugging him, mad with joy.

Marius took the stairs two by two, his heart racing. He didn't love Seraphina but was willing to give her another chance. *Hell, maybe we could have another child*. He grinned and opened her door, his voice freezing in his mouth.

She was in bed, her hair loose, tumbling down her back, riding a man, their moans interrupted by him bursting into the room.

Seraphina's face contorted in wrath as she turned around. "Who the hell..." Her eyes grew wide at the sight of that stranger with long, black hair, standing, holding the door, and her words got caught when she recognized him, his blue eyes wide in his pale face. "Marius..." It was just a whisper, and she jumped off the man in her bed, quickly hugging the covers to her breasts.

A cold sweat broke down Marius' back when he recognized Titus in the sheets, the other man looking at him as if seeing a ghost, but Marius' shock quickly turned to anger, Seraphina watching in alarm as his face darkened, that familiar blaze in his blue eyes searing into her.

She quickly tried to compose herself. "Marius... you're alive... we thought you were dead..." She faked a smile, smoothing her hair back. "Oh, gods... but you're here... this is wonderful... I was so worried..."

Tears welled up in her eyes and Marius felt a cool calm wash over him as he pushed the words out. "Get the fuck out of my house..."

Titus rose then, thinking it was directed at him, and decided not to speak, not to make matters worse. He started dressing, and Seraphina continued talking to Marius. "This is nothing, love... we were just having a bit of fun... I mean, I am... was technically a widow... but you're absolutely right... he should go now..."

Marius looked at her, his eyes cold. "Get the fuck out of my house... have you not heard me?"

Titus froze, and Seraphina looked at Marius, not understanding. "But... he's leaving..."

"Yes... he's leaving, and so are you."

Seraphina blanched. "What? You can't throw me out of my house..."

"This is not your house." Marius looked at Titus. "You fucked her? You can take her away... in fact, you are doing me a huge favor."

"Marius..."

"No... spare me your lies. Get out."

Seraphina got up, clutching the covers to her, her face contorted in rage. "You have no right to storm in here after a year and throw me out! I'm your wife! The mother of your child!"

Marius looked at her, cool. "I am divorcing you, wife. Now, get dressed, and leave with your lover."

"No!" Seraphina screamed, and Marius backhanded her, hard, sending her to the ground. Titus was there in an instant, holding her, Marius' face impassive. "This was long deserved, you, lying whore. Now get out. I won't say it again. If you don't leave, I'll kill you, and you know I have the right to."

Titus knew and started pulling her up.

Kyle arrived at this instant, alarmed by the shouting, and he stopped short behind Marius, his eyes wide.

Seraphina wiped her mouth, her eyes blazing with anger. "I'll go. Get my child. I'm not leaving her behind."

Marius' lips curled up into an evil smile. "Oh yes, you are. She is my daughter, and as her father, I have the right to keep her with me."

She paled, holding onto Titus. "You have no right... you can't..." But she knew he had, and her tears flowed, even if she hadn't cared about the little girl at all, not even naming her, or spending any time with her. She was not that easily defeated though, and she let the covers go, dressing, pulling on her clothes, spitting the words. "Fine! I'm leaving! But I'll be back! I'm not going into a divorce!" She stood in front of Marius, her cheek darkening with the blow. "Send my clothes to my parents' house. Thais!" She screamed the girl's name, and she came running, her face filled with fear. "We are leaving, Thais... come!"

She grabbed her hand, but Marius swatted hers away, making her hiss in pain. "The girl stays, she's mine. Get out."

Seraphina watched him, disbelieving. "She's my slave..."

"Nothing is yours in this house. Nothing. Now, get out before I choke you to death."

She understood then, looking into his eyes, filled with madness and wrath, and left with Titus, her head high.

Marius walked them down to the door, making sure they were gone, banging it shut.

He turned to Kyle, his eyes filled with hurt, shame, anger and the young man laced his arms around him, his breath on his neck. "I love you..."

Marius held him tight, fighting his tears, when his eyes went to Melissa, slowly approaching with the stunning one-year-old toddler on her arm, the little girl's dark eyes framed with jet-black bouncy curls, all the way down to her shoulders. Marius froze, and let Kyle go, walking cautiously closer, the little girl shy, her knuckle in her mouth, her head pressed against Melissa's neck.

Melissa's eyes were full of tears as she spoke softly to her. "This is daddy. He's back."

Marius' eyes filled with tears, but he didn't dare touch the child. Slowly, the little girl's head perked up and, curious, she reached her hand towards his gleaming blue eyes. Melissa let her go, his powerful arms lifting the toddler up, her soft little hands going for those eyes, then grabbing his long, silky hair. She smiled then, trying to catch the tears spilling down his cheeks. He hugged her softly, and she played with his hair, tugging the strands in her fists, making him grin wide, her fingers going to his teeth, poking, laughing.

Kyle watched them, floored, seeing Marius melt inside, holding her up by her body and making her whirl, the little girl giggling wildly, her laughter like pearls. Marius fell in love with her in an instant, a fierce instinct of protection rising in him, and he looked at Kyle and the slaves.

"She can't come back here. Ever. Send her stuff to her parents today."

They nodded, understanding.

He sat her on his arm, walking to Kyle, his other arm snaking around the young man, the child wedged between them.

"It's just you and I now, pet. I am not taking another wife."

Marius kissed him wide, and the little girl laughed, holding on to his hair, her chubby hand trying to grab their mouths, and they broke apart, laughing.

Kyle stood, breathless, a small smile on his face, looking up into those striking blue eyes in their silky black frame, utterly and completely in love.

TO BE CONTINUED

Avis Aureus - The Golden Bird - Book II (preview)

I

"We have to go to the palace." Marius dressed hastily, putting on a better-looking tunic and his sandals, whilst Kyle did the same. They strode downstairs, Marius waving Sixtus and Paulus over. "My ex-wife is not allowed in here, not her, not her parents, or her lover. Nobody actually. Just don't open the door, bolt it when we leave."

He went then to look for Melissa, finding her in the kitchen peeling vegetables. "My daughter?"

"She's sleeping, dominus."

Melissa looked at him, her heart in her throat. He was back and she was not sure what would happen. She had raised that child until now, with him gone and her mother not caring, but she also knew she had no right to continue, now that her father was here.

Marius watched her carefully, her drawn face and large eyes, just waiting with trembling hands which she quickly fisted in her apron.

"Did you take care of my daughter whilst I was gone, Melissa?"

"Yes, dominus... I raised her..." She blanched when she realized the audacity of her words and went to her knees, eyes downcast. "I didn't mean it! What I meant was that...I helped domina raise her..." She waited, her breath quickening and felt him step over and pull her up, cupping her chin, her large eyes full of tears.

"Don't kneel to me... you did raise her, I know Seraphina and heard enough to know that she didn't take care of her." He smiled. "Please continue taking care of her. I am back but will probably be quite busy, maybe sent away again, and she loves you."

Melissa's tears flowed, but she was unsure. "I am a mere slave, dominus... and you would trust her to me?"

He let her go, folding his arms. "You took good care of her, that's all that matters." He whirled and left, and she collapsed, sobbing with relief.

They walked to the emperor's palace, the spring sky glorious, a rich sunshine streaming down on the sparkling stones of the city. Marius looked care-free but determined, and Kyle wondered why he had insisted on taking him too. He feared the emperor and Marius' father, and had no wish to meet them, but he had no choice, and he followed the tall Roman, watching his hair flow around his muscled shoulders. It would be a matter of time that he'd have it cut, Kyle knew, and his heart wrenched.

In front of the palace, Marius announced himself to the guards and they looked at them, dubious. "Commander Marius is dead, as far as we know, and you don't look the part..."

They laughed and Marius' face flushed with anger. "I am Commander Marius, and you will pay for your insolence. Go, and announce me to the emperor."

The guards looked at each other, thrown by his commanding tone, and one of them shrugged. "Your loss if the emperor finds out you're an imposter."

He left then, and Kyle reached for Marius' hand, gently squeezing. "Try not to explode."

Marius chewed on his lip, sighing. "Fuck these idiots."

The guard went to the emperor's council chamber, Gaius there, as every day since Marius' disappearance, waiting for news, still hoping. The guard saluted the men and announced.

"Divine Emperor, a man claiming to be Commander Marius is awaiting to be let in, but he doesn't really look like the commander."

The men froze and the emperor prompted. "What does he look like?"

"Blue eyes, black hair, quite tall..."

Gaius shot to his feet. "My son!"

The emperor was more cautious. "He's alone?"

"No, divine emperor, he has a slave with him. By the looks of him, a Celt."

The emperor paled. "Let them in, now!"

The guard hurried out and went back to the gate, opening it. "Welcome home, Commander..."

Marius pursed his lips but didn't comment and they strode straight to the council room, the guards opening the doors wide.

Gaius looked at the men entering, his eyes growing wide at Marius' sight, his blood freezing, seeing a ghost of the past. *Those blue eyes. The long silky black hair flowing on the shoulders. Just like her...*

The emperor hurried to Marius, clasping him into a warm embrace. "Marius... my nephew... my blood... How...? We thought you died, son!"

He hugged him back. "I'll tell you all about it, uncle..." Marius then stepped aside to face his father. His father, unable to speak, his face blanched. Marius smirked. *As usual, loveless, old bastard...*

ALSO BY MAXIME JAZ

Avis Aureus - The Golden Bird Book II of the Omnia Vincit Amor trilogy, is available for pre-order! It will also be available on Kindle Unlimited.

https://getbook.at/Avis

Fall - a contemporary MM romance - available on amazon and Kindle Unlimited

https://getbook.at/Fall-MaximeJaz

About The Author

Maxime is a queer author who writes about guys falling in love in various places and times. Although the books could be labelled as MM romance laced with erotica, they do not fit a single genre, and are filled with drama, and sometimes darkness. Maxime likes to explore complex emotions, the journey to self-discovery, and living a life true to oneself, and their characters often struggle before finding happiness. Maxime often incorporates elements of their Hungarian and French origins in their works.

In their free time, Maxime likes to spend time with their family, ride their horse, or walk their dog on hikes.

Maxime writes next to a fulfilling career in international education.

All Maxime's links can be found here: Maxime Jaz | Linktree

GLOSSARY

A ll definitions are by Oxford Languages and Wikipedia. Words in order of appearance in the book.

Atrium: an open-roofed entrance hall or central court in an Ancient Roman house.

Toga: a loose flowing outer garment worn by the citizens of Ancient Rome, made of a single piece of cloth and covering the whole body apart from the right arm.

Salve: an ointment used to promote healing of the skin or as protection.

Posca: an Ancient Roman drink, made by mixing vinegar, water, salt and perhaps herbs. It was the soldiers, the lower classes, and the slaves who drank posca, a drink despised by the upper class.

Printed in Great Britain
by Amazon

42030711R00155